THE

SHANGHAI

MOON

ALSO BY S. J. ROZAN

THE

SHANGHAI

MOON

S. J. ROZAN

MINOTAUR BOOKS ⚹ NEW YORK

THE SHANGHAI MOON. Copyright © 2009 by S. J. Rozan. All rights reserved. Printed in the United States of America. For information, address St. Martin's Press, 175 Fifth Avenue, New York, N.Y. 10010.

www.minotaurbooks.com

Library of Congress Cataloging-in-Publication Data

Rozan, S. J.
    The Shanghai Moon : a Lydia Chin/Bill Smith novel / S.J. Rozan. — 1st ed.
        p.   cm.
    ISBN-13: 978-0-312-24556-6
    ISBN-10: 0-312-24556-4
    1. Chin, Lydia (Fictitious character)—Fiction.   2. Chinese Americans—Fiction.
3. Smith, Bill (Fictitious character)—Fiction.   4. Private investigators—New York
(State)—New York—Fiction.   5. Jewelry theft—Fiction.   I. Title.
    PS3568.O99S53 2009
    813'.54—dc22

                                                        2008033941

First Edition: February 2009

10   9   8   7   6   5   4   3   2   1

For Barbara Seranella
RIP, girlfriend

ACKNOWLEDGMENTS

As always, I'm grateful for so much, including help and support from:

Steve Axelrod, my agent
Keith Kahla, my editor

The Atlantic Center for the Arts
Art Workshop International

Steven Blier, Hillary Brown, Belmont Freeman, Eve Rudin, Max Rudin, Noah Rudin, James Russell, Amy Schatz

Betsy Harding, Royal Huber, Tom Savage, Jamie Scott

Susanna Bergtold, Nancy Ennis, Josh Paynter, Sui Ling Tsang, Joseph Wallace

Peter Blauner, for advice he probably doesn't remember giving

Ruth Gruber, for knowledge

Lee Hyla, for the right music and a lot of birds

Guillermo Kuitca, for understanding

B. G. Ritts, for priceless research

Jonathan Santlofer, for tea

THE

SHANGHAI

MOON

1

"I'm back."

I dropped my suitcase, slipped off my shoes, and listened to familiar Chinatown sounds spill in the windows. Horns honked, delivery vans rumbled. Mr. Hu's songbird trilled from the roof next door. I heard a child squeal with laughter and her grandmother scold in Cantonese: *Hold my hand, you bad girl, or that fish truck will squash you flat.*

And speaking of scolding in Cantonese, here came my mother.

"Who are you?" She shuffled from the kitchen and peered at me. "You look like my daughter, Ling Wan-ju, but I haven't seen her in a long time. She went to California. She said she'd be back soon, but she stayed. I'm happy she's having fun."

My mother's sarcasm could cut diamonds.

"Two extra weeks, Ma. And they're *your* cousins." I kissed her papery cheek, which she grudgingly allowed. "Have a good time while I was gone?"

"Your brother's children are very noisy." I have four brothers, but my mother rarely uses their names when she talks to me; I'm supposed to know which one she means. This time I did: Ted, the oldest. She'd stayed at his place in Queens while I was away.

"But you had the downstairs apartment to yourself, right?"

"I was fortunate it was empty. It's so dark, no wonder no one will rent it."

"I think Ted and Ling-an did a nice job on it."

"Too many rooms for one person. With such a big kitchen! Hard to find all the pots and pans."

"Did you cook?"

"Your brother and his wife both work so hard, come home late. They order from restaurants. So expensive! I made *har gow,* and long-life noodles."

"I'll bet the kids liked that."

"And so much lawn, so many useless flowers! I planted melons."

"You did?"

"Your nephew helped."

I could see that scene: my mother in a straw hat, plants dangling from each hand while ten-year-old Barry dug and mulched. Luckily, both Ted's kids adore her. They know her frowning and finger-wagging are scams to hoodwink malicious spirits into thinking her useless, disobedient grandchildren aren't worth stealing.

"Flushing. Pah!" my mother finished. "Too far away."

I sighed. She'd seen right through us. That apartment, far from being "fortunately" empty, had been built for her. My brothers and I think this fourth-floor walk-up we grew up in is getting hard for her to manage. But her refusal to leave Chinatown begins with a refusal to acknowledge she has anywhere to go.

Jet-lagged, I didn't have energy for this argument. "I'm going to unpack, Ma. Then I'll tell you all about the wedding."

"You could have gotten married yourself, you were there so long. Have you eaten?"

"Not yet."

"I made congee. There may be enough for two."

Detouring into the kitchen, I waved at old Chow Lun, leaning over the street from his usual windowsill. I lifted the lid from a steaming pot and found enough congee for an army. The table held bowls of chopped spring onions, pickles, and dried fish.

My mother's never liked fish in her congee. But I love it.

While I unpacked, I called my office phone. No messages. Not that I'd expected any. Work was slow, and anyway I'd been checking in daily from California. Now, that might sound like I was waiting for a particular call, but of course I wasn't. I especially wasn't waiting for a call from Bill Smith, my former associate, then partner; former close friend, then almost-I-don't-know-what, who'd done a vanishing act months ago after our last case together. The case, involving Bill's nephew Gary, had ended badly. As his partner and close friend, I felt terrible for him and understood why he wanted no part of anyone for a while. But as his partner and close friend, it made me furious to be one of the people he wanted no part of.

To the tune of my mother bullhorning Chinatown gossip across the apartment, I excavated my suitcase. I was down to the T-shirts when my cell phone rang. I grabbed it; the number was unfamiliar. Squashing down a pang of disappointment, I gave my name in both English and Chinese. Then I yanked the phone from my ear as an off-key tenor bellowed:

> *"The stars that hang high*
> *Over Shanghai*
> *Bring back the memory*
> *Of a thrill!*
> *I've been looking hiiiiigh, and I've been looking looooow,*
> *Looking for you, Shanghai Lil!"*

"*Stop!* Pilarsky, your singing has *not* improved."

"Hey, it wasn't 'Lydia the Tattooed Lady.' I thought you'd be happy. How are you, Chinsky?"

"Oh, I'm fine." I sighed. "How are you? What can I do for you? And what was that?"

"*Footlight Parade.* Busby Berkeley, Cagney, Keeler. One of the greats. And me, I could be worse. I'm still in business. Are you? If yes, it's not what you can do for me, it's I have a job for you."

"Doing what?"

"Do I know? A client wants someone who can, quote, operate discreetly in the Chinese community."

"So why did he call you?"

"Apparently, because I speak Yiddish. And he's a she."

"I don't—"

"I don't either. Come to the Waldorf at four and we'll both find out."

"Today?"

"Of course today."

"Well . . ." Chasing to a meeting with Joel Pilarsky when I'd just fought my way in from JFK wouldn't have been my first choice; but work is work. "Okay."

"Good girl. I'll be lurking behind a potted palm."

I bristled at the "girl," but Joel was on the far side of sixty, and I was in fact younger than two of his three daughters.

As I clicked off, my mother's face floated around the doorjamb. She must have been in the hall, responding to a sudden need to re-arrange the linen closet or straighten the family photos. "Who was that? You were talking about work. Was that the white baboon?"

"Bill? No. I haven't heard from him in a while." I busied myself with my suitcase. "That was Joel Pilarsky. You've met him. I helped him last year when he was looking for that Jewish lady who ran off with the Chinese restaurant owner."

"In Flushing, I remember! Nobody in Flushing is busy enough, so they make trouble for themselves."

Well, mentioning that was obviously a mistake. "Anyway, Joel has a job for me. I'm meeting him later."

"Today? He's sloppy. He gives you orders. And he sings. You get a headache when you work with him."

"Only when he sings." She makes a point of not listening when I talk about work, so how does she know this stuff? "And it's good to have work. Keeps me busy."

"Pah. Keep busy so you won't think about who isn't calling you."

"Ma! You don't even like Bill. And I haven't called him lately ei-ther."

"If you never call him again, your mother and your brothers will be happy. But for him not to call you? He values himself too highly. Make you go all the way to California."

"I went to California for Jeannie Chu's wedding."

"A month for a wedding?" Her pursed lips told me what she thought of that. Then she waved away the annoying gnat of Bill. "When do you have to go to your job today?"

"Two hours. Plenty of time to shower and change. But first, let's have some congee."

Probably taken in by the charcoal silk pantsuit that was my mother's handiwork, the Waldorf doorman actually smiled at me. In the carpeted, chandeliered lobby, three men conferred over PDAs, no doubt scheduling a very important meeting. A graceful woman rolled a suitcase toward the door. Even the two little boys waiting while their parents checked in wore button-down shirts and were behaving themselves.

In a club chair to my right I spotted Joel, not behind a potted palm but beside one. Silver pots and porcelain cups clustered on the coffee table between him and a neat, plump woman. Joel looked a little chubbier, a little balder than last time I'd seen him, but, with both his yarmulke and his tie askew, his hurried, preoccupied air was the same.

The woman, smiling and saying something, looked slightly younger than he. Allowing for facials, makeup, and the general care we women take of ourselves, that probably meant she was a few years older. She'd smoothed her graying hair into a neat bun. My mother would have approved of the twill cloth and conservative cut of her dark green suit.

Joel popped up, banging his shin as he came around the table. "Great to see you, Lydia. Lydia Chin, Alice Fairchild."

Alice Fairchild stood and shook my hand. She wasn't much taller than I: five-four, maybe, or five-five. "I'm delighted you're available, Ms. Chin. Joel tells me you're just the woman I need."

"I hope so. And please, it's Lydia."

Joel manhandled a chair over. "Sit. Have some coffee."

"Is there tea?"

"Oh, good!" Alice Fairchild reached for a pot. "I always feel so lonely among coffee drinkers. Lydia, how do you take it?"

"Milk, no sugar, please."

"I have to thank you both for making yourselves available on such short notice." She placed a tiny spoon on the saucer and handed me my tea. "As I was just telling Joel, he was recommended by a contact in Zurich. And of course you, Lydia, were recommended by him."

"Alice is an attorney," Joel said. "From Switzerland."

"Semiretired. I only take cases of particular interest now. My bread and butter was estate planning for fellow American expats. A little boring." She smiled. "But I have a rarefied specialty: recovery of assets for families of Holocaust victims. My office is in Switzerland for that reason: As Willie Sutton said about robbing banks, that's where the money is. Most of it. But from time to time, something turns up somewhere else." From a slim briefcase, she handed us each a set of papers. "If you don't mind, I'd like you to look at these."

On top was a Xerox of an old photograph. A teenage girl, in the knee-length skirt and round-toed pumps of thirties movies, stood with a boy a few years younger. One hand held down a hat threatening to take off in a wind that slanted his tie and stirred her curly hair; the other seemed to hold down the boy himself, who radiated affable impatience. Their conspiratorial smiles as they indulged the photographer reminded me of my brothers and me.

The next page was another Xerox, of a handwritten letter. A typed notation at the top margin said, "Jewish Museum, Holocaust archives. Rosalie Gilder to her mother, Elke Gilder, April 14, 1938."

"This looks like German," I said. "I don't—"

"Oh, I'm sorry," said Alice Fairchild. "The last page is the translation."

I flipped the pages. From neat typing, I read:

14 April 1938
Dearest Mama,

    I write from the deck of the *Conte Biancamano* as we are putting out to sea. A salt wind is blowing and the sun shines with a power I've never seen. Oh, how I miss you, Mama! From this moment I shall write often and tell you everything, exactly as you requested. Paul teases me that my inability to keep silent and my love of setting pen to paper would assure that you'd be flooded with letters, whether you'd requested them or not! And he's right, of course. Though this letter, and its fellows to come, could remain unwritten, could go to blazes for all I care, if only you were with us!

I couldn't write from the train, Mama. No one aboard could think of anything but how each passing meter brought us closer to the border. What weak conversation there was stopped completely each time the train did. Everyone was terrified that the Gestapo—who came aboard twice—would find something wrong in our papers, and remove us. Such downcast eyes and timid voices! Even mine, Mama, even mine. Choking on my fury—yes, and my fear— I sat, the soul of meekness, showing Paul's papers and mine as commanded, otherwise silent. But all the passengers were the same; even the youngest children sat frozen, clutching their parents' hands.

Until the border! As the whistle blew and the train chugged from the Italian customs station, such cheers erupted! Strangers hugged and champagne bottles appeared by magic. One gentleman jumped from his seat and burst into Italian song. I allowed Paul champagne because I imagined you would have, and took a small glass myself. Briefly we celebrated; then the tumult died down, as all of us, exhausted by worry and weakened by relief, turned to quiet conversations or private thoughts.

Are you well, Mama? I must tell you, as the train pulled out of the Hauptbahnhof I very nearly leapt from it and refused to leave Salzburg without you! But I forced myself to remain. You've made me responsible for Paul's safety and I intend to carry out my charge so you will be proud of me when you arrive. And I hope and pray that will be sooner than we expect. Three months is not fast enough! Please do

whatever you must—sell everything, badger the steamship
lines, cause a nuisance at travel offices—until you book an
earlier passage! Please, Mama, I won't rest until I hear
that you and Uncle Horst have cleared the border.

Now, as to Paul and myself, you mustn't worry. People
show great kindness when they learn we're traveling
alone. The situation on this ship, in any case, is quite extraordinary. Everything is teak, glowing brass, and thick
carpets. As we boarded this morning, streamers flew and
in the Grand Saloon the ship's orchestra played merry
tunes—quite well, I'm sure, but unnervingly discordant in
the circumstances. Our stateroom is small but well ap-
pointed. Our suitcases, though battered, are intact and holding up nicely. The passengers are looked after by stewards
who treat us as guests traveling for business or pleasure,
though fully two-thirds are fellow Jews in our situation—
refugees, let us use the word.

The emotions among us are so mixed, Mama, so hard to
describe! Relief. Sorrow. Anger. Fear for the future. Horror
and disgust, as we hear whispered stories of brutalities per-
petrated in Germany. Can it be that Austria, now that we
have lost our independence, could stoop as low? None believe it, but Mama, guard your tickets! If you and Uncle
Horst cannot find an earlier ship, then train it must be, and
please take great care until you depart. Urge Uncle Horst to
rein in his temper and live in a way so as not to be noticed—
oh, Mama, I'm serious but I laugh to see what I've written!
The very words you spoke to me! And here I repeat them to
you for Uncle Horst, as though you need them.

I can't wait for the day when we're together again! In
Shanghai Paul and I will ready a home, and when you arrive we'll rush to meet you. Perhaps, in years to come, bed-
time tales of the Chinese adventures of the Gilder family
will be told to wide-eyed children, who will then dream
wonderful dreams.

Paul sends his love, and promises to write though I
think he will not. But no matter; I will faithfully corre-
spond for us both. Please, please, Mama, come soon!!!

With all my heart,

Your Rosalie

In the silence I became aware of comings and goings in the Waldorf lobby. A bellhop pushed a luggage cart across the carpet. Well-
dressed men and women read newspapers and sipped coffee. If you
ignored the taxis beyond the doors, this could be the saloon of a great
ocean liner itself.

I looked at Alice Fairchild. "I don't understand. These were Jews
escaping the Nazis? But—they were going to *Shanghai*?"

"It was their only choice."

"What do you mean? I thought they went to other countries in Europe, or came here."

"Survivors did, after the war. But as the Nazis rose in the thirties,
countries all over the world closed their doors. Everyone knew what
was happening, but no government was willing to deal with a flood of
desperate refugees."

"Even the U.S.?"

"The U.S. had small quotas by country and looked at the Jews as
Germans, Austrians, Poles, wherever they were from. All the normal
paperwork was required."

"This is a surprise?" Joel asked me. "There were Chinese quotas,
too, you know."

"I know that. But I thought—"

"It was just you? Wrong."

I sipped tea to hide my annoyance that Joel had caught me out being ignorant, and in front of the client, too. "Well, but Shanghai? It
seems so . . . unlikely."

"I'm sure it did to them, too," Alice said. "But visas were relatively
easy to get, and often passengers off ships weren't asked for papers in
any case. Anyone who could get there could stay. It was the only
place."

"How many refugees went?"

"Twenty thousand."

"Twenty *thousand?*" Where had I been during world history class?

"The story's not well known." Alice read my mind. "It's been eclipsed by the war, the concentration camps. They began arriving in numbers in 1937. By 1942, fighting in Europe and the Pacific had closed the routes."

"But 1937—that's when Japan invaded China." I hadn't slept through world history completely, after all. "The Japanese let them in?"

"Shanghai's open port was what made it wealthy. That early, Japan wasn't planning on war with the West and saw no reason to change anything."

Alice looked at Joel, then at me. "Rosalie Gilder was eighteen, her brother Paul fourteen, when they fled Salzburg by train for Trieste, to board the *Conte Biancamano.* Their mother, Elke, a widow, and her brother, Horst Peretz, had tickets to Shanghai three months later by the overland route—Trans-Siberian Railway to a ship at Dairen."

I asked, "Why didn't they all go together?"

"Germany had annexed Austria a month before. Extermination wasn't yet the Nazis' plan for the Jews; they meant to force them out. They'd arrest Jewish men, and only let them go once their families produced travel documents. That happened to Horst. Elke was able to get train tickets, so he was released, but three months was a frighteningly long time to wait. She moved heaven and earth to get berths on a ship leaving sooner, and managed two. She sent her children. She hoped she and Horst could follow on another ship."

"Did they?"

"No."

"So they went by train?"

"They never got out."

My gaze fell to the photo again, sister and brother smiling on a windy day. I looked at Joel. His face was carefully blank. It occurred to me he must have grown up hearing countless tragic variations on this same story.

"In the letter you see a reference to their suitcases," Alice resumed briskly. "Jews who left weren't allowed to take much money, or anything valuable. Paul and Rosalie packed only clothing and a few household items—a pair of pewter candlesticks, for example."

"What happened to things people left behind?"

"The Nazis seized them. Most can't be traced. My work involves trying to recover the ones that can—paintings, antiques. In this case, though, that's not what I'm after. As Rosalie predicted, Paul turned out to be not much of a correspondent. But he was good with his hands. He'd built hidden compartments into the suitcases, where they concealed their mother's jewelry."

Joel raised his eyebrows. "That's why she says the suitcases are intact."

"Yes. She was telling her mother they'd held on to the jewelry. Earning a living in Shanghai was hard for the refugees, and these were teenagers. The jewelry was their safety net."

"What happened to them? Rosalie and Paul?"

"That's actually unclear. After the end of the war they can't be traced. You can imagine what chaos those times were. Record-keeping wasn't anyone's priority. Now, as I'm sure you know, Shanghai's in the middle of a building boom."

I nodded. That was something I did know.

"A month ago, excavation for a tower in what had been the International Settlement, in a place called Jiangming Street, unearthed a carved box containing five pieces of jewelry. I was able to identify it as Rosalie Gilder's." Reaching into her briefcase again, she handed us photographs of a necklace, two rings, and two bracelets. "I represent the grandchildren of Horst Peretz, Rosalie and Paul's uncle. He'd sent his daughter to live in Switzerland in 1935. She survived the war. My clients are her sons.

"The Chinese government considers anything found on their soil Chinese cultural patrimony, not to be removed from the country without permission. In this case, because the jewelry is so clearly European in origin, I was able to persuade them to negotiate. I went to Shanghai, and things were going smoothly until a few days ago, when the jewelry, and a midlevel official from the Shanghai Ministry of Culture, disappeared."

"The official ran off with the jewelry?"

"Oh, well, I don't know that, do I?" Her eyes sparkled. "But I have reason to think that he—Wong Pan is his name; this is his picture—arrived in New York two days ago." She handed us photos of a round-faced man.

"Is the jewelry very valuable?" I asked.

"By jewelry standards, no. Each piece is probably worth between twenty and forty thousand dollars. But for a Chinese bureaucrat, you can see the temptation. To my clients, of course, it's priceless.

"So now you can see why I need you both. Under most circumstances, if I were trying to sell antique jewelry in New York, I'd head to the Diamond District." She nodded at Joel. New York's Diamond District on Forty-seventh Street is almost exclusively the province of Orthodox Jews.

"Except maybe if you were Chinese." I began to catch on.

"Exactly. Then I might try Canal Street, even though I understand antiques aren't Canal Street's specialty."

"No, those shops deal mostly in new pieces. Still . . ."

"Yes, exactly. So I'd like you to show these photographs around and see if anything's turned up."

Joel studied the photos. "And if it has?"

"If you find someone who's bought any, let them know I'm in New York and interested in recovering it. Between us, the family's prepared to buy the jewelry back, to save years of headaches. You might stress I'm not the long arm of Chinese law."

"What if we get a lead on the bureaucrat? Wong Pan?"

"If he still has the jewelry, I'll be willing to deal with him. I'm not crazy about someone profiting from a stunt like this, but my charge is the assets. Now"—Alice sat back—"I have to tell you, I have another, more personal reason for my interest in this case. I was born in Shanghai. In those years."

Joel did the gallant thing. "How can that be? Someone as young as you?"

"You're a very sweet liar. My parents were American missionaries. We spent two and a half years in a Japanese internment camp after

Pearl Harbor. Of course I was very young—then." She smiled. "Most of my memories are from the camp, not Shanghai itself, and they're not particularly pleasant. Still, when this case came along, it did seem like something I'd want to see through. As if somehow it might, a tiny bit, redeem that experience. I'm not sure that makes any sense."

Joel said, "It does to me."

Personally, I had doubts about experiences being redeemable, but I kept them to myself.

We had more tea and coffee while the conversation turned to fees, expenses, and reports. Alice was Joel's client, so he took the lead, and that was fine with me. I listened, put in my two cents when it was wanted, and tried not to yield to the hypnotic combination of jet lag and the Waldorf.

Finally, retainer checks and receipts having been written and passed around, Alice said, "You'll have to excuse me. That Shanghai flight's a long one, and my poor body's not sure what day it is, let alone what time. And I've scheduled meetings with other clients over the next few days, since I'm in New York. Lydia, you just got back from California, didn't you? You're probably looking forward to the end of this meeting, too." I tried to deny it, but she had my number. "I'll go up to my room and let you two get started. Thank you."

Joel and I stood, shook her hand, and watched her cross the lobby.

"Well, Chinsky," Joel said, "ready to do the bloodhound thing?"

"Sure. Thanks for calling me in."

"Chinsky, as far as Chinese PIs, you're at the top of my list. I mean, it's a short list, but still."

"Gee, thanks." I had taken a few steps when I realized Joel was still staring toward the elevators, chewing his lower lip. "What's the matter?"

"I don't know. I feel like something's off."

"Like what?"

"For one thing, she's a shiksa. Her parents were missionaries. It's an odd profession for a shiksa, Holocaust asset recovery."

"Maybe she converted."

He gave me a pitying look. "Trust me on this, bubbaleh."

"Okay. But so? There must be money in it. She probably gets a per-
centage or something."

"If she finds anything. And she'd be on retainer, in case she doesn't.
But it's frustrating. Like she said, most assets can't be traced. When
they can, ownership takes years to prove. Half the time, you never do,
and you don't get your client's goods back. Everyone I know who does
that work thinks of it like a religious calling."

"She does have that air about her."

"Yes. The question is, why?"

"Because her parents were missionaries?"

Joel rolled his eyes. We turned and headed to the door. Casually,
Joel asked, "Speaking of work, how's your partner?"

"You're subtle as a ton of bricks, Pilarsky. I haven't seen him in a
while." As though it explained anything, I added, "I've been away."

"Mmm. I heard you guys were having problems."

"Did you? Where?"

"Around. It's true?"

"Why? You want to go into business with one of us?"

"With you, in a minute. We'd be unstoppable. Cute little Chinese
chick and a fat Jewish alte kacker, clients would be falling over each
other. No, seriously, it's just that you guys work well together. That's
not so easy to find."

That showed a surprising sensitivity, coming from Joel, but I didn't
want to get into it. "He seems to think I'm better off without him."

"Who asked him?"

"Certainly not me. Listen, is this important? Like, does it have to
do with this case?"

Joel smiled and suddenly bellowed,

> *"You're nothing without me!*
> *Without me you're nothing at all—"*

"*No!*" I put my hands to my ears. He stopped, and I asked, "What?"

"*City of Angels*. Coleman and Zippel. Last of the great Broadway
musicals, and it's about a private eye, too! You should see it, Chinsky."

"Where's it playing?"

"Nowhere. Closed years ago."

"Then how do I see it?"

"Your problem, kiddo. You need anything before we start?"

"No," I sighed. "I'm good."

"Okay." Joel smiled beatifically. "Go. Have fun."

2

It was too late to start working my way through the jewelry shops of Canal Street; by the time I got downtown they'd all be closed. I was tempted to go home to bed. If I did, though, I'd spring wide awake in a few hours and spend the rest of the night staring at the ceiling.

I headed for the dojo. I'd worked out in California, but that wouldn't cut much ice with Sensei Chung. All he knew was I hadn't been around for a month. I suited up, stretched, and offered to take a class of younger students through their forms. Sensei bowed, accepting the offer. I worked with the kids for forty minutes, until they, and I, were sweaty and panting. Then Sensei dismissed them and smiled, ready to show me why it wasn't a good idea to disappear.

I got home exhausted enough that I had hopes of falling asleep and getting back on New York time. I found my mother watching a soap opera on the Cantonese cable channel.

"Oh, will you be home for dinner?" she asked innocently. "I think there are vegetables." I peeked into the kitchen and saw mountains of chicken, broccoli, peppers, and ginger chopped and ready to stir-fry.

Sometimes this transparent kind of thing flips my switch. Our deal is, I'll live here as long as she lives here, so she won't be alone; but she doesn't get to give me a hard time about where or when I come and go. Or whether I'm home for dinner.

But I *had* been away a month. Besides, I was starving.

"Ma, it looks great. Let me change, and I'll cook."

"You make the chicken dry. Go shower. Dinner will be ready when you come out."

Which meant she'd already made two people's worth of rice.

Clean, dry, and full—truth be told, my mother's a great cook—I headed for bed at a ridiculously early hour. Which turned out to be a mistake. Sensei Chung's private lesson and my mother's stir-fry were no match for jet lag, and though I fell asleep before my head hit the pillow, by midnight I was, in fact, staring at the ceiling.

I tried deep breathing, Advil, counting sheep, and everything else I could think of, but I couldn't get any closer to sleep than a stone skimming the surface. Around two I gave up. I switched on the light and looked for something to do.

The image of the skimming stone brought to mind a vast ocean, and that brought a ship. I went to my desk and looked at the photos: the jewelry, Rosalie and Paul Gilder, Wong Pan. I reread the letter. I wondered if there were others at the Jewish Museum. I wondered what had become of Rosalie, of her brother. It wasn't relevant to the job I'd been hired to do, but I wondered.

Ah, the magic of what my mother refers to as the Interweb. A search for "Rosalie Gilder" on the Jewish Museum Web site brought me to Holocaust/Survivors/Documents/Shanghai/Gilder.

Rosalie Ruchl Gilder. Salzburg to Shanghai via the Conte Biancamano, *April 1938, age 18. Accompanied by brother Paul Chaim Gilder, 14. Letters to Elke Chana Gilder, mother, 1938–1941. Acquired 1967. In German. English translation available.*

There were fifteen more. I clicked on "English," then hesitated. Read someone else's letters? That wasn't right. *But these are historical documents,* I told myself. *In a museum collection.* Yes, but they weren't written that way. A young girl wrote them to her mother, who she never saw again.

In the end my curiosity overcame my scruples. It's one of the things Bill always liked about me. Though why I should care what Bill liked now that we didn't seem to be speaking, I had no idea.

I printed out the translations of the first half-dozen letters and curled up with them in bed.

18 April 1938

Dearest Mama,

This will be the briefest of notes, because the tender is leaving soon to take the ship's mail. But I can't give up the chance to describe the scene before us: We've docked at Port Said, and the setting sun is bathing the Sinai range with gold! Along with many fellow Jews, I stand at the rail, my heart stirred at the sight. Paul laughs at me, his skeptical sister; and truthfully, I have no idea which of the peaks before us might be Mt. Sinai itself. Nor does he, I might add. Nor do any of the crew seem to know, though they've made this voyage before.

The crew, by the way, treat us quite respecfully. An Italian steward confided, in poor but heartfelt German, that he was grateful to be at sea. On land, as he put it, "She's all gone crazy!" This cordiality extends to the ship's engineer, a Bavarian. He seems amused by Paul's fascination with the machinery, and is pleased to have someone with whom to discuss it in German. He's invited him to visit the engine rooms at any time. I take hope from the attitudes of these men that the madness sweeping Europe will soon come to an end.

But until it does, and despite my own impatience with the Talmud's more ridiculous tales and constricting injunctions, I stand at this rail with my fellow refugees, and declare myself a Jew.

Your Rosalie

You go, girl, I thought. I snuggled more deeply into my blanket and went on to the next letter.

23 April 1938

Dearest Mama,

I hope you and Uncle Horst are keeping well, and are at this moment racing to Trieste to board a ship! Paul points out that if you are, of course, this letter will miss you. But I won't mind having written in vain, if it means we'll be together soon. I would gladly repeat myself as we sit over coffee—or fragrant flowery tea, as taken by the Chinese.

Now, you ask, how is it I can speak about Chinese tea, still three weeks from China's shore? Mama, I've had the most fascinating encounter! Here is what happened:

As I wrote you, most of our fellow passengers are also refugees heading to the Orient with no more experience or knowledge of the place than we have. Many are families with children, who, with their natural high spirits, are treating this voyage as a great adventure. I don't mind—in fact I find their sunniness reassuring—but not all my fellow passengers feel the same.

Aboard also are some dozen Chinese men, returning home. They look like the illustrations in that lovely poetry book; if anything, more elegant and impressive, with their pale skin and slanted eyes. The two most elderly dress in long dark gowns; all the rest wear jackets and trousers, but still, they're quite exotic and I've had to be strict with Paul, that he must not stare at them.

Now, this morning, as I sat on deck with a novel from the ship's library—it's quite large, Mama, with books in so many languages!—I observed a young Chinese man run afoul of some boys playing with a ball. Almost knocked over by their pandemonium, he shouted that they were ill bred and worse behaved, and that as they were no credit to their families, they ought to be ashamed.

With my usual self-restraint I was on my feet in seconds. I thundered that it was he who ought to be ashamed, for frightening small children. He spun around, finger raised to scold me—then stopped, as if in confusion. Then he smiled, Mama, and bowed to me, a deep Oriental bow!

"Well," said he. "I was under the impression that with the exception of my countrymen, the passengers on this voyage were largely German and Austrian. I suppose I shall have to watch my tongue."

It was only then that I realized with astonishment what he'd grasped first—that we were both speaking English.

"If you intend to continue berating the children, indeed you will," I drew myself up and answered, as though conversing in English with a Chinese aboard an Italian liner plowing the Red Sea were an everyday thing. "Perhaps you'd at least consider insulting them in your native language, so they might learn something they'll find useful in their new home."

At this he smiled again, but looked quizzical, and inquired where their new home might be. When I told him Shanghai, he seemed truly surprised.

"Madame, Shanghai is under Japanese occupation. Civil war rages in the countryside, and foreigners abandon China on every ship that sails. I understood my fellow passengers to be refugees from oppression, but Shanghai seems an odd choice of new home."

"Choice? We are Jews, sir—we have no choice! The countries we leave hound us, steal from us, throw us behind bars. We're ordered into exile and would gladly go, but no place will have us—except Shanghai!" I swept my hand toward the boys. "These children leave home, family, and friends for an unknown place where the language, the streets, the very food will be wholly new to them. Yet they laugh and play. And you dare take them to task for it!"

Finally reining in the runaway horse that is my temper, I felt myself redden up to my scalp and was appalled at my effrontery.

The gentleman regarded me, his face grave. He asked if there were truly no other place for us. "I'd thought Shanghai was a transit port," he said. "A stop on the way to someplace more hospitable."

Surprised by the catch in my throat as I spoke, I told him "hospitable" was not a sentiment the world felt toward Jews.

He kept his gaze on me for another brief time. Then he turned to the boys, who'd been watching in part fear, part fascination. He bowed—at which they took a step back, as though afraid of what might happen next!—and requested that I convey his apologies. I told them in German they might continue their game but must take care not to disturb their fellow passengers, and I shooed them off.

The gentleman turned again to me, and again, he smiled. "I am Chen Kai-rong. Chen is my family name, and so, if we're to be friends, you must call me Kai-rong. I'd be honored if you'd take tea with me."

And that, Mama, is how I've come to know about Chinese tea!

I receded to my deck chair. Mr. Chen Kai-rong settled himself also and spoke to a steward. As we awaited our tea he glanced at my book. I'd been reading Thomas Hardy, to improve my English; he asked whether the author was a favorite of mine. When I told him Mr. Hardy was rather dark for my taste, he agreed, and asked what writer in that language I enjoyed.

And Mama, now you'll laugh, because what popped from my mouth was "William Shakespeare." All the times you despaired of me, devouring Wilkie Collins while *King Lear* gathered dust, and now to a stranger on the deck of a ship I tell such a fib! But this gentleman holds himself with such grace, Mama, his English is so good and his manners so refined! I wanted him to think well of me.

I then asked if there was an English author he particularly admired, and he responded with P. G. Wodehouse. Do you know this writer, Mama? I don't, and I told him so. His answer: "Well, I commend him to you. I think you'll find him compatible." Later, I sought out the works of Mr. Wodehouse in the ship's library, but they are not carried.

Our tea tray arrived, bare of milk, sugar, or lemon. The accompanying cakes were entirely unfamiliar. Mr. Chen Kai-rong instructed me to swirl the teacup to release the scent, as we do with wine. I found the tea's golden color and sweet fragrance appealing, and discovered it to be delicious, though I was less successful in enjoying the cakes.

"Never mind," he said. "At least now the very food of China isn't wholly new to you." At that I couldn't contain a smile, though I tried to conceal it. He continued, "I confess to a weakness for linzer torte, myself. Tell me, Miss Gilder, are all Jews as firm in their opinions and as outspoken as yourself? If so, Shanghai can look forward to some excitement."

"We are indeed firm in our opinions," I replied. "Though I think you and Shanghai will find most of my fellow refugees more capable of holding their tongues than I. Please accept my apology; I had no right to speak to you that way. But if we are to continue speaking, and even, as you hinted, to be friends, and if I'm to call you Kai-rong, you must call me Rosalie."

He nodded gravely, as though I had proposed terms for a political treaty. "Well, Rosalie," said he, "it seems I'm indebted to those young hooligans. If they hadn't tried to trample me, I'd not have discovered the pleasure of your company. To my regret, though, I now have an appointment to keep." He stood and bowed in farewell.

"Please wait, sir," I said before he could take two steps. My boldness makes me blush, thinking of it now, but Mama, the half hour we'd spent over tea was the only half hour since the train pulled out of Salzburg that I haven't been afraid. Can you understand that? I've been trying so hard to be brave, to look after Paul and be *responsible,* and really, Mama, I've been managing, please don't think I haven't. But this brief time spent with someone who is neither a frightened refugee, nor in the business of frightening refugees—I'd nearly forgotten what it was to converse, to speak of things beyond fear and loneliness and the horrors of our situation. So I called after Mr. Chen Kai-rong, and when he quickly turned back to me, I had to have something to say! I blurted, "Sir? My young brother and I go to China alone, with no more knowledge than we could glean from a children's poetry book. If you'd care to educate me about your country, so I'm not a total dunce when we arrive, I should like that very much."

He smiled. "I think, Rosalie, you stand no chance of being a dunce. But I'd be honored to talk with you about my country. Will you take tea with me again tomorrow afternoon? I can arrange for a group of rowdy children with dangerous toys, if that will entice you."

"I need no enticing," I told him, and the deal was struck.

So, Mama, soon I'll be what the British call an "old China hand." I'm looking forward to my education, but more than that, to another half hour with someone in whose presence I can forget that I'm afraid.

Stay well, Mama, and come soon!

Your Rosalie

As I slipped the printout onto my bedside table, I could almost feel the salt wind. I wondered what kind of tea Rosalie and Chen Kai-rong had been drinking: Osmanthus flower? Chrysanthemum? And did the Italian liner stock these teas for the Chinese passengers, or had Chen Kai-rong brought his own tea aboard? Maybe he'd found a favorite shop in Europe where he bought his Chinese tea, and now he was taking it home.

I fell asleep and dreamed of oceans.

3

"You slept well," said my mother: a declaration, not a question.

She's a restless sleeper herself. It was entirely possible she'd seen light under my door at 2:00 A.M. and was ostentatiously pretending she hadn't. Rather than get into that, I poured myself tea and called my best and oldest friend, Mary.

"Lydia! Are you back?"

"Almost completely. You have time for lunch today?"

"I'm on the eight to four, but I'll make time. My vic won't be any deader after lunch."

"You have a homicide?" I was surprised. Mary Kee is a Fifth Precinct detective. She does, or, as she says, undoes, extortion, robbery, and assault, but the precincts usually hand off homicides to the NYPD's specialized squads.

"Not exactly. An Asian John Doe in a Times Square hotel. Bad teeth, no money, no papers, so they think he might be an illegal. Midtown Homicide asked for someone from down here to help ID him. My captain doesn't like it, but he couldn't say no."

"Why doesn't he like it?"

"He thinks the special-squad guys are divas. Especially Midtown Homicide. They don't play well with others."

"Sibling rivalry in the NYPD? I'm shocked and appalled. Well, bring along the John Doe's photo. Maybe I know him."

"Oh, sure. Lydia, you've been away so long I'm surprised you still know your way around."

"For Pete's sake, it was one month! You sound like my mother."

"What? I take it back. See you later."

I did my dishes and got dressed for a day of gumshoeing. As an afterthought, I slipped into my bag the Rosalie Gilder letters I'd printed out last night but hadn't read. Then I headed out to see if I still knew my way around.

Rushing Chinese people and strolling tourists crowded the hot, bright sidewalks. I worked my way past open storefronts where ice-filled boxes displayed dozens of kinds of fish, past piled vegetable stands and restaurants with chickens glistening in the window. When I hit six lanes of snarled and honking traffic, I'd reached Canal Street.

Canal, running east-west through lower Manhattan, was once Chinatown's border, but those days are gone. On the immigrant floodwaters of the last two decades, Chinatown has spread north through what was once Little Italy and east through the formerly Jewish tenements of the Lower East Side. It's lapping at the blocks west, too, merging with Tribeca and SoHo in a jagged scramble of the newly come and the ultra hip.

I surveyed the glittering windows of the jewelry row along Canal. As Alice Fairchild had said, they don't go in much for antiques here. Chinese people value antiquities, but we generally like to know where things have spent the last, oh, five hundred years. Buying old things from strangers carries a risk: Unless you know what happened to the original owner and you're sure he or she didn't mind giving up the piece, you're in danger of acquiring some bad luck along with it.

Westerners don't seem to feel that way, and some of the Forty-seventh Street shops carry beautiful antiques. But a Shanghai bureaucrat on the lam might want to steer clear of the yarmulkes and black coats uptown and offer his ill-gotten goods to someone who spoke his language.

Literally.

Newcomers from other parts of China notwithstanding, a lot of Chinatown is still Cantonese. Including most of these jewelers. Wong

Pan was from Shanghai, and a government official. He'd speak Shanghainese by upbringing and Mandarin by necessity. That didn't mean
he wouldn't be willing to do business with Cantonese jewelers, and in
written Chinese he'd be able to, but I'd bet he'd try his own people
first.

So how would he find them? Most likely, by the shoe-leather
method. He'd go from store to store, asking which dialect the propri-
etor spoke. The real question was, how was *I* going to find them in a
way that would cancel out his two-day lead?

I headed east on Canal, to Golden Dreams.

"Ling Wan-ju!" Mrs. Chan, my mother's friend-and-rival, smiled
from her perch behind a case of jade bracelets. In the corner, incense
smoke twisted up from General Gung's altar.

"Hello, Auntie." Greeting her in Cantonese, I took both her plump
hands in mine. "How are you?"

"For an old lady, I'm well, thank you. You look lovely! California
must have agreed with you. I can understand why you extended your
trip."

Mrs. Chan and my mother sewed side by side at Mr. Leng's factory
the whole time I was growing up. If my mother was going to complain
to anyone about my being away, it would be Mrs. Chan. Of course, the
way she put it probably had to do with how invaluable I was to my
cousins, and how much more my help was needed, even after the wedding, than we'd expected when I made my plans.

"I had a good time, Auntie, but I'm glad to be home." I knew that
would get back to my mother, and I wanted it to. No point in her staying up all night worrying that I might relocate. "Auntie, I need your
help. Professionally."

Mrs. Chan's cheeks crinkled when she smiled. "Of course!" She sat
up straighter. Out of loyalty, most of my mother's friends disapprove
of my profession, but Mrs. Chan is different. She watches lots of TV
cop shows and likes the idea that I'm fighting crime.

"Auntie, I need to find jewelers who speak Mandarin or Shanghainese. Do you know any?"

"Oh, I don't know if I can help. I'm so busy here in the store, I have

no time to waste gossiping with other jewelers." Having established
her bona fides, she went straight on. "Of course, Mr. Lee, at Canal Diamonds, is from Beijing. And Old Wong at Harmony Jewelers, he
speaks a dozen dialects—anything for a sale, that old man. Yang
Nuan-yi's husband is Shanghainese, so maybe she's learned his dialect.
Or maybe not. If I were married to him I'd be happy for an excuse not
to talk to him. Mr. Chen at Bright Hopes is from Shanghai, but he's
been here many years." She kept that up for a full five minutes. I made
a list, excluding the editorials.

"Thank you, Auntie," I said, when she finally ran out of steam. "I'm
grateful for your time, and I won't take up any more of it. But I imagine you want to know why I'm asking."

"Oh, it's not my concern." Her eyes were wide with innocence, but
to head off a commiserating phone call to my mother about the difficulty of living with a daughter always in too much of a rush for common
courtesy, I showed Mrs. Chan the photos. She shook her head, at both
the jewelry and Wong Pan. "But I'll call you without delay if I see him,"
she promised, aglow at the prospect of striking a blow for justice.

I spent the rest of the morning working my way through Mrs.
Chan's list. I showed the photos and marveled at the variety of ways
people had for saying no. I'd gotten simultaneously halfway through
the list, halfway down the street, and nowhere when it was time to
knock off and meet Mary for lunch.

I headed to our favorite Taiwanese tea shop and slipped onto a
stool at a front table. I was a few minutes early, and Mary, being on
duty, was likely to be late. I almost ordered black tea, but the old man
at the next table swirled a pot of sweet-smelling osmanthus flower, releasing the fragrance. I ordered some of that and pulled the next of
Rosalie Gilder's letters from my bag.

28 April 1938
Dearest Mama,
    I write to tell you how proud you must be of Paul. Not
that his jokes and fidgets have been abandoned for sober
respectability. Staying in his chair for an hour at dinner is

still more than he can manage. It's as difficult as ever to convince him to read any book not a dry scientific text; fortunately he is able to practice his English on such wonders from the ship's library as *Capacitative Resistors: Design and Use*. And sharing a stateroom is turning out to be a matter of calling him back time and again to fold his clothes or mop up the lavatory.

But those are small irritations, and I'm ashamed to think how they once exasperated me. Among our fellow refugees we hear such tragic tales! A girl my age, Ursula Krause, from Berlin, goes to her uncle in Shanghai alone. Her father and brother were taken by the Gestapo, and she's heard nothing since—except a smuggled note from her brother begging her to leave while she could. Mama, my blood runs cold! I, the family skeptic, have found myself saying a prayer for Ursula.

Oh, Mama, I don't mean to upset you. Seeing what I've written, I nearly tore this letter to shreds. Please believe me: We're well, and being brave, and having adventures! But to tell you about those adventures only, to write about the sparkling waves and the salt breeze—those things are true, of course they are, but so is the terrible reason we're on this ship to see them.

Mama, I've just roused myself; I've been sitting for some time, wondering again whether to ball up this letter and throw it in the sea. But no. We are fine, but the world is not. If I can't sit beside you and talk about this, I must lighten my heart by sharing my thoughts over time and distance.

Let me go on, then; I started out to tell you that Paul has lately discovered new talents, and I know this will bring you a smile. He's become a model of patience and leadership—among the small children! It's as if the Pied Piper were aboard. Everywhere, he's trailed by a string of babies. He invents games for them, doctors their cuts and bruises, tells them fantastic stories to make them gape and laugh. To see the children happy eases their parents' minds; and so Paul, by carrying on in his silly way, renders a great service. This is a magical thing, and I hope, Mama, it makes you as proud as it does me.

I'll close now, as I see Mr. Chen Kai-rong approaching; we are to have tea and begin my lessons. I feel myself smiling. He wouldn't be wrong to think it's for the pleasure of seeing him; but it's also for the idea of *your* smile when you read about Paul; and practice for the smile I'll be wearing when I greet you and Uncle Horst in Shanghai!

Take care, Mama.

Your Rosalie

"Lydia? Are you okay? Wake up."

"What? Oh, Mary, I'm sorry!" I jumped from my stool and hugged my best and oldest friend.

"What are you reading?" Mary unslung her shoulder bag and pulled out a stool, her long braid swinging as she sat. When she was in uniform she'd complained about having to wear her hair stuffed under her cap. Since that was pretty much the only thing she didn't like about being a cop, now that she'd made detective and was in plainclothes, life was good.

"It's from my case. It's kind of sad." I gave her a brief rundown: Alice Fairchild, the Jewish refugees in Shanghai—which she'd never heard of either, just proving we went to school together—the excavation site, and the jewelry; and Rosalie Gilder, writing to her mother. "She was just a kid. Trying to be a grown-up and look out for her little brother, excited and scared and missing her mom. She keeps saying, 'I can't wait to see you again.' But she never did."

"God. That's awful."

"It was a long time ago. But it makes me feel like, how *dare* this Wong Pan guy steal her mother's jewelry? Like he stole it from *her*."

"What happened to her and her brother?"

"Alice Fairchild says it's not clear. I guess a lot of people can't be traced from after the war. But I'm starting to feel . . . protective. As though I knew her."

A young Chinatown-cool waiter—blond-streaked hair, tight black pants—appeared. We ordered tea eggs, chicken skewers, and lemongrass soup.

"Enough of the sad past." I folded Rosalie's letter and stuffed it into my bag. "Tell me about *your* case."

"Nothing much to tell. Guy was found shot in a hotel room. Wallet was gone. Registered as Wu Ming."

"'Anonymous'? Oh, great, a joker. Okay, show me yours, I'll show you mine."

We traded pictures.

Our quarries looked alike, if by that you mean they were both middle-aged Chinese men. Hers was thinner and wore short hair; mine was pudgy and had short hair, too, but grayer.

"Yours is better-looking," Mary said.

"Well, he's alive."

"I guess that's an advantage in a man. Is he wanted for something? Here, I mean?"

"Not that I know of. In China, for running off with the cultural patrimony."

"If he's not wanted here, I can't show his picture around for you, though. Sorry."

"That's okay. I'm not really looking for him anyway, just the jewelry." Our soup arrived, and we put our work away. Mary gave me the past month in her life, filled me in on gossip my mother hadn't gotten to, and asked about my family.

"My brothers are all thriving, in their own unique and bizarre ways," I told her. "And I've been back less than twenty-four hours and my mother's already driving me up the wall."

Mary nodded her sympathy. "She told my mom yesterday that you'd taken a case with a guy who irritates you so you wouldn't be thinking about Bill."

"Oh, for Pete's sake! Why does she *do* that? You'd think she'd be happy."

"She's your mother. You're not happy, she's not happy, even if what makes you happy makes her unhappy. Why don't you call him?"

"He doesn't want me to."

"So?"

"Listen, I'd love to sit and chat about my twisted professional and personal life, but I have jewelry to track down. And aren't you on duty?"

"Oh, nice sidestep. Well, whenever you want to talk about it, I'm here."

We gathered up our things and went out to show Chinatown photographs of men we didn't know.

The day got old and so did my search. Yang Nuan-yi, as it turned out, had learned her husband's Shanghainese dialect, but the only person she'd spoken it to lately was her husband. Old Wong at Harmony Jewelers recalled having a long conversation with a Fujianese yesterday, and just this morning threw two wealthy punks with that terrible Macao accent out of the shop for making a pass at his daughter, but all his other recent customers were Cantonese, or *lo faan* with no Chinese at all. White-haired Mr. Chen at Bright Hopes had a sharper nose than mine, and rounder eyes of a lighter shade of brown; he might be Eurasian, I thought, or from the western provinces. But he'd had no Shanghainese- or Mandarin-speaking customers in weeks, and I was beginning to think my smart idea wasn't so smart after all, when I slipped the jewelry photos out of the envelope to show him anyway.

His face paled. Staring at the photos, he felt behind him for his stool and sat heavily. "This is what he stole, that man?"

"Yes. Uncle, are you ill?"

"Where . . ." He trailed off. His assistant hurried over, but he waved her away. "I'm fine, Irene," he said gruffly. "See to the customers." The shop was empty, but she took the hint and went back to her post by the door.

I tapped Wong Pan's picture. "You've seen this jewelry, this man?"

"No." Mr. Chen mopped his brow with a handkerchief. "I would like . . . May I borrow these photographs?"

"They're copies, you can have them, but you need to tell me why. Has someone offered to sell you these pieces?"

"No."

"Then—"

"I have to make sure. I might be wrong. You will hear from me." He stood, collecting all but one photo from his counter. He handled them as delicately as if they were jewels themselves.

"Uncle, you really need to tell me what you know about this."

But Mr. Chen was through speaking to me. He carried the photos into his office and shut the door. I was left alone with the assistant and, smiling up from the counter, the black-and-white face of Wong Pan.

4

There's no such thing as a quiet corner in Chinatown, but I found a sheltered doorway and called Joel.

"Hey, Chinsky! Hope you're having better luck than I am."

"I'm not sure. But a strange thing happened." I told Joel about Mr. Chen. "He knows something, obviously."

"Excellent deduction, Watson."

"Give me a break. Are you going to call Alice?"

He paused, and I wondered if he was chewing his lip. "I don't know."

"Why not?"

"Why not? Because I don't have anything to tell her, because you didn't push him."

"Push him? He'd have totally clammed up if I'd pushed him."

"And if he'd clammed up, you'd have what less than you have now?"

"Nothing, but I might have less than I'm going to get when he calls."

"Or you gave him a chance to think about it and he isn't going to call and you're going to get nothing. Which is what you have now."

"Oh, Joel, come on! He's an old Chinese man. There was no way—"

"And you're a young Chinese woman and you were being polite. Dangerous in our business, Chinsky. Anyway, forget it. I'll call the client, she'll at least see we're wearing out shoe leather."

"I was—" *Drop it, Lydia,* I ordered myself. *While you're at it, stop reminding yourself that Bill would never have suggested you'd mishandled an interview with an old Chinese man.* I gritted my teeth and asked, "Okay, so how did *you* do?"

"Zippo. Blank stares on Forty-seventh Street. Hey, good name for a science fiction movie. So, what else you been up to?"

Joel's tone was conciliatory. Well, good. "I've read a couple more of Rosalie Gilder's letters. From the Jewish Museum Web site."

"You have? Why?"

"I'm not sure. I wanted to get to know her better, I guess."

"Ah, Chinsky. You never change. Okay, talk to you later."

After we hung up, I squinted down Canal. Just because Mr. Chen had nearly fallen over in a faint when he saw the photos, and just because I was irritated with Joel, didn't mean other jewelers might not have seen these pieces. I'd need to keep going, but that would have to be tomorrow. All along Canal, Closed signs were going up in store windows.

Hungry, thirsty, and tired, I headed to Pho Viet Huang for a bowl of noodle soup. I was annoyed at Joel for getting on my case, annoyed at my mother for being right about me getting annoyed at Joel, and annoyed at myself for having the sneaking suspicion Joel might be right, too. Joel Pilarsky and my mother—now there was an unholy alliance.

The soup was full of mint, bean sprouts, and beef, and after it I felt much better. I went to the park, sat on a bench, and spent twenty-five minutes on a conference call with my brothers. Ted's and Elliot's wives, Ling-an and Li-jane, were in on the call; Andrew's boyfriend, Tony, stayed out of it; and Tim's girlfriend, Rita, was too new to get mired in Chin family business. The subject was my mother, her stay in Flushing, and how we could leverage the experience into an argument for a permanent move. The conclusion we came to, as usual when the five of us discussed anything, was none at all.

"She was adjusting, she just needs time," was Ted's mild assessment.

"She seemed fine," came from Elliot, who's an emergency room doctor and tends to see all emotional states less dramatic than hysteria as the same.

"She liked the garden," said Andrew, who'd made the long trip to Flushing a couple of times during my mother's month there.

"She hated the whole thing," retorted Tim, who hadn't gone but is the one my mother calls to complain about the rest of us.

"Lyd?" Andrew said. "How did she seem when you got home?"

"Like the only way to get her to move to Flushing would be to stuff her in a box and load her on a van. Look, guys, it's good to have Ted's apartment there, but I think it'll be a while until we can talk her into it."

"That okay with you?" That was also Andrew. Tim wouldn't think to ask, and the others are afraid to, in case someday I might say, *No, I've had it with this.*

"Right now she seems intent on proving what an uninterested, privacy-cherishing housemate she is," I said. "I can deal, for the time being."

So we decided to do, say, and plan nothing. A classic Chin family outcome.

To stay on Sensei Chung's good side, I went down to the dojo. When I got home, my mother was watching the news on Cantonese cable. She looked up. "Have you eaten?"

"I had some soup. Is that shrimp I see?"

"To cook with spring onion." She added, "It was cheap."

Uh-huh. I knew what shrimp, one of my favorite foods, was selling for. "I'll chop the onion," I offered. It no doubt took iron self-control, but she didn't stop me.

Dinner conversation was mostly about my brothers, my niece and nephews, and, in expanding rings, various cousins whose exploits, troubles, or luck required discussion. After the dishes, jet lag suddenly clobbered me. I took an herb-laden bath. When I came out, barely able to keep my eyes open, I found my mother absorbed in a Hong Kong soap opera, one she's been following since I was in first grade. It's set in an apartment complex on Kowloon, and the cast must have changed ten times since it began. I kissed her; she kissed me back but kept an eye on a red door closing to ominous music.

5

In the morning I found my mother sewing on a blouse she was making for Ling-an.

"How did you sleep?" she asked as I put water on.

"Strange dreams. I think it's the jet lag. What's going on in Cloud Lake Mansion?"

"On television?" She seemed dumbfounded by the question.

"Is that girl marrying the rich guy her father wants her to? And what about that soldier, did he come back?"

"I didn't know you followed that show."

"Ma, it moves so slowly I only need to walk by once a month when you're watching to catch up. Did the politician's wife have the baby yet?"

She blinked. "No, but she's in the hospital, she's having problems. And that pretty girl is a fool. She'll marry that old man to make her father happy, instead of waiting for her soldier."

"She probably will, but I'm surprised you don't approve. Isn't she being properly filial, doing that?"

"Of course. But if her father were a proper father he would care more about her happiness than making a good business alliance."

"I guess he would. Do you want tea?"

"Yes," my mother said, and added, "Thank you, Ling Wan-ju."

· · ·

I hit Canal Street, heading for Bright Hopes to see if Mr. Chen was ready to talk to me, but before I got close, my cell phone rang. When I answered, that bellowing tenor blasted my ear:

> *"'Pretty lady with the flower,*
> *Won't you give a lonely sailor*
> *'Alf an hour?'*

"Sondheim, *Pacific Overtures.* Chinsky! Come up here right away."

"Now? But I was—"

"Whatever you're doing, drop it. Something's fishy, and I want to talk about it."

"What is?"

"Come up here."

"Just tell me—"

"Chinsky! *Now!*"

Then a click. I stood for a moment, fuming. Who the hell was Joel Pilarsky to give me an order and then hang up? I almost called him back just to say that. *Yes, well, chill, Lydia. Just go up there.*

We certainly did have to talk.

I got in gear and trotted to the N train, reaching the platform in time to see red taillights. Served me right for arguing with myself. Well, so Joel would have to wait. Served *him* right for pushing me around. When the train finally came, the ride was shorter than the wait had been.

Joel's office was in midtown, in a 1930s building with complicated corridors and cranky steel windows. Its elevators grumbled and its terrazzo floors sagged. Joel claimed he didn't move because the place was such a dump the landlord paid the tenants, but I knew the truth. From the day we met, I'd seen Joel's impatient know-it-allness for what it was: a smoke screen for his secret identity as a hopeless romantic. Like most romantics, he was disappointed in little and big ways dozens of times a day, and like most, he kept trying. These rabbit-warren hallways, these glass-paneled doors with names in gold, creaking onto small rooms with vast Manhattan views—what could be a more romantic place for a private eye? *Joel Pilarsky,* I thought, *you don't fool me.*

I got a nod from the lobby guard. My last case with Joel—the runaway wife and the noodle king—had been only a year ago, so maybe he recognized me. More likely he just hoped he did so he wouldn't have to tear himself from the *Enquirer*'s coverage of a spaceship landing in Pittsburgh.

The elevator muttered all the way up as though I'd interrupted its lunch break. On Joel's floor I walked the maze, left-right-right-left. I knocked and pushed his door open. There was an outer office, as though Joel had a secretary, but he didn't, just a part-time bookkeeper to send out the bills. I walked through to the inner office, saying, "Pilarsky, this place is a mess. If you're going to make me drop everything and run over here, the least you could do—"

I stopped. Joel was sitting in his office chair, but though his eyes were open he wasn't looking at me.

Or at anything, anymore.

I tried. I ignored the oceans of blood soaking his shirt and felt his neck for a pulse, though I knew he wouldn't have one. But it was the by-the-book thing, and Joel would have been disappointed in me if I hadn't done it. I looked around, taking in the open drawers and file cabinets, but I didn't touch anything. I used my cell phone to call the police and then I waited in the corridor, so no one else would make the mistake I had, of touching the doorknob, maybe screwing up the killer's prints. And I left Joel's eyes open, and his yarmulke on the floor where it had fallen, though I wasn't sure that was okay, at all.

6

"Here, drink this."

Mary held a takeout cup with a dangling Lipton's label. I sipped, hoping tea would clear my fog. I felt as though I were seeing through the wrong end of a telescope and hearing through a closed door. And standing in sludge.

"Sit down," Mary ordered.

"The forensics people—"

"Then in the hall." She led me to the corridor and pointed at the floor.

Why hadn't I thought of that? I sank down and leaned against the wall, closing my eyes.

"They'll be through with you soon." Mary's voice came from beside me. "Then you can go."

"I missed the train."

"What?"

"Joel told me to get up here, and I was so mad at him for ordering me around that I didn't hurry. If I'd caught the train that was pulling out, I'd have been here in time."

"To get killed, too?"

I opened my eyes. "To stop the killer!"

"Maybe not."

"I was talking to Joel on the phone!"

"And maybe the killer was right outside, waiting for him to hang up."

"Still—"

"No 'still.' It's not your fault. The point is now to catch the person who did this."

I stared at this best friend, this cop. When, I wondered, had Mary stopped understanding me?

A small, sharp-featured man stepped out of Joel's office. His gold shield was clipped to his pocket, and I knew someone had told me his name, but I had no idea what it was. He stopped when he caught sight of the badge hanging around Mary's neck. "Who're you?"

"Mary Kee. Fifth Precinct."

"What're you doing here?"

Mary pointed. "She's a friend of mine."

The uptown cop frowned. "Your name's familiar. Do I know you?"

"We spoke on the phone. Your Asian John Doe from the hotel."

"Right! You're supposed to be ID-ing him."

"I'm working on it."

"Here? Now, I need the witness."

"I'd like to stay."

"I'd like you not to."

"She's a friend of mine. She's upset."

"And you're off your turf. I'll be nice." He showed me a bunch of teeth, which was probably a smile.

Mary looked to me. I shrugged. She said, "When you're ready to go, I'll take you home," and walked away down the hall.

The detective watched her, then turned back to me, notebook in hand. "You worked for Pilarsky?"

A preface would have been nice, I thought. Your name, how sorry you are. "Not exactly." My voice sounded dull. Well, maybe I'd bore him, and he'd go away. "We're both freelance. He called me in on a case. Before that I hadn't seen him in a while."

The detective had stopped writing, as if to let me finish babbling. "So, on *this* case, you worked for him."

"I guess."

"What's the case?"

"Stolen jewelry." I gave him a summary, finding it hard to stay focused. I kept seeing Joel standing outside the Waldorf, bursting into off-key song.

"Any way that could be related to this?" On "this" he nodded toward the office. I could read the skepticism in his lifted brows.

"I don't know. When he called, he said something was fishy."

"What was?"

"He didn't tell me."

Nodding as though he'd expect Joel not to tell me, he asked, "This jewelry—very valuable?"

"Not really, though it's probably worth more than a Chinese civil servant could hope to see."

"I thought everyone was getting rich over there, now that they took all our jobs. What's 'not really'?"

I stared at him. "Around twenty thousand, each piece."

"Gee, sounds valuable to *me*. Must be nice to be you. What about Pilarsky? Why would someone shoot him over it? Did he have it?"

Mulgrew, I suddenly remembered, that was his name. Not that that made me feel any warmer toward him. "Detective Mulgrew? It's *missing*. That's why we were hired."

"So maybe Pilarsky found it."

"He told me something was fishy. That wouldn't be fishy."

"Fishy. Uh-huh." He lifted his eyebrows again. "His wallet's gone. And laptop and cell phone. And the place was turned over. You want to know, I make this for a robbery. How much cash did he keep in the office? A lot?"

"I don't know. Just a robbery?"

"Some days, the bear gets you. We have three unsolved robberies in this neighborhood, last two months. Just like this. Daytime, high floor, vic alone. My theory? Messenger with a jones, just delivered whatever, now he's in the building. Finds a one-man show, easy pickings."

"Did anyone get killed in those others?"

"Maybe the vics didn't put up a fuss. Would Pilarsky have? Instead of forking over?"

I gritted my teeth and nodded. "He could get—indignant."

"Civilians." Mulgrew shook his head.

"He was an ex–Port Authority cop."

"Oh, really?" He spoke with the thick condescension the NYPD reserves for the lower cop orders. I wanted to slug him. "What about you? You ex-PA, too?"

"I've always been private."

That got me an even more patronizing "I see." Then: "Did Pilarsky go armed?"

"No. He shot someone on the job once and he didn't like it."

Mulgrew wrote that down, too, and flipped the notebook shut. So much for Joel. An ex-PA cop with a never-been-a-cop girl employee, unarmed because he was squeamish about shooting people, arguing with a stickup artist in his one-man office. What did he expect? Case closed.

"They have their own ambulances," I said.

"What?"

"Orthodox Jews. There are special ways you have to handle the body." Actually, I wasn't sure Joel cared. He'd told me once about the ambulances, but I didn't remember him saying to make certain he was carried away in one. But he had said I should get up here fast, and I hadn't. In case the ambulance thing was important to him, I wanted to get it right.

Mulgrew hissed a sigh. "I think the Department can handle the protocol. Okay, go. Wait—what about you? You don't carry, right?"

"I do sometimes, but not now." I opened my jacket and showed him. Before he could ask, I opened my bag, too. He waved it closed as though I were trying to sell him something.

"So you do and Pilarsky didn't?" Clearly for him that was backwards, just wrong.

"I shot someone once, too. I didn't like it either. But I'd have liked it less if he shot me."

Mulgrew smiled.

I still wanted to slug him.

7

Mary drove me back to Chinatown. Somewhere past Fourteenth Street I roused myself to ask, "Can I call Alice?"

"The client?"

"I assume that charming Mulgrew will follow up with her?"

"He thinks there's probably no connection. He's hoping for the messenger with the jones who can close this and the three open robberies at the same time. But he'll go through the motions."

"Then I'd like her to hear it from me. He doesn't have the greatest bedside manner. Or any kind of manner. The bear gets you. Jerk."

"I guess it's okay." Mary's tone said that as a friend she agreed and as a cop she'd rather I didn't call. I ignored the cop.

As it turned out, though, it didn't matter. "No answer." I pocketed my phone. "I left a message on the room phone and her cell, just to call me."

Mary nodded. The cop was probably relieved. "You want to go home?"

"No, thanks, to my office." I couldn't face telling my mother about this, not yet.

Mary dropped me on the west end of Canal. "Should I come in?"

"No, I'm fine."

"You forget I've seen you when you're fine. But okay. Call me if you need me?"

"You know I will."

She went back to work and I went in the street door that bore a nameplate for Golden Adventure Travel, but not my name. My office was the second one inside. As long as my clients came out with brochures about cruises through the Guilin mountains, who was to say where they'd really been?

I waved at the travel ladies as though this were a normal day. "Welcome back!" Andi Gee called, looking perplexed when I didn't stop to chat after a month away. I'd have to mend that fence later, but right now I needed to be alone.

Unlocking my door, I stepped into the dusty stillness of a room long unused. I opened the window and put the kettle on. After I splashed cold water all over my face, I stared into the mirror, but the eyes looking back were hard to take.

A random robbery? I dropped into my chair. Would that be better, or worse? Worse, I decided. The good news would be, it wasn't something I should have seen coming. The bad news was, I still should have gotten up there right away. And if it didn't have to do with our case, then I wouldn't be able to have a hand in catching the son of a bitch.

When my desk phone rang, I almost jumped out of my chair.

"Lydia Chin. Chin Ling Wan-ju," I told it in English and Chinese.

"It's Bill."

Months, I marveled. *For months I've been checking the readout to see who was calling; this is the first time I didn't.*

"I'm sorry about Joel," he said.

"How do you—"

"Mary called me."

"Mary did?" My best and oldest friend? Sandbagged me like that?

"Can I buy you a cup of tea?"

"I . . . I don't think—"

"Please."

Just that, just "please." Anything else—any long explanation, any attempt at apology, especially any excuses—and I'd have hung up. But there was just that one "please," and silence.

"Come to my office," I said. "I have tea here."

• • •

Some things surprise you, but some don't. Bill showed up carrying a large black coffee. The offer of tea had been an olive branch, but that didn't mean whatever peace terms he was proposing would include him drinking any.

"Long time," I said, shutting the door behind him.

He sat in the chair across the desk. Were there really more lines on his face than last time I saw him?

"I'm sorry," he said.

"About Joel? Or about the long time?"

"Both."

"Who the hell asked you?"

A pause. "If I shouldn't have come—"

"Oh, shut up."

He did.

I sipped my tea. Jasmine, what my mother used to give us when we didn't feel well. "It's just, I don't think it's okay that you get to make that decision unilaterally."

"What decision?"

"About who isn't good for who and who could do better without who and who should stay away from who and who gets back in touch with who. And don't tell me some of those 'whos' should be 'whoms.'"

"They should, though."

"I know!"

He drank his coffee. "Listen: I fucked up big. I needed time to think about that. If I—"

"When did I ever not give you time? Did I ever crowd you? Why couldn't you have called and said, 'I need time. I'm going to the cabin, I'm locking myself in my apartment, I'm shooting myself into space?' Just to call and acknowledge I still existed. Why couldn't you do that? Before you went off to meditate on what a fuckup you are?"

"Because I'm a fuckup." He raised his gaze; I met it silently. Without a word, long and steadily, we held each other's eyes.

Then, because I know that face so well, I saw him fighting a smile.

Dammit, I wanted to yell, *this isn't funny*! And it wasn't. But what was, was how hard he was working to stifle it. *Bet you can't,* I thought, and felt my own mouth twitching.

And suddenly there we both were, cracking up. Howling, gasping for breath, astonishing a month's worth of dust and gloom. I laughed so hard tea slopped out of the mug I held. Until in an instant I felt a change, a spin-around: Now I wasn't laughing, I was sobbing.

Bill jumped from his chair, came around the desk, and held me, an awkward manuever since I was sitting down. The clumsiness of it struck me as hilarious, and I was laughing again, and then crying, and both, until I didn't know anymore what kind of shudders were convulsing me.

Finally, the storm let up. I pushed Bill away, stood, and made for the bathroom. I went through the cold water routine again, this time spending longer for less result. When I came out, Bill was back in his chair, halfway through a cigarette.

"Who said you could smoke in here?"

"You changed the rules?" He held the cigarette over the ashtray, prepared to stub it out.

"No. But you're lucky I still have that."

"The ashtray? Yeah, but you hid it. It wasn't easy to find."

"You're supposed to be a detective." I dropped into my chair.

"As such I have a question."

"Which is?"

"When did you start using four-letter words?"

"I haven't, as a rule. But some situations demand extreme measures."

"Like me."

"Yes, I'd say you're one of those situations." I paused. "Bill?" I said, more gently. "How's Gary?"

Bill looked into his coffee. "Coping."

"Better than you?"

He shrugged.

As badly as things turned out in that case, they'd have turned out worse if Bill hadn't been there, and people—including Gary—told him that, but it didn't comfort him. I think the reason Bill disappeared after that was that he didn't want to hear anymore how it wasn't his fault.

So I didn't say it now.

"If you talk to him," I said instead, "give him my love."

Bill nodded.

I got up and poured more tea, to give myself a chance to figure out some really smart, articulate words for what I wanted to say next, but I was lost, really. All I could come up with was exactly what I meant: "What do we do now?"

"About what?"

"Well, it was lots of fun cracking up with you, but we still haven't gotten past the part where we haven't spoken in months because you're a four-letter-word. And Joel's still dead." I tried for matter-of-fact, but I felt my eyes mist.

"How about," Bill said, "we put the first item on hold and work on the second?"

"Meaning what?"

"Mary said you think Joel's murder may be related to the case you're working, but the homicide cop who caught it doesn't."

"Speaking of Mary, wait until I get my hands on *her*."

"That's between you two. What I'm proposing is, if you want, I'll work with you on this. We can follow up whatever you think needs following. If you're right maybe we can light a fire under the cops, and if you're wrong we'll find that out."

"I'm right."

"You usually are."

"Boy, you must be seriously feeling guilty, to say something like that."

"You're right about that, too. Deal?"

"Is this why you called?"

"Yes."

"Because you thought I needed help?"

"No. Because I wanted to help you."

And that was like the "please" when he'd first called.

Probably the sensible thing to do would be to let the cops handle Joel's murder. I could focus on Rosalie Gilder's jewelry, assuming Alice Fairchild still wanted that. Bill speaks a number of languages, but none of them is Yiddish or Chinese, so if I took that route I could throw him out and count myself lucky to be rid of a fuckup.

But it was Joel who'd said we worked well together, Bill and I.

8

I laid the situation out for Bill: Alice Fairchild and the Waldorf, Joel summoning me to his office because something was fishy, Detective Mulgrew's unsolved robberies. I showed him the photos: the jewelry; Wong Pan, who stole it; Rosalie Gilder and her brother, Paul, smiling on a windy day. I gave him Rosalie's first letter to read.

"There are others," I said. "At the Jewish Museum."

"Have you read them?"

"Some."

"Do they help?"

I felt an odd, unexpected comfort: the same feeling I'd had dropping my suitcase in my own apartment after a month away.

"Not really, except to get to know her. It made me want to get her jewelry back even more, though."

"Can I have them? I'll read them later."

"I'll print you out a set." I clicked on the computer and had just gotten to the Jewish Museum site when the phone rang. I didn't recognize the number, so I answered in both languages. "Lydia Chin, Chin Ling Wan-ju."

"Whatever," a dismissive voice countered. "Where's your client?"

"Detective Mulgrew?"

"Two points. Where is she?"

"I have no idea. She's not at the Waldorf?"

"If she was why would I be calling you?"

Because you're as charmed by me as I am by you? "If you tried there and her cell phone, I have no idea."

"It would be good if you did."

"I thought you said Joel's death had nothing to do with her."

"I don't like witnesses running out before I talk to them. Makes them look bad."

"Running out? Did she check out of the hotel?"

"No, and her things are still in her room. But she's not turning up."

"You were in her room?"

"Oh, gee. Shouldn't I have done that? Look, when you hear from her, you're going to let me know right away, right?"

"Anything you say."

"Because I don't like people helping witnesses run out, either." He hung up on me.

"Mulgrew can't find Alice," I told Bill. "He thinks that makes her look bad. I can't tell him where to find her, so I look bad, too."

"Did she check out?"

"No."

"Then what makes him think she's not just in a meeting or something, with her phone off?"

"Probably because so many people avoid him all the time, it's his first guess."

"She may not even know he's looking for her."

"Or she could be in trouble. Maybe that's what was fishy." I tried Alice's cell and the Waldorf myself but just got voice mail. I pulled her card from my wallet. "I'm going to call her office in Zurich. Maybe they know how to reach her."

"You can do that, but it's eight at night there."

I did it anyway, and all it got me was a woman's voice, speaking German, saying nothing I understood except "Alice Fairchild." I tried to leave a message, but the phone clicked off.

"How's your German?" I asked Bill.

"My Dutch is better. Why?"

I made the call again and handed him the phone.

"The office is closed for two weeks," he said. "Please call back."

"That's why it won't take a message?"

"Who wants their voice mail clogged with two weeks' worth of calls?"

"Who can afford to blow off business for two weeks? Wouldn't your clients drop you if you did something like that?"

"My clients drop me for all sorts of reasons."

"Yeah, like you don't have that smart, dependable Chinese partner anymore."

"And they know it's my own fault. Maybe all the clients she cares about have her cell number."

I was trying to think what to do when the phone rang again. It was another unfamiliar number, and I considered letting it go to voice mail, but at the last minute I answered, drawing out both names in case it was Mulgrew again.

"Ms. Chin? This is Leah Pilarsky calling." The voice was tentative. "You don't know me. I'm Joel Pilarsky's sister-in-law."

I felt as if the sun had suddenly gone down. "I'm so sorry about Joel."

"Thank you. We all loved him. Ms. Chin, Joel's wife, Ruth, asked me to get in touch with you. She got a call from someone looking for Joel, someone who didn't know . . . Anyway, Ruth thinks it has to do with the case he'd just started, with you. Joel always spoke highly of you, and Ruth is sure he'd want you to go on. Do you want the number?"

Joel spoke of me at all? And, highly? "Yes, I do, please. Was it Alice Fairchild?"

"No. A man called Friedman, Stanley Friedman." She gave me a number. "Do you know him?"

"No, but I'll call him right away. Thank you very much. And please tell Mrs. Pilarsky how sorry I am."

I briefed Bill while I dialed.

"Friedman and Sons, you've reached Stanley Friedman." The voice had an Eastern European accent.

"Mr. Friedman, my name is Lydia Chin. I worked with Joel Pilarsky. I understand you called him?"

"Yes, I did. You're his partner? My condolences to you."

"Thank you." I let the inaccuracy slide. "Mr. Friedman, do you have information you wanted to give Joel?"

"I'm not sure I do, I'm not sure I don't. Yesterday when he came here, he spoke to my son, I was out. I only just now saw the pictures he left."

"Do you know something about the pieces in them?"

"Something. Ms.—Chin? A question: Maybe it's possible for you to come here? The telephone is a fine instrument, but some things are better face-to-face."

"I completely agree. Where's here?"

"Thirty West Forty-seventh Street. Third floor. Friedman and Sons."

"I'll be right up."

I hung up and looked at Bill. He was already on his feet.

For the second time that day I took the N uptown. Weaving along the crowded Diamond District sidewalk, Bill and I parted for three bearded, black-coated Hasidim and eddied around a Latino couple holding hands at an engagement-ring display. At Number 30 a minimal lobby led to a no-frills elevator. On the third floor, a camera peered from the ceiling and a buzzer clung to the wall by a door labeled FRIEDMAN AND SONS. I buzzed and it buzzed back.

In a windowless but brightly lit room we were greeted by a man with warm blue eyes and white hair under a black yarmulke. "Ms. Chin, I'm Stanley Friedman. Thank you for coming."

I introduced Bill—as my associate, not my partner; he looked at me sideways and I thought, *So sue me*—and we all shook hands. Stanley Friedman gestured us to chairs around a book-piled coffee table. Luscious color photos of rings, bracelets, and necklaces decked the walls.

"These are your work?" I asked. "They're beautiful."

He smiled. "My father, of blessed memory, was a real jeweler, an artist. So are my sons. In between is Stanley Friedman, a peasant. I choose the stones and run the business." He lifted an envelope from the table and slid out photographs I recognized. "Now, Ms. Chin, I ask you a question: These are the pieces you and your partner, may he rest in peace, were looking for?"

"Yes. Have you seen them?"

"No."

"No? But—"

"Again, I ask you a question: These were all?"

"All?"

"Nothing else?"

"Not as far as I know. Should there have been something else?"

"Should, I can't say. I'll admit to you, when I saw these pictures, I got excited. I thought probably it was just Friedman being romantic, and it wouldn't be true, but if it was, how wonderful to be part of it! But then I find the man who brought the pictures is murdered, and I think this: The chances of it being true are greater, and wonderful it's not."

"Mr. Friedman, I'm sorry, but I don't follow you."

He turned one of the photos over. On the back a bulleted list covered the facts of the case: Rosalie Gilder's name, and Elke's, Horst's, and Paul's; the date of Rosalie and Paul's arrival in Shanghai; Wong Pan's name, the date the box was dug up, and the date the contents disappeared.

"My son is a precise man," Stanley Friedman said. "This is the information your partner gave him. It's correct? These pieces were Rosalie Gilder's?"

He spoke Rosalie's name with an odd familiarity.

"Yes, it's correct."

He leaned forward. "Ms. Chin, your partner. He had found these pieces?"

"I don't think so."

"Possibly, you may need to think again." From the coffee table Friedman picked up a thick book. "*Legendary Gemstones of the World.* Scott and Huber, 1992. A reference in my field. May I read an entry?" He slipped on half-glasses and opened to a bookmark. "'The Shanghai Moon. A disc of white jade streaked with green, set in gold, surrounded by diamonds. The surface of the jade worked in a pattern of clouds and magpies, China, Tang Dynasty (618–907); the diamonds of nineteenth-century origin, reportedly bar- and princess-cut.' Ms. Chin, Mr. Smith, do you know this gem?"

"No," I answered.

But Bill said, "Yes."

"You do?" I was surprised, though Stanley Friedman didn't seem to be.

"When I was in the navy, in Asia," Bill said. "It's a brooch, right? And it's lost. It was the Pacific seaman's equivalent of the Brooklyn Bridge. If you were particularly clueless, some guy would always offer to sell you the Shanghai Moon."

"A brooch," Mr. Friedman agreed. "And lost. Listen to Scott and Huber. 'One of the more recent pieces in this volume, the Shanghai Moon is also the most mysterious. Its story is unverified, but there is general agreement on the basic facts: In Shanghai in 1941, a young couple brought a jade disc and a diamond necklace to a jeweler whose identity has been lost. The couple were a Jewish refugee from Salzburg, Rosalie Gilder—'"

"*Rosalie?*"

Mr. Friedman stopped, peering over the glasses.

"I'm sorry!" I said. "Go on. That gem is *Rosalie's*? Who was the man?"

The jeweler went back to the page. "'Rosalie Gilder, and a Shanghainese named Chen Kai-rong. Secretly—'"

"Kai-rong! Oh! Oh, good! No, I'm sorry, go on."

He lowered the book. "Ms. Chin? You don't know the Shanghai Moon, but you know these people?"

"I've read some letters. Her letters. From when she met him. That's all. Please go on."

"Letters?"

"At the Jewish Museum. In the Holocaust archives."

"Ah." He nodded slowly and resumed. "'Secretly betrothed, the pair asked the jeweler to combine the jade, an heirloom of the Chen family, with the stones from the necklace, which had been Rosalie Gilder's mother's. The resulting brooch was known as the Shanghai Moon. Worn by the young woman at their wedding the following year, the Shanghai Moon was seen only rarely after that. It was variously reported sold, stolen, or destroyed; the most fanciful rumor had it in the possession of a German officer's widow in a Japanese internment camp. None of these stories was ever proved true. It remains most likely that Rosalie Gilder Chen, or in any event the Chen family, re-tained possession of the brooch throughout the war.'

"'Jewish refugees leaving Shanghai after the war took with them rumors of the Shanghai Moon's splendor, as did repatriated European and Japanese nationals. How many of these people had actually seen the brooch is unknown, but its legend grew.'"

Here Stanley Friedman looked over his glasses, then went back to reading. "'For four years following the Second World War, civil war raged in China. Occasional accounts of sightings of the Shanghai Moon reached the West, none verifiable. In 1949, as the Bamboo Cur-tain fell across the early days of the People's Republic, the brooch was said to be in Kobe, Japan; in Bangkok; and in Singapore. Over the years stories have put the Shanghai Moon in such places as Taipei, Hong Kong, and San Francisco, and collectors have followed; but to date every search has been fruitless.'"

Finished, Friedman took off his glasses and passed the book to us. The glossy white page opposite the entry was conspicuously empty except for these words:

THE SHANGHAI MOON
VALUE: UNKNOWN
(NO ILLUSTRATION)

I looked up at Stanley Friedman. "This is what should have been with Rosalie's jewelry? The Shanghai Moon?"

"Should, who can say? But this story, I heard it when I was young. Even then, I was a practical man. I paid no attention. It was a legend, you see, this gem." He folded his glasses and slipped them into his pocket. "So for sixty years, no one sees these pieces that were Rosalie Gilder's. Everyone starts to think like Stanley Friedman: They're a myth, the Shanghai Moon's a myth, it's all a romantic story from bad times. But now? Suddenly, here they are, these pieces, and suddenly, your partner's killed. These, they don't look to me like something worth killing over. Especially, they're not worth killing someone who hasn't found them."

"But the Shanghai Moon is?"

"Would I kill for it, or would you?" Stanley Friedman shrugged. "But if your partner had caught its scent—Ms. Chin, there are people who've been looking for the Shanghai Moon for a very long time."

9

"It must be what Joel meant," I said to Bill as the elevator started down. "He must have heard about the Shanghai Moon."

"Maybe. But why would that be 'fishy'?"

"Because Alice never told us about it?"

"She might not know. Just because it was Rosalie Gilder's doesn't mean it was found with this other jewelry."

"True. But when the heirs were notified about the find, wouldn't they have asked?"

"Maybe they never heard of it either."

"That's a stretch. *You've* heard of it."

"It was one of those back-room legends in sailor's bars."

"With which you're quite familiar, I'm sure."

"Legends?"

"Bars. Did you ever meet anyone who saw it?"

"Not that I recall. Just guys whose buddies, captains, and pawnbrokers had. The drunker guys were, the more spectacular they claimed it was."

"By which you mean the Shanghai Moon."

"Don't tell me," he said as we issued onto Forty-seventh Street, "that besides taking up the use of four-letter words, you've developed a dirty mind."

"Without you around someone had to provide the smut." I sagged against the building, dismayed at the rush hour crowds. "God, I'm tired. I feel like my tank's empty."

"You've had a hard day."

"No kidding."

"You want a cup of tea?"

"Can I go home to bed?"

"Sure."

"No, I can't."

We started along the block, looking for a place to try the tea option. We didn't make it to the corner before my phone rang. I flipped it open and answered, sticking my finger in my other ear to hear better. What I heard was "Lydia? This is Alice Fairchild."

"Alice!" I practically yelped. "Where are you? Are you all right?"

"Yes, of course." She sounded surprised at the question. "Lydia, what's happened? I've been in meetings, and I just got your messages. A police detective has been trying to reach me, too. Have they found Wong Pan? And the jewelry?"

"Oh," I said. "No, I'm afraid not. Alice, there's some very bad news. I'm sorry, but . . . Alice, Joel's dead."

I heard her quick breath. "What? Oh, my God! What happened?"

"Someone shot him. At his office, this morning."

"*Shot* him?" Her voice rose a few notes. "This morning? But I just spoke to him this morning. Who? What happened?"

"They don't know. That's why the police want to talk to you."

"To me?" A pause. "They can't be thinking this has anything to do with the jewelry?"

"They don't know."

"But how? I don't see— Had Joel located it?"

"I don't know."

"Had he found Wong Pan?"

"I don't know, Alice. He called me, but he just said to come up. I don't know why."

"Oh, my God. What if he'd found Wong Pan, and Wong Pan— Yes, of course I'll talk to the police, if it would help. I'll call that detective right away. Will you come?"

"To see Mulgrew?" The idea did not fill me with delight.

"You might remember details I've forgotten. Of our discussion. Something that might have sent Joel off in one direction or another."

I had to admit it was a good idea.

"I'm almost back at the Waldorf," she said. "I'll call him now."

"I'm nearby. I'll meet you there."

I relayed this conversation to Bill, who'd steered me into a notch in a facade and planted himself between me and the surging crowds. We headed toward the Waldorf. Our steps fell into rhythm, as they often did; as it often did, that surprised me, Bill being thirteen inches taller than I am. "Hey, by the way," I said, as we neared the hotel's doors. "Thanks."

"For what?"

"Showing up."

For a moment, he didn't speak. Then, "I was afraid it was too little, too late."

"Almost. Not quite."

I got no smile this time from the Waldorf's doorman, who probably thought I shouldn't be running around in wrinkled linen when I had that nice silk suit. Or maybe he didn't like the looks of Bill. Bill can clean up well, but in general he's not a Waldorf kind of guy. Nevertheless, a call from the desk to Alice's room got us an invitation up to a floor where the corridor was plushly carpeted and the walls layered in molding. I clinked a little brass knocker; the door opened right away.

"Oh, Lydia!" Alice pressed my hands in quick sympathy. "This is so terrible. I'm so sorry about Joel."

"Thank you. Alice, this is a colleague of mine, Bill Smith. Bill, Alice Fairchild."

They shook hands. Alice asked Bill, "Did you know Joel?"

"Yes."

"Then my condolences on your loss, too. Sit down, please. Coffee and tea are on the way. Or would you like something stronger?"

"Aren't we going to the precinct?" I asked.

"The detective's coming here."

"Mulgrew?"

"You sound surprised."

"At him, for being so accommodating."

"I think he thinks I'm a delicate lady of a certain age who might get rattled in a police station. Where he got that idea, I have no clue." Her eyes twinkled. "But I'm sure it's more comfortable here than there."

The room was populated by carved furniture, brass lamps with pleated shades, botanical prints on striped wallpaper. Street sounds drifted up, muffled by glass and the soft purr of air-conditioning. I sat in a flowered armchair, but Bill leaned near a window, where he could look both into the room and out over New York.

"Tell me what happened," Alice said.

I gave as clinical an account of Joel's death as I could manage. Her hand went to her mouth when she heard I was the one who'd found him.

"That's horrible! Oh, Lydia, I'm so sorry."

"He called me. He said something was fishy. He told me to rush up there."

"Fishy? What was it?"

"I don't know. I never found out. But if I'd done what he said—"

Bill shifted on his perch, about to break in and give me a hard time for giving myself a hard time, but Alice spoke first. "It's so natural," she sighed. "To blame ourselves when something terrible happens. I think it's comforting in a way. It makes us feel there's something we could have done if we'd been smarter, or faster, or whatever it is. Sometimes thinking we've failed is less frightening than admitting we were helpless."

My face burned. I felt like I'd caught sight of myself in a mirror, and I didn't look so good.

"But Lydia," Alice went on gently, "you say the police think it was random, a robbery. Couldn't that be true?"

"Yes, of course," I sighed. "Trying to make it part of this case may just be me. An odd kind of wishful thinking."

The door knocker clinked. Bill checked the peephole and let in a waiter rolling a room service cart. By the time Alice signed for it and sat down, I was ready to be all business again. I wasn't at all sure she was right about failure being better than helplessness, but obviously best by far was to put up with neither.

"Alice, you said you spoke to Joel this morning. Did you call him, or did he call you?"

"He called me." She handed me a cup of tea, milk, no sugar, and just the right amount of milk, too. She poured coffee for Bill, who took it back to his windowsill. "He knew I'd be in meetings today. He just wanted to touch base before I was unavailable."

"Did he say anything was wrong?"

"No, nothing. He said you were both proceeding along the lines you'd started yesterday, and he'd check back later."

"Did he mention anyone he was planning to talk to?"

"No. I'm sorry. That's not very useful, is it?"

"Anything that fills in the gaps is useful," I said, more to make her feel better than because it was true. "Before Mulgrew gets here I want to ask you something else, though. Have you ever heard of a piece of jewelry called the Shanghai Moon?"

"No, I don't think so. What is it?"

"Apparently, Rosalie Gilder was married in Shanghai. To a Chinese man she'd met on the ship. Why are you smiling?"

"Chen Kai-rong? Was it he?" To my nod, she said, "Oh, how sweet! She talks about him in her letters. They're in the museum's archives. You can call them up on the Web site."

"I've actually read the first few," I said. "Jet lag. I couldn't sleep last night."

"When I read them I couldn't tell if it was obvious to either Elke or Rosalie that Kai-rong was courting her, but it was to me. You're telling me they married? That's marvelous! How do you know?"

"One of the jewelers Joel left photos with recognized Rosalie's name and knew the story." I told her what we'd learned in Stanley Friedman's showroom.

"The diamond necklace," Alice said, when I was done. "That's what happened to it!"

"What diamond necklace?"

"As nearly as my clients know, Rosalie and Paul took seven pieces of jewelry to Shanghai. Five are in this find. One was a ruby ring, which Rosalie sold—you'll see if you read the rest of the letters. She also mentions a diamond necklace. I've been wondering where that was. Wondering even if Wong Pan palmed it before the contents of the box were known, though I don't see how he could have. The Shanghai authorities would never have allowed him to open it alone. But this would answer that question."

"That question, yes," Bill said from across the room. "Not the question of the Shanghai Moon."

Alice shifted to look at him. "You think that might have been in the box? But it's the same problem. How could he have stolen it without anyone knowing it was there?"

"Maybe it wasn't," I said. "Maybe someone just thinks it was."

"And that person killed Joel? But why?"

"They thought he knew something he wasn't telling? Things were stolen from his office. That's why Mulgrew's thinking robbery. But what if that was just opportunistic? What if the real point was to search the place?"

"I suppose that's possible. But to find what?"

"Whatever they thought Joel knew?"

Alice nodded thoughtfully. Bill sipped coffee thoughtfully. I wished I had a thought or two, but I had only questions. "Alice, didn't you grow up in Shanghai? Mr. Friedman says this brooch, the Shanghai Moon, is famous. You've never heard of it?"

"I was born there, yes, but I was four when we were sent to the internment camp. When we were released three years later, we took the first ship home we could get." She stirred her tea. "These aren't memories I return to very often. As you might imagine, the camp was a bad place. Heat and mud in summer. Clammy cold in winter. Nothing was clean and there was never enough food. Everyone was sick, worse and worse as the war ground on. A lot of people died. The land was so swampy they wrapped bricks in the binding cloths—there were no coffins—so the bodies wouldn't rise back to the surface. But sometimes it didn't work. You'd see a hand, a leg . . .

"I was a child. That was my entire world. *Our* entire world. If outside the camp there was someone called Rosalie Gilder, and she married someone called Chen Kai-rong, and they had a brooch created to celebrate, we wouldn't have known. Then, once we came to America, everyone tried to put Shanghai far behind."

I said, "That sounds terrible. I'm sorry."

"It was. But we lived, and came here, and prospered. Many didn't. Still, you can see why Shanghai may mean something quite different to me from what it meant to Rosalie Gilder."

"Yes, of course."

From the window, Bill said, "What about your clients? They never told you about the Shanghai Moon?"

"No," Alice said, frowning over that. I frowned, too; the question seemed a little insensitive right at the moment. Although I had an insensitive question of my own I'd been looking for a time to ask.

"Alice, Joel was wondering something. About you. It made me wonder, too. I don't mean to offend you—"

"No, please. If you think it will help discover what happened to Joel."

I didn't see how it could, but it seemed like something I should find out, because Joel had wanted to know. "It's this: Why do you do the work you do? Holocaust asset recovery?"

She smiled. "You mean as a gentile? Don't worry, I've been asked that before. The camp . . . It was the war that sent us there. We lost so much, as so many people did. As I grew, I learned that what we'd been through, horrible as it was, wasn't the half of it. I hated that war. But a war that's over is an elusive enemy. My sister urged me to put it behind me, and I tried, but I couldn't. I felt—as we were saying earlier—angry and helpless. When the asset recovery movement started to grow, I saw it as a chance to right some of those wrongs."

"Joel said most people who do the work you do see it as a religious calling."

"Did he? I suppose, in a way, I do. And not all my clients are Jewish, you know. Most are. But Catholics, Hungarians, Poles, homosexuals, Gypsies—that war had many victims."

"Wouldn't your argument really have been with the Japanese?" Bill asked. "That's who put you in the camp."

"There's no reparations movement against Japan, except on behalf of 'comfort women.' But Germany and Japan were allies. Prying stolen treasures out of German hands is about the best I can do. For me, it's enough."

When there's not much you can do, something still beats nothing. Well, I could second that.

The desk phone rang. Alice spoke and then, slipping the receiver back, told us, "Detective Mulgrew's on his way up."

"Maybe I'll make myself scarce." Bill rose from his perch.

"You'd deprive yourself of the pleasure of meeting Mulgrew?" I asked. "And the pleasure of more of the Waldorf's coffee?"

"Good as the coffee is, from what I hear the one doesn't begin to make up for the other. And the NYPD doesn't like crowds."

That was true. Also, certain elements in the NYPD don't like Bill. Mulgrew seemed to be the type who'd check around and find some way to get on my case later about the company I keep.

Under Mulgrew's hand even the door knocker sounded scornful. If Mulgrew was enchanted to see me, he hid it well, but he didn't boot me out. He even tossed the occasional question at me, though the ones he asked Alice sounded less sharp in tone, less accusatory in content. Maybe that was because she poured him coffee as soon as he sat down, and put two chocolate cookies on the saucer.

Not that he had many questions. The pro forma nature of this interview couldn't have been more obvious. What did you hire the deceased to do, did he give you any indication he was worried about anything, what did you talk about this morning, can you think of anyone who'd want to hurt him?

"Well, only Wong Pan. If Joel had found him."

"The Shanghai guy? What about it, had Pilarsky found him?"

"He didn't say he had," Alice admitted, "but maybe after I spoke to him—"

"He didn't get any calls or e-mails. He made three calls: his college roommate, you, and you." Mulgrew turned to me. "Did he say anything about finding this guy?"

"I'd have told you before if he had, Detective."

"I'm sure." Back to Alice: "Any idea where I can find this Wong Pan?"

"If I had," Alice said with a small smile, "I wouldn't have hired Joel and Lydia. You do have his photo?" She started for her briefcase, but Mulgrew waved her back to her chair.

"Yeah, she gave it to me," he said. I sincerely hate being referred to as "she" when I'm sitting right there. "But unless he also pulled the other three jobs in that neighborhood, my money's not on him."

"You will look for him, though?"

"Sure." Mulgrew reached for a lemon bar, devouring it, as he had the other cookies, in a single bite. This was not a detail man. "Thanks for your time." He stood. "Call me if you think of anything else." He started toward the door.

"The Shanghai Moon," I said.

"What?"

"A legendary lost gem. It belonged to the same woman the rest of this jewelry belonged to."

He stared at me. "A legendary lost gem."

"It's famous."

"Oh, a *famous* legendary lost gem. And it was part of this find?"

"No." I was already regretting opening my mouth. But he irked me, his dismissiveness, his put-upon air. "Or, maybe. We don't know."

"You don't know. So why are you bringing it up?"

"Someone may have thought it was."

"And the connection between that thought and Pilarsky's murder would be?"

"I don't know."

"Did Pilarsky have it? Or know where it was?"

"I don't know."

A pause. "All right, I'll check it out."

Hah. I could just bet what that meant. Mulgrew barking across the squad room: *Hey, any of you ever heard of some jewel called the Shanghai Moon? What about this mutt Wong Pan, from China, where they stole all our jobs?*

Alice walked to the door and opened it for him. "Thank you for being willing to come to the hotel, Detective."

"My pleasure, ma'am. Not often I get to see how the other half lives."

When we were alone again, I said, "Well, you won his heart."

"He's not so bad."

"Yes, he is."

"Just overworked, I think. Most policemen are overworked. Not that you seem exactly fresh as a daisy, if you don't mind my saying so."

"I'm exhausted."

"You've had a terrible day. Why don't you go home? Take a long hot bath. Something relaxing, maybe lavender. It'll do you a world of good."

"You know, that sounds great." I stood. "We can talk in the morning."

"Yes, but I think not professionally."

"What do you mean?"

"Until they catch whoever killed Joel, or until we can be sure his death had nothing to do with Rosalie Gilder's jewelry, I can't think of letting you go on."

My jaw dropped. "You can't think of stopping me! Joel would hate that, giving up!"

"I'm not talking about giving up, but until we know it's safe, we have to let the police take over. I'll call my clients. I'm sure they'll agree."

"But that's just wrong! Mulgrew's not really looking for Wong Pan, and he didn't care at all about the Shanghai Moon!"

"He may be right."

"He's not right."

"All the more reason to back off, then, and let his investigation lead him to that conclusion. Really, Lydia, I can't allow to you endanger yourself. Recovering this jewelry isn't worth that. I'm sorry, but it's my decision."

"But to just give up—"

"Oh, Lydia, please don't make me say it."

"Say what?"

Her sympathetic look didn't alter her unambiguous words. "You're fired."

10

I called Bill the the second I disembarked from the Waldorf. "We're fired!"

"What you mean 'we,' Chinese woman?"

"Be serious! This is bad!" I told him about the interview with Mulgrew, and its aftermath.

He asked, "What are you going to do?"

"Are you kidding? If you think there's any *possible* way I'm going to forget it and let Mulgrew just go through the motions, you're every bit as—"

"I didn't say, 'Are you going to forget it?'" he broke in. "I said, 'What are you going to do?'"

"Oh. Well, when you put it that way." I rubbed my eyes. "I apologize. I shouldn't be taking it out on you."

"That's what I'm here for. Though I'd be curious to know what I'm every bit as."

"I'll never tell. But I'm curious to know something, too. Why did you do that thing you do, sitting off to the side so you can observe someone?"

"I do that?"

"You know, when I play innocent with you, it's silly. When you do it with me, it's absurd. Yes, you do that. When you don't trust someone. Do you have a problem with Alice?"

For a moment he was silent. "There's something peculiar about her. Joel said so, too."

" 'Off' is the word he used, and that was because she does this work and she's not Jewish."

"And she explained that. But there's still something."

"Any idea what?"

"No."

"Have you eaten yet?" my mother called from the living room as I slipped off my shoes in the vestibule. It's a standard Chinese greeting, the hospitable inquiry of a famine-prone land. It's no more looking for a real answer than "How are you?" is in English. But the thought of food right now was enough to curdle my stomach.

"I'm not hungry. Ma, I need to tell you something." I sat on the couch next to her.

"Ling Wan-ju? What's wrong?" She shut her Hong Kong fashion magazine, which she studies for ideas for outfits for my sisters-in-law and me.

"It's Joel, Ma."

"The one who sings."

"Ma, he's dead."

Her lips compressed into a thin line. She patted my hand. Then, hands back in her own lap, she asked, "What happened to him?"

"Someone shot him."

"Who did that?"

"I don't know."

"Was it because of your case?"

Nothing like the head-on approach.

"I don't know that either. The police don't think so." She nodded and minutely relaxed. I could have left it at that, but I didn't want to lie to her. "I do, though."

"Do you?"

"Yes. The client does, too. She wants me to stop."

A few moments of silence. "Are you in danger, Ling Wan-ju?"

"I don't know."

"But it wouldn't matter, would it?"

"Ma—"

"No, it would not. And what the client wants will not matter either. You will do what you think is the right thing for your friend, even if you must do it all alone."

I wasn't going to be alone, but this would have been a particularly bad time to bring up Bill.

"No, you will continue. You will not consider the consequences until they happen."

"I have no choice, Ma."

She looked across the room to the cabinet holding my father's collection of mud figurines: fishermen, farmers, a young woman weaving. People living the lives their parents had lived, and their parents' parents, unchanging, peaceful, and unsurprising. She stood. "You have a choice, Ling Wan-ju: whether to eat dinner or not. I have *jyu sam tong.*"

Pig's heart soup, for reviving the fainthearted. As I followed my mother into the kitchen, I wondered, how had she known?

My mother and I watched a Cantonese soap opera while we ate, a costume drama full of drums and cymbals, Tang dynasty outfits, and complicated hairdos. Trying to follow the story absorbed my attention, as had the running around I'd done all day. It wasn't until I was alone in my room that the image of Joel open-eyed in his chair flooded back into my brain.

I stood in the middle of the floor, feeling my breath knocked out the same way it had been by the actual sight. I closed my eyes, didn't try to muscle the picture away, but let it rush in like a tide until, like a tide, it could ebb again.

It did. But tired as I was, there was no way, after that, I was going to be able to sleep.

So I turned my computer on and Googled "Shanghai Moon."

I didn't learn much more than I had from Mr. Friedman's book. No Web site had photos, or even a good description. All agreed the Shanghai Moon's whereabouts were unknown; few agreed on its last known location. In a chat room I found a breathless account of a brooch seen at an audience with some Bhutanese royals; could this be the Shanghai Moon? Two curt responses: no, and no way. The jade described was apple green. The setting included sapphires. The poster, someone scoffed, must be a newbie even to ask. On another site someone calling himself MoonHunter reported on a private jewelry auction at a swank hotel in Kuala Lumpur, which he'd been invited to by a collector friend. He dwelled a little long, I thought, on the VIP status of the attendees, the lapis fountain, the free Moët, and the stunning waitresses, but that was probably because he had to admit that in the end he'd caught no sniff of the Shanghai Moon. Now that he was in the private auction world, though, he just knew he was on the right track. I didn't know much about private jewelry auctions, but it rather uncharitably occurred to me that anyone so impressed with celebrities, fountains, and waitresses—and who had to be invited into their presence by someone else—was, just possibly, a gasbag.

After an hour of surfing, I got tired of rehashes of the same rumors. Also, the aroma of greed, the focus on the guessed-at value of the brooch, began to bother me. Where was Rosalie in all this, these discussions of colors of jade? Where was Chen Kai-rong, where was the reason the Shanghai Moon had come into existence in the first place?

I logged off. It was possible this was nothing but a big waste of time anyway. Strictly speaking, only Stanley Friedman's book even suggested a connection between Joel's death and the Shanghai Moon. Fingering the jade pendant my parents gave me when I was born, I crawled into bed and fell asleep.

11

The *Wonder Woman* theme song jarred me out of an indistinct, menacing dream. "Oh ho," I mumbled, finding the phone and sinking back into the pillow. "Hi, Benedict Arnold."

Mary said, "Sorry to call so late."

I checked the clock: not quite midnight. "I'm surprised you have the nerve to call me at all."

"You're mad I told Bill about Joel."

"Good guess."

"But that means you know I told him, which means he must have called you."

"No wonder you have that gold shield."

"So what happened?"

"He wormed his way into my office and into the case."

"And into your heart?"

"Not so fast, sister."

"Okay, but you're working together again?"

"Until we find out who killed Joel. Then I'll see how he's behaving."

"So I did the right thing."

"You think I'd admit that?"

"I wouldn't, in your position. Anyway, I really hope it works out. But Lydia, that's not why I called."

"If you're checking up on me because of Joel, I'm okay, truly."

"I still don't believe that, but I'm glad to hear it. But that's not why either."

There was a tone in her voice I was finally awake enough to hear, and I didn't like it. "Mary? Is something else wrong?"

"It sort of is. We identified my John Doe."

"Hey, if I weren't mad at you I'd say, 'Great'! Did it make you look smart? Who is he?"

"Not that smart. He's Chinese, but not an illegal. Not an immigrant at all. Lydia, he's a cop."

"A cop? You mean from another department, or from like the FBI?"

"I mean from China. From Shanghai."

"A cop from *China*?"

"They'd made contact a few days ago, brass to brass, to say he was coming, but that kind of thing doesn't trickle down to precinct level until the out-of-town cop gets here. This guy never got that far. Shanghai got in touch when he missed a check-in call home."

"What was he doing here?"

"Chasing a fugitive."

"And you're calling me in the middle of the night to tell me this. Wait—the light is dawning. It was my fugitive? He was after Wong Pan?"

"Yes."

"Oh boy."

"Oh boy, what?"

"Probably nothing. But there may be more going on than you know about." I told Mary what Stanley Friedman had told us.

When I was done she was silent for moment. "You're kidding. A mysterious lost fabulous jewel?"

"Just keep an open mind."

"If you say so. But you don't know if Wong Pan has this jewel."

"No."

"Or if he does, if Joel knew that."

"No."

"Or if it has anything to do with this at all."

"What happened to that open mind?"

"It's still ajar. Right now I need to speak to Alice Fairchild. She doesn't answer her phone at the Waldorf or her cell. How do I find her?"

"Mary, it's midnight! Maybe she sleeps with earplugs. If you want her, go over there and bang on the door. That's what Mulgrew would do. Speaking of Mulgrew, did you tell him about the Chinese cop? That's his case, too, isn't it?"

"Teed him off. He told me I should have figured it out sooner."

"*You* should have?"

"And he's still clinging to his messenger theory on Joel."

"He thinks this can possibly be coincidence?"

"More like hopes. He did promise they'll check the forensics at Joel's office and the cop's hotel room."

"Well, I guess that's all we can hope for. Mary? What was his name?"

"The Chinese cop?"

"Yes."

"Sheng Yue. Why?"

"I don't know. He's dead. We should at least be calling him by his name."

After we hung up I stared at the ceiling for a while. I thought about Joel, drinking coffee at the Waldorf; about Alice, remembering how I took my tea; about Rosalie and Kai-rong on the deck of an ocean liner. I thought about calling Bill, and while I was thinking, I suddenly found the room bright with sun. And though I hadn't noticed myself sleeping, I'd woken with an inspiration. I groped for my phone and speed-dialed Mary. "The cop from Shanghai. Sheng Yue. His hotel room's the one that was registered to Wu Ming? 'Anonymous?'"

"Good morning to you, too. Yes, that's right."

"Why would a cop do that?"

"I wondered that. Probably, Wong Pan knew the Shanghai police were on his trail. Wong Pan's a civil servant, he might even know Sheng Yue personally. So just in case."

"Right," I said. "Thanks."

"Lydia! Do *not* hang up! It sounds lame to me, too. What are you thinking?"

"I'll tell you if it works out."

"No."

"Then come with me."

"It's a quarter to seven!"

"So what? Your shift starts at eight. Think of it as overtime."

Twenty minutes later we were at the Midtown Suites, Mary knew what I was thinking, she'd made this official business, and she was telling me I was lucky she was letting me tag along.

"It was my idea!"

"You're lucky you have good ideas."

At the desk, Mary showed the pudgy, bleary-eyed clerk her gold shield. "You had a homicide here a few days ago."

He nodded. "Five twenty-five. A Chinese cop, I hear." His look said he was savvy enough to know that's why two more Chinese cops were in his face right now.

"Were you on duty when the man who took that room checked in?"

"Of course. This is my shift. Midnight to ten."

"Is this him?"

He peered at the photo. "Of course. Why?"

Of course. The photo was Wong Pan's.

Out on the sidewalk, Mary called Mulgrew and read him the riot act. I was impressed; my regret was that I couldn't hear Mulgrew's end. When Mary lowered the still-smoking phone, she told me, "He says Sheng Yue answered the description of the registered guest."

"Meaning he was Chinese."

"This desk clerk who checked him in lives out in Jersey and was off by the time they found the body. Mulgrew asked if anyone still on duty had seen the registered guest. A room service waiter brought him a burger the night before."

"He made the ID?"

"Yes. But guess what? He's a Mexican illegal himself. Mulgrew said don't worry, they weren't INS, just was this the guy with the burger or not?"

"He said it was?"

"Maybe he even thought it was. Mulgrew never should have bought it without corroboration. An illegal ID-ing a bloody corpse in a roomful of cops? What kind of police work is that?" Mary's face was flushed with both anger at, and embarrassment for, her department. "So you were right. The room was Wong Pan's. Sheng Yue must have traced him to it. I'm going to need that photo."

I handed her the envelope. "Mary, what about phone calls from the room? If it was Wong Pan's, they may mean something."

"They might have, but there weren't any. Maybe he didn't make any. Or maybe he has a cell."

I thought about that. "What are the chances of a midlevel Shanghai bureaucrat on the lam having a cell that works in the U.S.?"

She looked at me. "You know, it's a shame you picked such a sleazy profession. You wouldn't have made a bad cop." She called Mulgrew again. A few crisp sentences and she was off the phone.

"That was fast."

"Right now he's so afraid of how bad I can make him look that he'd run over and paint my apartment. I told him to check the records for all the pay phones two blocks in every direction. That'll take a while, though. Do you want me to call you when I hear?"

"Why did that sound like a question?"

"I'm going to the Waldorf now, to talk to your client. No, you can't come."

She was all set for an argument, but I couldn't see any point in explaining I no longer had a client. "Okay," I said. "Let me know what happens." I waved and walked off before her curious brow-furrow turned into a suspicious frown.

In the absence of any brighter ideas, I headed back to Chinatown. I needed to think, so I decided to walk. While I was walking, I decided, the way I used to when I was thinking, to call Bill.

"Smith," he mumbled, his voice raspy.

"Chin."

"Hey! Like old times."

"Yes, me up and in action early and you waking from a sound sleep only because the phone rang."

"It's a good thing we're working together again. I almost had to buy an alarm clock."

"You remember I told you Mary was working a homicide?"

"I thought if you found Mary she was going to *be* a homicide."

"Get serious. Her victim's a Chinese cop. From China. Sent over here to find Wong Pan."

Bill was silent for a moment. "I'd guess he found him."

"Better, or worse. The hotel room he was killed in? It was Wong Pan's." I gave Bill the story. "They're checking the pay phones in the area. And I—hold on, a call's coming in." I switched lines and answered, in both languages. The caller replied in English.

"Good morning, Ms. Chin. This is Chen Lao-li speaking. From Bright Hopes Jewelry. If it is convenient, please come to my shop this morning."

I stopped short. *Oh, Lydia!* I'd forgotten all about the jeweler, sweeping my photos off his counter. "Mr. Chen! Do you—"

"We open at ten. I look forward to our meeting." He hung up.

I clicked back to the other line and was surprised to find Bill still there. "Why didn't you hang up the way you always do when I put you on hold? I'd have called you back."

"I'm trying to behave."

"This is unnerving."

"That call?"

"No, you. But the call, too. It was Mr. Chen."

"Chen . . . The jeweler? Who knew the photos?"

"That's the guy. I forgot about him. How stupid is that?"

"Right. After all, you had nothing on your mind yesterday."

"Don't try to talk me out of it. Anyway, he wants me to come there. He opens at ten."

"It's not ten yet?"

"It's not even nine. And you're up. Imagine that."

"Well, in celebration of this miracle, want me to come with you?"

I considered. "I think not, thanks. Whatever he wants, he might be willing to open up to a nice Chinese girl, but it would probably be better if you weren't there."

"It usually is."

Chances were I was right and Bill shouldn't come along. And this was our SOP, to work separately when it seemed like the results would be better. And Bill was a four-letter word who hadn't called me in months.

So it was surprising, the little pang of loneliness I felt after we said good-bye.

12

Somewhere on my walk downtown, the day slid from fresh promise into muggy fact. I wiped my forehead and put on my sunglasses. By the time I hit Canal, traffic was at full stampede, giving out with honks and rumbles the way a herd of cattle might bellow and stamp.

Even though I'd walked, I was early. I watched through the window at Bright Hopes as the young assistant flicked on lights and lit General Gung's incense. At the stroke of ten she unlocked the door and smiled to find me at it.

"Lydia Chin. I was here yesterday? I've come to see Mr. Chen."

"Yes, he's expecting you. I'm Irene Ng, by the way. Please follow me."

Irene Ng led me through the shop, lifting a gate in the back counter. She knocked on Mr. Chen's door and then opened it for me. Mr. Chen and another man stood from low lacquered stools. On the table before them, along with my photos, sat a tray of sweets, tiny teacups, and a gourd-shaped pot. A flowery fragrance filled the air.

"Chin Ling Wan-ju, welcome." Mr. Chen bowed, using my Chinese name but speaking in English as we had yesterday. "This is my cousin, Zhang Li."

I bowed to Mr. Zhang as he did to me. Older and bigger than Mr. Chen, full-faced and balding, he had classic Han Chinese features that made Mr. Chen's rounded eyes and sharp nose more apparent. "An honor to meet you," I said. Formally, with both hands, he handed me his card, so formally, I took it and did the same.

In some way I didn't follow, this had become an occasion. Mr. Chen seemed to have recovered enough from yesterday's vapors to regard me intently, almost hungrily. It wasn't the guilty look of a man nervous about being caught with contraband goods. It might be, it occurred to me, the look of a man who'd already bought some and was interested in buying more.

I was intrigued. If I hadn't had pressing things on my mind, like murder, I'd have played it their way, letting them spin it out until I saw what they wanted. Under the circumstances, though, that would be disingenuous to the point of fraud.

I sat, thanking Mr. Chen when he handed me tea. Courtesy dictated that I try it and comment on its deliciousness, allowing him to tut-tut and me to insist, but I skipped all that and went straight in. "Mr. Chen, I'm not sure why you called me, but since yesterday the situation has changed."

"Situation?" His surprise may have been due to what I'd said, or to my rudeness in cutting so directly to the chase.

Mr. Zhang, the cousin, was giving me an odd, appraising look. Maybe he was having trouble with the language. "Should we continue in English?" I addressed them both. "Or in Cantonese?"

At that Mr. Zhang smiled. "Please, in English. Our Chinese is the Chinese of Shanghai. We learned English there as boys, when learning came easily. In America, my cousin has been able to conquer your Cantonese dialect in a way that has eluded me. Of course, he is younger and his brain more agile."

Mr. Chen waved that away. "Neither of us has been young for some time, cousin. But"—to me—"I have had this shop for many years. My customers provided my education. What do you mean, Ms. Chin, that the situation has changed?"

"Yesterday, when I brought you these photographs, I was working with an associate trying to find that jewelry. I'm sorry, but there's no good way to say this. He's been killed."

Both men stared at me. Mr. Zhang recovered first. "Killed?"

"I'm afraid so. And another man, too: a police officer from China, following the thief."

"They were killed because of this jewelry?"

"I don't know. Once you tell me what you know about it, I'll have a better idea."

It seemed to me Mr. Chen's hand trembled slightly as he set his teacup down. Mr. Zhang said, "Yes, of course. And please accept our condolences on the loss of your associate."

"Thank you."

"Before I speak about this jewelry," he continued, "it is important that I understand the entire, as you say, situation. Perhaps you could tell us again why you are looking for it?"

No, you answer my question first! I wanted to shout. But yesterday I'd insisted to Joel that pushing was no way to handle an old Chinese man. "These pieces were in a box excavated in Shanghai recently. They've been stolen. My late associate and I were hired by a client who believes they've been brought here to be sold."

"Who is your client, and why is he looking for this jewelry?" Mr. Zhang asked. "Is he from the Shanghai authorities?"

Oh ho, I thought. *You do know something, and you don't want to get in trouble.* "No. The client's a woman, a Swiss attorney working for heirs of the original owner."

Mr. Zhang exchanged a look with his cousin. "Who are these heirs?"

"I don't know their names. The original owner was a Jewish woman from Salzburg, Elke Gilder. Her daughter, Rosalie, brought the jewelry to Shanghai. The heirs are Elke's brother's children."

Mr. Chen started to speak but was stopped by a look from his cousin. Notwithstanding the fact that we were in Mr. Chen's shop, Mr. Zhang was clearly in charge. "Do these photographs represent the entire contents of the box?" he asked.

"As far as I know."

"Was anything else found?"

"Anything else." I eyed the two men. "You mean the Shanghai Moon?"

Mr. Chen froze, as though any movement might break something. Mr. Zhang, though, just said mildly, "Yes. The Shanghai Moon."

"I heard the story yesterday," I told them. "That the Shanghai

Moon might be in the company of these pieces. I also heard that these pieces aren't worth killing over, but the Shanghai Moon is."

Mr. Zhang smiled. "You've cleverly sidestepped my question."

"As you have mine."

His smile grew delighted. "I'm unused to being clever, but I suppose I have. Ms. Chin—the Shanghai Moon? Was it there?"

"I don't know," I admitted. "If it was found, my client wasn't told."

Mr. Zhang inclined his head. "Thank you for indulging me." Something passed between the two cousins then; I couldn't read it, but they'd reached a decision. "I hope," Mr. Zhang said, "we are able to answer your questions as fully as you have answered mine." He sipped some tea, waiting.

"Well, to start with, let's go back to this question: Have you seen these pieces?"

"Yes."

I nearly jumped off my seat. "Wong Pan, the man who stole them, he's been here?"

"No."

"But—"

Mr. Chen spoke. "We have seen them."

"Why didn't you—"

He raised a hand. "Yes, we have seen them. But not for sixty years. They are my mother's."

13

Under the bright lights in the jewelry store office, I stared from one old man to the other. "Your mother's?" I said. "But these are Rosalie Gilder's, that she—" I stared again: Mr. Chen's rounded eyes, his sharp nose. *Oh*, I thought. *Oh, oh, oh.* "Rosalie Gilder? She was your *mother*?"

"Yes. Do you—"

"Chen," I breathed. "Chen Kai-rong. He's your father."

Mr. Chen gave a bow of his head. "It does me honor to acknowledge them. I'm surprised to find you know their names, however."

"They were in the book. Where I read about the Shanghai Moon. But of course, Rosalie's—Miss Gilder's, I mean"—I corrected myself, not wanting him to think I was taking liberties—"my client told me her name. And I found Chen Kai-rong's name in her letters."

"Your client's letters?"

"No, your mother's."

A pause. "My mother's—"

"I suppose," Mr. Zhang interrupted gently, "Ms. Chin means the letters at the Jewish Museum?"

"Yes, exactly."

"Oh," said Mr. Chen. "Yes, of course." He nodded a few times. "Yes, at the museum."

Not sure why his face had clouded, I said, "I apologize if you feel I've invaded your mother's privacy. But she was a fascinating woman." A thought struck me. "Mr. Chen, is she—" *Not that way, Lydia.* "I'd be thrilled to find her still with us."

Mr. Chen smiled sadly. "As to that, I must disappoint you."

It was true, I did feel disappointed. *Though really, Lydia,* I pointed out to myself, *if Rosalie were alive, she'd be near ninety*. But to me she was a scared, brave young woman I'd just met, and grown fond of.

I looked at Mr. Zhang, the cousin. "Is your relation in the Chen family line?"

"Yes. My mother, Mei-lin, was Chen Kai-rong's sister. But Ms. Chin, this is not the time for reminiscence. We have more urgent matters before us."

"The jewelry." I nodded. "You haven't been offered it?"

"No."

"But you want to find it before it's sold."

Mr. Chen answered that one. "Yes, of course. Anything that was my mother's is precious to us." Again the smile. It faded and he said, "However, the piece not pictured here . . . the Shanghai Moon . . . you've heard nothing?"

"No. I'm sorry. If it was your mother's, I understand how much it must mean to you."

He nodded. The hungry look was gone from his eyes, replaced by a stoic disappointment.

"My cousin has been searching for the Shanghai Moon all his life," Mr. Zhang said.

"When it disappeared, what—" I was stopped by a tiny shake of Mr. Zhang's head. He cut his eyes toward his cousin, who, with an air of resignation, was pouring tea.

What was Mr. Zhang telling me? Not to ask any more questions in front of Mr. Chen? What could that mean? Nothing in that story could be news to Mr. Chen. Mr. Zhang shot a look at the phone on the desk. Got it: He'd call me later. Well, okay, for now. I had his card, too.

"Gentlemen," I said, "whether or not what happened to my associate and the police officer has anything to do with the Shanghai Moon, it still may have to do with the rest of this jewelry. If you hear from Wong Pan, or anyone else who wants to talk about these pieces, will you let me know?"

"Yes, of course," said Mr. Zhang, and Mr. Chen nodded. "But there is still another matter."

"What's that?"

"The heirs."

"What about them?"

"You say you don't know who they are."

"I don't know their names. They're grandchildren of Rosalie's uncle, Horst Peretz."

Mr. Chen lifted his eyes to me. "Ms. Chin, are you familiar with Jewish naming practices?"

I shook my head.

"My father chose my Chinese name. My mother gave me a European one. Horst Chen Lao-li. An odd name, is it not? Ms. Chin, Jewish people do not name babies for living relatives, in case the Angel of Death, coming to collect the elder, should make an error. When my mother named me for her uncle Horst, she knew he was gone. She gave me his name so he would be remembered. There was none other to remember him: He died childless."

It took me a moment to process this. "Then who are these clients?"

"Whoever they are, they are not who they claim to be," said Mr. Zhang. "That in itself is worrisome, wouldn't you say?"

14

I called Alice as I headed back to my office but only got her voice mail. *Come on, Alice, pick up! Your clients are bogus!* Could this be what Joel had meant by "fishy"? But how would he have known? I left a message to call me, then switched directions for the subway, to go up to the Waldorf and bang on the door myself. Before I'd gone two blocks, my phone rang the *Wonder Woman* song.

"Lydia, we were right."

"We're always right. About what?"

"A few days ago a pay phone a block from Wong Pan's hotel made a call to the Waldorf."

"To the Waldorf? *Wong Pan* called *Alice*? But she never said anything. She wasn't even positive he was in New York."

"The call was short. He might have tried, didn't get her, and hung up. The point is, he knows where to find her."

"If it was him. All you have is a pay phone calling the Waldorf."

Mary ignored my magical thinking. "I'm here, but she's not. Have you heard from her?"

"Here, the Waldorf? You're there? And she's not? Now you're worrying me. I just called and got voice mail. I was about to go up there. Was that pay-phone call before the Chinese cop was killed or after?"

"His death can't be pinned down that exactly, but it was probably within a few hours. Let me know right away if you hear from her."

"I will. And Mary? I have a couple of other bombshells." I told her about Mr. Chen, Rosalie's son, and Mr. Zhang, Rosalie's nephew, and about Alice's clients, not Rosalie's relations at all.

"Oh," Mary said slowly. "Oh, Lydia, I'm not liking this."

"Me either."

"I'm going to alert the sector cars to look out for her. Meanwhile, Shanghai's sending a new cop over."

"They are?"

"Hey, it's a homicide of one of their own, plus a theft from the Chinese people. It wouldn't surprise me if they sent a whole squad. Inspector"—a pause—"Wei De-xu. The e-mail says, 'Inspector Wei is one of Shanghai Police Bureau's most esteemed officers.' I'm going to the airport in the morning to collect him."

"How come you get to go? Instead of someone from Midtown Homicide?"

"Captain Mentzinger's squeezing this. Technically, once the John Doe was identified, I was done, but he wants me to stay with it. After the screw-up on the room, Midtown can't really object. They're saving face by saying it's okay for me to collect this guy because I can talk to him."

"In Shanghainese?"

"What do they know? Besides, would Shanghai send a cop here who didn't speak English? But don't tell them."

After we hung up I redirected myself again, back to my office; there was no point in going to the Waldorf if Mary was already there and Alice wasn't. At the office I put on water for tea and called Bill, repeating for him everything I'd told Mary and what she'd told me. His reaction was a lot like hers: He didn't like the sound of things either.

"That seems to be the consensus," I said. "What are you up to?"

"I'm waiting for a call. And reading a book."

"A history of Shanghai?"

"Am I that transparent?"

"I'm afraid so. What call?"

"A friend of a friend. An expert on modern Chinese history. I'm hoping he can give us some background."

"That's very enterprising."

"Am I stepping on your toes? I don't want—"

"No, I meant it. Did I sound sarcastic?"

"I wasn't sure."

I was taken aback. Bill, unable to read the tone in my voice? "No, I think it's a great idea. Let me know if he calls."

"Where will you be?"

"I think I'll do some reading, too. I'm going to print out the rest of Rosalie's letters."

"They've been public property for years. You won't find anything in them that Chen and Zhang don't already know."

"Well, it's not like I'm looking for a map with a big X on it. But Mr. Chen caught me flatfooted when he said he was Rosalie's son. I don't want that to happen again. Right now the letters are the only thread I have."

I took my tea to the easy chair and settled in.

29 April 1938

Dearest Mama,

Well, your ignorant Rosalie is only slightly less ignorant today, as regards China. But having sat with Chen Kai-rong yesterday long into the afternoon—over coffee and linzer torte, which I'm afraid I devoured greedily; he suggests we alternate the foods of our peoples, a charming offer—I am considerably less ignorant about my new friend.

He made, I must say, a valiant effort to unravel the history of forty centuries. But I became hopelessly lost among the states and dynasties. My floundering amused him, which he tried to hide. (And failed!) His own family traces its roots to a time called "the Warring States"—two thousand years ago, Mama! When our people had already been scattered for millennia, when Christianity was about to rise and scatter us again—Chen Kai-rong has visited the graves of his ancestors from that time!

I confessed to envy, and a wistful longing for a similar homeland. Our books tell us the history of our people is as long as China's, but what Jewish family knows the names of its forebears beyond half a dozen generations, or could find their graves?

Chen Kai-rong questioned me about Zionism, and though he pleaded ignorance, he was well informed on the subject. I told him I consider Zionism a collective opium dream of the Jewish people; and then I quickly apologized for the mention of opium, as I understand the drug to be a scourge of the Chinese. The Chinese people carry many burdens, was his answer, and opium, though a curse, at least provides a temporary joy.

The conversation having taken this doleful turn, I moved to another subject entirely, asking how he came by such a fine command of English. English, he said, is the lingua franca of commercial Shanghai. Since I have been finding the prospect of conducting myself in Chinese a daunting one, you might imagine my delight in hearing this! Kai-rong attended the Shanghai British School and has spoken English since he was a boy. He now returns home from two years' study at Oxford. I asked what his field had been.

"I was reading law," was his answer. "Though from what I hear, law is a discipline very much needed in Shanghai at the moment, and very little in demand." He fell silent, staring over the water.

"I'm sorry," I ventured. "I seem to be touching today only on subjects that distress you."

At this he stirred himself. "No, no, I'm the one who must apologize. I was . . . brooding." And he smiled.

"Over what, if I may ask?"

"Ah, Rosalie. You've left a country where your people have lived for centuries, but are no longer welcome. I fear I return to one."

"How can that be? You're a Chinaman going to China."

His smile broadened. "First, you must not say 'Chinaman.'" (Mama, this word has no German equivalent, but is in common use in English. I never knew it was offensive before this.) "It's a word used by Europeans and carries a condescending odor. You'll find more friends in Shanghai if you say 'Chinese.' I know this seems trivial—"

I assured him it did not, having been myself rudely awakened in the past months to the pain words can cause. "I can't pretend to understand the nuance, because my English is so poor," I told him. "But if the word offends you, I shall strike it from my vocabulary!"

"I and my countrymen thank you. And permit me to say, if you're able to slip 'nuance' so neatly into a sentence, you must stop thinking your English poor."

I thanked him for the compliment (though, Mama, his English really does outshine mine) and asked what he meant by being unwelcome in China, whether he referred to the Japanese occupation.

"The occupation, yes; though I can understand foreign invaders better than I can the puppet government—Chinese so hungry for power and wealth that they take orders from invaders, against their own people."

"But what of the government this puppet one replaces? Is there no resistance movement of loyal Chinese, working to retake the country?" I was of course thinking, Mama, of the situation at home, of those loyalists who refuse to accept Herr Hitler's Anschluss.

"What they replaced," Kai-rong replied, "was hardly a government. Chiang Kai-shek and his Nationalists are two-faced thieves who betrayed the Republic many years ago, before it could take root. And half the country, in any case, was never under their control—and isn't under Japanese control now. It's strangled by warlords. Greedy thugs to whom 'China' is an abstract concept, while wealth is a concept they understand." He paused, sipping coffee; I had no idea how to respond. And then, Mama, he made this extraordinary statement: "As painful as your situation is, Rosalie, there may be an advantage in having no country to fight over. Your traditions are long and beautiful, and your spiritual nature has flowered in the absence of the distractions of politics and the necessity, once power is gained, to keep a grip on it."

I was amazed by this, and had to answer: "Also in the absence of safety, and often of food to fill our bellies!"

Surprised, he said, "Did I sound patronizing? I apologize."

My indignation vanished and I began to laugh, pointing out we were apologizing to each other with every third breath!

"You're right," he said, "and if that's my fault, I apologize." He laughed with me.

Then he grew pensive and added, "But it seems we have something to envy in each other's history, if not in each other's circumstances. Come now, there's still linzer torte to fill your belly. And I can return, if you want, to the Northern Song, and pick up where we left off."

I sighed. "Yes, please, though I don't think it will do much good. But first, you never gave an answer to my question: Is there in China a resistance movement against the Japanese?"

I thought he wouldn't reply, but at last he said, "Yes. There is. Fighting to regain China for the Chinese people."

"Will they win?"

"If you're asking me to tell the future, I can't do it. But I can tell you this: History is on the side of China. Now pick up your plate and let's return to history."

And we did. Not that, as I say, I've managed to learn much about the past. But I've learned enough about Chen Kai-rong to look forward to the future—tomorrow's lesson, accompanied by fragrant tea and curious Chinese cakes.

Stay well, Mama!

Your Rosalie

3 May 1938

Dearest Mama,

I haven't written for some time, I know, but as I've been told there will now be no mail service until we reach Singapore, I feel foolish putting pen to paper to produce a letter that will sit on my bureau for days. Paul applauds this lack of enterprise on my part, seeming to feel it justifies his own, though I have a number of previous letters to point to, which makes me feel quite superior but has little effect on him.

But this morning I awoke feeling melancholy, Mama, and missing you greatly. Perhaps the fog which enshrouds us affects my mood. People speak softly; even the children are subdued. We're less than a week from Shanghai. I believe the enormity of this undertaking has at last forced itself on our understanding. I have had glimpses of it over the past weeks, but have resolutely refused to acknowledge it, preferring the luxury of the ship, the exhilaration of new acquaintances, and the adventure of sailing into the unknown. But the fog brings about an odd sensation. There is little wind, and in no direction can anything be seen beyond the rail. At home a chill fog precedes a change of weather, but this warm, featureless mist seems as though it might continue forever. Ah, and there you have it, Mama: I've said "home," and the word fills me with sadness.

When I look toward the future, excitement and curiousity lighten my trepidation. My new friend, Chen Kairong, has taught me much about his country. It's clear he loves his homeland deeply and longed for it when he was away, equally clear he knows China's shortcomings and is eager to see them corrected. His devotion in spite of all he thinks wrong is reassuring, and I hope his feelings will color my own. In this way, I find myself already connected to Shanghai; but when I turn toward the past, my feelings are exactly opposite. I'm no longer connected, but uncoupled and adrift. My every happy memory is shaded by a forlorn longing for the home we've lost.

Mama, have you written to us? I understand the fast liners are few and I do not expect a letter from you on each tender that meets us; and yet, as Paul asks, if that's true, why do I continually put myself in the path of the steward who distributes the passengers' mail? I should dearly love a letter, Mama. But much much more, I should love to find you and Uncle Horst on the ship that follows immediately behind this one.

I'll seal this letter now, and lay it on my bureau until tomorrow, when the tender sails out from Singapore. Perhaps by morning the fog will burn off, and I'll be

Your strong and sunny Rosalie, again.

9 May 1938
Dearest Mama,

Yesterday we arrived in Shanghai.

What a place this is!

How to tell you? How to begin? It's all so strange, Mama, and we're so unprepared! On shipboard Chen Kai-rong painted such vivid word-pictures that I felt quite ready to step into life as a practiced "Shanghailander." But oh, how wrong I was!

Though I'm finding great difficulty, Mama, in putting words to this experience, nevertheless I'll try, so things won't be as strange for you when you arrive; and also so you'll have an idea what Paul and I, in this dizzying world, are feeling.

The night before last, in a thick mist, we bore down on

the mouth of the harbor. Everyone ran to the rails, though for some time nothing could be seen. The air became electric when ships loomed from the fog: two liners at anchor, gunships of many nations, and our first sight of the square-sailed junks and flat sampans of the Orient.

We dropped anchor to await the turn of the tide. The kitchens put forth a sumptuous banquet of fish, goose, and dumplings. Not knowing what our situation would be from that moment forward, I ate my fill and encouraged Paul to do the same. (Though he needed no encouragement; as costly as this passage was, I don't believe that in the end the Lloyd Triestino Line has made any profit on Paul.) Stewards stacked luggage on deck, and many emotional farewells and promises of continued friendship were made. Neither Paul nor I slept that night; had we, I believe we would have been the only passengers to do so.

As the sun rose the engines rumbled, and the ship was on the move. We made our way up the Whangpu, as the river is called where it flows through Shanghai. Though the fog was thick, we refugees once again jammed the rails, straining for a glimpse of our new home.

That "glimpse" came first not as sight, but as scent. Though "scent" is too gentle a word: This was a full-on reek, a riot of tangled odors that, had it been noise, would have deafened us all. Imagine, Mama, the sea at low tide; add diesel oil, rotting vegetables, and the smoke from a thousand factories, and stir into a haze of damp heat! Such was our first impression of our new home.

As the fog burned off we saw the shore. In contrast to the report of our noses, our eyes suggested a dreamlike scene. We floated past fields and rice paddies dotted with low huts and with farmers trudging behind what Kai-rong informs me are not oxen but water buffaloes. Soon, though, we approached the outskirts of Shanghai, and oh! what a disheartening sight! The area we passed, called Hongkew, suffered much in the Japanese invasion. The devastation, drifting smoke, and rubble, and the poor souls wandering through them, were not encouraging omens.

Next came the wharves. Junks, sampans, and rafts crowded the water, riding our wake or fearlessly crossing before us; how we failed to swamp them, I cannot say. On the docks all was chaos. Trucks loaded and unloaded and automobiles inched along. The rickshaw, that odd vehicle of the Orient, could be seen, with men pulling like horses at its rails. But the chief element of the boiling, eddying commotion was people, oh so many people! A few wore European dress, but most, both men and women, rushed or trudged or sat about in short trousers and conical hats. I felt dismay at the sight of such a dense and endless crowd; but also, a strange exhilaration that made me impatient to join them.

Next came into view grand buildings in the European style. The streets, though still bustling, became less frantic. Kai-rong gazed upon his home city for the first time in years. The light in his face strengthened my resolve to try to love this place.

Kai-rong informed us we had reached the Bund, a riverfront promenade lined with banks, office blocks, and grand hotels. This is the heart of the International Settlement, an area that by treaty is governed not by China but by the foreign powers whose subjects reside there. And this word is not our German *Bund,* as one might expect, but Hindustani, and meaning "dock." (Do you see how much I've learned, in these few weeks? Though I haven't yet learned to love Chinese sweets.)

Our engines quieted; we were met by pilot boats. Paul ran to join a group of friends his own age at the bow, to be the first to see our dock. Spying a garden along the Bund, I asked Kai-rong if it was as lovely as it appeared. He said he thought it must be, but he's never been inside, as Chinese aren't allowed.

Mama, my heart froze. I saw before me the "Jews Forbidden" sign at the gate of the Mirabell Garden the last time you and I tried to go for our accustomed Sunday stroll.

"But how can that be?" I was vehement, Mama; I think I wanted him to say he'd been making some odd joke, or I'd misunderstood. "How can that *be*? This is China! This area may be *governed* by foreigners, but surely they cannot—"

"They can. By treaty they can and for a hundred years they have. A mile behind that"—indicating the Bund—"and thousands of miles beyond, is China. The International Settlement and the French Concession might as well be Europe. Though I can tell you, Rosalie, I was never treated with as much disdain in Europe as I have been here in the city where I was born."

This saddened me, Mama, more than I can say. Looking with dismay across the water, I asked whether he meant to tell me the international areas, so prosperous and attractive, are entirely closed to Chinese.

"Oh, by no means," he answered with a wry smile. "Just this 'public' garden, and the gentleman's clubs, sports clubs, and private dining establishments. A million people live in the International Settlement, half a million in the French Concession. Of those, if more than sixty thousand are European, well, then, as they say in England, I'm a Chinaman."

I smiled also, and asked, "Sixty thousand people rule the lives of one and a half million?"

"But isn't that how things are done everywhere? In China's treaty ports the disparity is sharp because the rulers are foreigners. But"—again sweeping his hand—"in those thousands of miles, for thousands of years, it's been millions of peasants sweating and starving while aristocrats sip tea. In most of the world, the few govern the many."

"Now, take care what you say, or you'll be thought a Bolshevik."

"Oh, hardly. In fact," said he in ironic tones, "my own home is in the International Settlement. My father trades in cotton and silk, as his father did, and his. I'm expected to continue this dynasty."

"Are you? And yet in your voice I hear something else."

He turned to me, briefly silent, and quite somber. Then he smiled. "Your hearing is acute. Come, let's find your brother. When the gangway is lowered, chaos will descend with it."

Mama, I'm told the lights will soon be turned off in this place where we're staying. I'm quite exhausted. I'll end here and post this letter tomorrow, hoping it crosses the path of the ship on which you and Uncle Horst are steaming toward Shanghai right now! Though were I assured you were on such a ship and would never see this letter, I'd still continue my account. I'm oddly comforted by the attempt to decribe this extraordinary place for you. To envision your smile as you read makes me feel less alone than, surrounded by the crowds and ceaseless bustle in this room and in Shanghai, I know myself to be.

                                        Your Rosalie

Crowds and ceaseless bustle. That was Chinatown; that was Mary and me and the thirty-six other kids in our tumultuous first-grade class; that was my parents, my mother's older sister, and my four big brothers in our walk-up apartment. I wanted to tell Rosalie, *Don't worry, once you get used to it it's kind of fun.* I reached for the next letter; maybe she'd found that out herself. But my hand had to detour to pick up the ringing phone.

"Ms. Chin? This is Leah Pilarsky. Joel's sister-in-law. I'm so sorry to bother you, but . . ."

"Please call me Lydia." I wrenched myself back to this familiar room. "And you're certainly not bothering me. Is something wrong?" *Besides the obvious,* I thought.

"That's why I'm calling. I'm not sure you can help, but we don't know where else to turn. It's about—Joel's body." Her voice caught. "I'm sorry, it's just such an odd thing to say, his body . . ." After a tiny pause she went on. "Lydia, I don't know if you know this, but our religious laws call for burial within twenty-four hours of death."

"I think I did know that. But that's already past."

"Yes. We also prefer not to do autopsies, but in cases like this, the rabbis permit it. Our laws are ancient, but we do live in the modern world." Her tone was ironic, almost amused. In better times she was probably the funny relative, full of mordant humor. She was also, clearly, the competent, steadfast one you turn to in times like this. "We've been told the autopsy's been done. But they won't release the body."

"Why not?"

"They say with violent crime it's protocol to wait a few days. I understand that, but it's a problem. Ruth is having a terrible time. She's clinging to the rituals and laws—well, that's what they're for, to give you something to hold on to in bad times. She's become obsessed with the funeral: a kosher burial, starting the shiva period. It's the last thing she can do for Joel, and she really needs to do it. But all I get from the medical examiner's office is 'as soon as we can.' I started to harangue them—sweetly—and they let it slip that if the police okay the release, it can be expedited. So I talked to that detective, Mulgrew."

"Ah. But that was like talking to a stone wall in a bad mood, right?"

"Exactly." I heard that faint amusement again, and I was glad I'd caused it. "Lydia, I know you don't work for the city—"

"But you're hoping I know someone who does. I'll call you right back."

I clicked off and punched my speed dial.

"Hi, Lydia. What's up?"

"Detective Mary Kee, this is your lucky day. Special offer, improve your karma with one easy phone call."

"Oh, no."

"Oh, yes. Double karma points if you act without delay." I told Mary about my conversation with Leah Pilarsky.

"What are you saying? I'm supposed to deal with that?"

"They'll release the body on an okay from the NYPD."

"Not from me. I don't have the rank and it's not my case."

"No, your captain does and it's Midtown's."

"Oh, now—"

"You didn't want your apartment painted anyhow."

"You want me to call in my chips for *this*?"

"To help a grieving widow. Like I say, the karma's real good."

Silence; then a sigh. "I can't believe I'm falling for this. Call me back in ten minutes."

I picked up the next letter, thinking, *See, there's something to be said for ceaseless bustle.*

12 May 1938

Dearest Mama,

We've been here three days. At the beginning, sensations flew at me so fast my head spun; but now I believe I'm finding what sailors call "sea legs"—the knack of taking a ship's motion into account as you move about. The streets and buildings of Shanghai don't move, Mama, but I promise you they are the only things here that don't. All is constant, frantic activity, day or night. It requires attention and a steeliness of will to step out one's own door onto the churning streets. Though in truth it might be more difficult to do so, were the place we're staying not, on a smaller scale, an exact mirror of Shanghai's chaos.

Oh, that sounds so ungrateful! And I'm not, Mama, really. The people who received us are doing the most they can with resources stretched to their limits. We'd be on the streets if not for their kindness. The reception of refugees is managed by a number of committees supported by wealthy Jewish families—British citizens from Bombay—who have seen the need and responded generously. Nevertheless, the need is so great, and so rapidly growing, that this generosity results in conditions which, while providing minimally for us, underline the dismal reality of our situation.

But Mama, reading over what I've written, I find I'm failing you as a journalist; my complaining has superseded my obligation to be your eyes and ears. I'll stop my grumbling instantly, and take up my account from the moment the gangplank connected with the dock.

So, then: We descended in the same orderly chaos in which we'd boarded, though with considerably more trepidation. A small number of passengers were met by relatives or friends who'd come here earlier. (As you and Uncle Horst will be, by us!) Kai-rong had a car waiting, and offered to take Paul and myself to our destination. But we didn't know our destination! So he left us with careful instructions on how to find him, and went off, his driver employing the car's horn (with little success) to blast a path through the crowd. I watched until his car was swallowed up; then with Paul I joined the stream of refugees along the wharf. We had been told of a meeting point and were making for it, but before we reached it we were found and warmly greeted by men and women speaking German.

From here, the story becomes less fairy-tale-like, and more befitting the truth of our situation.

We were escorted onto open trucks—trucks, Mama!—and carried through the bumpy streets to our new home. Some people sat on luggage as we inched along, but most crowded the truck's sides as we had the ship's rail, to see Shanghai close-up.

Alas, the sight was not encouraging. Narrow lanes, torn

pavement, low doorways; windows that were no more than gaping squares, having shutters but no glass; hanging wash; women stirring pots outdoors; children practically naked; men carrying burdens on poles across their shoulders. Debris, and worse, swirled through open gutters. Everywhere, the smells that had greeted us on shipboard, concentrated tenfold; and everywhere, the dense, swampy heat. People who had dressed their best for disembarkation removed coats and loosened starched collars, and it became a contest, whether one's hat was better used to shade one's face, or fan it.

As we lurched on we learned our destination: Hongkew! That desolate bombed area we'd floated by on the *Conte Biancamano.* Which, half a week behind us, now seems like just a dream.

Finally we came to a halt. Gentlemen helped ladies from the trucks, and we faced our new home.

This shelter—there are a number, and they are called "Homes," a well-meant but mocking title—fills an abandoned warehouse. Walls are bare brick and floors are concrete and all are in bad repair. On the ground floor are kitchens, a dining hall, and a medical clinic. Large rooms upstairs serve as dormitories, partitioned by hanging bedsheets. Beds are double-decked bunks or military cots; mine is in the family section, while Paul has been assigned to the room for bachelors. He's proud to have been placed with the men and not with me as he would be if considered a child; but Mama, I believe he's lonely, as I know I am.

The kitchen produces barely adequate and unpalatable meals, which nevertheless we're grateful for. Sanitary facilities are shared, and there is no hot water. Never can you find a moment's silence: Some child is always crying or some adult talking or coughing. If couples argue, everyone hears; and if they whisper tenderly to each other—the same.

So you can see why finding a place of our own—which from what I'm told is likely to possess many of the disadvantages of this Home but will have one great advantage, privacy—has suddenly become my heart's desire.

And I suppose I'll have to continue this account tomorrow, because once again, as—but not at all like—when Paul and I were children in the nursery and you came to kiss us good night, the lights are about to be put out.

Good night, dear Mama.

Your Rosalie

16 May 1938

Dearest Mama,

I know I have not written for days, but it's so hard to put into words the bewilderment of our daily lives.

The thick, damp heat is unforgiving. Noise is constant, with many sounds unidentifiable and therefore disconcerting. Hongkew's narrow lanes are so like each other that getting lost is inevitable and finding your way again all but impossible. Yesterday, searching for a vegetable market, I became so hopelessly confounded in an area all Chinese that I was almost brought to tears, rescued only by a Polish refugee child. She spoke no German, so could not direct me, but took pity and led me to a main avenue. In Shanghai the avenues bear English signs, and so I was able to locate myself. I returned to the Home grateful, though carrotless.

The streets are overwhelming, Mama. The heat and crowding combine to assure that life is lived out of doors, and thus publicly. Beggars abound, both adults and children, a sight I have not gotten used to; but also shoemakers, dentists, druggists, teahouses, and public letter-writers—a lending library, Mama, of Chinese books, attached to shelves by strings just long enough to reach nearby benches! All are on the streets, and one is expected to step around them, as work takes precedence over passing by. Everywhere we hear the competing shouts of vendors, the clack of mah-jongg tiles, and the clangs and mournful strings of Chinese music, as these are also activities for the street.

All this, I think, would be exotic and strange, and yet I'd square my shoulders and get on with learning to recognize a streetcar stop and distinguish the currency—as well as adjusting to boiling the water, and peeling what little fresh fruit I find—were it not for the intermittent intrusions of sounds and smells from home. Acrid smoke carries the stench of sewage and the unfamiliar aromas of Chinese spices—but then we catch a whiff of coffee or cinnamon from some lucky refugee's kitchen. These things are not unavailable here, only beyond most refugees' reach. People will save for weeks to buy enough coffee to brew a single pot, which they'll sip slowly, not knowing when they'll taste it again.

Mama, it's these familiar things that make the heart pound. One feels as if in a dream, where the real and fantastic exist side by side, where it's no good to determine to get on with anything, as one could be lifted into the sky, or houses in a lane could turn to trees in a forest, at any second.

Oh, I sound so foolish! And yet this is how I've felt this past week, as I make my way around Shanghai. More than once I've stopped still and tried, as I do in frightening dreams, simply to will myself awake. The Nazis never marched into Austria. Paul and I never fled to Shanghai—Shanghai, how absurd!—leaving you and Uncle Horst behind. The Nazis themselves don't exist, but are monsters of my imagination. But my efforts result in no effect: I'm awake and all this is only too real.

Now you'll worry I'm going mad. Please don't fear. As long as I have Paul to look after I'll keep my feet on the ground, I promise. And I don't hesitate to admit I've been greatly aided by my friend, Chen Kai-rong. Though he

made sure I had his address before we parted, I'd decided
not to contact him until Paul and I were no longer living in
these squalid, communal conditions. Pride, I suppose, made
me want to meet him again as an equal, as aboard the ship.
But two days ago, Paul and I were summoned from the roof
where, on the lines that crisscross it, we were hanging out
laundry. (This in itself is almost a joke, Mama, because
nothing dries in Shanghai.) The child who'd run to fetch us
said a Chinese gentleman was at the door in a fine car, asking if he'd found the Home in which the Gilders stayed. I
hesitated, but Paul—who does not find laundry entrancing—
let out a cheer and galloped down the stairs. I followed, to
find Kai-rong standing beside a Mercedes-Benz. He quite
beamed when he saw us, and I'm afraid I did the same,
though propriety might have demanded a more restrained
response. He requested the pleasure of taking us to tea. I
was embarrassed by the state of my hands, my hair, my
dress; but I couldn't refuse Paul this treat. We set off, ig-
noring the pursed lips of some of our fellow residents, who
seem to think a refugee girl entering a Chinese gentleman's
car can mean only one thing, even with her younger brother
at her side.

My discomfort at having been discovered in our meager
circumstances found no echo in Kai-rong, who was full of
practical questions: Was the food passable, were we learning our way around, did we understand the bank notes? We
spent a lovely hour at a lakeside teahouse occupied, except
for Paul and myself, exclusively by Chinese. Paul devoured
the tea cakes; as for me, even the mediocrity of my recent
diet hasn't increased my enthusiam for these dainties. But
the tea was sweet, and swans floated by, and I suppose I'm
growing used to Chinese music because I found the quartet
quite pleasing. Kai-rong explained the instruments and their
tuning, we discussed Mozart and literature, and I was very
sorry when we had to leave.

Kai-rong had his driver take us back on a wandering path, as he pointed out landmarks to familiarize us with our new home. The tour was enlightening; but it was the comfort of Kai-rong's presence that made me feel, as on shipboard, connected to this time and place.

Your foolish, but entirely rational,

Rosalie

23 May 1938

Dear Mama,

We've been here two weeks and it seems a lifetime.

Who could ever have imagined? The Pesach tales of oppression, which I once dismissed as part myth, part ancient history, and wholly unrelated to our enlightened age, have risen from the pages of the Haggadah to come howling after us. Once again we're fleeing, scattering to the winds. Over the thin kasha soup and rough bread that serves as dinner at the Home, one hears of relatives making for Australia, Argentina, the Dominican Republic—oh, Mama, I don't believe I could find that island on a map, and yet it's rumored that, alone in the world but for Shanghai, its doors remain open.

And reverently people speak of the Promised Land, America. America? Which issues only a miserably few visas to refugees, desperate as we are? Why does anyone believe America will be more hospitable once they pry open its doors? And yet so many plan and scheme and hope: A former employer who fled to Chicago will send for them, or cousins in New York will sponsor them, and the gates of paradise will swing wide.

No, I say. Shanghai is mystifying and often harsh; nevertheless, it's welcomed us. Until insanity is overthrown and our homes restored, my home is here.

Oh, what a demagogue I've become! I'm sorry; worry over you and Uncle Horst, over the future, over how to know I'm doing the right things for Paul—over whether I'll find kasha soup in my bowl again tomorrow—combines with a helpless anger, and leads to a darkness I haven't known before.

Others feel this darkness, too, the result of worry and the inability to find work, a place to live, decent food—to take any action in any direction. At the Home you see people—a small number, but real—who sit all day in the canteen or on their cots, who have little to say and will not try the streets of Shanghai, who no longer spend effort to stay clean and groomed—and it is an effort here, Mama, but one I force myself to make and demand of Paul. This darkness thickens imperceptibly: I didn't realize I had fallen into its shadow until our outing with Kai-rong. For the brief period of that afternoon, Shanghai seemed not like a frightening dream, but merely a *place*. Bizarre and mystifying, admittedly, but nevertheless a solid, daytime place whose streets and customs could, with application, be understood.

I'm telling you this, Mama, because I want you to understand a decision I've made: after wrenching consideration, I've determined to sell Grandmother Gilder's ruby ring. I'm afraid to stay too long at the Home, afraid of what the dreariness will do to my heart and Paul's. The price of the ring should enable us to pay what's called "key money"—pure extortion, but every landlord demands it—and also, I hope, to pay Paul's school fees when I find him a place. He claims to be perfectly happy in his truancy, and asks that I not sell anything for his sake; but I don't believe him. He hasn't seen the inside of an incomprehensible science text since we left the ship, so how could he be happy? And even if he were, nevertheless he should be in school.

Accordingly, tomorrow I'll set off into the French Concession—a beautiful area, with villas on tree-lined streets, as opposite to Hongkew as you can imagine; Kai-rong took us through it. The finest shops are there, and Kai-rong has given me the names of jewelers of good reputation. I'll search one out, and return to Hongkew richer, though, I think, much poorer also.

I've chosen the ring because it's mine. Yes, I remember my vow to renounce sentimentality; but to regard *your* jewelry, Mama, as mineral banknotes isn't easy without you here to tell me to do it! Until you come, I have nothing but your photograph and my memories. These include watching you dress for elegant evenings, and the magical moment when you fixed the diamond necklace at your throat and became Queen Mama, and I became Princess Rosalie. That necklace especially, but also the gold bracelet, and the others—yes, yes, I will sell them if I must, I won't let Paul starve! But if there's a way, I would dearly love to see you, when you are here in Shanghai, as Queen Mama once more!

I hope you approve of my decision, Mama; and if you don't, I can't wait to hear you tell me so yourself.

Your Rosalie

The alarm on my cell phone beeped. Ten minutes? That's all? I felt like I'd been in Shanghai, walking beside Rosalie, for weeks.

When I called, Mary picked up right away. "You owe me, girlfriend. And you owe Captain Mentzinger, too."

"Was he mad?"

"You mean how much do you owe? Actually, it was another chance to stick it to Midtown. Remind *them* they owe *us*. Still—"

"Okay, I just entered it in my karma ledger."

She gave me the details, and I called Leah Pilarsky. "Midtown Homicide is contacting the medical examiner. You should be able to pick up Joel's body by the end of the day." She was right, it did feel weird to say "Joel's body."

"Oh, Lydia, thank you! This will mean so much to Ruth! If there's ever anything I can do for you—"

"Just let me know when the funeral is. I'd like to be there."

"Of course! We can plan now for tomorrow. I'll call you. Now I'd better go. So many people have been calling, people who need to travel in—cousins from Seattle, his old partner in Florida, his college roommate in Zurich. I have to let them all—"

"Leah? Who's in Zurich?"

"Joel's college roommate."

"The roommate's in *Zurich*?"

"He's lived there for years. David Rosenberg. He publishes a business magazine."

"I'd like to talk to him."

"Yes, of course. But the police already talked to him."

"I'm sure." Three calls, Joel made the morning he died. Alice, me, and first, his college roommate. Mulgrew had said that. He hadn't said the roommate was in Zurich.

I called the number Leah gave me, but David Rosenberg, as it turned out, had already left for New York.

"He wanted to be with Ruth," Rosenberg's wife explained, in accented English. "His plane will land eight at the morning. No, no, that is my time. In New York it will be night."

"Tonight?"

"Yes."

I called Leah. "If you hear from him, will you ask him to call me?"

"Yes. And if not, the funeral's tomorrow at ten." She gave me the details.

"I'll be there. But that's not a nice thing, to bother Mr. Rosenberg at the funeral."

"You'll come back to the house afterward. You can talk then."

All right. Joel's friend in Zurich; that sounded like movement. Feeling a little less stuck, I went back to Rosalie.

24 May 1938

Dearest Mama,

I admit to an odd feeling of satisfaction today. I set off to sell Grandmother Gilder's ring, and returned unsuccessful.

But the very reason for my failure is the main source of my gratification.

This afternoon I approached three of Shanghai's finest jewelers. Each made an offer, but I did not like their prices. They were low, Mama, they were the offers of men taking advantage of a young woman in need. And so, thanking each, I turned on my heel. With every abandoned transaction I found, to my surprise, a growing sense that life here might not be beyond my control after all.

Do you understand that, Mama? Until today disorientation and uncertainty have made me progressively more passive, deflated, and defeated, in ways I've not always recognized. But dealing, in German and English, with these arrogant men, and scorning their offers (politely, always politely!) began to restore me to myself.

Which sense was then magnified by the adventure that ended my day! As I left the third jeweler's shop, the sky darkened and a torrential downpour swept in—that happens often here, as though the very air, impatient of the thick dampness, is trying to throw it into the gutters. Waiting beneath a colonnade for the sky to lighten, I noticed a foreign-language bookstore. What choice had I but to enter? I discovered shelves of volumes in English and German, as well as French, Spanish, Polish, and Russian. There was no question of a purchase—where would I keep anything, I whose home is a cot behind a bedsheet? and with what would I buy it, I who am selling a treasure?—but it cheered me to be in the presence of so many books. I was searching for the works of P. G. Wodehouse when voices erupted. A Chinese in military uniform was upbraiding the clerk in English. The clerk's helpless "*Bitte?*" made it clear he didn't speak the language, but the officer seemed to take his befuddlement as a deliberate affront. The officer's rudeness was unfortunate, for his broad shoulders and erect bearing cut a handsome figure.

Before I was aware of myself I'd offered my help. The clerk accepted gratefully, but the officer disdainfully inquired whether I was employed in this establishment. I apologized for intruding and began to walk away.

"Wait!" he ordered. Now, Mama, you know how well I respond to orders, but I told myself he was a military man, so perhaps it was natural to him. And as I didn't like to leave the poor clerk to be abused again, I turned.

The officer, bowing stiffly, introduced himself as one General Zhang. It seemed a young lady of the general's acquaintance had expressed a desire to improve her English. "This fool's idiocy has made me lose my temper. I should not have permitted myself the indulgence."

On that poor excuse for an apology I would have given him a cold good-bye, but the clerk was following our exchange with eager eyes. Perhaps, I thought, I could enable a transaction that would leave the general's money in the clerk's hands, and bring joy to a young lady. If my assistance gratified the general also, that couldn't be helped.

I inquired after the young lady's tastes, concerning which the general was poorly informed. Left on my own, I suggested various English and American poets. General Zhang settled on a volume of Elizabeth Barrett Browning in a costly binding. In German I recommended the clerk double the price, but though he smiled, he didn't do so.

The general offered to repay my kindness by taking me to my next destination in his waiting car. The steady rain made the offer tempting, but the general's eye had taken on an odd look. I thanked him, saying I hadn't concluded my business in the bookshop. He declared he'd wait. I begged him not to trouble himself and turned back to the shelves. The general, after a moment, swept out.

During this operation a mustached European entered, shaking off an umbrella. He listened so closely as I extolled

my poets that I thought I might make a second sale; but after the door slammed behind the general, this gentleman addressed me in English: "Splendid, my dear, simply splendid!"

Astonished, I laughed.

"Robert Morgan, at your service. Londoner by birth.
Washed up on these shores a decade since. This misbegot-
ten establishment, I'm sorry to say, is mine. Drinks money
like water. I can't afford to chuck out blighters like General
Zhang, though I'd dearly love to, and I know Walter would
also, eh, Walter?"

Walter, the clerk with no English, didn't follow a word.
Mr. Morgan repeated the salient points in German, making
him laugh.

"This young lady saved my hide, sir."

"Yes, well, I can see that. Perhaps the young lady will
pause from doing God's work rescuing doomed clerks, and
favor us with her name?"

"Rosalie Gilder, sir."

"Well, Rosalie Gilder, I hope you won't say no to a cup of
tea."

I did not. For the next half hour, to each customer who
entered, Mr. Morgan celebrated what he called my "adroit
handling" of General Zhang. "Sent him away with his tail
between his legs!" At first I demurred, as it was never my
intention to offend my hosts, the Chinese; but I was informed the general was a well-known and widely despised
collaborationist in the "puppet government" army. By the
time the storm abated and I began the long trek to the
Home, not even the prospect of kasha soup could dampen
my pride in having bested four arrogant opponents in one
afternoon!

Be well, Mama!

Your adroit
Rosalie

27 May 1938

Dearest Mama,

I have found a job!

I'm quite delighted, so please don't be angry. I know we agreed I should try to continue my studies, but that won't be easy. The number of universities here is small, smaller since the Japanese have closed some down. The number that give instruction in a language I speak is smaller yet! I have a wild idea of someday studying alongside the educated Chinese. The students, whom I glimpse in streetcars and cafés, are a fascinating group: animated in their discussion and chic in their dress. That dream will have to wait, however, until I've mastered more Chinese than "Good morning," "Thank you," and "Your tea cakes are delicious." (This last was taught me aboard ship by Kai-rong and is my first lie in Chinese.)

But Mama, flights of fantasy aside, Paul's education must come first. I have my secondary diploma, but he hasn't, and he won't be able to go on to medical studies once the world regains its senses unless he takes up classes very soon. The daily tasks of living here, I'm learning, demand more time and energy than at home. Paul and I can't both be in school at once, at least until you arrive. Once you do, I'll abide by your every instruction! (And what a change that will be, I can hear you say!) Until then, I must do what I think best.

The position I've taken, that of English tutor, comes from a not surprising source, but one that I admit gave me pause. My student is to be Kai-rong's younger sister, Mei-lin. When Kai-rong first suggested the idea I bridled, thinking his offer thinly disguised charity. But he explained that his sister is largely confined to the family house and grounds, as is the Chinese custom for unmarried women of a certain class, and is greatly in need of society. He maintained he was determined to find her a tutor from among the European community, and would account it a favor if I, with whom he is already acquainted and in whom he feels he can place his trust, were to accept the position, freeing him of the responsibility of discovering and interviewing strangers. As he, who has done so much for us, was asking this, I hardly felt I could refuse to consider it. I agreed to take tea at the Chen home and meet my potential charge. Accordingly, this afternoon Paul and I, in our finest clothes (and to hear Paul tell it his starched collar threatened any moment to choke the life from him) presented ourselves at the gates of the Chen villa. And oh, Mama, within those gates, what a life is led! There are gardens with flowering shrubs, willow trees, emerald lawns, and a fish pond; the mansion is in the European manner, with wide halls and many rooms. The marble floors are carpeted in Persian rugs and the walls hung with scrolls of forests, storks, and misty mountains, plus beautiful, flowing calligraphy. Tea was served in a parlor whose furniture is a harmonious blend of Chinese antiquities and European pieces in the modern style. In addition to Kai-rong and his sister, we were joined by their father and a woman of a certain age introduced only as Mei-lin's "amah," meaning governess. Apparently I needed to pass the inspection of the assembled multitude before the position was to be mine. Given Paul's appetite for the napoleons, apple squares, and linzer torte spread before us, I feared we would be ejected from the premises; but the senior Chen, with dry humor, instructed the houseboy to inquire of the cook what additional sweets might be on hand. Soon we were presented with a new tray, of Chinese tea cakes. I pleaded an appetite already satisfied by the first wave of dainties; but everyone was approvingly impressed by Paul's appreciation of their cuisine. Mama, these are such charming people! Educated, well spoken, and welcoming. Mei-lin, who is sixteen and quite effervescent, is indeed anxious I should come to her, though I suspect my exotic status here in Shanghai and the tales I

can tell of the wider world are as much of an attraction as
the opportunity to improve her English.

Before the afternoon was out we had settled on a
schedule—I will be visiting three times weekly—and a wage,
which I consider high but which Kai-rong claims is standard
for such services. Paul is welcome to accompany me anytime, I am told. The schedule will permit me the time required to accomplish the errands of daily living and to keep
house (as soon as I find us one!), and the wages will be a
great boon. And as Mei-lin's company promises to be agree-
able, I could see no reason to refuse this position; and thus,
Mama, I am employed!

Your professorial

Rosalie

30 May 1938

Dearest Mama,

A letter from you! You have no idea how my heart
pounded when, calling at the Main Post Office, I found the
General Delivery clerk—who by now knows me well and is
apologetically weary of disappointing me—smiling and
holding out a letter as I approached his window. Oh, Mama,
I sank onto a bench and opened it then and there! And
though it's nearly three weeks since you wrote it, I read
and reread every word. I'm vastly relieved that you and
Uncle Horst are well; and at the same time terrified to hear
how things are at home. The speed and zeal with which our
neighbors have taken up the Nazi cause is horrifying; your
report of the destruction of Herr Baumberg's shop and the
treatment of his children made me ill. Mama, Mama, you
must make every effort to stay out of sight, and to leave
Austria as soon as possible!!!

You write that my stories of our travels bring you joy
and relieve your worry. Very well, I'll go on telling them,
though the situation at home makes the hardships we've

found seem so trivial. We are poor; we are crowded; we are hot and sometimes hungry. But many in China—the Chinese, Mama, whose country this is!—are much worse off than we. Yes, Shanghai has its own misery and perils. But Mama, please believe we're well, as happy as possible under the circumstances, learning to negotiate our new home with daily increasing confidence. And we can walk down the street, not entirely without fear—I won't lie—but at least knowing that any danger we encounter is encountered by all. We're never menaced here solely because we're Jews, and it breaks my heart to know that, in my beautiful Salzburg, this is no longer true.

Waiting eagerly for your next letter, and your arrival!

Your Rosalie

2 June 1938

Dearest Mama,

The tone of your letter and its awful news have been weighing on my mind, along with the uncertainty of your situation. Reading it when I first had it in my hands, I felt as if you were sitting beside me; but I can no longer ignore the fact that you wrote it weeks ago, and I have no real knowledge of *today*. I just pray—I pray, Mama, can you imagine?—that the thugs who found Herr Baumberg don't find you, that you and Uncle Horst pass invisibly through your days until your train leaves for Dairen—or better still, that you've long since left Salzburg for an ocean crossing or an earlier train!

As you ask, I'll continue my account of our days—because I have no other way of doing anything you ask. As I imagine my letter in your hands, I see you in the parlor, safe and comfortable; and so I'll keep writing until I truly see you, hot, weary, and bewildered, as we all are, but *here,* in Shanghai.

So to the news: Mama, I've sold the ruby ring. Oh, it was

a sad moment! To see it placed on velvet in a glass case, to catch a stranger's eye. But I comfort myself the price of it will enable Paul to resume his schooling, and the two of us to find a measure of privacy and a life closer to normal. And the transaction was made less painful by the extraordinary kindness of the jeweler, a refugee himself. Presciently assessing the situation in his native Germany, he brought his wife and children to Shanghai five years ago. He understands we do not sell our possessions lightly. His patience and gentle good nature were reassuring, and the sum he offered fair. With it, Paul will soon return to his test tubes and electromagnets, and—with luck—I will find us a room with solid walls.

Be safe, Mama!

Your Rosalie

10 June 1938

Dearest Mama,

I apologize for my silence. For over a week I've been incapable of anything but collapse at the end of each day— but for many wonderful reasons! First: I've found a school for Paul. He'll attend the Shanghai British School, to be educated in English—hurrah, Mama, for your insistence on "Treasure Island" and "Robin Hood!" This good fortune was made possible by Grandmother Gilder's ring; and by Kai-rong, who suggested the place, and, as an alumnus, had a word with the headmaster. (I believe, Mama, he was prepared to pay the school fees himself, but after I ignored his hints to that effect, he gave the subject up and waited until I told him we had the sum in hand.)

And equally important: We've found and moved to a place of our own!

I say "we," but it was Paul's doing, I having been a total failure at the project. Since a few days after our arrival here, Paul has been busy in an unexpected and enterprising way. Once we began somewhat to understand the city, he and I embarked upon serious negotiations, coming eventually to an agreement over where he may venture and which streets, on the other hand, he may under no circumstances cross. (I felt the dangers of Shanghai's streets to be less than the dangers of being confined all through the day in the wretched Home; I hope you'll agree.) The streets on which he is allowed he wanders daily, in the company of other boys. He returns with odd treasures—two fresh apples, a bicycle tire—for which he has traded yesterday's treasures. Today's will be assessed, and, if not eaten (and I believe if he put his mind to it he could eat a bicycle tire) will be taken tomorrow to some shopkeeper of his acquintance who needs precisely that item and will offer in trade another item which Paul knows is needed at a shop across town. A yuan or two often finds its way into Paul's pockets in the course of these transactions. The yuan is almost worthless, but with a pocketful of them certain items may be obtained: Yesterday, in celebration of our new home, Paul presented me with a single gingersnap! Mama, I was touched to tears. Something to which at home we gave not a second thought here becomes a gem to be marveled at. I did marvel; then I shared it with him, and in four bites it was gone. One does not save food in Shanghai. Refrigerators are unknown except to the wealthy, and too many of God's creatures—flies, worms, mice, and rats—are as interested in your comestibles as you are.

Oh, but how far afield I've flown! But you see, flies and rats aside, I'm happy today, and want to share that happiness. Paul's trading expeditions led to the discovery of the rarest treasure of all: a room to let. The owner of a typewriter shop in the International Settlement which he supplies from time to time with screws and bolts had lost a tenant, bound for Australia. As he remembered Paul inquiring about rooms, he telephoned to the Home requesting the honor of Paul's presence. We set off immediately! The room in question is the rear of two above the shop, facing a courtyard used for cooking and washing, as I imagine we will use it. It is not large—nothing in Shanghai is large, Mama, nothing! with the exception of the banks and great villas—but it is irregularly shaped, with an alcove for a bed. So Paul and I will have privacy now not only from the population of the Home but, up to a point, from each other! We have a basin with cold running water and wonder of wonders, in the hallway, shared with the room at the front, a water closet! Indoor plumbing, whoever would have thought that something to aspire to? But the norm is a bucket, whose contents are taken off each morning by night soil collectors. So a flush toilet, shared with but one other family, is very heaven! The past days have been a matter of scrubbing and airing, of negotiating the price of beds, chests, and linens, of finding coolies to pile them on carts and push them through the streets. This morning we said our good-byes at the Home, with little regret. Friends we've made we'll continue to see, and as for kasha soup, I hope never to see another bowl!

And Mama, it is Shabbos here. Though I do not expect to continue observances, it does seem fitting that on our rickety table in our odd-shaped attic I have set out the pewter candlesticks. I've sent Paul out with a few yuan for candles; when he returns, we'll light them, and say a *barucha,* in thanks for our new home and in hopes to see you speedily in it!

Stay well, Mama.

Your Rosalie

17 June 1938

Dearest Mama,

Oh, I am tired! But I could not go to sleep without writing to tell you what a lovely dinner we've had!

Dinner, you say? I'm writing about a meal?

Well, first, a meal in Shanghai is not a small thing. Wait, that's phrased incorrectly: Often it *is* a small thing: some rice, a carrot boiled with an onion, and there you have it. (Though I have not yet had to resort to kasha.) But after a complicated transaction that began yesterday with a shoemaker's awl and proceeded through several shopkeepers, Paul marched triumphantly up our stairs this afternoon with a chicken! Plucked, cleaned, and ready for the stewpot, the bird became the centerpiece of a Shabbos dinner at which we had our first guest. No, Mama, I am not taking up religion, I assure you. But Kai-rong had expressed a desire to attend a Shabbos dinner, and after his kindnesses, how could I say no? We lit candles, washed, and said the correct prayers, Paul explaining the meaning of the various rituals to Kai-rong. (And he has absorbed much more from his bar mitzvah preparation than I'd have suspected!) We ate chicken, stewed with onions on our charcoal stove in the courtyard, and challah, a great delicacy, purchased from a Viennese bakery. I even managed to sauté some thin Chinese beans into a reasonable side dish. Kai-rong brought linzer torte and a pound of coffee! We sat and ate and talked in our tiny room, at which Kai-rong showed no dismay but also, to my relief, no false cheeriness. We never ran out of conversation, the three of us, and the hour at which Kai-rong finally took his leave would have scandalized our neighbors, had they not been scandalized already by the fact of his unchaperoned presence. Luckily, I and Paul—who in any case considers himself as much of a chaperone as we could ever need—remember your own attitude toward the opinion of neighbors, and are fashioning ours after it.

Mama, it was so lovely, to have a guest for dinner, as we used to at home; it made us feel, nearly, that this could be home, too. All that's missing is you and Uncle Horst, but

the day is fast approaching when your train leaves! Oh,
Mama, I cannot wait to see you again!

> Your tired but happy! Rosalie

That was it.

That was *it*?

Apparently so. I'd reached the end of the stack of printouts. Suddenly Rosalie was silent. Her romance, her marriage, the birth of her son—I wanted to follow her through that. I knew her now, and I wanted to stay with her. But I couldn't. She was gone.

I stared into the dimness of my office, feeling the cloud that had begun to lift rolling back in. In my growing affection for Rosalie, my joy in watching her find, as she said, her sea legs in Shanghai, I'd almost let myself forget that at least part of her story had a tragic ending.

Elke and Horst never made it out of Austria.

That must be why the letters stopped. Rosalie must have learned there was no one to write to.

15

I don't know how long I sat there, feeling simultaneously terrible for my eighteen-year-old Rosalie and like an idiot for caring so much. *Terrific, Lydia. Here you are, all depressed over a sad story from sixty years ago. What's wrong with you?*

Well, it could be what was wrong with me was the sad story from yesterday.

All right, that was enough. If the moroseness in here got any thicker I'd need a cleaver to cut through it. There had to be something I could *do*.

Zhang Li, now. Mr. Chen's cousin. Hadn't I not pushed him for long enough?

I dug out his card and called. A pleasant woman told me in Cantonese that I'd reached Fast River Imports, but the boss was out and she didn't know where to reach him or when he'd be back. I gave her my name, which did not make the boss miraculously reappear. Whether that meant he really wasn't there or he was ducking me, I had no idea. I asked her to have Mr. Zhang call me at his earliest possible convenience and hung up.

All right, that hadn't worked, but I still had to get out and move. Maybe I'd pop up to Mr. Zhang's office, just in case he was one of those people—there were a lot of them, actually—who didn't know how much he wanted to talk to me until he saw me, and saw me, and saw me.

Joel would have laughed, would have said, *Chinsky, hold your horses.*

Have a little patience, he'd have suggested, lots of doors were still open. I just had to wait until David Rosenberg got in, until Zhang Li called me back, until Wong Pan tried to peddle Rosalie's jewelry up the street here.

Joel would have mentioned something else, too, though. *Chinsky? What exactly are you up to? Did you miss it? We've been fired.*

Yes, well, maybe it was time to take that up with the client.

Alice's cell rang three times, and then, just as I was starting to grit my teeth, she answered. "Lydia! How are you doing?"

"I'm fine," I said. Which was true, if you didn't count the sudden visions of Joel with blood all over the front of his shirt that flashed into my brain every few hours. "Fine."

"I'm glad," Alice said. "I hope you're calling with good news. Have the police found anything?"

"No, but I have." I ignored the "good news" part. "Alice, I called you before. Did you get my message?"

"You did? I'm sorry. I have eleven new messages, and the truth is, I was too dispirited to even look at them."

"We need to talk," I said. "Where are you?"

"Washington."

"*Washington?*"

"I have friends here. I thought it might help to come down and see them."

"When will you be back?"

"Tomorrow or the next day."

"But you haven't checked out of the Waldorf?"

"It's tourist season. I have the room booked for two weeks. If I give it up I'll never get another. I'll call you when I'm back."

"No, wait. This is really important. Have you spoken to your clients in Zurich?"

"Yes, I told them what had happened. They agreed we should suspend the search for the jewelry until Joel's murder is solved. I'm sorry, I know—"

"Alice, what do you know about them?"

"About the Kleins?"

"That's the name they gave you?"

"What do you mean?"

"They told you they're Horst Peretz's daughter's sons?"

"Yes, of course."

"Alice, Horst Peretz didn't have a daughter. He never had any children."

A pause. "Lydia, what are you saying?"

"That's why I asked what you know about them."

"What do you mean, Horst never had children? How do you know that?"

"Because Rosalie did. She and Chen Kai-rong had a son, and I've met him, and he told me."

A much longer pause. "You've met him? He's still alive? He's in New York?"

"Yes. He recognized the jewelry photos."

"Oh, my God. You're sure? Rosalie's son?"

"Yes. When you get back I'll introduce you. But then—"

"Yes, I follow you. Then who are my clients?"

"Right. So you can see—"

"Have you told this to Detective Mulgrew?"

"You can't believe he'd care. But Alice, there's more. The police found Wong Pan's hotel."

She caught her breath. "They found him?"

"No, just where he'd been staying. But he seems to have tried to call you. At the Waldorf. He didn't get you, did he?"

"Wong Pan? Of course not. What do you mean, he seems to have tried to call me?"

"A pay phone near his hotel called the Waldorf."

"Oh. But that could be coincidence."

"It could. There's another thing, though, and it's bad: The police think Wong Pan killed someone. A cop from Shanghai who'd followed him here."

"The Shangahi police followed him?"

"But the cop was murdered. In Wong Pan's room."

"My God. Lydia, this is . . . But then, you *have* spoken to the police."

"Not to Mulgrew. To a detective friend of mine, who's . . . involved."

"Lydia, I want you to listen to me. I need to think about this. About the Kleins. I'll call them in Zurich as soon as it's morning there. And I'll come back to New York tomorrow and we'll talk. But this is important: If what you're saying is true, you have *got* to stop."

"Stop what?"

"Lydia! Stop working on this case! Tell Detective Mulgrew, tell your detective friend, and then leave it alone. If Wong Pan killed someone, if my clients are lying to me—whatever this means, one thing that's clear, the situation is dangerous. It sounds likely now that Joel's murder may well be part of this case. And I want you out of it! I won't be responsible for you getting hurt."

"Alice, this is my choice. You're not responsible, but I can't just—"

"Lydia, I fired you to keep you safe. You must stop."

"I don't feel like I can."

"What do you want me to do, get a restraining order?"

I came to a screeching halt. "What?"

"This is my business. I hired you, I fired you, and now you won't leave it alone. If it's the only way I can keep you out of danger, I'll do it. Please, Lydia. I just don't want anything to happen to you."

"You can't do that," I said, wondering if she could.

"Lydia, please. Leave it alone until I get back tomorrow. We'll decide how best to move forward from there."

I sighed and rubbed my eyes. "Will you call me as soon as you're back in New York?"

"Yes."

"All right. I'll talk to you tomorrow."

I clicked off. It was possible my voice sounded a little more resigned, a little less resolute, than I felt. Alice could interpret that however she wanted. I never actually said I'd give up the case, though, and she couldn't quote me as saying I had. Because, in fact, she was wrong on one particular.

She hadn't hired me. Joel had.

16

I called Bill, got voice mail, told him we were fired again and to call me. Then I gathered up my things and started to move.

In five minutes I was back on the other end of Canal. Outside Bright Hopes I paused, letting my gaze sweep the rings, the necklaces, and the ridiculously adorable gold zodiac animals on a Plexiglas Milky Way. This was the bridge between earth and heaven, where the Weaver Maid and the Shepherd meet once a year for all eternity, brought together by their steadfast love.

Behind the jewels and silly animals, Irene Ng's smiling face appeared. She came around and opened the door. "Did you want something? Mr. Chen's not here, but I'd be happy to help you."

"I wanted Mr. Chen, so I guess I'm out of luck. Is there somewhere I can reach him?"

"He didn't say. I'll tell him you were looking for him."

"What about his cousin? Zhang Li?"

"Oh, I have no idea. He comes here a lot, but his business is on Mott Street. Do you want me to call him for you?"

That sounded like a good idea. Zhang Li might be in to Irene Ng even if he wasn't in to me.

But no. Smiling apologetically, she put the phone down. "Fay doesn't know where he is or when he'll be back."

Well, at least Fay's story was consistent. "Thanks." I peered into a case of rings. "I'll bet you enjoy your work. Around these beautiful things all day."

"Oh, yes! I'm just learning, but I love it. Mr. Chen knows every-thing about stones and settings. And he's nice, very patient even when I'm being hopeless. Mr. Zhang says Mr. Chen's mother was just like that."

"They seem very close, Mr. Zhang and Mr. Chen."

"Yes. Like brothers."

I had to smile. "I have four brothers. Do you suppose when we're all old we'll get along that well?"

"I'm not sure age helps." She cocked a dubious head. "From what I hear, Mr. Chen and Mr. Zhang were always much closer than Mr. Zhang and his actual brother."

"Mr. Zhang had a brother?"

"Has. A half brother, about ten years older. The same father, differ-ent mothers." To my surprised silence she said, "C. D. Zhang. You don't know about him?"

"I certainly don't. Tell me."

"Oh, there's nothing special to tell. He imports jewelry. His busi-ness is a few blocks down Canal Street."

"He's *here*?"

"He's been here much longer than Mr. Chen and Mr. Zhang. He actually sponsored them to come. He was so happy when they asked him to help, he told me once. But I don't think it's worked out the way he wanted."

"Why not?"

"I think he thought they'd all be, you know, family. Hang out to-gether. Mr. Chen and Mr. Zhang, they do that, kids and grandkids, that kind of thing. At Thanksgiving and Chinese New Year they in-clude C. D. Zhang, but otherwise, they just aren't that close with him."

I left Irene Ng dusting jade bracelets and hurtled down Canal. Mr. Chen and Mr. Zhang might not be close *with* C. D. Zhang, but close *to* was a different matter. My phone call barely got to C. D. Zhang before I did. On the second floor of a wide-windowed building not far from my office, a secretary with a frizzy Chinatown perm ushered me through the boss's door. "Lydia Chin," she announced in English.

"The private detective!" A tall, spry old man jumped from behind a flat monitor remarkably at home on an antique scholar's desk. "So intriguing! Please, come in."

Bony and quick, with broad shoulders and a lined and leathery face, C. D. Zhang was clearly older than both his half brother, Zhang Li, and his cousin, Chen Lao-li. He gestured me to a thin-armed rosewood chair of the kind I'd seen in museums and always wondered whether they were comfortable.

"I appreciate your seeing me, Mr. Zhang." He'd greeted me in English, so I guessed it was the language of choice.

"How could I resist? *The Maltese Falcon! Farewell, My Lovely!* When I was young, schoolboys in Shanghai were weighed down with dull books for our English lessons, but among ourselves we put those lessons to better use. Oh, the intrigue! The romance!" His black eyes sparkled. "Of course, in those days detectives were tough-talking, two-fisted men."

"Some still are." I sat; the chair creaked but fit me pretty well. The door opened, and the secretary brought in a tea tray. While he poured from a sleek white pot into sleek white cups—the Western kind with saucers and handles—I looked around.

The rosewood chairs and the scholar's desk were the only things in the room older than I was. Everything else—lamps, desk chair, credenza—was relentlessly minimalist-modern. Bookshelves lined two walls, interrupted by certificates of membership in importers' and appraisers' associations. The roar of traffic charged through steel-framed windows along with the midday sun. On my right hung the only other evidence of the past: a colossal black-and-white photo of prewar Shanghai. A full moon gleamed over the neon of the Cathay Hotel and laid a broken path along the sampan-clogged river. Its round glow was dittoed down the Bund in the headlights of boxy cars. A black ocean liner rode the horizon. I found myself listening for the lap of waves, wondering whether the passengers found the harbor's complicated scents exciting or disturbing.

"That was a long time ago."

"Oh, I'm sorry!" Startled back to Canal Street, I said, "I've never been to Shanghai. It seems so fascinating."

"Oh, it was!" C. D. Zhang held out my tea, smoky and strong. "Wild. Intoxicating. As a boy I was in love with the streets of Shanghai. Endlessly I pestered my amah to take me outside our villa walls. I didn't understand half of what I saw or heard, but what chaos! What cacophony! She'd buy me an ice or a bit of fried eel. Women in silks would smile from rickshaws. I can still see it: Coolies with carrying poles darting between limousines. Dazzling bar girls, Sihks with turbans, English bankers sweating in tweeds. Ships and cargo! Temples and gongs! Shops, soldiers, crowds. Banners and neon in the hot damp air."

"That's very poetic, Mr. Zhang. I feel like I'm there."

"No, you're too kind. It's just the truth. If it sounds like poetry, credit the Shanghai of my youth, not myself." His smile turned wry. "Now the Cathay is the Peace Hotel. Our villa houses the Bureau of Water Resources. I hear they park in the side garden, where my father's banquet tent stood."

"Do you go back?"

"Why would I? Everything I remember, and everything I had, is gone. But you're being polite, Ms. Chin. You're a private eye, on a case! You haven't come to discuss Shanghai."

"No. Well, in a way maybe I did. I want to ask you about the Shanghai Moon." *Go ahead, Lydia, jump right in.*

C. D. Zhang was silent for a long moment. "The Shanghai Moon." Then his face cleared. "Ah, I see! I think you've been talking to those two old men."

"Your half brother and your cousin? Yes."

"Li and Lao-li," he smiled. "One madder than the other. They've spun you their tales, and now you're caught up in the romance of the Shanghai Moon."

"I did talk to them, about—something else. But they never mentioned the Shanghai Moon until I found it in a book and asked. In fact, they never mentioned you."

"And why would they?"

"Because you're Mr. Zhang's half brother?"

His smile remained, but it softened. "My brother and I have never been close. The difference in our ages, plus other factors—not least, the war our childhoods shared—conspired to keep us at arm's length. I'd hoped, when Brother Li and Cousin Lao-li came to this country, things might change, but I suppose it's not easy to set one's feet on a new path."

"Still, we were talking about the past. I'd have thought they'd have said something. With you being right down the street here."

"Ms. Chin, if your business with Li and Lao-li concerned the Shanghai Moon, I promise you nothing else was in their thoughts. They'd have no reason to mention me. It would surprise me to hear they told you anything at all."

"Why is that?"

"My cousin has been searching for the Shanghai Moon obsessively and all his life. It's not in his nature to share news of it."

"Well, it was his mother's. I understand it's very valuable."

"Yes, both those things are true. But neither riches nor family pride are what draw him. Cousin Lao-li seeks the Shanghai Moon as a way to recover his past. As though it were a portal he could walk through. He chose jewelry as his life's work solely to dwell in the world of the Shanghai Moon."

"Mr. Zhang, you're in the jewelry business yourself."

"Yes! One of many interesting ironies in our lives, I suppose. But my reasons are quite different. I see you wear a jade *bi*, Ms. Chin."

"My parents gave it to me."

"To safeguard you through life! Do you know why?"

"Jade is supposed to have protective qualities."

"Supposed so, by we Chinese. To the Tibetans, it's turquoise; for the Romans, it was opals. And diamonds are forever!" He waved his hand toward the shelves. "In a flood, my beautiful books are soaked to pulp. In fire, this desk, seven hundred years the support of scholars, is ash. You and I will one day be dust, though mine will form sooner and yours will be prettier. But your jade? The diamonds in this ring? They *will not* change! Burn them, drown them, bury them for a million years: immutable! Smash them to bits—each bit will still be pure: a tiny speck of diamond or jade. Everything changes, Ms. Chin. Water becomes sweet tea and then grows bitter as it steeps. There is no immortality for us. The nearest we can come is to be in the presence of gems."

"Mr. Zhang, I have to repeat myself: You're quite a poet."

"And I repeat myself: It's just the truth."

"But isn't that why Mr. Chen wants the Shanghai Moon? To touch that immortality?"

"My cousin's search is for the Fountain of Youth: a very different obsession. My brother indulges him. Fools, the pair of them."

Immortality and the Fountain of Youth: I wasn't sure I saw such a great difference. "Fools," I said, "but family. Mr. Chen's assistant told me you sponsored them to come here."

"As you say: family. That was forty years ago. I'd heard nothing from them in twenty years, since my father and I had left China. I didn't even know if they still lived. Suddenly, from Shanghai, a letter! It brought greetings from my cousin, whom I had never met, and my brother, and wishes for my good health. It told of a storm fast approaching, to engulf all China in chaos and destruction. If possible"—the wry smile again— "my brother and cousin would prefer to ride out the storm in America. They asked for my help. Such was their good fortune that my father had recently died."

"Why was that good fortune?"

"Sad to say, my father's capacity for ill feeling increased as he aged."

"But Zhang Li is his son."

"And Mei-lin's. And he and Loa-li were both raised by Kai-rong. My father and Kai-rong had not exactly brotherly feelings toward one another."

"But not to help his own son because he didn't like his brother-in-law?" That would take a very hard man. Suddenly, I had another thought. "General Zhang! Rosalie Gilder met him at a bookstore. It's in her letters. He's not—"

"My father? Yes. Shanghai society was a small and insular world.

The book Rosalie found him was for Mei-lin. It was the beginning of their courtship." He smiled. "I've read that letter. Rosalie took a fast dislike to him."

"Oh, but I'm sure she wasn't seeing his best side."

"No, his everyday one. And for his part, he didn't much care for Rosalie's proud nature. Or her temper."

"Was that part of the problem between your father and Kai-rong?"

His glance rested on the Shanghai photo. "Part of it, yes. But surely, Ms. Chin, we're getting far afield from the reason you've come?"

Reluctantly, I said, "I suppose so. Your brother and your cousin— the storm was the Cultural Revolution?"

"They hadn't been here six months when the first clouds burst. They've made new lives, but like so many, their hearts remained in China. In a China that ceased to exist. That's the meaning of their search for the Shanghai Moon." His smile grew sharper. "Beware, Ms. Chin."

"Of what? The search is dangerous?"

"Not in the way you mean. Men have lost their lives in it, it's true. But it's a living death. No one's seen the Shanghai Moon for sixty years, but everyone's gotten word, gotten wind, everyone knows some-one who's heard from someone who saw something glitter in a dusty shop. They throw away their money and their time and in the end have nothing."

"All those people over all these years, finding nothing?"

"Oh, not so many. Most men, even jewelry men, have more sense than to chase a ghost. But through the years, enough. A jeweler in Antwerp who spent his savings rushing here, there, and everywhere, ending with pockets as empty as his hands. A Singaporean of enor-mous wealth, already the owner of three of the world's great jewels. Ah, your face betrays your fascination! The Shanghai Moon, casting its web.

"But now you must tell me: Why are you asking about the Shang-hai Moon? And since those two old men didn't send you, why have you come to me?"

"Mr. Zhang, you say the search for the Shanghai Moon isn't dangerous in the way I meant. I'm not sure that's true. You also say there are always rumors about it—have you heard any lately?"

"No, I haven't. Why?"

"A client hired me to trace some jewelry recently found and then stolen in Shanghai. Rosalie Gilder's jewelry. The Shanghai Moon may have been there."

The racket of traffic crowded into the space his silence made. A flock of pigeons swooped by. I wondered if C. D. Zhang had chosen this corner for its chaos and cacophony.

Quietly, he spoke. "Have you seen the Shanghai Moon?"

"No."

"No." He nodded. "This is how it always goes. 'It's possible.' 'It could be.' 'I think, I heard, I was told.' But in the end . . .'"

"Mr. Zhang? What would the Shanghai Moon be worth?"

He fingered his teacup. "There are no accurate records. It would have to be appraised."

"Sixty years," I mused. "I wonder if there's anyone still around who ever saw it."

"As a boy in Shanghai"—C.D. Zhang looked up—"I saw it myself."

I stared. "You did? Oh, of course! You were family!"

"Despite the mutual aversion between Chen Kai-rong and my father, yes, we were. But I adored my stepmother, Mei-lin. And more than that I adored being family. I was a lonely boy, a dreamy child in a strict and practical household. I barely remembered my own mother, who died before my third year. My amah and tutors were capable but cold. The social reverberations of Rosalie Gilder and Chen Kai-rong's marriage were known to me, a boy of ten, but I didn't understand or care. I was excited that it gave me more family to be part of."

"Were you at the wedding?"

"I was. Rosalie Gilder wore the Shanghai Moon at her throat." His eyes found the nighttime photo. "Though by then it was already legendary. You read about it, you say. So you know its story."

"I know it was made from an antique jade of the Chen family, and stones from a necklace that had been Rosalie's mother's."

"Its legend started before it was made. Please understand what an extraordinary event this engagement was in Shanghai. Of course Europeans had always taken Chinese wives. The exotic bride—a mark of wealth and power! And Chinese men with fortunes kept European mistresses. British girls, Germans, White Russians. And Americans! Very popular, American girls. And yes, some Jewish refugees took Japanese officers or rich Chinese as lovers. They were poor and times were hard. They did what desperate girls have always done, and though few approved, no one was surprised. But *marriage*? A Chinese from a noble family and a refugee? It's hard to say which community was more appalled."

"Mr. Zhang, the book I read said the engagement was secret."

"In Shanghai everything was secret, and every secret was known! Over the charcoal stoves in their alleys, the Jewish women whispered that Rosalie Gilder couldn't be blamed for taking an easy path to good meals and clean clothes—which meant they blamed her deeply. Among my father's friends, the wives muttered and the men shook their heads. The Chen lineage, that had served every emperor of the last thousand years, diluted with European blood? The prophecies ran wild: the fury of the Chen ancestors, how their retribution would strike!"

"But the marriage went ahead."

"It did. And nothing worse happened in Shanghai than what was happening every day. Rosalie Gilder, with her brother, moved to the Chen villa. Where, briefly, they lived a life more comfortable than most of their fellow refugees."

"Why briefly?"

"The marriage took place in April of 1942. In early 1943, to please the Germans, the Japanese ordered the Jewish refugees to relocate to Hongkew, where they could be controlled and watched. Many already lived there, but many lived and worked elsewhere. Then, with one stroke, businesses were closed and families uprooted. Twenty thousand Jews, many with no way now to make a living, confined together with a million of the poorest Chinese in a single foul square mile."

"That sounds horrible."

"Horror, Ms. Chin, is relative. The Germans wanted the refugees exterminated. The Japanese, for their own reasons, didn't care for that plan. The ghetto was a compromise."

I supposed, given the choice, he was right. "And Rosalie and her brother had to go?"

"As Chen Kai-rong's wife, Rosalie Gilder might have been excused. But as it happened, Chen Kai-rong fled Shanghai shortly before the edict was to take effect. That angered the Japanese."

"Fled? What do you mean? He abandoned her?" This couldn't be right.

"Ah, Ms. Chin! It was wartime. His loyalty was questioned, he offended a Japanese corporal on the Garden Bridge, a Japanese officer wanted his limousine—I don't know. But he was gone. So Rosalie and her brother went to live in Hongkew. Taking with them," he added, "my brother, Li, who was not yet two."

"Your brother? Why?"

"Because my stepmother, Mei-lin, had disappeared, never to be seen again."

"What do you mean, she disappeared?"

He gazed at me evenly. "It was wartime."

Just like that, I thought. *Your mother disappears forever, and the answer is* It was wartime.

"Why didn't your brother stay with your father and you?"

"By the time Rosalie went to Hongkew we also were long gone. To Chongqing, where my father, changing allegiances, joined Chiang Kai-shek's army. As, within a few years, I did myself."

"You don't seem old enough to have fought with Chiang Kai-shek." I'd seen the remains of the Nationalist army marching defiantly through Chinatown every October, and though C. D. Zhang was not young, those men definitely had years on him.

"I joined up at fifteen, not the youngest in my brigade. To my surprise, military life suited me. Soldiers are family, dependent on each other. People helped me and expected me to help them. I could be useful, you see! And appreciated for it! An unfamiliar situation in my life until then.

"However, my talents, such as they were, were more logistical than martial. I was valued in my unit because I could provide. We always ate. Sadly, in actual battle, I was a poor soldier. A disappointment to my father in that as in so much else. But Ms. Chin! Again we stray. My military career, not even a footnote to an addendum to history, is not why you're here. I fear we're caught up in the romance of the past. Always more alluring than the mundane present."

Mundane? Shanghai's shadows vanished in an instant: Joel was dead, and the Shanghai Moon might be to blame.

"You're right." I put my teacup down. "Can we go back to the Shanghai Moon? You saw it. What do you think it's worth?"

"I saw it, yes, as a boy. But childhood memories are unreliable."

"Still. You're an expert in this field, after all."

"Ah, such barefaced flattery! But all right, I'll take that bait. As described—as its legend has it—the value of the Shanghai Moon would approach two million dollars. More, if collectors let their hearts rule their heads. And they always do. That truth has brought me a good livelihood. But I deal in gems I can hold in my hand! The Shanghai Moon is a shadow. A quicksand. Tread carefully."

"It may be too late for that. Mr. Zhang, I'm not the only investigator hired to look for Rosalie Gilder's jewelry. The other was shot dead in his office."

The traffic must have stopped for a light, because the room went silent. "Shot dead?" C. D. Zhang paused. "And the search for Rosalie Gilder's jewelry was the cause?"

"I'm not sure of that," I admitted.

"And you're not sure the Shanghai Moon has reappeared, even if it was."

"No, but—"

"Exactly my point. The Shanghai Moon attaches itself to danger, to romance. The way a shadow attaches itself to substance. My cousin is sure, no doubt."

"I don't know."

"Oh, I can promise you he is. If he hasn't said as much, it only means he thinks he's close to the Shanghai Moon and wants to keep it for himself. It's always the same."

"You're saying he was freezing me out?"

C. D. Zhang just smiled.

"Will he try to freeze your brother out, too?"

"Well, he hardly can, can he?"

"Why not?"

"My cousin's wasted a great deal of money on this wild goose chase over the years. That money has all been my brother's."

"Zhang Li's been financing him? I didn't know that."

"Does it surprise you?"

"Yes. He seemed more, I don't know, down to earth."

"They're both mad, not just the one. Although Brother Li lives in less of a dreamland than Cousin Lao-li, perhaps precisely because the money's his. He's seen through some of the more absurd hints and of-fers, over the years. Chases Lao-li would have dashed off on if he had his way. And this, Ms. Chin, sounds like another of those. That a long-vanished jewel should be involved in a recent killing . . ." He fixed his eyes on me. "But it doesn't matter, does it? You're caught in the web."

My cheeks grew hot. "I'm trying to solve a murder." Which didn't mean he was wrong, but I ignored that. "The book I read said the Shanghai Moon disappeared in the last days of the civil war. I asked them—Mr. Chen and Mr. Zhang—about that, but they wouldn't talk about it. Can you tell me anything?"

"The gem's disappearance?" He shook his head. "My father and I didn't return to Shanghai until a Communist victory was clearly in-evitable. Even then we were there just hours, racing for a ship for Taipei. My final memories of Shanghai are dark ones: dodging down alleys and lanes, running to meet my father on the *Taipei Pearl*, ahead of the slow, silent march of Mao's soldiers toward the Bund."

"How old were you?"

"By then, eighteen. Ms. Chin, let me ask you: Where was Rosalie Gilder's jewelry found?"

"In a construction excavation."

"In Hongkew?"

"No, in the area that used to be the International Settlement. On Jiangming Street. Mr. Zhang? What is it?"

C. D. Zhang had gone still. "If I'm correct, what is now Jiangming Street was once Thibet Road. The Chen family villa was at Number 12."

"You mean . . ."

A long pause. "The story, the romantic one the wives whispered, was that Rosalie Gilder was never without the Shanghai Moon, wearing it always hidden on a chain around her neck. But there was another rumor, counter to that and equally persistent, that she didn't take it to Hongkew. She was said to never lock her door, to underscore the fact that the brooch wasn't there."

I thought about this. "If she'd buried her jewelry before she went to Hongkew, why wouldn't she dig it up once the war was over? The Jews didn't have to stay in Hongkew after that, did they? Couldn't she go back to the villa?"

"She could, and she did. But after the Japanese surrendered and left China in 1945, tyranny was replaced by anarchy as Nationalists and Communists tore at each other's throats. Treasure of any kind was better buried, denied, declared already stolen. And after 1949, with the revolution blazing a glorious path into China's future, it was both vulgar and perilous to admit to wealth."

"So do you think it could be true?"

"I think, Ms. Chin, that each tale of the Shanghai Moon's reappearance is credible to those who want to believe." Then, slowly, came a different smile: indulgent, almost conspiratorial. "I will admit, however, this tale is more compelling than most. What will you do now?"

"I'm not sure. Your brother may yet talk to me: He said he would, though that may have been just to get me to leave. But I don't know how much use he'd be. Any memories either of them have that could help in the search, they'd have followed already. As you say, childhood memories are unreliable, and they were both very young."

"Yes." C. D. Zhang nodded. "They were young. And I suppose Dr. Gilder is too old?"

"I'm sorry?"

"Dr. Gilder. He and I are nearly of an age, though we barely know each other. I understand his mind has been slipping for some time now. So I suppose he's of no help?"

"Who's Dr. Gilder?"

"Paul Gilder," said C. D. Zhang, surprised. "Rosalie's younger brother."

17

"You still have that car?" I asked Bill the second he answered the phone.

"What car?"

"Any car."

"Sure. Why?"

"Pick me up. We're going to New Jersey."

Teaneck, specifically, our goal was. Where Dr. Paul Gilder, eighty-four, lived with his granddaughter's family.

"It never crossed my mind he might still be alive," I said as I snapped my seat belt. "Much less near here. He's like a fairy tale character. I didn't expect him to be real."

"I wonder if he'll be happy to know that." Bill pulled the car into traffic.

"According to C. D. Zhang he doesn't know much. His granddaughter said the same thing: He's in and out. Why are you stopping here?"

"So you can get a cup of tea for the drive. I'm well trained."

"Very. But please, no. I've spent the whole day with old Chinese men. You have no idea how much tea that involves."

As we drove I told Bill about my phone conversation with Paul Gilder's granddaugher, Anita Horowitz. "I came clean with her: told her I'd spoken to Mr. Chen, Mr. Zhang, and C. D. Zhang, told her about the Chinese cop and Joel, and about Wong Pan and Alice. The whole thing worried her, but she's willing to let us speak to Paul.

Though she doesn't see how he can help. He's only lucid sometimes, for one thing, and anything he ever knew, Mr. Chen and Mr. Zhang would know."

"Maybe not, if they were just kids when the Shanghai Moon disappeared."

"No, but since they came here in 'sixty-six they've been in touch with him. They'll have pumped him long since."

Bill's GPS led us to a neat raised ranch with bright plastic toys dotting the lawn. A dark-haired woman answered the doorbell.

"You're the detectives? I'm Anita Horowitz. Paul Gilder's granddaughter." As she stood aside to let us in, a toddler clomped up. She looked from one of us to the other and offered Bill half a cracker.

"Thank you." He accepted it gravely.

"This is Lily," Anita Horowitz said. "Lily, these people are here to see Zayde. Can you show them where he is?"

Lily ran off. As we followed, Anita Horowitz smiled at me. "You'll be pleased to know you have a sterling reputation."

"I beg your pardon?"

"After we talked, it occurred to me I should find out more about you. I called our lawyer and asked him to check around. I was prepared to send you packing, but he called back with a glowing report."

"Well," I said, straightening. "I'm pleased to hear it."

"Now you, on the other hand . . ." She turned to Bill, but still with a smile.

"Don't worry about it," I said. "I'll keep him in line."

We came to a glassed-in porch, where Lily leaned against the knee of an old man in a wheelchair. He was smiling at her, smoothing her hair.

"He's usually not sure who she is," Anita Horowitz whispered. "He's always asking her if anyone's taking care of her. He's relieved to see me with her, though half the time he doesn't know who I am either. Wait here a minute." She crossed the room and crouched next to him. "Zayde, some people are here to see you." He looked up with interest, and she gestured us in.

"Dr. Gilder," I said, pulling over a chair, "I'm so pleased to meet you."

He peered through thick glasses. I tried to match his crumpled face to the photo of the young boy grinning next to Rosalie, but I had trouble. He looked up at Bill, then back to me, frowned, and leaned forward. A slow, marveling smile lit his face. "Mei-lin!"

I glanced at Anita, then back as Paul Gilder's stiff fingers grasped my hand. "I'm so glad to see you, Mei-lin! Oh, my goodness, so glad! Why has it been so long?" His voice was weak, his English German-accented: "gled" and "vhy." "And who is this? Ah, I know. An American, a soldier."

"Navy, sir," said Bill.

Paul Gilder shrugged. "Soldier, sailor. You're very welcome in Shanghai, my friend. Mei-lin." He searched my face. "You're all right?"

"I—I'm fine."

"When we didn't hear, we feared . . . It was said the general . . . but enough! Rumors, all rumors. Such a relief! Where is Rosalie? Does she know you're back? Have you seen your little Li? What a handful he is! Oh, he'll be so happy to see you!"

"I . . ."

"Zayde," Anita said, leaning toward him, "this is Lydia Chin. From New York. She wants to ask you some questions."

Paul smiled. "Anita, my dear. Have you met . . ." Confusion seeped into his face. He looked from her to me. "Mei-lin? How is it . . . Anita . . ." He trailed off.

"This is Lydia Chin," Anita patiently repeated. "She wants you to tell her about Shanghai."

"Shanghai, yes, Mei-lin has come back to Shanghai." But his voice was uncertain, and his gaze wandered into the garden.

Anita stood and spoke softly. "I'm sorry. I didn't think he'd be able to help you. I don't want him getting upset."

"I understand." I squeezed Paul's hand. "I'm happy to have seen you. I'm sorry, but we have to go now."

He turned and met my eyes. "Mei-lin. Wait."

"Zayde, they have to go," Anita said.

"But Mei-lin's book. Haven't you come for your book?"

"What book, Zayde?"

"In the chest. With . . . with the letters." His brow furrowed. "Rosalie kept it safe for you, as you asked. And I . . . after Rosalie . . ." He set his chin, determined to go on. In a firm voice he spoke to Anita. "In the chest."

"The red chest?"

"Of course."

"All right. I'll get it."

She left the porch, Lily thumping after her. I stayed sitting by Paul. I didn't intend to ask him anything, just to be companionable. But he suddenly spoke. "Have you seen Kai-rong since you've come back? I don't know where he's gone . . . he wasn't hurt badly, you know. They hadn't had time." He smiled at me. "You saved his life. You were very brave."

I said, "I've never been brave."

He laughed, and suddenly I could see the fourteen-year-old in the garden. "Mei-lin, when did you learn modesty? How will we get used to such a change? Never mind. Kai-rong and I are lucky to have such sisters."

Anita came back with a shoebox-sized chest of lacquered wood. A lock clinked against a bronze disk. "He brought this from Shanghai," she whispered. "He never opens it."

My breath caught. A box from Shanghai, that Rosalie Gilder's brother has had all this time and never opens—could it be? *No, Lydia, that would be too easy.*

"Where is the key?" Paul asked Anita.

"You have it, Zayde."

"I have? Ah." His stiff fingers worked into a pocket and brought out a key ring. He carefully separated keys, until he found the smallest. "This," he told Anita. "It sticks," he added. With a little jiggling— it did stick—Anita opened the box, releasing a swirl of rosewood and age.

Inside, a string-bound bundle of letters nestled on a small book, but the box held nothing else. I caught Bill's eye; his shrug told me we'd been thinking the same thing. Paul lifted out the book and shut the box. No one spoke while he gazed at the book's once-rich leather cover, now mildew-spotted and flaking. Then he presented it to me with both hands, the formal Chinese way.

"I've waited . . ." Again, the confusion. "I've waited a long time to return this, Mei-lin." Briefly, his eyes closed.

"I'm very grateful." I glanced at Anita, who was looking worried. "You're tired," I said to Paul. "We'll go now. Thank you very much."

"I am tired. Lately I'm often tired. But Mei-lin. You'll come back?"

"Yes, of course."

"It was an honor to meet you, sir," Bill said.

Paul Gilder, his arm wrapped around the box, looked at Bill. "Mr. American Sailor."

"Yes, sir?"

"If you're keeping company with Mei-lin, be careful of the general."

"The general, sir?"

"He's a dangerous man. We thought . . . After Mei-lin went to Number 76 . . . Just keep an eye out."

"Sir? Number 76?"

"Very brave. Mei-lin, you were very brave." Paul nodded. Lily ran over and leaned into his knee. He looked at her in surprise, then smiled. "Lily."

"Please," Anita whispered.

Leaving Paul cradling the rosewood box, Bill and I followed Anita to the living room. She said, "I'm sorry. I was afraid he wouldn't be much help."

"He thought I was Mei-lin. Kai-rong's sister. Do you know what he meant about her being brave?"

"I barely know her name. I told you on the phone, he's never talked much about Shanghai."

"Or the Shanghai Moon?"

"That, never. The first I heard of it, I was eleven. My Hebrew School teacher invited Zayde to come talk about the Shanghai ghetto. He said he would if I did research and could give the facts—how many refugees, from where, things like that." She smiled. "I wasn't very bookish, and he was trying to help. Anyway, I found a reference to the Shanghai Moon, and that it had been Great-Aunt Rosalie's. I was a little girl with my head full of princesses, so I loved the idea of a romantic lost gem, but when I asked Zayde he just said it was gone." She looked through the doorway at her grandfather and her daughter. "He said wherever it was, it was cursed, and he wished it had never existed. He said the important things about Shanghai were the Yiddish theaters and the coffeehouses, that people had bar mitzvahs and seders and lit Shabbos candles for ten years on the coast of China, and I should remember that and forget this nonsense about gems. That he didn't want to hear about it again." She paused. "It was the only time he was ever short-tempered with me."

"So you don't know what happened when it disappeared?"

"No. The only times I heard it mentioned were when Cousin Lao-li visited. Rosalie's son. Even then they hardly ever spoke about it."

"Do you see him often, Chen Lao-li?"

"More often now, since we moved here. He comes for holidays and the kids' birthdays, things like that. I grew up in California, so when I was little I didn't see him much. I wasn't born yet when they came here, he and his cousin, but my big brother used to tease Zayde about how excited he'd been when he got the letter that they were coming. He flew to New York three days early, so if he got delayed he'd still be there to meet them."

"I wonder why they didn't ask him to sponsor them?" Bill said. "Instead of C. D. Zhang, whom one of them didn't know and the other didn't like."

"They did, and he tried. But he wasn't a close enough relative for the INS. So Zayde tracked down C. D. Zhang. I have the feeling they might not have contacted him at all if they didn't have to."

I asked, "When did Dr. Gilder come to this country?"

"In 1949. He was one of the last refugees to leave. Very few stayed, but Zayde had been planning to. My father used to say we all could have been Chinese."

"Why didn't he?"

"Stay on? Well, I suppose he had less reason to, after Rosalie died."

18

I stood in Anita's living room stunned, as though I'd gotten a phone call full of bad news. Not my Rosalie! *Oh, Lydia, get a grip!* I demanded. *You already knew she was gone.*

Yes, but not so young! I found myself negotiating. *Not so soon! Couldn't she have had a life of happiness with Kai-rong first, and died a contented old lady?*

"Are you all right?" Anita eyed me with concern.

"Yes, I'm sorry." I drew a breath. "It's just, I've been reading Rosalie's letters at the Jewish Museum and I got very fond of her. I didn't know she died so young."

"I read the letters, too. Zayde donated them around the time Lao-li and Li came to this country. I think I would have liked her."

"Do you—can you tell me what happened?"

"How she died? I just know it was near the end of the civil war. Those last days are something Zayde absolutely never talked about. Do you think it's important?"

"I don't know." *Maybe not to the case,* I was thinking. *But to me. It is to me.*

For a moment, we were all silent. I looked at the book Paul Gilder had handed me. "Do you know what this is?"

"He's never mentioned it. I didn't even know the box existed while I was growing up. My father brought it with Zayde's things when Zayde came to live here, but all he knew was it had papers in it."

"May I look at this?"

Anita nodded. Carefully, I opened the cover. Flakes of leather drifted off the spine. On thick paper flowed column after column of beautiful calligraphy. The first characters on the first page, twice the size of the others, read, "Kai-rong is back!"

Back, I thought. *From England? Just off the* Conte Biancamano?

"Can you read that? What is it?" Anita asked.

"I think it's a diary. The pages are dated. This first one's May eighth, 1938. That's the day their ship docked in Shanghai—Rosalie, Paul, and Chen Kai-rong. Anita, what are the letters in the box?"

"I don't know. I could try to take a look, but not right now, I don't think." Paul, with the box on his lap, was running his hand through a set of bamboo chimes. When he stopped, Lily pointed; when he clattered them again, she laughed.

"If you could, it might help. Anything from that time. And I'd like to try to translate this."

"I don't know . . . What if he asks for it? Now that he's been reminded."

"We'll Xerox it," Bill suggested. "Then you can put it back. It won't take long."

"Well." Anita smiled. "All right. After all, that he gave to you."

"Can you really read that?" Bill asked as I got back into the car. We'd spent twenty minutes at the Kinko's in the mall, and then I'd returned the book to Anita, thanking her profusely and trying not to look like I was running out the door.

"Why wouldn't I be able to?" I airily traced my finger down a column of Chinese characters.

"Because if it was written in Shanghai while Paul Gilder was there, it's probably in the Shanghainese dialect, which, though Chinese characters carry no phonetic information and therefore can be read by anyone literate, still may be different enough in the vocabulary formed by those characters to baffle a speaker of one of the other Chinese dialects, say for example Cantonese."

I stared at him. "What are you, Wikipedia?"

"What's that?"

"Never mind. How do you know all that, what you just said?"

"Anybody trying to impress his Chinese *associate* into thinking he wasn't a total loser would have gone out of his way to know that. So can you read it?"

"Anyone trying to impress her *lo faan* associate into thinking she was a genius wouldn't admit it if she couldn't."

"I already know you're a genius."

"Oh. Okay, then, I can read it, but I have to guess at some words. But there's no question it's Mei-lin's diary. Listen how it starts: '*Kai-rong is back!!!*' That's written extra big, with emphasis. Then it goes, '*What—*' uproar, I think that's the word. '*The houseboys airing his rooms, Cook racing to market, the kitchen maids peeling and chopping. I wanted to go meet his ship but of course Father and Amah said no.*' Doesn't that sound like family?"

"Not my family, but I see what you mean."

I scanned the page. Modern Chinese is written in simplified characters, but at the Mott Street Chinese school my brothers and I had (with varying degress of grumpiness) gone to Saturday mornings, the teachers had been educated before Mao's reforms. They'd proudly taught us the old ways. And these strokes—made with a pen, I thought, not a brush—were particularly crisp. "Okay," I said, "now listen."

"You're about to show off?"

"I am. Any objection?"

"None."

So as we drove toward and over the gleaming Hudson, I read the entry out loud. I stumbled occasionally, but generally, I think I did my Chinese teachers proud.

"'*Father sent bodyguards, so I'd have been perfectly safe, but it's not the danger, I know it's not! The docks are like every place I want to go: A decent young lady can't be seen there.* SO old-fashioned!!! *A decent young lady can't go* anywhere *except the homes of other decent young ladies. Even then her amah goes with her! A decent young lady is the same as a prisoner!*

"'*So I'm sitting, waiting. Sitting, waiting!! Amah sent me to work on my*

embroidery—an ancient, useless art! Though I am rather good at it. But I
stuck myself twice when I thought I heard the car. So I threw that aside to
start this book.

"'I haven't put a stroke in it since Kai-rong sent it from Italy. Father
wanted me to fill it with calligraphy—another useless art I'm good at! Copies
of famous poems. Amah thought that was a lovely idea. I didn't! I know why
Kai-rong sent it: So I could keep a journal the way European women do. Un-
til now it's been empty, because what could I write about? What ever happens
behind these walls? But now that Kai-rong's back, things will change! Father
and Amah listen to him. He'll tell them I'm grown up! He'll make them let me
go out! I'll finally, finally, finally get out from behind these walls! Kai-rong's
come back to rescue me!!!'"

That was the first entry. I took a breath.

"Boy," said Bill.

"No kidding."

"Girls just wanna have fun, huh?"

"Hey, give her a break! In the old days women could spend their
whole lives locked up in the house. And Shanghai was a dangerous
place. You're the one who's reading a book about it."

"Doesn't say much about girls locked behind walls."

"What does it say?" I was realizing I didn't know much about wartime Shanghai. "If it doesn't make me sound like not a genius to ask."

"Every word you speak makes you sound like the genius you are.
Mostly it says the opposite: the place was a nonstop end-of-the-world
party. Everyone who didn't run when the Japanese came was franti-
cally dancing and drinking, pretending nothing had changed."

"Party like it's 1936? All during the war, they did that?"

"What we mean by 'the war' was different in Shanghai. Until
'forty-two, the only way you could tell there was war in Europe was
when Europeans snubbed each other in the streets."

"But the Chinese civil war? And the Japanese invasion?"

"The civil war had been going on for years. When the Japanese
came, Mao wanted to unite with Chiang Kai-shek to fight them, but
Chiang wasn't interested. That worked for the Japanese. Chiang went
inland to push Mao north, and Japan set up puppet governments and

occupied the coast. Everyone left Europeans alone and Europeans made money. Until 'forty-two, that was 'the war' in China."

"And in 'forty-two?"

"December 'forty-one was Pearl Harbor. A few months later the Japanese locked Allied nationals—English, Belgians, Dutch, Americans—into internment camps."

"That's where Alice Fairchild was, one of those. So the party was over then?"

"No. Things got ugly, but the party went on."

"Who was left to party?"

"To start with, lots of Japanese. And Germans. Vichy French. Neutrals—Swedes, Spanish, Portuguese. Filipinos, Indians. White Russians. Wealthy Chinese."

"Indians? Weren't they British citizens? And Filipinos—"

"They were Asian. The Japanese didn't lock up other Asians, no matter whose citizens they were. They wanted to be loved when they took over that half of the world and Germany took over the other. They didn't intern the Jewish refugees, either. Japan had no argument with them. To make Germany happy, they moved them to a ghetto—"

"In Hongkew. In 1943. Rosalie and Paul went there. What, you think you're my only source of historical information?" I looked at the Xeroxed pages. "So here's poor Mei-lin, in 1938, in the middle of a wild party, and she can't go."

We exited the bridge. Bill asked, "How many entries?"

I flipped through. "Hard to say, but the last one's dated 1943. After that the pages are blank. Oh . . ."

"Oh, what?"

"Oh, I'm being stupid. You saw how it threw me when Anita told us Rosalie died so young. I just remembered C. D. Zhang saying Mei-lin had disappeared. I asked him what happened and he said, 'It was wartime.'"

"So you're worried about her, too?"

"How stupid is that? I hardly know her! I mean, obviously I don't know her at *all*—"

"It's not stupid. It's one of the best things about you."

"How I get carried away?"

"No," he said. "How you care."

I shot him a suspicious look, but he was concentrating on the road as though he were new in town.

After a moment I looked at the papers again. *What a day this has been!* She could say that again, I thought. To Bill I said, "I have an idea."

"Good, I like ideas."

"I'm really hungry."

"That's less an idea than a description of your existential situation."

"It was the preface. I'm suggesting we find someplace for a snack and I read to you."

Fifteen minutes later I was guarding two stools at the stainless steel counter of Tai-Pan Bakery. Bill was at the register paying for eight-treasure rice and vegetable dumplings. Tai-Pan had not been chosen lightly. It had two virtues: The food was great, and it was on Canal smack in the middle of Jewelry Row. In fact, it was directly across from Mr. Chen's shop.

"And the point would be?" Bill had asked when I'd suggested it.

"Mr. Chen said he hadn't been approached by Wong Pan. That doesn't mean he won't be, or anyone else won't be."

"You think Wong Pan will show his face, if he killed that Chinese cop?"

"He still needs to sell the jewelry."

By the time Bill brought the tray over, I'd swept the counter clear of crumbs and provided us with chopsticks. After an urgent dumpling, I took Mei-lin's diary from my bag.

"Keep your eyes open," I instructed Bill. "If you see Wong Pan, kick me or something."

"Really?"

"I don't think so. Are you ready?"

"Can't wait."

I narrowed my eyes. "You're not laughing at Mei-lin, I hope?"

"Absolutely not. I'm looking forward to this. I've never read a girl's diary. Even from sixty years ago, she still might give me some idea how you people think."

"Us people, Chinese?"

He shook his head. "You people, women."

"Not happening," I informed him. "Okay. This second entry's the same date. Once she started this journal thing, I guess she got into it." I studied the characters and began to read. "'*What a day this has been!*' That's written big, with emphasis, like before. She's pretty excitable, I guess. '*The moment I put my pen down this morning, the car rolled through the gate. By the time I'd rushed downstairs the houseboys were fighting over the honor of carrying Kai-rong's luggage. Number One Boy had to shout at them— they almost came to blows!*

"'*Kai-rong swung me around and told me I looked beautiful! He hasn't changed, his eyes still twinkle! Of course I've changed. I was a child when he went away, I'm a lady now. Father and Kai-rong greeted each other formally, with bows and flowery words. (Father frowned at Kai-rong's European suit. I thought it looked wonderful!) When Father asked about the voyage Kai-rong said it was pleasant. Only* pleasant? *A month on the ocean, where you can see for miles, no walls anywhere—only* pleasant???

"'*We had tea in the garden listening to Kai-rong's stories. His life is so exciting! He brought gifts—a leather case for Father, Spanish hairpins for Amah (she said he was foolish to spend money on nonsense). For me—British shoes!! With high heels! Black satin for evening, red leather for day! I jumped up and hugged him in a not very ladylike way. Father disapproved of the shoes, but when he saw how happy I was he didn't forbid me to have them.*

"'*After Father went to lie down, Kai-rong asked* me *to tell* him *about what* I've *been doing. Nothing, I said, nothing nothing nothing! Embroidery, calligraphy, playing the pipa and feeling about to explode! Since the Japanese came Father says the streets are so dangerous I can't go* anywhere! *Although I'm allowed to call on the Feng sisters, and Tsang Sui-ling, and how can the streets be dangerous except when I'm going to them?*

"'*Kai-rong promised to speak to Father and Amah, though he also agrees the streets are more dangerous than they used to be. I said he'd been home half a day, so how would he know? That made him laugh. Be careful what you wish for, he told me, it might come true. I said that was just more ridiculous*

old musty advice that doesn't mean anything. If I wish for something it's be-
cause I want it to come true! He laughed again and asked how the shoes fit. I
said, Perfectly! But it's a shame they'll live out their lives inside these walls in-
stead of being seen and admired. Then he asked if I thought they'd get enough
admiration at the Cathay Hotel. And was Friday too soon for them to be ad-
*mired? It took me a moment to understand—*He's taking me to dinner at
the Cathay Hotel!!!

"*'It's late now. Everyone's sleeping, except me. Today was so exciting, and*
the life I'm starting now that Kai-rong's back is even more exciting!! The way
I feel right now, I may never sleep again!'"

I paused for breath. "The way *I* feel right now, I need caffeine just
to keep up with her."

"Good." Bill got up. "We need to pay rent on the counter."

"Any action on the street?"

"Nothing but. No one who looked like your boy, though. It would
be a hell of a stroke of luck if he just strolled past."

"I know. But do you have anything better we could be doing?"

"Than eating and reading a girl's diary? Nope. What can I get you?"

I took over the task of peering out the window until he got back.
A typical Chinatown afternoon: wall-to-wall people, mostly Chinese,
but also bargain-hunting uptowners and map-wielding tourists, all
shopping their little hearts out. Umbrellas, uglyfruit, toys, T-shirts,
salmon, and sunglasses flew out of storefronts and street stalls into
plastic bags, and good hard American cash flew the other way. Heavy
traffic in and out of the jewelry shops, too, but nothing out of the or-
dinary.

Or almost nothing. The one interesting thing I spied was Clifford
"Armpit" Kwan, a distant cousin of mine—not distant enough, according to my mother—peering into jewelers' windows. I shared my
mother's opinion of Armpit: He and I had had some run-ins at family
gatherings in the past, when he was a nasty brat picking on the littler
kids and I was an adolescent Lady Galahad riding to the rescue. Now
he's a grubby stoner perpetually on the fringe of one or another Chinatown gang. None of them really wants his useless behind, but occasionally he'll get a one-day contract when some huge display of muscle

is called for, or some gang's franchise player is unavailable on account of being, say, in jail.

The gangs provide protection. This means they guard shops against theft and vandalism, caused, if you don't pay, mostly by the gang you didn't pay. I wasn't sure whose real estate this block was, or which lucky gang had Armpit's services these days. But I didn't like it. Armpit, never devoted to beauty, was unlikely to be merely indulging his joy in sparkly things. It occurred to me some fed-up jeweler could have stopped paying, and his protectors might be planning to show him his mistake. I made a note to mention this to Mary. If, on her info, the cops were ready when a gang did a smash-and-grab, it could do her career some good.

"Anything?" Bill distributed cups and pastries.

"Relatives."

"Mr. Chen's?"

"Mine. Are you seriously going to eat that?"

"Why, just because it's blue?"

"There can't be one real ingredient in it."

"Sugar. Come on, what happens next? Does her brother take her to dinner?"

"You really want to hear more?"

"You bet I do."

I sipped the milk tea he'd brought—my aversion to tea had faded, but a great deal of sweetened condensed milk seemed important— and bit into an almond cookie. "Okay. Just don't laugh at her, and don't take your eyes off the street."

"You got it, boss."

I read down the column on the next sheet and found myself smiling. "They went to dinner a few days later."

"Was it great?"

"Her word is 'grand.' *'Oh, the Cathay is so grand!'* She talks about the marble, the carpets, the chandeliers. And the air-conditioning. It was so cold she shivered. But air-conditioning's modern, and she likes modern."

"Did she wear the shoes?"

"She did. *'I'd practiced for days, so I swept smoothly past the Sikhs at the door. (One winked at me! Of course I pretended not to notice.)'* "

"Of course."

"You *are* laughing!"

"Never. If I'd have been there I'd have winked at her myself."

"And she'd have ignored you, too. *'I wanted to go into the bar, but Kai-rong refused. Women are permitted there—but he said I wasn't. He can be so much like Father! When we were shown to our table he ordered champagne. It was delicious, though I'm not sure I care for a drink with bubbles. As we sipped we played a game: guess-the-nationality. I picked out Britons, Frenchmen, Dutchmen, Russians. Kai-rong wouldn't give me credit for Americans because they're too obvious.'* Hey, that was a definite snicker!"

"Only at the obvious Americans. Remember, I was a Yankee sailor in Asia myself."

"Oh. Well, all right, but watch it. *'There were Japanese everywhere, perfectly well behaved. When a mustached man entered, I guessed he was Italian, which made Kai-rong laugh.'* "

"*He's* laughing at her."

"He's her brother, he's allowed."

"I'll remind you next time your brothers laugh at you."

"You'd better not. *'It was Sir Horace Kadoorie, a wealthy Jew from Bombay. How am I supposed to know what Jews look like? I don't know what anyone looks like unless they call on Father. And the famous Sir Horace is small and dark. The only Indians I've ever seen are those gigantic Sikhs. Kai-rong kept laughing and said I'd seen other Jews and Indians on the streets, but I probably thought they were all Italians, too. I'd have thrown my champagne at him but my glass was empty. If I were allowed on the streets I could learn to tell people apart! He said the Bombay Jews are originally from Baghdad, which accounts for their coloring and size, and that not all Jews look like them, either. When I asked how he became such an expert on the subject of Jews, he blushed! And then said out of nowhere how much he was enjoying the string quartet.'* "

I glanced up at Bill; he was grinning but silent. Well, I hadn't said he couldn't smile.

" *'I thought the quartet was boring. I wanted to hear the Filipino jazz band in the nightclub. But I didn't say that, so he wouldn't think I'm ungrate-ful. One day soon I'll play him my jazz records, and show him the American dances the Feng sisters taught me (while Amah was gossiping with their cook!).*

"'*So many people came over to welcome Kai-rong home! Some asked who his companion was. When he introduced me eyebrows flew up. "This is little Mei-lin?" they'd say—if they knew I even existed! One Frenchman said he suddenly regretted not calling on Father while Kai-rong was away. Each time someone complimented me, I gave them a distant smile, to show I was pleased to meet them but really, one meets so many people, doesn't one?'*"

"I knew it!" Bill broke in. "This girl doesn't get out much, but she knows how to make men feel small. You're all born with that talent, aren't you?"

"No, but we develop it early, after we've met a man or two. Shall I go on?"

"Please."

"'*Once each one left I made Kai-rong tell me all about them. The French-man, he said, is a wine importer, and I could thank him for the champagne that was making me tipsy. I told him I wasn't tipsy—'*"

"She was too."

"Granted. '*—and asked about a sad old woman. She's a Russian countess! Here since the Bolshevik Revolution. Kai-rong says all the White Russians are aristocracy of some sort, which doesn't keep them from jobs as waiters and seamstresses. He suggests I take a lesson from that. Just like Father! And I can sew, though I'd like to see him wait on tables.'*"

I took a tea break. "I can sew, too, by the way."

"I know you can. And I'm a lousy waiter, but a hell of a short-order cook. So when the revolution comes, we're in business."

"What a relief. '*We ate roast beef and Yorkshire pudding. It wasn't the first time I'd had them, and I told Kai-rong he needn't think it was: The Tsangs keep an English cook. I don't like roast beef—it seems rude to serve such a big, unflavored slab of meat—but Kai-rong says it's the most British meal of all. The evening raced by like a kaleidoscope of dinner jackets and silk gowns. I was so happy to be there! Probably because of the excitement, some parts are hazy.'*"

"Or the tipsiness."

"Shush! *I remember meeting a bookseller called Morgan, and a Dutch doctor. Two dashing soldiers approached us together: a German officer named Ulrich, and his friend General Zhang. They both kissed my hand!*'

"I don't know the dashing German," I interrupted myself to tell Bill, "but the dashing General Zhang is the guy she eventually married. C. D. Zhang and Zhang Li's father. But you need to read Rosalie's letters. He doesn't come off quite so well. *Three school friends of Kai-rong's sat and drank champagne with us; we all found each other amusing, oh how we laughed! They excused themselves, with winks they thought I didn't see, saying they were off to Madame Fong's. When I asked who that was, they roared. After they left, Kai-rong's only answer was that Madame Fong is no one I'll ever need to know. He thought I had no idea—but of course I do! She must be a courtesan, and his friends were off to a flower house! I asked Kai-rong if he'd ever been to Madame Fong's. He opened his mouth with no sound, like a carp. I laughed so hard I cried.*' Is that what they called them when you were a sailor?"

"Who called what?"

"Flower houses."

"How would I know?"

"Uh-huh. *When we were leaving (the Sikh winked again!) Kai-rong asked if I'd enjoyed myself and whether I was happy. I said yes yes yes! I had a wonderful time!*

"*'But if by happy, he meant satisfied—no, I'm not satisfied. Tomorrow I'll be expected to resume my life as prisoner. Calligraphy, embroidery—no no no no no!!! Crowds, music, laughter—this is the life I want! And the life I'll have.*'"

Turning the page, I found a new date, which meant a new entry. I closed the book and took a breath.

"You're stopping?" Bill protested. "I want to know if she got it."

"Got what?"

"The life she wanted."

"You'll have to wait. This translation stuff is tiring, you know."

"Even for a genius?"

"I'm immune to flattery."

Barely audible above the swirling voices and Cantopop Muzak, my phone chirped the ringtone of an unfamiliar number. Who invented this device, I wondered, and did he really do us a favor? Well, maybe he did. The caller turned out to be Anita Horowitz.

"When Zayde was dozing I opened the box. There's a set of letters. They're mostly from Rosalie to her mother, but they're in German, so I can't read them. And there's one from someone else to her, in German, too. That one was mailed to her in Shanghai, General Delivery, but the ones to her mother don't have addresses or stamps. They were never mailed."

"No?" I thought about that. "Anita, I'd love to read them." For the case, of course. Strictly for the case. "May I?"

"If you think it would help. I can make copies when I pick up my son from Little League. Zayde won't notice them gone for that short a time. Can you come out and get them?"

"Absolutely! Thanks!"

When I clicked off, Bill asked, "What are you so excited about?"

I told him what Anita had found. "Though I have to admit I'm not so excited about driving back out to New Jersey right now. And I think my mother wants me home for dinner."

"Your mother always wants you home for dinner."

"Yes, but . . ." He was right, of course. At a loss to explain what was different now, I settled for "I've been away." Which, I realized, was the same nonexplanation I'd offered Joel about Bill.

"I'll go."

"Back to Teaneck? By yourself?"

"It's my fate. To be alone, solitary, by myself, while you—"

"Don't start that stuff."

"Oh, okay. But I'm the one who reads German. I'll go get the letters and settle in with my German-English dictionary."

"Sounds cozy."

"Not as cozy as—oh, right. Never mind. You go home and rack up karma points by having dinner with your mother." He gave me a smile and a kiss on the cheek, and left me at Tai-Pan.

19

I called my mother on the way home to ask if we needed anything. She seemed a little thrown; maybe it was the "we." She recovered fast, though, and assigned me choy sum, peanuts, and soft tofu.

Making tofu's a cottage industry in Chinatown. Everyone has a favorite back room, basement, or fourth-floor walk-up where someone's granny stirs vats and scoops the silky stuff into a container you bring along. The place I like is a Baxter Street hole-in-the-wall. If the route there took me right by Bright Hopes, was that my fault? I told myself I wouldn't go in unless I saw Mr. Chen out on the shop floor.

I didn't. In fact, the shop was already closed. I turned up Baxter, but I was hit by a nagging sense I'd seen and ignored a familiar face. I don't like to be rude unless I mean to be, so I looked over my shoulder, scanning the choreography of the street. No, I was wrong.

No, I was right. Not someone I knew. But a familiar round face, with what must be a seriously guilty conscience: As soon as our eyes met, he was off.

"*Wong Pan*!" I surged past three teenage girls whose linked elbows dammed the sidewalk. "Wait!"

For a fat man, he could move. He cut through traffic and I charged after, jay-running across Canal. "Wong Pan!" Had he found Mr. Chen? Had they spoken, made a deal? Knowing Wong Pan was likely a killer, would Mr. Chen do that?

For his mother's jewelry? Damn right he would.

"Stop!" I yelled, but of course Wong Pan didn't stop. No one stopped him for me, either; by the time my shouts registered, people had already sidestepped out of his way. I was gaining on him, though. He slipped down Walker and turned on Lafayette. Just before the courthouse I went into overdrive, did a broad jump, and got hold of his shirt. I spun him around and threw us both off balance. He grabbed me, we did a jig, neither of us fell, and then one of us felt a gun in her ribs.

I stopped moving. "You won't shoot me here."

"I shoot you where I have to." He put an arm around me. His gun lurked under my jacket. "Smile like you glad see me."

"I *am* glad to see you. I've been looking for you. You killed my friend." I showed my teeth in imitation of Mulgrew.

"I kill you, too. Stay away. Don't wanting more trouble."

"No, you have enough already. This would be the time to turn yourself in."

He laughed like ice cracking. I was never so lonely for my gun in my life. "Sorry, your friend." He shoved his moon face close to my ear. "All I want is get my money, go away. You leave me alone, no one else get hurt, too. You don't, remember this: For me, nothing to lose."

A sudden hard push and I was face-to-face with a brick wall. By the time I spun around, Wong Pan was gone.

I don't know if it was true about the karma points for eating dinner with my mother, but I hoped so, because I needed them. Mary, hearing what had happened, hit the roof.

"You let him get away?"

"He pulled a gun and mashed me into a wall!"

"So? You were okay with chasing him down the street without calling us, why not try for the collar, too?"

"I didn't have time to call you!" *Stop, Lydia. Breathe.* "You're right. I'm sorry. But Mary, anyway, now we know for sure he's here. And that he killed Joel."

"That's supposed to make me feel better, a known killer on the loose?"

"And we know he knows about Mr. Chen."

"No, we don't."

"What else was he doing down here?"

"What you thought originally he'd be doing. Trying to sell his jewelry."

"Rosalie's jewelry."

"What?"

"Nothing. But what if he does know about Mr. Chen? Or finds out? They could have a secret deal."

"You're asking me to put a surveillance on Chen?"

"I wouldn't ask you for the time of day."

"You wouldn't get it, either. But it's not a bad idea. Even if it was yours. You think you can stay out of trouble until morning?"

She hung up without my answer. I think she was afraid of what I'd say.

On the way to actually pick up the tofu, I called Bill and filled him in. Unlike Mary, he was neither surprised nor annoyed that I'd chased an armed suspect down the street.

"It's unlike you to lose him, though."

"It's the jet lag. Do you think I should warn Mr. Chen? Tell him not to do business with him and call if he turns up?"

"Of course."

"Do you think it'll do any good?"

"No."

It especially wouldn't do any good if Mr. Chen didn't pick up his voice mail, because that was as close to him as I got.

Dinner, though delayed, was delicious. I didn't tell my mother about Wong Pan. We talked about some cousins in the Philippines she'd just heard from, and others in Sidney who never write. I mentioned seeing Clifford Kwan, at which my mother heaved a major sigh about the grief Clifford caused *his* mother by being willful and selfish. Sensing landmines, I steered the conversation elsewhere: the progress of the melons in Ted's backyard. After dinner she cleared the table while I did the dishes, with minimal instruction from her on which was the dish sponge as opposed to the counter sponge, and how hot the water had to be.

The sky's vibrant blue had softened to lilac and I'd just dropped the sheaf of diary Xeroxes on my desk when the *Bonanza* song rang out. "I'm going to have to give you a new ringtone," I told Bill. "That one's getting on my nerves."

"If I apologize, will you meet me uptown?"

"I won't accept that apology because you had nothing to do with the ringtone. Does that mean I can stay home?"

Apparently it didn't. "Half an hour. At Columbia. To see a friend of a friend."

Once, you had to pass a gate to get onto the Columbia campus, a placid academic island amid Manhattan's surf and riptides. Now university buildings line Broadway and the side streets, too. But the gate still stands, opening ornamentally, if unnecessarily, to the old quad. I met Bill there.

"It took a lot of blind faith to get me out again tonight," I informed him.

"I appreciate that. Dr. Edwards called me right before I called you. He's a busy guy, but he has time tonight after his evening class. You okay?"

"Why wouldn't I be?"

"Something about your face meeting a brick wall."

"I'm fine. Just a little furious. This Dr. Edwards is who?"

"Remember I said I was calling a friend? One of the handball regulars is a Columbia prof."

"This is him?"

"A friend of his. The go-to guy on modern Chinese history."

A lamplit brick walk, a security guard, and an elevator later, Bill and I poked our heads into a book-lined office. Book-paved, and pretty much book-furnished, too, except for the computer on the desk and the Manchu ancestor painting on the wall. Though if the rangy sixtyish man whose cowboy boots rested on the desk was Bill's friend's friend, they weren't his ancestors. Unless black Africans had come farther along the Silk Road than I knew. Admittedly, they weren't my ancestors either: The eyes and hair were the same, but the pale skins and formal silks marked these people as aristocrats, from a time when my ocher-faced forebears would have been lucky to find burlap to tuck around themselves while they worked the fields.

At the rap of Bill's knuckles the man lifted his eyes from a lapfull of papers. "Hey! You Smith? This your partner?" He swung his boots off the desk and shook hands with us both. "William Edwards." He bustled around, shifting books to the floor. "Go on, sit. They'll behave."

"The books?" Bill asked.

"They like chairs better, but they're adaptable. So you're a friend of Larry's?"

"Handball."

"Is he as cutthroat there as here?"

"He kills me."

"And then stands over your corpse and cackles, right? So. Larry the molecular biologist tells me you're interested in a minor CCP official from the early years of the People's Republic. Like he knows what that means. He doesn't know what any sentence means that doesn't include the words 'electron microscope.'"

"He says you're the expert."

"Wonder what that's gonna cost me? But hey, a call for booklarnin'! Let's get it done before Google digitizes everything and I'm obsolete."

"I'm sorry," I said. "A minor CCP official?"

Professor Edwards tapped the pile of books at his elbow. Some had English titles, some Chinese. From what I could see they were summaries of reports on this, minutes of meetings of that, and proceedings of plenary sessions about the other. "When Larry speaks, I jump. Reason I didn't call until tonight, I was busy looking your boy up."

"Our boy?"

"Chen Kai-rong."

"He's in there?" I was surprised.

"References to him. Sketchy, but better than a poke in the eye. You guys are really detectives? How come you're interested in stuff I can't even get my students to care about, and if they don't care they don't pass?"

Bill looked to me to take the lead, so I said, "We have a case. Everything about it seems to point to what went on back then, but we don't know much about then. I didn't even know Chen Kai-rong was a Communist Party member, much less an official."

Dr. Edwards nodded. "Intelligence Services. Though even with that, his background would've made him a shooting gallery duck during the Cultural Revolution. Reading between the lines, he was in for some serious re-education in the countryside, *and* he'd have been wiped from the historical record. But he was lucky, he died."

I wasn't sure that meant Chen Kai-rong was lucky, but if it meant there was information on him, maybe we were.

"When did he die?"

Professor Edwards consulted a sheet of scribbled notes. Like the books, some were in English, some in Chinese. I guessed it had to do with the text he was taking them from. "In 1966. Just as the Red Guards picked up steam. According to the Party press release, 'he struggled heroically against a short, powerful illness.' That wording would've meant heart disease or cancer."

"Any reason to think otherwise?" Bill asked.

"Hah! You mean foul play?"

"I'm not sure what I mean. Just wondering."

"I don't think so. They had other press releases for that. Worded one way, they did it; another way, someone else did. I'd say this fellow died of natural causes."

"What in his background would have brought the Red Guards down on him?" I asked. "His European wife?"

"That wouldn't have helped, though it looks like she was long dead by then. You know about her? Rosalie Gilder? I didn't find much on her, besides letters cross-referenced at the Jewish Museum."

"We have those."

"Cool. I did dig up an internal CCP report that says they had a son, who by the way Chen sent to the U.S. not long before he died. Chen died, I mean, not the son. That was a good call—the Red Guards wouldn't have found a Eurasian endearing. And furthermore, Chen was raising, and also sent here, a nephew, his sister's son, whose father was a Nationalist general who further furthermore had been a collaborationist general—and was once accused of being a Commie spy, which the Red Guards *would* have liked but it was a big fat lie—before he, the general, switched horses in mid-war."

"Wait," said Bill. "I'm lost."

"Larry always complains about that, too. It's the dazzling footwork."

"I followed the son and the nephew," I said, "but the General? General Zhang was accused of being a Communist?"

"In 'forty-three. He was fingered to the Japanese as a Red spy. He escaped and ran like hell to Chongqing to prostrate himself and his money at the feet of Chiang Kai-shek. Listen, you know all these people? What do you need me for? Did Larry send you here to flatter me for some nefarious reason? He wants my chair, tell him he's gonna have to learn Chinese."

"I'll mention it," Bill said. "We do know something about these people—General Zhang, Chen Kai-rong, and Rosalie Gilder. A little about Kai-rong's sister, Mei-lin, too. We're trying to fill in the blanks."

"What's blank?"

"For one thing, we know Kai-rong left Shanghai in 1943," I said. " 'Fled' was how it was put. But not why."

"Hah! I can help you with that. *And* the answer to your first question—the stain on his revolutionary rep—is in the answer to this one, too! There, was that melodramatic enough?" He yanked out a volume and with a warning finger dared the rest of the pile to crash to the floor. It didn't.

"Okay." He flipped pages. "In my hand, a compendium of intelligence reports from the U.S. Navy base at Qingdao. Where the beer comes from. German breweries nationalized by Mao. Irrelevant to your boy, but the best thing about Qingdao. During World War II, the U.S., as I'm sure you know"—with a stern look that said he was sure we didn't know—"was in China, training and supporting Chiang Kai-shek's troops against the Japanese. After the war Chiang went back to the brawl that really interested him: arm-wrestling Mao. Chiang showed us love, so we stayed, in the business of holding Chiang's coat, until even the blind—meaning the U.S. military—could see Chiang was headed for the hard fall. Then we cleared out, end of 'forty-eight. With me so far?"

I felt like turning down the speed on the fan, but there wasn't any fan. "Yes."

"The U.S. Navy not being allowed to blow stuff up, they needed a hobby. They whiled away their time seeing which trusted comrades were double-agent material. Your boy was one they looked at."

"Chen Kai-rong was a double agent?"

"No. They thought about flipping him, but they changed their minds." He tilted his chair back, clomped his boots onto the desk, and cleared his throat theatrically. "'August 30, 1948. File report on Chen Kai-rong, Lieutenant, People's Liberation Army (formerly Red Army). Born: 1917. Home: Shanghai. Father, Chen Da, merchant. Mother died 1929. Sister, Chen Mei-lin, born 1922, married 1939 to Zhang Yi, General, Nationalist Army, formerly General, Army under Wang Jingwei.' You know who that was?"

"The puppet government leader," Bill said.

Oh, you're so smart, I thought. *I bet you just read that yesterday.*

"I just read that yesterday."

"In my book?"

"Yes."

"Ding ding ding ding ding! So you get it, this General Zhang was a collaborator. 'Chen joined CCP secretly, 1935. Sent by father to Oxford, 1936. Returned to Shanghai 1938. Married Rosalie Gilder, Austrian Jewish refugee, 1942. One son, Lao-li. Also raising sister's son, Zhang Li.

"'Chen holds Lieutenant's rank but work for CCP has been in intelligence. In guise of war profiteer, made numerous trips to Japanese-occupied territory 1938–1943, as courier between Red Army and

Shanghai CCP station. Very successful in concealing CCP involvement during that time. However, February 23, 1943, arrested, presumably on a tip (unconfirmed) and taken to Number 76.'" Dr. Edwards looked up. "Number 76. You know what that was?"

"No," I said, though the phrase sounded familiar.

"Seventy-six Jessfield Road. Prison nominally run by the Shanghai Municipal Police. But like everyone else with power, the police were in bed with the Japanese. The Japanese liked to keep the puppet government focused on the Communists because it kept them from focusing on the Japanese, who were, you know, occupying the country? So they encouraged the police to pick up Commies and beat the daylights out of 'em." He went back to his reading. "'. . . taken to Number 76. Chen thought to have list of CCP agents in Shanghai. Preliminary interrogation'—that would've involved rubber hoses—'produced no results. Interrogation interrupted by call from Japanese military headquarters, requesting on behalf of German military attaché Major Gunther Ulrich that questioning of Chen be suspended. Chen sent back to his cell.' Hmm. Wonder why?"

"Why they agreed?" Bill asked.

"No. Why the Germans wanted them to stop."

"Major Ulrich was a friend of General Zhang's," I said, thinking back to Mei-lin's diary. "General Zhang was married to Mei-lin by this time. Maybe he asked his friend to do his brother-in-law a favor."

"If he did," the professor said drily, "it gets filed under No Good Deed Goes Unpunished. Listen: 'Later that evening Chen's sister, Mei-lin, arrived at Number 76.'"

"Paul!" I turned to Bill. "That's who told us about Number 76."

"Who's Paul?" Dr. Edwards demanded.

"Paul Gilder. Rosalie's brother."

"The brother's still alive?"

"He's got Alzheimer's, or something like it. He thinks I'm Mei-lin. We can't really question him, but he started talking about those days, rambling. We didn't understand most of what he said, but he mentioned Mei-lin going to Number 76 and being brave. I wonder how much of this is in Mei-lin's diary?"

"Her *diary*?"

"It's in Chinese. I've just started translating it. He—Paul—had it all these years. No one's read it. But it stops—"

"No one's read it? An undiscovered primary source? Calloo callay! Can I see it?"

"I—I suppose so."

"She supposes so! Oh heavenly joy! What else you got?"

"Nothing." I wasn't ready to admit to Rosalie's unread letters; I was queasy about us reading them ourselves. "Except some old men who were there."

"Military men?"

"No. The sons."

"Whose sons?"

"Everyone's. Kai-rong's, Mei-lin's—"

"The son and nephew Kai-rong sent here?"

"Yes. And General Zhang's older son."

"By his first wife?"

"You know about him?"

"I know about everybody. These men are still around? You'll introduce me?"

"Well, okay, yes. Though I don't know—"

"Whether they'll talk to me? That's my problem. Cracked some tough nuts in my time, I have. Okay, on that basis, and even though Larry sent you, I'll go on." He picked the book up again. "Now pay attention. Because we're getting to the 'brave' part, I bet. 'The sister stated to the captain in charge at Number 76 that her brother was not a Communist spy, but her husband was.'"

"My God," I said. "Was that true?"

"Have patience. Quoting again: 'She offered to turn over husband's list of CCP agents if her brother was released. Police officials considered locking her up, taking list by force. Decided against that, fearing her father had influence with Japanese. Chen Kai-rong freed. Sister handed over list, handwritten, not in Chen Kai-rong's hand. Three men on it previously suspected by SMP, so authenticity seemed probable. SMP went forward with plan to round up agents, then General Zhang. When agents' homes and businesses raided that night, however, all had fled. Chen Kai-rong, Mei-lin, General Zhang also gone. Chen's Austrian wife briefly arrested, released soon after. Appeared to have no inkling husband was CCP. Credible: Jewish refugee, no knowledge of Chinese politics, likely married him for his money.

"'Chen reportedly made his way north to Red Army. General Zhang turned up in Chongqing with older son. Reported to have put his personal fortune at Chiang's disposal as token of earnest repentance at having served puppet government and evidence of sincere resurgence of patriotism.'" The professor looked up. "Some of these navy guys had dry senses of humor." Back to the book: "'Zhang in Nationalist military, commanding army brigade, since. No further word on Mei-lin.

"'Assessment of potential usefulness of Chen Kai-rong to U.S. interests: low. Later intelligence suggests Mei-lin's statement false. Probably had two intended results: to free brother and discredit husband. Domestic relations reported not good. List likely to have been Chen's, as suspected, copied over in her hand. Further reports indicate agents on list tipped off, probably her doing. Interrogation of Zhang servants indicated general, Mei-lin, and older son fled hours ahead of SMP raid. Driver said Mei-lin tried to break away, forced onto train. Not with general and son in Chongqing. Zhang presumed to have killed her.'"

I couldn't help it: "Oh, no!"

Dr. Edwards peered over the book. "She screwed him. Ruined him. He was a high-ranking collaborationist and she fingered him for a Commie spy. It cost him his whole fortune to buy his way into Chiang's army, where he actually had to fight battles and stuff. You bet he killed her."

He went back to the book while I thought about Mei-lin. *Be careful what you wish for.*

"'Chen reported to have returned secretly months later, in and out of Shanghai since. To this date, has managed to elude Nationalist capture. Presumed to be continuing CCP intelligence work.

"'Recommended action: none. Continue surveillance. No contact unless situation changes.'"

Dr. Edwards plopped the report down. "The end. So. Does that tell you what you want to know?"

"Yes. And no," I said. "Chen Kai-rong really was a Communist all along?"

"Looks that way. But remember, in those days they were the good guys. The peasants were starving, and Mao's people were their only hope. And you want towering heroism, you can't do better than some of these early Communists. That's how revolutions are. Before politicians get hold of them." Dr. Edwards looked wistful.

"While we're bemoaning the perversion of the insurrectionist spirit," Bill said, "tell us this: Are there details in there about his wedding?"

"His wedding? *His wedding?* I'm giving you blood and thunder and you want shoes and rice?"

"I'll take that as a no."

"Don't. You're looking for sweet domesticity, I got your sweet domesticity right here. U.S. National Archives. Unbelievable what's maintained at taxpayers' expense. Who reads German?"

"I do," said Bill, while I shook my head.

Dr. Edwards, looking not at all surprised, handed Bill a sheet of paper. "From *Die Gelbe Post.* One of the ghetto newspapers. Anyone want a Coke?"

He strode off to the vending machines. I craned my neck to see what Bill held: a photocopy of a blurred newspaper page. Rosalie Gilder's name headlined one column. I hoped for a photo, but no. "What does it say?"

"It's from May 1942. Just an announcement. Rosalie Gilder married Chen Kai-rong—it calls him 'a Chinese gentleman'—in a civil ceremony before a judge. As Chinese law requires for foreigners' weddings, the ceremony was held in a public place, in this case the Café Falbaum on Tongshan Road. At a reception afterward, guests were served wine, schnapps, tea, espresso, red bean cakes, and linzer torte."

"Does it—"

"Yes it does. The bride wore a simple white dress and the groom a silk scholar's robe. The bride, at her throat, wore a brooch of jade and diamonds."

"That's all?"

"That's all."

"What's all?" Dr. Edwards dumped an armful of Coke cans and bags of peanuts on the desk. He handed out mugs, poured his Coke, and dropped in a handful of peanuts. The Coke fizzed and foamed. I stared.

"Only way to do it, where I come from."

"Me, too." Bill did the same.

"I never in my life saw this before," I said. "It's disgusting."

"I thought I heard Dixie in your voice," Dr. Edwards told Bill. "Where y'all from?"

"Louisville."

"Bah! You ask me, that's the west. Macon."

They raised their foaming concoctions and toasted each other.

"Now that we're kissin' cousins," Dr. Edwards said, "suppose you elaborate a little more, why you care about this fellow?"

Bill and I took turns explaining and sipping Coke. I ate my peanuts the normal way.

"Well, by gosh and by golly." Dr. Edwards pitched his empty can into the trash. "The Shanghai Moon! You can't be in my business and not have heard of that. Pretty much everybody thinks it's a myth. Or that maybe it was real once, but it's gone gone gone. However, it's my experience that, with the exception of Larry the molecular biologist, pretty much everybody's wrong."

"You do have your uses," I told Bill as we emerged from the lamplit Columbia campus into the real world.

"I do. Another would be to drive you home. Unless you want to stop for coffee or something?"

"No, I'm exhausted. I just want to get somewhere quiet and absorb all this. You think it's true?"

"They may have some details off, but the outline's probably right. Some of it may be in the diary."

"It would explain why Mei-lin gave the book, and her son, to Rosalie. And why she never came back. But why didn't C. D. Zhang tell me any of this?"

"If your father had murdered your stepmother sixty years ago, would you tell a stranger? And in fact he might not know. He was a kid himself."

"That navy report is public. Anyone can read it."

"It's not on the front page of the *Times*. He'd have to have gone looking for it, and why would he?"

"Well, he's read Rosalie's letters, so he's interested in his own past. And he didn't even tell me they all left together. I think I'd like to talk to him again."

"You can do that second thing tomorrow. First thing, I'll pick you up for Joel's funeral. Eight thirty."

"You think we need to be there right at ten? Jewish time is like Chinese time, I thought."

Joel always said our matching fondness for starting events late was one piece of evidence—he had others, like the emphasis on literacy, on family, on food—that the Chinese are among the lost tribes of Israel.

"I don't know," Bill said. "I'm not sure that really goes for funerals."

20

The thin morning air had already begun to heat and congeal when I came outside to wait for Bill. The night before, he'd suggested we bring our respective undiscovered primary sources to read on the drive today; Joel's Long Island town was more than an hour away. I suspected him of wanting to take my mind off where we were going as much as he wanted to hear voices from sixty years ago, but that was okay with me.

"You're early." I climbed in the car.

"And you're ready. Does that show impatience, or faith? There's tea and a sesame bagel in the bag there."

"Wouldn't impatience be proof of faith?" I checked out his charcoal suit and clean-shaven face. "You look good. Almost suave."

"Considering how early I had to get up and how late I went to bed, I'll take that as a high compliment."

"Don't get carried away. Why did you go to bed so late if you knew you had to get up so early?"

"I was working. My boss is a slave driver."

"You don't have a boss."

"My partner, then."

"Oh, you have a partner?"

For answer he gave me a glance, then said, "The envelope at your feet."

I checked the floor, and sure enough, a manila envelope lay in the space a taller person's legs would have taken up. "What's this?"

"Translations of Rosalie's letters."

"Written translations? That's what you stayed up all night doing?"

"Of course. Don't tell me you didn't stay up translating Mei-lin's diary. That was what kept me going through those lonely hours: the picture of you burning the midnight oil while the candle dwindled down—"

"If I had midnight oil, what would I need a candle for? Anyway, I didn't."

"You mean I'm a step ahead?"

"Not likely. I got up at five and read through most of it."

"Five? What's that?"

"Someday you'll have to check it out, dawn. It's kind of pretty." I opened his envelope and pulled out a scrawl-covered yellow pad.

"Listen," he said. I glanced up: His tone had changed. "What's in there—it's not very cheery."

"I guess I didn't expect it to be."

He nodded. "The top one isn't Rosalie's. It's to her, from a neighbor."

I took a look. Bill's handwriting isn't particularly legible, but I'm used to it.

He headed the car over the Manhattan Bridge as I took a sip of my tea and began to read.

12 June 1938

My darling Rosalie,

It is with a heavy heart that I put pen to paper tonight. I hardly know how to tell you of the events that have occurred here. My dear, prepare yourself: Your dear uncle Horst is no more. I have no further facts than this: Attempting to go to the aid of an elderly rabbi who had been set upon by a mob, he would not obey a soldier's command to back away and let the mob go about its business. They exchanged angry words. Without warning, the soldier drew his pistol and fired. For what consolation it may be, those who saw say the bullet pierced Horst's heart and he died instantly; he did not suffer. Rosalie, I am so sorry. But it is my painful duty to tell you that the troubles of the past days do not end there. Oh, my darling! Your mother was arrested hours later as she was preparing to go claim your uncle's body. On what pretext I do not know—it has become a common thing here for Jews, for Catholics, for supporters of Chancellor Schuschnigg, to fall into the arms of what now passes for the law. I saw the police mount the steps of your home, and watched them lead your mother out. I ran and asked where she was being taken, and went myself to that police station, where after a few hours' wait I was allowed to see her. She was unharmed, but she is being sent to a work camp and they would not tell me where. As you would expect of your mother, she was much more composed than I. She asked me to take some things from your home, as she fears, and with reason, I'm afraid, that her possessions will be confiscated before she is released. I returned quickly and retrieved what she requested: your letters from Shanghai, and the tickets for the train to Dairen. I took also some family photographs—the one of you and Paul at the Mirabell Gardens the day we all went together; your parents' wedding portrait; and some others. At your mother's request I've given one of the train tickets to Herr Baumberg for his eldest son, and will keep the other for your mother, praying she will be released in time to use it. Her instructions were that if she is not, I should give it away also. She also asked that I request of Herr Baumberg that if possible he arrange for a proper Jewish burial for Horst, which I have done. Klaus and I will remain in Salzburg until she is released, or until the date of the train's departure. Then, Rosalie, whether or not your mother is on that train—which I dearly hope she is!—we will leave for Switzerland. We will go to Klaus's brother in Geneva, and Klaus will start a practice there. We have been discussing the unhappy possibility of this step since February, and are now prepared to take it:

We feel we can no longer remain in a country that treats its citizens so. Klaus is traveling there tomorrow to make our arrangements, and I shall give him this letter to send to you, because I find I am distrustful now even of my beloved country's post. Oh, Rosalie, Rosalie, I am so sorry! With you I mourn your dear uncle, and I pray for your mother's rapid release. I hope the day comes very soon when you are reunited. And that the day comes even sooner when this wicked, murderous, usurping government is overthrown and we live in sunlight once again!

Please keep yourself and your brother well, my dear. I hope to be able to send you more and much better news very soon.

With much love,
Hilda Schmitz

When I finished reading, I looked at Bill, then back out the window. "I guess this is what Mei-lin meant."

"When?"

"She mentioned Rosalie's terrible news, how bad she felt for her, but she didn't say what it was." Almost afraid to turn to the next sheet, I asked him, "She didn't, did she?"

"Who didn't what?"

"Hilda Schmitz. Send better news."

"There aren't any more letters from her."

And we already knew there wasn't any better news.

"What are the rest of these?" I asked. "If her mother was in a camp?"

"Rosalie kept writing. She responded to that one, not to the neighbor but to her mother. After that there are only a few more, when big things happened."

I hesitated, then pulled out the next sheet.

5 July 1938

Oh, Mama, Mama! I've received a letter from Frau Schmitz with news so horrible I cannot bear it! Mama, I cry for you, for Uncle Horst, I feel my heart will break! Please, please, keep yourself safe, I pray, yes, *pray*, I *beg* God to prove His kindness by releasing you unharmed and bringing you to us here!!!

Mama, I cannot send this letter but I cannot help but write it. I'm reaching for the comfort I've found these months as I imagine you reading my words; that comfort is all but gone, only the faintest warm breath of it remains, and in the heat of Shanghai I've gone so cold! I don't know what to do, I can't think at all. But this, but this, Mama: we will say kaddish for Uncle Horst, I will go to a rabbi and learn what must be done and we will do it. And beyond that, I don't know, except we will continue with all our hearts to hope and pray!

Ever, ever,

Your Rosalie

"Damn," I breathed.

Bill didn't answer. I slipped that sheet behind the others and took a look at the next one.

"Three years later," I said, and read it.

25 June 1941

Dearest Mama,

I am to be married.

Oh, Mama, how different this is from the way I hoped to tell you such news! Racing breathlessly into the parlor—or tiptoeing into the garden as you prune your roses—even, Mama, asking your permission, certainly your advice—so many ways I've daydreamed about this moment since I was a child. And to tell you like this, in a letter from across the world, a letter I cannot even send—! My eyes fill with tears as I write. Where are you, Mama? Are you well? Are you utterly alone? Not you; no, not you. Your humor and good sense will draw people to you as they always have, however bad the circumstances. I comfort my heart with the certainty that you have found friends.

The entire world is mad. It's only when I'm with Kai-rong that I feel again my memories are memories, not consoling fairy tales of a time that never was. It's no small thing, in days as dark as these, to have found someone who makes me remember the light, and even believe it will return. Some around us are counseling us to wait until the madness passes. But how long will that be? And more—how will it pass, unless we refuse its hold, and defy it?

So Kai-rong and I will marry. I will pray every minute for the miracle of your arrival to share our joy, and make it complete. Please, Mama, please, wherever you are, give me your blessing.

Your Rosalie

2 October 1941

Dearest Mama,

Oh, I hope and pray that wherever you are, you are well, you are safe. As the fourth Rosh Hashanah passes without word of you, my heart aches, Mama. I did not attend services because I could not bear to hear the shofar blown, remembering what pleasure you have always taken in the sound of it. Paul did go; he regularly helps form the minyan at a shul near us, and has embraced our traditions in a way I cannot, though I admire him for his dedication. I admire him for much, Mama. What a fine young man he has become! You will be proud of him, Mama, so proud.

I'm writing now to tell you of a decision my heart has brought me to. Kai-rong has given me a gift: a carved jade disc that has been in his family many hundreds of years. He gives it with the blessing of his father; I'm to wear it on our wedding day to mark the uniting of our families, and I will do that with joy. But the union of two families cannot be marked by a precious object of one family only. I've determined to remove this jade from its setting and add to it the stones from the Queen Mama necklace. The jade represents many generations of Kai-rong's ancestors, and is therefore precious to him. The necklace represents you, and is therefore extraordinarily precious to me!

My beloved Kai-rong, having heard my reasoning, is in complete accord. Tomorrow we'll take the jade and the necklace to Herr Corens, the jeweler in Avenue Foch who bought from me the ruby ring. He's a lovely man, Mama, and quite an artist. He will make for us a new piece, a brooch, I think. It will tell tales: of steadfast love over time and distance, of generations of ancestors revered, of the joining of two proud traditions, and the union of two devoted hearts. It will be beautiful, Mama. And when I wear it, I will have both you and Kai-rong ever with me, no matter where you are.

I pray every day for you, Mama.

Your Rosalie

21

"There's Kleenex in the glove compartment," Bill said.

"We're going to a funeral. I brought my own." I wasn't exactly crying, but my vision had blurred. "You're right. These aren't very cheery."

"There are just a few more."

"I'm not sure I can take it."

"You want me to summarize?"

"In a minute."

I wiped my eyes, then laid the papers on my lap, gently, even though they were only Bill's scribbled translations. "Have you ever been to an Orthodox Jewish funeral?"

"Yes."

"What goes on?"

"Same as anyplace, but in Hebrew."

"If they don't bang gongs and walk around the coffin with incense, it's not the same as the funerals I know."

"Basically, though, it is. Prayers, songs, a eulogy. No sermon, I don't think. You know we won't be able to sit together? They separate men and women."

I nodded; somewhere, I knew that, though I hadn't thought about it. I felt a pang of anxiety, which made me mad. *Boy, Lydia, first you're not sure you ever want to talk to this guy again, and now you're fretting because he'll be sitting on the other side of the synagogue?* "Will the coffin be open?"

Bill's eyebrows lifted at my sharp tone, but all he said was "No."

That was good; Chinese coffins usually are, and I find it creepy. Maybe in the old days it was okay, a chance to see your loved one looking peaceful as you said good-bye. Today funeral homes embalm and use makeup and when you see your loved one he looks like someone else. I didn't want to see Joel looking like someone else. But when the last time I did see Joel—the office, the blood—flashed behind my eyes, I decided Bill's distraction tactic was a good one.

"The rest of Rosalie's letters. What are they about?"

He looked over at me. *Just don't ask if I'm all right.* It worked, because he didn't. "The next one's about the wedding," he said calmly, just two investigators talking over a case. "At the Café Falbaum, the way the professor's article said. The one after that, very brief, that she's pregnant. She imagines her mother singing to the baby. Then she writes about Kai-rong's arrest; she's frantic, but Mei-lin has a plan. She says the cost of getting Kai-rong out will be high, but she knows her mother will understand."

"What does that mean?"

"I don't know. Then she writes about his escape, and how she's taking care of Mei-lin's son until Mei-lin comes back. The next one tells why they have to move to Hongkew. She's worried her mother won't be able to find them there."

"Oh, God, Bill."

"I know. And then one about the birth of her son, and how she's naming him Horst but because he's growing up in China they'll use his Chinese name, Lao-li, which means 'labor is truth.'"

"It can also mean 'truth is hard work,' you know."

He nodded. "The last letter is on Lao-li's first birthday."

"No more?"

"That was October 'forty-four. The Japanese surrendered in August of 'forty-five. The war in Europe was over by then, and the Red Cross lists of concentration camp confirmed dead began to reach Shanghai in the fall. By Lao-li's second birthday, Rosalie must have known her mother was gone."

I slid the papers back into the envelope. "Poor Rosalie."

"She was pretty tough. Most of that time, Kai-rong was away. She was on her own with those two kids—she and Paul. Her father-in-law gave them money, so I guess they ate as well as anyone in the ghetto, but toward the end of the war no one in Shanghai had much to eat."

"But Kai-rong kept coming back? The way the navy report said?"

"In the one about the baby, she says he held his son soon after he was born. So he must have been slipping in and out. I don't get the idea, by the way, that she didn't know what he was up to."

"What makes you think that?"

"She says she misses him, but what he's doing is important and she's proud. I don't think she'd say that if he were just on the run."

We drove in silence for a while. A sense we'd missed something kept waving at me for attention, but when I looked right at it, it disappeared. This section of expressway cut through a residential area. A young woman pushed a baby carriage; on the next block a much older woman, thin and bent, carefully picked her way down the sidewalk. I wondered if they knew each other, if the old lady cooed at the baby when they met in the supermarket aisle.

"Up for reading?" Bill's voice, solid and real, pulled me back.

"I'm sorry, what?"

"Mei-lin's diary. You brought it, right?"

"Of course. We had a deal." I reached into my shoulder bag for my own manila envelope with the stack of Xeroxes. I'd flagged some entries, but I hadn't made a written translation the way he had. That struck me as not very nice of me. "It starts off well, but it wouldn't win any Pulitzer for cheeriness, either. I didn't make it quite all the way to the end, but I don't think it gets any better." I turned to the first flag. "Let me catch you up, and if we have time I'll translate the last few." Maybe simultaneous translation would make up for my lack of written pages. "This one's a couple of weeks after what we read yesterday. The thrill of dinner at the Cathay has worn off and it's beginning to dawn on her that nothing's really changed. Then something happens. General Zhang—she calls him 'dashing' again—comes to tea."

"To see her?"

"Umm, *'He found himself in the neighborhood and sent his card in.'*"

"Oh, sure."

"Her father asks Kai-rong to join them and sends for her, too. She's overjoyed and figures it was Kai-rong's idea because it couldn't possibly be her father's. She runs and puts on the red shoes, and then takes her time going downstairs. She says she knows just how to behave."

"And that's how?"

"'Polite, but cool and distant.'"

"Oh, for Pete's sake! You see? She's overjoyed, but she gives him the frost anyway."

"She goes beyond that. 'Kai-rong tried to tease me—so childish! I ignored him. Father inquired about the general's family. He's a widower, with one son. He admitted to being lonely, but said with a smile that one must bear what one can't change. I felt for him—I know about loneliness! We discussed art, music, and literature. The general's very cultured, with opinions on everything. When Father and Kai-rong spoke he listened respectfully—and to me, also! Though I was careful not to express strong ideas. He asked to see my calligraphy, and praised it! He said it was refreshing to see a young woman accomplished in the traditional arts. He's a bit old-fashioned, actually. For one thing, he doesn't like American jazz. Although he said he was willing to try it again, and invited Kai-rong and myself to the Cathay's nightclub! Oh, I wonder if Father will agree? He smiled, as though the general were joking, but maybe Kai-rong can persuade him.*

"'Twice I felt the general watching me when Father was speaking. I kept my eyes downcast, of course—but I could barely supress my giggles! I hope the general didn't notice. He stayed a long while and promised to call again. I hope he does!! It was as though he brought a cool breeze when he came through the door. While he was here, I could breathe.'"

"Well," said Bill. "That's our Mei-lin."

"And for your information, the frost worked. The general came back."

"Of course it worked. I never said it wouldn't work. We fall for it every time."

"So if you fall for it, why should we stop using it?" I looked around. High walls fenced in the expressway. There was nothing for me to see, and nothing to think about except where we were headed. I went back to Mei-lin's world. "This is a week later. *'General Zhang came to tea again—and brought me a gift! Last week the subject of foreign languages came up. The general speaks French and English, like Kai-rong, and Father speaks those and German, too. When the general asked me—I waited until he asked!—I said I only speak English, and poorly. Kai-rong looked sour and told the general I was being modest. I denied that. Father was only too willing to come to my aid—he said I'd never suffered from modesty, so it must be true! He never believes I can do* anything! *If he'd take ten minutes to speak to me in English he'd know better, but that would waste his valuable time.*

" *'But the general spent* his *valuable time buying me a beautiful book! To improve my English, he says.'* "

"So the false modesty worked, too."

"You want to know the truth? Pretty much everything works."

"We're that easy?"

"Sorry. *'It's a book of poems by Elizabeth Barrett Browning, love poems, in fact they made me blush when I read them years ago. Of course I didn't say I knew them. Father was pleased, though Amah pursed her lips when she saw the author was a woman. Kai-rong looked even more sour than last week! He'd been planning to go out, but changed his mind when the general arrived. I don't know why, because he was out of sorts—if he wanted to be somewhere else, why didn't he just go? But Father seemed delighted the general had come, and said he hoped he'd be a frequent guest. And the book is so beautiful! I can't wait to show the Feng sisters. A gift from an army general!'* " I broke off and demanded, "What are you smiling about?"

"I guess we have tricks that work, too."

"Oh. Well, maybe."

"Uh-huh. What happens next?"

I flipped the pages. "Next is a few days later. You'll love it. *'A wonderful thing! Kai-rong's found me an English tutor! It's odd, because when General Zhang was here Kai-rong insisted my English was good. Which it is! And now over dinner, he proposed this idea. He's met a young Jewish refugee he says is very refined and would be good company for me, as well as an excellent teacher. A European woman coming here—I'm so excited! For all I care she can teach me circus juggling. Father waved the proposal away, saying it would put ideas in my head to make me disobedient. But Kai-rong said study-ing English won't give me any ideas I can't get in Chinese. Of course Father disapproves of my having any ideas at all. But I thought of an argument! I suggested—respectfully, of course—that a better command of English could increase my value as a wife. Kai-rong made a face, and Father asked why. Then I had to force myself to sit still while they argued about marriage in-stead of my tutor! Kai-rong says I'm too young to think about marriage. Fa-ther pointed out Mother was seventeen when Kai-rong was born and I'm very nearly sixteen now. They went back and forth while I obediently ate my meal. By the end of dinner the discussion had turned around! Father became convinced improving my English will make me more marriageable and de-creed it should be done at once. Kai-rong looked unsure whether he'd had a victory. But he's bringing the tutor tomorrow!'*

"Now, from tomorrow: *'My tutor came today! Oh, I do like her. Right from the moment we met, we laughed! She says my English is much more 'En-glish' than hers. She's afraid after a short time with her I'll sound like an Aus-trian. I told her that would suit me—if I'm not allowed to travel, at least I can sound as though I had! She brought three books. Two novels—one English and one American—and poems by an American named Walt Whitman. We'll read them together. It will be such fun! Though today we began the poems and I don't like them very much. I don't understand what they're saying. But it's not the books, or speaking English, that I'm looking forward to. It's having a visitor! And such an exotic one! She can tell me—of course in English!—about the country she's from and the places she's visited. Also, about the part of Shanghai where she lives and the streets she travels to come here, which are as out of reach as Europe, to me!'"*

"Sounds like the start of a beautiful friendship."

"Yes, but it's not enough for Mei-lin."

"Why? It turns out they don't get along?"

"Oh, they do, really well. She loves it when Rosalie comes. Some-times she brings Paul, and they laugh even more when it's the three of them. They sit in the garden and drink lemonade and eat red bean cakes."

"Rosalie doesn't like red bean cakes."

"Paul loves them, though. I wonder if he still does? We could go back to New Jersey and take him some." I flipped through the papers to my next flag. "Okay, this is a few weeks later. Rosalie's been coming and going, and the general dropped by once more, with his son."

"C. D."

"Correct. She and the kid hit it off right away—he's a live wire, impulsive, but well-mannered and fun. Besides that, nothing much happens. Kai-rong takes her to the theater once, and to dinner a couple of times. She likes it, but each time it reminds her how stuck she is. Still, she's in a pretty good mood. Then things start to go downhill."

"Why?"

"Because: '*Father and Kai-rong had an argument today. I didn't mean to overhear, but I couldn't help it. I was in the garden practicing calligraphy. Teacher Lu is coming tomorrow and I haven't touched my brushes all week! I told Number One Boy to set my table by the acacia tree. Kai-rong and Father were in Father's study. They must not have seen me through the blossoms. I'd have left, but they might have noticed me getting up, and they'd have been so embarrassed!*'"

"Considerate of her."

"As you say. '*I tried to concentrate on my brushstrokes, but I couldn't shut out their raised voices. I didn't make out everything, but I heard enough to know that Kai-rong doesn't like General Zhang. I don't know why—he's so handsome and cultured! But Kai-rong doesn't want him coming here. Father thinks the general's connections among the Japanese could be helpful to us. Kai-rong said his connections to the Japanese are exactly the problem, and Father snapped at him in that tone he uses with me all the time, but almost never with Kai-rong. He said Kai-rong's never been practical and obviously there's no reason to hope he's changed.*

"'*But apparently he has changed, because I heard the next part clearly, and I didn't like it at all: Kai-rong's leaving soon! He wants to go to the north, on business! He says there are opportunities there. I hoped Father would stop him, but though he's skeptical, he's pleased Kai-rong's showing an interest in business— something he never cared about before! So he's letting him go. When I heard that, my hand jerked and my calligraphy was ruined. What will I do? To be locked up here again without even Kai-rong's news from the world? No conversation, no outings, even the few I've been allowed? Just Father, Amah, calligraphy, embroidery—I can't bear it! How can he leave again so soon? How can he leave me here to suffocate like this?'*"

As I flipped the pages, I waited for a wisecrack from Bill, but it didn't come. So I read the next flagged entry, from two weeks later. "*'It's been a week since Kai-rong left. No one's come here. The sun's an exhausted orange glow in an unchanging gray sky. The nights are moonless, starless. The air's thick with moisture but there's no rain, just languid drizzle. A storm with wind, lightning, thunder—even a monsoon, oh how welcome that would be! But the air feels as I do: trapped, weary, barely able to move.'*"

That brought the delayed wisecrack. "Uh-oh. Prose getting purple there. Wonder whose books those were that Rosalie brought?"

"Not Hemingway's, I bet." I lowered the papers and looked out the window. The sky over Long Island seemed a changeless gray itself. I couldn't argue with Bill about Mei-lin's heavyhandedness, though I had a feeling she wasn't exaggerating how she felt. "She snaps out of it a little whenever Rosalie comes, and she's really touching when she hears about Rosalie's terrible news. But generally, she's so desperate that the world's going on without her, she doesn't focus on much else. How close are we?"

"To Lake Grove? Another half hour, I think."

"This is tiring, this reading and translating. And I want to get to the part I haven't read. Can I paraphrase like you did? You can probably guess, anyway."

"Kai-rong keeps coming and going, General Zhang keeps showing up, coincidentally when Kai-rong's out of town, and finally he asks her to marry him?"

"He doesn't ask her anything. He asks her father. Her father's delighted and so's she. She can't wait to have her own home, her own servants, her own car to go wherever she wants in. Rosalie's not enthusiastic. She wants Mei-lin to hold out until she falls in love. Mei-lin's impatient with that whole idea. In fact she's surprised to hear it from a woman in Rosalie's position, which she admits is worse than hers in a lot of ways."

"A lot of ways? What ways isn't it worse in?"

"Rosalie can come and go anywhere she wants in Shanghai. Don't worry, the irony isn't lost on me."

"It is on Mei-lin, I'll bet."

"Entirely. So Kai-rong rushes back and tries to stop her from marrying the general, but their father orders him to shut up and get with the program. In the end he doesn't have much choice. After a certain amount more grousing, he behaves like a filial son and brother and stays in Shanghai for the wedding banquet. Which apparently was the social event of the season."

"Was it, um, 'grand'?"

"You liked the Cathay, you'd have loved this. Billowing silk tents in the garden, red lanterns everywhere, mounds of lilies. Clear sky, full moon. A ten-course banquet with gallons of whiskey, and champagne supplied by the Frenchman. A Chinese orchestra taking turns with the Filipino jazz band from the nightclub at the Cathay."

"So she finally got to dance to it."

"She did. It's not traditional at Chinese weddings for the bride to dance, but strictly speaking it's not traditional for her to have met the groom, either."

"*That's* why there are so many of you! Because brides don't know what they're getting into."

"You're not so far wrong. Anyway, Rosalie and Paul were there, and Kai-rong's school friends, and the Feng sisters. In fact, most of Shanghai, it sounds like. The best man was the general's German buddy, Major Ulrich."

"They have a best man at Chinese weddings?"

"This was a mixed affair, a civil ceremony with a judge and then the banquet. Very modern. Mei-lin danced like crazy. She danced with her husband, and his son—"

"That must have been cute."

"He'd had lessons and could do all the new dances, which the general couldn't. And she danced with Major Ulrich, and with Kai-rong. And she noticed Rosalie dancing with Kai-rong, more than once. And she also noticed that neither Rosalie nor Kai-rong seemed able to stop smiling while they danced. Which she puts down to happiness for her."

"Well, it was her wedding day."

That was not only not a wisecrack, it was downright sympathetic.

"Plus," he added, "she was no doubt tipsy again."

"Oh, good. I was afraid you were getting all warm and fuzzy on me."

"What? When?"

"Never mind. You understand it takes her three or four days to report on all this."

"Because it takes her that long to get over the hangover."

"Partly that," I conceded. "But also, no one had prepared her for her wedding night."

"Wasn't that her Amah's job?"

"Her amah just told her she wouldn't like it but it wouldn't kill her."

"There's a ringing endorsement."

"Can I get points for not making any of the obvious remarks?"

"How many do you want?"

"How many do I need to make up for not bringing you a written translation?"

He threw me a quick glance. "That's Chinese guilt working. I hadn't even noticed."

"There's no such thing as Chinese guilt. Anyway, Mei-lin might have been better off just with her amah's advice. At least she wouldn't have been looking forward to it and she wouldn't have felt duped. Unfortunately, the Feng sisters told her it was fun."

"From experience?"

"I doubt it. I think they were repeating what they'd heard in the Shanghai equivalent of the locker room."

"Women talk like that in locker rooms?"

"You cannot really think men have a monopoly on baseless boasting?"

"Don't disillusion me. I liked my image of women linking arms in sisterhood, unencumbered by the foolish need to impress one another."

"Oh, get real! You think we wear four-inch heels to impress *you*? Anyway, the general did not impress Mei-lin."

"He couldn't—?"

"Oh, he sure could. Fast and rough. He was drunk, he hurt her, it was over before she figured out exactly what they were supposed to be doing. He rolled off and fell asleep, snoring. Like the rumble of a delivery van, she says."

"She sounds almost amused."

"She sounds like that for the next six months. Desperately amused. Trying to convince herself life's wonderful and marrying the general was a great idea. She goes on about how marvelous it is to be mistress of an elegant villa. Practically catalogues its treasures. And all the places she goes. Shanghai's best department stores. The racetrack, the one they let Chinese into. Theaters, restaurants, nightclubs. She makes the rounds in her chauffeured car. She hangs out with other Chinese officers' wives, with Japanese and German women, and wealthy British women who compliment her English."

"Sounds great."

"No, it sounds like something that gets old fast. The women treat her like an amusing child. They play cards and mah-jongg and don't seem interested in much. Most of their conversation is gossip, except for their complaints about their husbands, and even when they're complaining they're bored. Half of them are having affairs with the husbands of the other half. The general lets her spend all the money she wants, but either he doesn't notice what she buys or he doesn't like it. She has a big house with servants, but she feels like a ghost there. No one listens to her about where to move the furniture or what to have for dinner. The servants beg her not to worry about matters of such insignificance, and the general orders her to stop interfering with the servants.

"Her buddies, the Feng sisters, are so jealous that she can't bring herself to admit to them life is anything less than fabulous. After a while, when she starts to acknowledge she's not ecstatic, the only one she'll talk to about it is Rosalie."

"Rosalie still comes to tutor her?"

"That's one of the many things the general doesn't seem to care whether she does, so yes. And she goes with Rosalie and Paul to concerts by refugee musicians and to the Yiddish theater and the Jewish coffeehouses. She has a favorite table at the Café Falbaum. You can't see the street from it, and all you hear around you is German and Yiddish. Even the signs and the menu are in Yiddish. Everyone is European, and it smells of cinnamon, exotic to her. She pretends she's far away from China and she loves it. A couple of times she spends the general's money to buy coffee and pastry for everyone there."

"The general doesn't mind?"

"He doesn't care where she goes. What he likes is showing her off. He wants her to dress well and impress his friends. At first she's flattered, but then she starts complaining the general thinks everything about her reflects on him—her English, her calligraphy, her legs. He takes credit when she does something well and gets mad when she screws up. He lets her get in a few sentences when they go out, like a talking dog, while he beams. Then he tells her to shut up. She wonders whether being ignored the way her father did might not have been better."

"The grass is greener."

"Well, maybe. Though the general does seem to be getting more and more short-tempered. He wants her to do everything right, but she can't figure out what everything is or how to know if she's doing it right. The only bright spot is the general's son. He makes her laugh."

"She's not that much older than he is, is she?"

"By now he's ten. She's just turned seventeen. She helps him with his schoolwork, especially his calligraphy, showing him the different styles. The boy's tutor compliments her. She writes how she can't wait to have children of her own. But they won't have tutors, she says. She'll send them to school, so they can be out in the world. Then she gets pregnant."

"When are we up to?"

"Spring 1940."

"What does the general think?"

"He's pleased and very proud—of himself. And he tells her now she'll stay home until the baby's born."

"Oh, no."

" 'Oh, no' is right. Her whole reason for marrying him flies out the window. To be stuck at home was bad enough, but to be stuck at *his* home! But he absolutely won't have her seen in public in her condition. They fight about it more than once. Finally he doesn't want to fight anymore, so he smacks her."

"Shit."

"It's the first time, but not the last. She gets more and more desperate. She's alternately belligerent and weepy. He doesn't think either is charming. In fact, he doesn't think she's charming at all, with her big belly and swollen feet. He leaves her locked up at the villa and starts tomcatting around with some White Russian torch singer from the Cathay's nightclub."

"From the Cathay? That's particularly low."

"When the baby's born he gives Mei-lin an emerald bracelet. Within two weeks he's demanding sex again. She writes how beautiful the bracelet is, all sparkling and glamorous, but she can't bear to wear it unless he orders her to. She'd give it, and everything else, to have her old life back. The only thing she wouldn't give is the baby. They name him Li. It's a word with a lot of meanings, but the character she writes it with means 'power.' She's allowed to go out again, and mostly she goes to her father's house. Rosalie comes over and they play with the baby in the garden. Sometimes Paul comes, sometimes she brings the general's son along—he adores his little brother, too—and sometimes Kai-rong's there. Kai-rong never says 'I told you so,' but one day he goes to the general's villa and, I gather, threatens bad things if he ever sees another mark on his sister."

"How does the general react?"

"Like any coward. From then on when he's mad he storms around and curses Kai-rong, but he doesn't hit Mei-lin again. She can't stop being scared, though. That's pretty much it for a long time, I mean years. The entries get shorter and fewer, more time between them. There are a couple of high points, especially Rosalie and Kai-rong's wedding in 'forty-two, but Mei-lin just gets lonelier and sadder and the whole thing is pretty depressing."

"Is that why you stopped?"

"No, I stopped because you were early."

"By ten minutes. You'd have had the rest done in the next ten minutes?"

"Of course I would have. First of all, I'm a genius. Second, I only had half a dozen left, and most of them are short."

"Well, genius, you have just about those ten minutes now, if my navigation's right."

"Then shush."

I scanned the last diary pages. The first four were more of the same: Mei-lin unhappy, trapped, and frightened. Then came the next to last. I could see the sharp change even before I read the words: Elegant calligraphy suddenly melted into shaky trails of characters. "This is February 23, 1943. She writes Kai-rong's been arrested as a Communist spy. Even her father can't get him out. They've taken him to Number 76, and she knows what that means. She's begged the general to do something, but he won't."

"Won't, or can't?"

"Won't. He has the juice, but he says traitors like Kai-rong are scum and deserve to rot. She can't believe it—a collaborator like him calling Kai-rong a traitor. Then she says she's hated the general for a long time, but never more than now.

"That entry ends there. The next one—the last—is from the next morning. Totally different. Even her handwriting changes, back to that beautiful calligraphy again. She writes she's got a plan. Here:

"'I spoke with Major Ulrich. I said I'll bring the list the police want. He's promised to stop them from hurting Kai-rong, and also to say nothing to the general—though his price was high! And would be higher if he knew everything I'm planning, which of course I didn't tell him! Though I don't believe he'd stop me out of loyalty to the Japanese or friendship for the general. Such a nasty man.

"'But Rosalie agreed to his price, for Kai-rong! What choice is there? As soon as the car's ready I'll take little Li to his Aunt Rosalie—they love each *other so much! He won't cry when I leave him there. If Kai-rong really does have this list, I know where he keeps it: in that leather case he's shut quickly, twice, when I entered his room without warning. The first time was years ago, soon after he came home. He teased and made a game of it, he keeping his secret, me trying to guess. I said it was letters from his secret love. He turned red as a rose! That was the moment I knew he did have a secret love. Oh, what days those were, when we laughed! I had so much, and I didn't know! I thought I was miserable, locked inside the villa walls. Kai-rong warned me, but I wouldn't listen. Of course he was right—I had no idea what misery was.*

"'The second time was less than a month ago. Rosalie was with Cook when I arrived, so I went to see Kai-rong. He swiftly closed the case as I entered. Our game of years ago came flying back, and jokingly I demanded to know what was in the secret case. I suppose I was hoping to recapture that time. But he didn't even smile. He said I must never ask, and never say a word to anyone that the case was here.

"'I've never asked myself what Kai-rong was doing on his trips to the north. More than once Father told Kai-rong he was wrong, that there was no wheat or salt, no kerosene or coal to be brought from Russia or Mongolia. He wanted Kai-rong to give up this idea of northern opportunity and stay in Shanghai, but Kai-rong insisted and kept traveling. I thought he was only stubborn. As I've always been, right or wrong.

"'I think Rosalie knew. She said she'd been afraid something like this would happen—why would she be, if she had no idea, if she thought it was only business he was traveling for?

"'I hear the gravel crunch—the car's rolling up the drive. Soon the houseboy will come to say the driver's ready, and Amah will bring little Li. I look at these pages and feel like laughing. How many times did Teacher Lu tell me the practice of calligraphy would steady my nerves? He made me so angry—all the old ways made me angry! And yet, why have I been rattling on, writing down every thought in my head, if not to calm myself for the day to come?

"'I'll pack up my pens now—if I can't find Kai-rong's list, I swear I'll invent one! Rosalie will be ready. I won't tell her my fears. What good would that do? She's beside herself with worry as it is, and with the new little one growing inside her she has more than enough to think of. Major Ulrich's price is very hard on her, but she'd give any treasure, all treasures, to save Kai-rong.

Oh, how I wish I'd just once felt a love like that! The value of the thing will mean nothing—though it's everything to that German vulture!—but the tie to her mother will make it painful to give up.

"'Here's the knock on the door. So many pages in this book still empty! Maybe they're fated to stay that way.*

"'*And maybe not. Soon, we'll see.*'"

Stunned, I read the last lines again, and again. "My God! Bill!" I finally stammered. "'*The value of the thing will mean nothing, but the tie to her mother—*'"

"I'm with you."

"Major Ulrich. Who *was* he? What happened to him?"

The car's rhythm changed; I looked up and needed a moment. Bill was pulling into a parking lot. Dark-clothed people flowed slowly down the path to a synagogue's open door. "Go on in," Bill said. "I'll call Professor Edwards. Maybe this is a trail he can follow."

So I left Bill outside under the gray sky, while I put my hat on and went in to say good-bye to Joel. And to Mei-lin, too.

2 2

I understood nothing that went on at Joel's funeral except the rabbi's eulogy, which was in English. He praised Joel as a devoted family man, a tireless member of the synagogue he'd helped found, an enthusiastic Hebrew school teacher, a volunteer always ready. All of which he probably was, though I'd heard him find fault more than once with his slacker son, and grumble about another insufferably boring Men's Club meeting. The only thing the rabbi said about Joel's professional life was that he was "well respected." Joel would have rolled his eyes at such bland anonymity. What he was, was a damned good investigator who got a kick out of his work. And taught me a lot. And had an annoying habit of giving orders and sticking his nose into everyone's personal life. But the Joel I knew, the rumpled, dogged detail man always ready with uninvited advice, who started or ended every conversation with some awful off-key rendition of a Broadway song, that Joel wasn't mentioned. You change in death; I'd noticed this before. It's as though the whole you isn't good enough to deserve all this sadness, so the suspect parts get pared away until you're something more wonderful-sounding, though flatter and a lot less you.

Besides the eulogy, everything else was a matter of Hebrew prayers. When the congregation quieted, the cantor's voice rose, then hushed, swelled, fell away again. A chill went through me. Here was a sorrow too deep for speech, an ancient grief that could only be told in song. That sorrow, I thought, wasn't just for Joel. Five thousand years of tragedy called through that voice; and yet it also was for Joel, for this one, unique loss.

I tried to follow, doing what everyone did, as far as I could. At times the congregation stood, or responded to the rabbi in unison. More than once the entire thing seemed to break down into what I had a sneaky feeling might have been Joel's favorite part: a murmuring, swaying, every-man-for-himself chaos. Every-woman-for-herself, too, where I was; a low curtain divided the room down the center, women on the right, men on the left. I could see Bill over there, wearing a black yarmulke. I took one quick peek to find him and turned away, because I wasn't sure it was okay to look over the curtain. At that, I heard Joel's exasperated voice in my head: *Chinsky, if it wasn't okay, we'd have put a higher curtain.*

Oh, give me a break, Pilarsky, I thought, as I had so many times, and was surprised to find the woman next to me giving me a quick hug. She held out a pack of Kleenex. Finally it dawned on me I was crying. *Good going, Chinsky, that's some detective work.*

I thought about suggesting to Joel that he could only stay in my head if he promised not to sing, but maybe it's impolite to set conditions on the dead at their own funerals. So I sat a little longer, and stood a little more, and Joel had nothing else to say, and then we must have come to the end because people started filing out.

In silence and with me wielding Kleenex, Bill and I drove to the cemetery in a line of cars. We stood as a pine coffin with a Star of David on the lid—a box that looked too small for Joel—was lowered. There were more prayers, and some people spoke, including Joel's now-grown slacker son who broke down in tears and couldn't finish. Joel's wife, Ruth, and his children wore black ribbons on their lapels; the rabbi ripped each one in half. Rending the garments, a funeral custom among my people, too. Ruth lifted a small carved box and poured a stream of sand into the grave. "From Israel," whispered the kind woman I'd been sitting beside, who turned out to be a cousin of Joel's. "It's a mitzvah to be buried with soil from the Holy Land. Joel brought it back with him years ago. But not from Jerusalem," she added with a smile. "From the beach."

Everyone was offered the chance to throw a shovelful of dirt into the grave. I wasn't sure, if I were Joel, that I'd see this as an act of friendship, but I took a turn. In the heavy, damp air, that simple exertion pulled a trickle of sweat down my spine. Then it all was done. We left Joel there and made our way to the gate.

"Lack of cheeriness seems to be the order of the day," I said to Bill as I climbed into the car.

"You okay?"

"I keep wondering about this." I tapped the envelopes. "Whether Joel would be happy we're following a hunch. I think more likely he'd chew me out for letting my imagination run away with me."

"Well, let me ask you this. Was he always right when he chewed you out?"

I gave Bill a long look. "You know, for the Marlboro Man, you're pretty smart."

"Speaking of which, would you mind if I had a cigarette?"

"Of course I'd mind. It's not good for you. Though I have to admit, if I smoked, I'd be puffing away right now."

"You mind when I do things that aren't good for me?"

I stared. "I take it back. Smart. What was I thinking?" I closed my eyes and leaned back against the headrest, just feeling the car roll along for a while. Then I asked, "Listen, assuming Joel would be wrong and the Shanghai Moon's a good hunch, did you get Dr. Edwards? What did he say?"

"He has no idea about Major Ulrich beyond what we already know, but he's intrigued. He's going to put a graduate student on it and get back to us."

"When?"

"Soon. She's his ace researcher, so it just depends what there is to find."

"Great. Can I nap?"

"Sure, but only if you want to stay in the car while I talk to the roommate from Zurich. We're here."

I sat up. "Here" was the Pilarsky home, where Ruth and her family would be sitting shiva for seven days. Strictly speaking, we weren't here. Cars already lined both sides of the street; Bill had pulled into a space a block away. He was opening his door when I asked, "Do you think I should go in?"

"What?"

I smoothed my black linen skirt, which suddenly seemed very wrinkled. "Maybe they blame me."

"Blame *you?*"

"I was working with him. I was on the phone with him right before."

"Do they seem to? His sister-in-law called you to go on with the case."

"But maybe—"

"Lydia? I don't think they're the ones who blame you."

I looked away. "If I'd rushed up there like he told me to—"

"You couldn't have—"

"But he told me—"

"Did you ever wonder why he called you in?"

"On this case? Because I'm Chinese."

"Did he only call you in on Chinese cases?"

"No. But—"

"Did I ever call you in on a Chinese case?"

"No. But—"

"You don't do what people tell you to."

"What?"

"That's you, all the time. You don't, and by and large it's a good thing. I know your mother hates it. In a daughter it's probably irritating."

"That's an understatement."

"But a partner—an *associate*, fine, whatever—who doesn't follow directions is a huge plus. I like knowing if you make a move, it's because you really think it's the right one. Not somebody told you to. Even me."

This was seriously new to me. I said slowly, "Joel was always on my case for not doing things the way he would have."

"It can be frustrating day to day. And he did have that mentor thing going, with you. But he didn't stop calling you."

"As opposed to you."

"No, hey. Okay. I stopped calling you because—"

"That's not what I meant."

"What isn't?"

"Calling me. We'll talk about that later, maybe." I saw, on his face, the resolve to explain himself warring with the relief of not having to. It was almost funny. "What I meant, you don't get on my case. About how I do things. One of the last things Joel said to me was 'You and Bill work well together.'"

"Did that come as news?"

I thought about it. "Not news. More like one of those pop-up reminders on your cell phone screen."

"My cell phone doesn't have those."

"Yes, it does; you just don't know how to make them work." I opened my door. "Let's go. We need to pay our condolences, and find this guy from Zurich."

As I walked toward the house I heard, *Good going, Chinsky*.

23

I'd never paid a shiva call before, so I didn't know what was normal after a Jewish funeral, but the chaos in the house, I thought, would have appealed to Joel. A small boy, shirt untucked, chased an older girl who kept slowing down so she wouldn't lose him. Women ferried from the kitchen to the dining room with casseroles, salads, breads. Men poured glasses of whiskey or juice. People stood, sat, ate, talked. No one rang the doorbell; you just walked in. Except for the contents of the casseroles, and the black cloths draping the mirrors, it was just like dropping by after a funeral at Wah Wing Sang.

I spoke to Ruth, who sat on a plain wooden stool in her living room. I'm not sure what I said, though "sorry" came into it a lot. I introduced Bill and she thanked him for coming. As I was offering my sympathy to Joel's son—I told him Joel had talked a lot about him, which made him smile—someone tapped my shoulder.

"Lydia? I'm Leah. I'd have recognized you anywhere."

I turned to find an angular, gray-haired woman smiling beside me. "Well," I said, shaking her hand, "I do sort of stand out in this crowd."

"Not just that. Joel described you perfectly."

"I'm afraid to ask."

"'Small, quick, restless.' He also once said, 'Much smarter than she knows,' but I'm sure by now you know."

"She doesn't." Bill arrived with a beer, and a seltzer for me. "But it won't help to tell her."

I was afraid I was going to have to squelch this debate about my

IQ, but Leah waved over a stocky bald man from across the room. "This is David Rosenberg. From Zurich, that you wanted to talk to. David, this is Lydia Chin, the investigator Joel was working with. And this is her partner, Bill Smith."

In less somber circumstances I'd have objected to Bill's unauthorized promotion back into his old job, but in less somber circumstances he'd have smirked. As it was, we all shook hands, and Leah, after suggesting we might have more privacy on the screened porch, left us. We settled ourselves in creaky wicker chairs and watched some kids making a mess of their good clothes by digging in the dirt. A few overgrown shrubs symbolically marked the boundaries of the Pilarsky backyard. Toward the rear rose a surprising and well-tended vegetable patch featuring an even more surprising scarecrow dressed in an old gray suit of Joel's.

"That's a little spooky," I said.

"His daughter Amy once said it was scary how many years Joel could wear the same suit," David Rosenberg said. "So Joel wondered if it would scare the birds, too."

"Does it work?"

Rosenberg gazed at the scarecrow with a sad smile. "I don't think Joel ever scared anything, in person or in effigy. Leah said you have questions for me?"

"Yes. You were one of the last phone calls Joel made. Not long before he died." I tried for clinical detachment, but I could hear I hadn't made it. "Alice Fairchild said she'd gotten Joel's name from a contact in Zurich. Could that have been you?"

"Yes. She called me a few weeks back to ask if I could recommend an investigator who knew his way around Forty-seventh Street. Because I'm originally from New York."

"Is that why Joel called you? Something about the case?"

"I wish I could say something that could help you, but we really didn't talk about much of anything." Rosenberg looked out at the scarecrow again, maybe thinking if he'd known this was his last conversation with his friend he'd have made sure to cover all kinds of topics. "I've already told this to the police. He called to thank me for sending Alice his way. He asked about her. I've known her for years, slightly. To say hello at cocktail parties, that sort of thing. She didn't say why she needed an investigator, and I didn't think it was right to ask."

"When Joel called, how did he sound? Was he upset, worried?"

"No. Nothing about the conversation seemed urgent. He sounded in a good mood."

Bill asked, "Can you remember that conversation in any detail?"

Rosenberg shrugged. "I'm a journalist. Remember is my middle name." He closed his eyes and, one hand going back and forth as though he were following a Ping-Pong game, he started to mutter.

"... hey, David, how are you ..."

"... hey, great to hear your voice ..."

"... how's Ingrid ..."

"... how are Ruth, the kids ..."

"... when are you coming to New York ..." At that David Rosenberg paused but didn't open his eyes. "... met with this Alice Fairchild day before yesterday, wanted to thank you ... interesting case, Shanghai ghetto, stolen jewelry ... called in that Chinese girl ..."

"... the one with the mother? ..."

"... yeah, keeps me young ... this Alice Fairchild, you know her well? ..."

"... no, just hello, good-bye ... she asked about a PI a few weeks back, gave her the best I knew ..."

"... gave her the only you knew, bubbaleh ..."

"... well, if you know the best, who needs the rest? ..."

"... you say that to all the boys ... she tells me she was born in Shanghai herself, missionary family ..."

"... I know, met her sister a few years ago, like Mutt and Jeff ..."

"... asset recovery, strange work for a shiksa ..."

"... someone has to do it ..."

"... she say anything about the clients? ..."

"... no, nothing at all, just she needed a PI ..."

David Rosenberg's hand drifted to a stop, and he opened his eyes.

"That's it. I'm sorry, but that really was it. I had a meeting to prepare for. He promised to think about coming to Zurich with Ruth, maybe in the winter. And we hung up."

For a few minutes we all sat in silence, watching a sparrow singing from the scarecrow's shoulder. I hoped it was belting out the bird version of some Broadway song.

"Does that help at all?"

"I can't see how," I admitted. "He called me a few hours later and told me something was wrong, but I don't see anything in your conversation that would make him think that. I'd found out something odd about the clients, and I thought maybe he'd learned it, too, but if you didn't tell him, I'm not sure how."

"What was it?"

"About the clients? That they're not who they told Alice they were." I explained about Horst Peretz and Horst Chen Lao-li. "That's true, right?" I suddenly thought to ask. "About Jewish names?"

"Yes, it's true. But Joel didn't hear anything about the clients from me."

"Well, thank you. If you think of anything else, could you call me?"

"Of course. So you really do think Joel's death is connected to this case? Ruth tells me the police don't."

"They might be right. But they'll have to prove it, before I stop."

Rosenberg smiled. "That's exactly what Joel would have said."

David Rosenberg returned to the crowd in the living room. Bill and I stayed on the porch. The day had grown grayer and heavier, and the kids had come back indoors. No one scolded them for getting their clothes dirty.

"That morning, before he called you," Bill said, taking out a cigarette, "there were only those two other calls. Rosenberg and Alice. If whatever was 'fishy' had come up the night before, wouldn't he have called you then?"

"Probably, yes."

"So if there was nothing in that conversation with Rosenberg—"

"Then whatever it was must have been in the call to Alice? Well, but that may not be true. He might have found something on a Web site. His laptop's gone, so we don't know where he surfed. Or he might have met someone for a quick cup of coffee. Or just put something together in his head. It doesn't have to have been on the phone."

"Granted."

"But it would be worth knowing what he and Alice talked about in detail anyway, is that what you're thinking?"

"That, and also, how Joel sounded."

"Well, in the process of firing me again, she did say she'd call when she got back today. I guess she's not back yet."

"Possible. But let me remind you, you also implied you'd give up the case."

"Ah. And if one of us was fibbing, maybe the other was, too? You think it's okay to call from here?"

"Yes. You think it's okay to smoke?"

"No."

I dialed Alice, got voice mail, and left a message. "I bet she's ducking me."

"She's probably tired of firing you."

"So she should stop. What does 'Mutt and Jeff' mean?"

"Sorry?"

"Mr. Rosenberg used it about Alice and her sister. It's one of those cultural references I don't get, right?"

"It used to be a comic strip. Two guys very different from each other. They stopped running it more than twenty years ago, so if you don't get it it's probably because you're young, not because you're Chinese."

"You say that as though it makes my ignorance better."

"Well, youth is a condition that will change."

"Oh, thanks."

Leah Pilarsky stepped onto the porch bearing a plate of rugelach. "I thought you might be hungry. Did you talk to David?"

"Yes, thanks. Though I'm not sure how much good it did." I stood. "Leah, thank you. We'd better go now. If I can do anything, will you promise to call me?"

"And you'll tell us if we can help in your work? I know Joel would want that."

I promised I would, thinking that what Joel would really want would be for me to find the bastard who killed him. Silently, I promised I'd do that, too.

24

As we drove back to the highway, I pulled Bill's papers from the envelope.

"You want to read those again?" he asked. "You're not depressed enough?"

"Well, for one thing, you paraphrased some, so I haven't actually read them. But also, I keep having this feeling there's something we missed."

"What kind of thing?"

"I don't know." I started to go over his translations of Rosalie's letters again. He was right, they were depressing, but he was also right, I was already depressed. I scanned the ones I'd already read, and was about to slip the last of those back in the envelope and start the first of the ones I hadn't, when I reached its final paragraph.

"Bill!" I yelped. "This is it! What we missed! It's the jeweler!"

"What jeweler?"

"Mr. Friedman's book said the name of the jeweler who made the Shanghai Moon was lost. But here it is! Corens, Herr Corens." I whipped out my cell phone.

"What do you—"

I waved to shush him as I heard, "Friedman and Sons, you've reached Stanley Friedman."

"Lydia Chin, Mr. Friedman. Do you know a jeweler named Corens? A refugee also, German, I think. He was in Shanghai the same time as Rosalie Gilder."

"No, I don't think so. Why?"

"Is there an association, a jewelers' organization—"

He chuckled. "There are dozens. But the grapevine, it's better. Shall I check for you?"

"Would you? It's important." I thanked him, pocketed the phone, and, in answer to Bill's skeptical glance, said, "I know, I know, it's a long shot."

"Even if he finds him. What could he tell us? And if he's still alive, he'd be close to a hundred."

"Right on all counts. But it's a door."

And it was a door that wasn't locked, because as I was finishing the last of Rosalie's letters, Mr. Friedman called back.

"Yaakov Corens, from Berlin, was in Shanghai from 1933 to 1945," Mr. Friedman told me. "He emigrated to Australia, one of the first to leave after the war. He died in 1982."

"Oh." That deflated me. "Well, maybe that's not a useful lead after all. But thank you. How did you find that out so fast? That's some grapevine you jewelers have."

"Don't be impressed. Two phone calls, that's all I made. One to a friend, he retired as secretary of the International Guild of Jewelry Artists a few years ago. He knows everybody. He knew Yaakov Corens."

"And the other?"

"To Beatrice Gardner."

"Who's that?"

"Yaakov Corens's granddaughter. She inherited her grandfather's shop, which was her mother's before her. She's a jeweler herself."

"Oh, Mr. Friedman! Thank you so much! Can you give me her number? But you didn't have to call all the way to Australia. Let me pay for that call."

"For you, Ms. Chin, if I had to call Australia, I would call Australia. But for this, it was unnecessary. Yaakov Corens left Sydney and came to New York in 1963. Beatrice Gardner has a shop across the street."

• • •

So there we were, back on Forty-seventh Street.

Nothing much had changed since the day before yesterday. Couples stopped to peer in windows; messengers locked bikes to lampposts. A chain-draped rapper with rings on every finger came out of a store grinning, glinting gold teeth. Hasidim in flat hats went by deep in discussion, pockets full of fortunes in stones they'd exchanged on a handshake. Or so I've been told. That all these men really carried riches on their persons struck me as doubtful. But the part I liked wasn't the value of the stones, anyway. It was the handshakes.

We found Sydney Gems and Gold in a street-level shop near the end of the block. A young woman smiled and asked if she could help us. From the back counter an older woman said, "It's all right, Shana. I think I'm expecting these people." Like the younger woman's, her crisp white blouse had a buttoned neck and long sleeves.

"Beatrice Gardner?"

"That's correct. Ms. Chin?"

"Lydia. And this is Bill Smith. Thanks for seeing us."

"You come with the recommendation of Stanley Friedman, quite enough for anyone on this street. What can I do for you?" She smiled warmly and shook my outstretched hand. She gave Bill the same warm smile but didn't offer her hand, which didn't seem to surprise him.

"We won't take much of your time," I said. "I'd like to ask you some questions about your grandfather."

"Yes, Mr. Friedman told me that. Zayde Corens, of blessed memory. May I ask why?"

"Mr. Friedman didn't say? It's about when he lived in Shanghai. He had a jewelry shop on the Avenue Foch, didn't he?"

"Yes, that's correct."

"We found his name in a letter written by an Austrian refugee girl. Rosalie Gilder. Does that name mean anything to you?"

"So." She looked somberly at us. "People are still searching for the Shanghai Moon."

"Then it's true! Yaakov Corens? He made the Shanghai Moon?"

Beatrice Gardner refolded her hands. "Mr. Friedman says you're asking questions for an important reason, and it would be a mitzvah to help you. But if all you want is the Shanghai Moon—"

"No, that's not it," I said quickly. "We do think the Shanghai Moon might be here in New York, but we don't want it, not really. Someone we know, another detective, was killed, and the Shanghai Moon may be involved. So we need to know as much about it as we can."

"Killed?" She paled. "Someone was killed?"

"A friend of ours. Finding who killed him is the reason we're asking these questions. So you see, it is important."

She didn't answer me right away. "And the Shanghai Moon? Why do you think that?"

I told her as much as I thought she needed to know: the find, the fugitive bureaucrat, the letters. She frowned, not at me but into her counter of sparkling gems, as though discussing the situation with them. Finally she looked up and nodded. "I suppose, by now . . . Yes, all right. Zayde Corens made the Shanghai Moon. But he never spoke about it."

"He didn't? He didn't tell you the story?"

"Oh, the story he told. Rosalie Gilder and . . . Chen Kai-rong. Did I say that correctly?"

"Better than I said 'Yaakov Corens,' I think."

Smiling, she said, "Zayde Corens was a dreamer, a romantic. He told the story many times. He had only daughters, and his daughters had daughters. And I have daughters." She threw a proud glance at the young woman across the shop. "Zayde loved the story of Rosalie and Chen Kai-rong and told it over and over. The jade, the necklace, how they asked him to combine them. How in a time of trouble and loss, hunger and fear, these two young people wanted a lasting symbol of love and of family. Some were offended by this match, Zayde said. But in the face of the horrors and uncertainties around them, to be asked to create an emblem of hope was to him a great and humbling honor. My grandfather was more proud of that piece than of anything else he ever made."

"Then why do you say he never spoke about it?"

"He told the story, but only in the family, and he said it was our family's secret. And he would never speak about the Shanghai Moon itself."

"You mean about what it was worth?"

"Even what it looked like. He'd only say, like the moon, round and glowing for children to dream about. Sometimes people, collectors mostly, who knew he'd been a jeweler in Shanghai, would ask him about it, though you're the first in a long time. He'd say he could tell them nothing about the Shanghai Moon, except that if it existed he didn't know where it might be."

"Did they think he did?"

"They were always hoping."

"They came because they knew he'd made it?"

"No. Just because they knew he'd been in Shanghai. Written records from that time aren't so good. If anyone said they'd heard he made it, he denied it. What could they do?"

"Didn't anyone know, anyone who was there?"

"Not so many knew even in the ghetto days who made the Shanghai Moon. Most were too poor, too hungry, too desperate for news of family they'd left behind, to spare attention for such a thing. The story of Rosalie Gilder and Chen Kai-rong was a fairy tale. Or a scandal, depending on who was telling and who was hearing. And to someone looking for the Shanghai Moon years later, what good was the man who made it? Zayde was paid for it and parted with it in 1942."

I gazed at a tray of unset rubies and sapphires as I mulled this over. Bill spoke up. "Why wouldn't he talk about it? Did he ever tell you?"

"Oh, yes." Her smile grew soft. "When I was a child that was my favorite part. He was asked not to."

"By whom?"

"A Chinese gentleman."

I looked up. "Who was this gentleman?"

"Zayde wouldn't say. It was part of the secret. The story went that a mysterious Chinese gentleman came to the shop one afternoon."

"In Australia or in New York?"

"No, here, into this very shop. He and Zayde had tea and talked for a long time. After that day Zayde never spoke about the Shanghai

Moon outside the family again. The gentleman, he said, had asked
him not to. More than that, the reason for it, Zayde wouldn't say."

"Did the man threaten him? Did he seem frightened?"

"Oh, not at all. Sad, perhaps. Yes, a little sad. When he told us at
dinner about the gentleman, his eyes sparkled as usual—he was a romantic, as I said, and a showman, too; he knew the effect of a story
like this—but he had that cheery air adults sometimes wear when
they're hiding distressing things from children."

"And you didn't see the Chinese gentleman?"

"No, I was just a child, six years old."

"Around when was that?" Bill asked.

"You're asking me to tell my age?" Her eyes widened in mock horror. Then she smiled. "It was 1967. Early spring. I remember, because I
liked the story so much I wanted to dress like a mysterious Chinese
gentleman for Purim. But Zayde said if I did, the gentleman wouldn't
be mysterious anymore, and he was part of our family secret. So I
dressed like a pirate, to throw everyone off the scent." She paused,
then added, "I admit the story got more elaborate as my sisters and I
got older. So maybe the gentleman wasn't so mysterious, or maybe he
and Zayde didn't talk for so very long. But without doubt it was after
that visit that Zayde started to deny to everyone but us that he'd made
the Shanghai Moon at all."

2 5

"So this mysterious Chinese gentleman," I said to Bill as we headed back to the subway. "One of ours?"

"Ours being Mr. Chen, Mr. Zhang, or the other Mr. Zhang?"

"Right."

"Why would they?"

"Why would anyone? Why would you want the jeweler who made the Shanghai Moon not to talk about it?"

"And why wait twenty years to ask?"

"Maybe it took him twenty years to figure out who the maker was."

"If he was one of ours, wouldn't he know?"

"Not necessarily. Two of them were children when it was made, and one wasn't born yet."

Bill lit a cigarette, took a puff, then stopped in the middle of the sidewalk. "Oh, for God's sake. Even if they did know. Two of them weren't here."

I looked at him, and then, with new respect, at his cigarette. "Of course. Mr. Chen and Mr. Zhang came in 'sixty-six. Then it would have taken them time to find him."

"But what about C. D. Zhang? When did he get here? If he sponsored them, he was a citizen already, so he must have been here a while."

"But he was a kid, too, when it was made, and of them all, he'd have been the furthest out of the loop. So he might have needed Chen and

Zhang to get here before he found out, assuming it was him who cared. 'He,' right? Aren't you going to tell me to say 'he'?"

"I wasn't, no."

"Good thing, too. So it still could have been any of them."

"Or someone else."

"You think?"

"No."

I flipped my cell phone open. It was time we stopped getting the runaround from these Chinese gentlemen.

Which was an opinion apparently not shared by Mr. Chen or Mr. Zhang. Both Irene Ng at Bright Hopes Jewelry and Fay at Fast River Imports were sorry to inform me their bosses were not available. "I really have to speak to him" and "I know he's ducking me" didn't make either man magically reappear.

"Why won't they talk to me?" My complaint to Bill was rhetorical, but his answer made sense.

"You're representing someone whose clients wanted that jewelry enough to lie about their identity. Chen and Zhang are sure to have their own networks in the jewelry world, and I'll bet they're trying to track down Wong Pan themselves."

"Well, there's still one Chinese gentleman left. And we wanted to talk to him anyway." I poked in another number and spoke to another secretary.

Miraculously, I heard, "Hold, please," and then C. D. Zhang's energetic voice: "Ms. Chin! Good afternoon!"

"Good afternoon to you, Mr. Zhang. I was wondering if you had a few minutes?"

"Of course! What can I do for you?"

"I'd like to come speak to you."

"Is this a part of your quest for the Shanghai Moon?"

"And other things. I can be there in twenty minutes."

"Such industry! Please, come! Though beyond what I told you yesterday I don't see how I can help you."

"I'll explain when I get there."

"Ah!" A tiny pause. "Have you made new discoveries?"

"Mostly I've found new questions."

"This is quite exciting! I'll be expecting you."

C. D. Zhang and the sleek white tea set were waiting when we arrived. I introduced Bill, and a smile creased C.D. Zhang's face. "Mr. Smith. Now, you more closely fit my preconceptions of a private eye."

"It's a liability," Bill said.

"Not in all situations, I imagine. Now, please! Sit down! Tell me your new discoveries!" He poured tea and passed cups around.

"We've come across some information," I said. "Facts I wanted to ask you about." To be polite, I tasted my tea before I began. This was not the smoky tea from yesterday but a flowery jasmine. Delicious, I thought, and said so, and Bill agreed, though I was sure it was too sweet for him.

I decided to lead with yesterday's question, to soften him up. "Mr. Zhang, you told me Rosalie Gilder took your brother to Hongkew because his mother, Mei-lin, had disappeared. Forgive me, but sir, what you didn't say was that she disappeared with you and your father. When you escaped the Municipal Police, who were coming to arrest your father for being a Communist spy."

C. D. Zhang stayed silent for a long minute. His face slid from buoyant to rueful. "He wasn't, of course."

"A spy? No, Chen Kai-rong was."

"Yes. The Communist cause, as miserable a failure as it became, was guided in those early days by idealism and ideology. Those were not goods in which my father traded. Tell me, how did you learn this?"

"We've been doing research. There's a navy intelligence report that lays out the incident based on interviews with former members of the Municipal Police. Why did you let me believe you had no idea what happened to Mei-lin?"

"You came here to unearth the Shanghai Moon, not the disgraceful secrets of my family. What happened to my poor stepmother isn't part of the story of the Shanghai Moon."

"I think it may be. Can you tell us about it?"

"In what way could the two possibly be related?"

"I'd rather you told the story first. So your memories aren't tainted by what I think."

His glittering eyes regarded me. "And if I do, you'll tell me why?"

"Yes."

Another few moments; then he put his teacup down. He folded one hand over the other and let some time go by before he began. "My stepmother did indeed leave for Chongqing with my father and myself, and not happily. I was frightened, not because of our rapid flight—I was twelve, young enough to be excited, not old enough to fully comprehend the danger—but because my stepmother was so wretched. I thought that was because we didn't take the time to fetch my brother at the Chen home, and wondered why we didn't. My father, of course, explained nothing."

"How did he know to run? Did Mei-lin tell him?"

"No. He was warned—in your profession you'd say 'tipped off.'" He gave a wan smile. "A bought-and-paid-for friend in the SMP."

"What happened after you left Shanghai?"

"We boarded a train for the interior, rattling over the miles in air electric with Mei-lin's misery, my father's anger, and stiff silence. Late at night my father and Mei-lin left our compartment. He returned without her. I knew my father's fury, and even in the weak lamp from the corridor I could see it was best to play at being asleep. But I didn't sleep that night, though my father did. I heard his snores. In the morning I asked where my stepmother had gone. My father said she'd betrayed us and now she'd left us. I asked if she'd gone back to Shanghai, and when we would be going back. My father replied that I'd be punished if he heard my voice again before we reached Chongqing."

"So you never knew what happened?"

"I never knew, and for years I wouldn't let myself imagine. But it's clear." He looked at me sadly, and I had to agree.

"And after that?"

"After that? Where the train line ended, my father bribed the border guards. From filthy cafés he hired drivers. At one point we rode hidden in an oxcart. If not for my father's smoldering fury and my loneliness, it would have been thrilling. Finally we arrived in Chongqing. We set up house. A new amah—young and beautiful—and new tutors. My father, as always, gone much of the day, and I more lonely than before. I missed my stepmother. I missed my small brother, who made me laugh. It was a long time before I let go of the idea that Mei-lin had returned to Shanghai. I pictured the garden at the Chen home, the acacia in bloom, everyone playing, happy together. I was consumed with envy! But of course I said nothing to my father. He, in a change of heart I only understood years later when I learned the reason for our flight, had joined the army of Chiang Kai-shek. I did the same myself when I was of age, though as I said, my value increased with my unit's distance from actual combat. But my lack of military talent pales beside my father's political judgment. He had a genius, apparently, for picking the losing side. In a three-way war, he chose it twice.

"Now." C. D. Zhang's smile re-emerged. "That's our sordid family story, and I'm ready to be enlightened. Where in all this is the Shanghai Moon?"

Well, we'd made a deal. Before I could start, though, Bill asked, "Could you just tell me one more thing? How did you and your father get out of China?"

C. D. Zhang waved an arm. "I've told this to Ms. Chin. I thought partners shared everything! Our escape was dramatic, but not unique. With companions from my unit, I reached Shanghai scarely ahead of Mao's barefoot soldiers. My father had gone earlier, to negotiate passage on the *Taipei Pearl*—one of the last ships. I nearly missed boarding it. A frantic crush streamed up the gangway, many losing their footing, plunging into the oily water. My father, on the deck, screamed at the crewmen repelling the mob to let me board. As though they were troops under his command! Of course they ignored him. As my friends and I fought our way to the top of the slope, a desperate sailor unhitched the gangway from the ship. I leapt, crashing onto the deck as the steel plates fell away below and sent hundreds into the river. My companions were among them. With screams still echoing we set course for Taipei."

His sharp eyes flicked to me. "Ah, Ms. Chin, you look so sad! The past is gone. Those hundreds are long dead, and many worse things have happened since those days, and many better ones, too. As for my father and myself, when the ship reached Formosa—or as we now say, Taiwan—Chiang's men settled in to await the day, sure to come soon, when they'd regain the country. My father mocked them as fools. He said China and the past had both betrayed us and he wanted nothing more to do with them. We continued to America, to start new lives in the land of opportunity! Where, for a man who told any who'd listen that he'd turned his back on the past, my father spent a good deal of time tending his garden of bitter memories."

"One of those memories was Mei-lin's betrayal?" My synapses suddenly made a connection. "That's why he wouldn't have wanted you to sponsor your brother and your cousin?"

"Yes, Ms. Chin. Exactly." C. D. Zhang offered the teapot around. I accepted; Bill declined. "Now, you've heard my story and wrested from me a dark family secret. The very least you can do is tell me why. Do you suppose Mei-lin had the Shanghai Moon with her when we left, and my father unwittingly . . . discarded it?"

"No, that's not it," I said. "Do you remember a German friend of your father's, a Major Ulrich?"

"Major Ulrich, of course. A sneering fellow, not so different from my father. Why?"

"He's the man who stopped the Municipal Police from beating Kai-rong. To get him to do that, Mei-lin and Rosalie may have promised him the Shanghai Moon."

A flush of excitement crept into C. D. Zhang's face. "Ms. Chin! New discoveries indeed! How did you learn this?"

"We've found some documents. Mei-lin's diary and some other things. Papers no one's seen before."

"My stepmother's diary! And other things?"

"Yes."

I didn't elaborate, and after a moment he asked, "Where did you find them?"

"As an academic told us, it's unbelievable what's maintained in government archives at taxpayers' expense." That was deliberately misleading and I felt bad about it. But Paul Gilder could have handed any of these men his rosewood box at any time over the years. If he'd chosen to keep it secret, it wasn't my business to give him away. "There's a lot of material, apparently, that hasn't been translated."

"And something you found says Major Ulrich had the Shanghai Moon?"

"No. The documents seem to say he was promised it. It's not clear whether he ever got it."

"Ulrich . . ." C. D. Zhang's brows knit in thought. "He died not long after we arrived in Chongqing, I think. We were sent word. He was part of the escape plot?"

"Just that limited role, it seems, to keep Kai-rong safe while Mei-lin worked out the rest of the plan."

"And you don't know whether he actually got the gem," he mused. "Although if he had . . . that would explain . . ."

"Explain what?"

C. D. Zhang kept his gaze on the nighttime photo. He spoke quietly. "As I told you, the rumor persisted that Rosalie Gilder always wore the Shanghai Moon at her throat. But when her body was laid out for burial, it wasn't found. My cousin and my brother have always assumed it to have been stolen when she died. I never agreed. I've thought it must have been hidden in the gardens of the Chen villa—as we now see her other jewelry was. But if she and my stepmother gave it years before to Major Ulrich, that would explain why it wasn't found."

"Stolen when she died? Who by?"

"She died during a robbery near the end of the war. Li and Lao-li have always thought the robbers took the Shanghai Moon with them."

"Do you know anything more about that? Rosalie's death?"

He paused, then shook his head. "There was no law toward the war's end. Money had no value, and life even less. Any object that could be traded for rice, fuel, or passage out of China was stolen and stolen again. We had been hungry so long we no longer felt hunger, just desperation and fear. It was a terrible time and drove many mad."

Poor Rosalie, I thought, escaping the nightmare of Europe only to have to live through, and die in, times like that.

"But if you've come to ask if my stepmother ever said anything about Major Ulrich," C. D. Zhang said, "I'm afraid she didn't."

"I admit I was hoping. Mr. Zhang, think back. Couldn't there be anything, maybe something that didn't make sense at the time?"

He smiled. "I suppose there may be. Not much made sense to me at that time. However, nothing my stepmother said stands out. But Ms. Chin, your documents. Is it possible they hold something? Something you haven't recognized? Would you like me to look at them?"

"I don't think there's anything there. Mei-lin's diary, for example, stops the day you left Shanghai. She gave it to Rosalie. Along with your brother."

I watched his face as this sank in. "Her most precious things."

"Yes."

"All these years," he said slowly, "I thought it was a quirk of fate that my brother was at Rosalie's home when we fled and was left behind."

"No. I think Mei-lin was afraid of what might happen."

"What my father might do, you mean."

"Yes."

"Yes. And your other documents? They stop then, too?"

"No, some are from years later. But none seem to be able to tell us much about Major Ulrich."

We sat in silence for a time, or as much silence as we could find between the traffic noise and the cooing pigeons. "Well, it does no good to brood, does it?" C. D. Zhang finally said. "Ms. Chin, I'm sorry your new discoveries seem to lead to a dead end."

"Maybe not quite. There's another incident I'm curious about. Do you know a man named Yaakov Corens?"

"No, I don't think so."

"A jeweler who died many years ago. He had a shop in Shanghai when you were there. He made the Shanghai Moon."

"He made it?" If this wasn't news to C. D. Zhang, he'd missed his vocation as an actor. "Ms. Chin! That's remarkable! This is also in your documents?"

"Yes. We were able to track Corens to New York and speak to his granddaughter. But this is the odd part. In 1967, someone reported to have been a, quote, Chinese gentleman visited Corens's shop. They had tea together, and the gentleman asked Corens never to discuss the Shanghai Moon with anyone." I watched him closely as I said this. His expression was one of intense interest, but if anything I was saying was familiar, I couldn't see any sign.

"Why? And who?"

"I was hoping you'd know."

"I certainly don't! But this is astonishing! Who could he have been?"

"Your brother? Or your cousin?"

"But why? I was under the impression they had no idea who the maker was."

"I don't know. It's very strange. But if it wasn't you—"

"I assure you it wasn't."

"Then it must have been one of them. I think"—I looked at Bill—"we should go ask them."

26

The first call I made when we hit Canal Street was to Mr. Chen.

"I'm sorry, he's still not here," Irene Ng said.

"Is that true, or he just told you to say that?"

"Oh, no." She sounded hurt. "It's really true."

"I'm sorry. I didn't mean to offend you. I'm just getting really frustrated here, not being able to find either him or his cousin."

"Why don't you try Mr. Zhang again? I just spoke to him. He's back at his office."

By "try," Irene Ng probably meant "call." I didn't call. Bill and I were on Mulberry Street before you could say, "He's back at his office."

On the ground floor of Number 43 was a funeral-goods store, its window full of paper clothes, furniture, and money to burn for the dead. The second-floor buzzer read FAST RIVER IMPORTS. I buzzed it, and Fay's tinny voice asked who I was. When I told her, there was a short silence. Then she came back and said Mr. Zhang wasn't in.

"Oh, yes, he is," I said, mouth close to speaker. "And if we can't talk to Mr. Zhang, we're going over to Mr. Chen's shop and not leaving until we talk to *him*."

More silence. Finally, a buzz. I yanked the door open and took the stairs two at a time, Bill right behind me.

A thin young woman sat behind a desk in a wonder of file folders, paper stacks, and sunshine. We didn't have to ask again for the boss: Zhang Li was waiting in his inner-office doorway. He smiled and bowed. "Ms. Chin. I apologize if I seemed reluctant to speak with you."

"Seemed? Mr. Zhang, you've definitely been avoiding me." I bowed back, annoyed with myself to feel my irritation fading fast. I introduced Bill, who shook his hand. It occurred to me I might want to teach Bill to bow.

"Yes." Mr. Zhang spoke contritely. "I suppose I have been. Please, come with me. Fay, please bring tea."

The clutter in Mr. Zhang's office was as impressive as in the outer room and went way beyond paper. Delicate porcelains peeked out of shipping crates. Soldiers from the terra-cotta army stood to attention on the floor and windowsill, reproduced in eight sizes from half-real-life to thimble. Jade bracelets, bronze coins on red ribbons, cricket cages, and embroidered shoes spangled every surface, as though a wave of Chinese culture had crashed over this room and beached them all.

"Samples of my wares." Mr. Zhang sounded both rueful and proud, like an indulgent uncle apologizing for rambunctious nephews. "Please, sit."

Stools and a low table occupied a clearing, as in Mr. Chen's office. These were glazed ceramic, the kind you'd find in a garden. Before we'd settled, Fay entered and set down a lacquer tea tray.

"You and your cousin are both lovers of tea," I said as Mr. Zhang poured.

"I think you are also, Ms. Chin?"

"Yes, I am." I took the lidded, saucerless cup.

"And you, Mr. Smith?"

"I'm learning."

Pushing an old Chinese man might be the wrong way to get anywhere, but over the millennia people who've wanted to know things from old Chinese men have concocted other tactics. I said, "This tea smells lovely. Delicate and tropical. Did you and Mr. Chen develop your taste for fine teas in Shanghai?"

Zhang Li smiled. He knew what I was doing. "Hardly. Our boyhood years were war years, our adolescence the early days of the

People's Republic. Most often, tea then was a cloudy, bitter drink, something to keep you warm when you had no heat, or make you forget you had no food."

All right. Going that far was a signal he was ready to talk. So I did the polite thing. I backed off, sipped, and said, "Your tea is refreshing and sweet."

"I'm glad you find it so. Dragonwell, a favorite of mine. Mr. Smith? Do you enjoy it?"

"It's subtle. I'm probably missing the nuances. But yes, it's very good."

We all sipped again. Zhang Li carefully replaced the lid on his cup and said, "Now, Ms. Chin. You have questions about the Shanghai Moon."

"Yes, we do. But first: You and your cousin have both been avoiding me. Is it because Wong Pan's found you and you're negotiating for the jewelry?"

"Ms. Chin! Of course not! You've said the man's a killer. We'd have let you know at once if he'd contacted us."

"Maybe *you* would have. But your cousin?"

"I promise you."

"Good. Because he's here. In Chinatown. With a gun. Even if he doesn't know who Mr. Chen is, if he's going from jeweler to jeweler he'll find him. So make sure you don't lose my number."

He nodded, looking worried. Good; let him take this seriously. "Now, Mr. Zhang, I do have questions. One is why you stopped me from asking questions yesterday. And why you never mentioned your brother. And why, years ago, you asked Yaakov Corens to keep silent about the Shanghai Moon."

That last was a shot in the dark. I wouldn't have been surprised to get wide-eyed innocence, either real or feigned. If Zhang Li denied it, what could I do? But he didn't. He gave me a long, quiet look and a soft smile.

"Ms. Chin, I must remember you if I'm ever in need of investigation services. Yaakov Corens. That gentleman passed away twenty-five years ago. A lovely man, truly a gentleman."

"So we understand. An excellent jeweler, too."

"Indeed. Fine work, precise and delicate."

"He made the Shanghai Moon."

"Yes, he did."

"And you went to him in 1967 and asked him not to speak about it. And your brother never knew you'd found him. Did you tell your cousin? And why did you ask Mr. Corens to keep quiet?"

Mr. Zhang sighed. "To answer this, and the other things you've asked, I must tell you a story both long and sad. Shall I?"

In my head rang out: *This is a question?* Before I could say anything, Bill spoke. "If it's going to be long," he asked Zhang Li, "do you mind if I smoke?"

Zhang Li rummaged on his desk, lifting a geomancer's compass to find an ashtray, which he handed to Bill. "Most of my customers smoke. It's a habit Chinese people seem unwilling to abandon."

"Lydia doesn't like it, though." Bill got up. He perched on the windowsill beside a terra-cotta soldier, who took the intrusion stoically.

Zhang Li turned back to me. "Do you share an office? This must make your partnership difficult at times."

"You don't know the half of it," I said.

Zhang Li nodded, his smile fading as he stared at nothing. After a moment he began.

"It is natural for the passage of time to soften difficult memories and ease pain. For me, this has happened. For my cousin, it has not. When the Shanghai Moon vanished, I was nine years old, he a boy of six. The Shanghai Moon was only part of Lao-li's loss that day. He also lost his mother. Rosalie Gilder died in the . . . incident . . . when the gem disappeared. The pain those memories cause my cousin gave rise, many years ago, to an agreement between us that we should never, ever speak of it. To each other, or to anyone."

"Is that why you've been avoiding me?"

"Yes. The current circumstances may justify my breaking that vow, but not causing my cousin the pain that would surely be his if I spoke of it in his presence."

"Current circumstances" including, obviously, my threat to go over and camp in Mr. Chen's shop.

Cradling his tea, Zhang Li looked over his shoulder to Bill, then back to me. "The days at the end of the civil war were dark and hard. We—Aunt Rosalie, Uncle Paul, Lao-li, and myself—were living with Grandfather Chen in the villa in Thibet Road, to which we had returned after the Japanese surrender. In former times, the avenue had been elegant and serene, the villa well staffed and luxurious. Shanghai had never been a placid place, but in the International Settlement a certain order was kept. In my earliest memories I see wide, bright rooms, soft carpets, and scroll paintings of scholars' huts among pines. But by 1945, when we returned, all but one of the servants had fled. The automobiles and carpets had been sold to buy rice and cooking fuel. Where manicured lawns had swept up to the house, scrawny chickens scratched the dust between sweet potato vines. The acacia tree still bloomed, but flowers had given way to carrots and onions. The paintings and family treasures that remained were buried under the gardens in places only my grandfather knew. This situation continued through the next four years, until war's end. Things then became more normal—you might say, more civilized—but the elegance never returned."

Zhang Li, I could see, was circling, reluctant to close in on a subject that was still painful no matter what he said about time and memories. "You came back after the Japanese surrender," I said, helping him circle. "You'd been living in Hongkew, in the Jewish ghetto, is that right?"

"Yes." He looked at me curiously. "How did you know that?"

"We've spoken to your brother. Mr. Zhang, why didn't you tell me about him yesterday?"

"You came to ask whether my cousin had been offered Aunt Rosalie's jewelry. What reason would we have to mention my brother?"

Asked directly like that, I couldn't think of one, but it still felt weird. Maybe Mr. Zhang saw that in my face, because he said, "My brother brought us to America. For that we will always be grateful. But since our arrival—and it is now many years—we haven't been

close in the way of families. At first I tried to involve myself in his activities, and him in ours. But neither I nor my cousin has ever felt
comfortable in his presence. I tried to ignore my feelings and extend
the hand of friendship as family ought, but we never forged the bond
I know my brother was hoping for."

"He told me that. He still regrets it."

"For that, I'm sorry."

In the pause that followed, Bill rubbed out his cigarette but didn't
leave the windowsill. With a small sigh, Zhang Li resumed his story.
"In early 1943, the Japanese ordered the Jewish refugees to relocate to
Hongkew. Uncle Kai-rong had been arrested, then released, and had
left Shanghai. Grandfather Chen tried to intercede on Rosalie's
behalf—she was pregnant, you see—but the Japanese wouldn't hear
him. I, of course, did not have to go to the ghetto, and Grandfather
Chen would have preferred that I stay with him; but I had been en-
trusted to Aunt Rosalie by my mother, and she refused to leave me. I
doubt"—he smiled—"that a Chinese daughter-in-law would have defied
Grandfather Chen as Aunt Rosalie did. But she sat with him and argued,
matching him point for point, in the way of her tradition. And one
morning she and Uncle Paul packed boxes, hired rickshaws, and trun-
dled me off to Hongkew."

"Why did your grandfather let it happen?"

"Things had gotten steadily worse for Shanghai's Chinese. The alliance with Germany had hardened Japanese hearts, never warm toward Chinese to begin with. But the Japanese respected the Jews. They
created the ghetto but refused what to the Germans was the logical
next step: extermination. They kept strict control over the ghetto with
identity cards and curfews, but they managed Hongkew with a lighter
hand than they did the International Settlement. Wealthy Chinese like
my grandfather were in danger of being arrested, their property confiscated. My grandfather had already lost his factories and warehouses, as
the Japanese took what would aid their war effort, or what their commanders fancied. Aunt Rosalie made the argument that I was safer in
the ghetto than with him."

"Was that true?"

"How am I to know? I did survive the war, so perhaps she was right. So did my grandfather, but not without being jailed twice. He paid large bribes to secure his release. What would have become of me if I'd been there, either to be taken away with him or left with the one remaining houseboy, I don't know.

"In any case, soon after we set up house in Hongkew, my cousin was born, at a hospital the Jewish refugees had built for themselves. Although my grandfather's own life grew more and more difficult, he sold family treasures on the black market to help look after us. For Hongkew, our quarters—four people in two rooms, with cold running water and a flush toilet under the stairs shared with just two other families—were luxurious. He sent food also, and books, and he came to see us. But he could not bring us out of the ghetto.

"Then in 1945 the Japanese surrendered. The ghetto was opened. Uncle Kai-rong came back and moved us to the villa. He left again, returning every few months. Until finally he came home for good, at the civil war's end."

Zhang Li refilled our teacups, rising to take the pot to Bill. When he sat again, I thought maybe he'd circled enough. "Mr. Zhang?" I asked. "The Shanghai Moon?"

He nodded and again looked off into nothingness. "By the war's last days, wild chaos reigned. Shanghai was one of the last cities to fall to Mao's army and therefore one of the last refuges of the desperate remnants of Chiang's. Nationalist soldiers rampaged through the steets. They stole food because they were hungry, money to buy passage to Taiwan, clothing so they could discard their uniforms. They stole anything. They burned, they smashed, they beat, ravaged, and killed.

"It was a matter of time until our villa was struck. Three armed men . . ." He stopped to swallow some tea. In a voice creaky and fast, he said, "They burst in. Rags hid their faces. They rounded us up— Grandfather, Uncle Paul, Aunt Rosalie, Lao-li, the old houseboy, and myself—and demanded our precious possessions, even as they gaped at the empty walls and bare floors."

Zhang Li's unsteady hands clinked the lid off his teacup. "Forgive me. This is the first time I've spoken of that day. As children, even allowing ourselves to think about it put Lao-li and myself in terror of calling down more bad luck, of causing the loss of someone else dear to us. We've never spoken of it, and I've done everything I could to avoid revisiting it in my own mind. The oddness is this: Through the years that day has come back at times, unbidden, as terrible moments will. I've always thought every detail engraved on my memory so deeply that I'd never forget a single sight, a single sound. But when I look closely, to try to explain it to you, events appear jumbled and confused. Sounds evade my hearing, sights are inexplicable. I find only fragments." After another moment: "I remember this: Grandfather ordered the intruders out. There was shouting. Their leader swung at Grandfather with his rifle butt. Grandfather slumped and there was blood . . . Uncle Paul ran at them, screaming they could see for themselves we had no riches, everything was gone. One of the men punched his stomach, knocked him down. Lao-li was shielded, as I was, behind Aunt Rosalie, but at the blood, the blows, the shouts, Loa-li began to scream.

"In my next memory, one of the men has seized Lao-li and is slapping him repeatedly. Aunt Rosalie threw herself on him, this man. A second man tore her away, but she didn't stop shrieking and struggling. It took both the men to force her to the ground. All this time the leader was beating Grandfather and shouting for treasures.

"Then the old houseboy—Number One Boy, who had been with the Chen family for decades, a thin man made skeletal by hard times—Number One Boy lifted a stool and smashed one of the men holding Aunt Rosalie down.

"The man crumpled. The other released Aunt Rosalie and ran at Number One Boy. Aunt Rosalie, hair wild and clothing torn, scrambled to her feet.

"The leader shouted, spun around, and fired." Zhang Li's eyes closed. He was silent so long I thought he'd finished, and I wondered whether I should say something, but Bill caught my eye and shook his head. Finally Zhang Li spoke again.

"Aunt Rosalie fell. Everyone turned to stone. Then Number One

Boy seized the fallen man's rifle and fired at the leader. But he was a houseboy, not a soldier. He missed his mark. The leader shot back, also wide, splintering a chair. The fallen man crawled to his feet. Their leader shouted an order, and they all turned and ran. Number One Boy chased after. I heard more shots, and finally silence. Number One Boy didn't return.

"After that . . . I have a picture in my mind of myself and my cousin kneeling beside Aunt Rosalie, in silence. I thought he'd reach for her, try to embrace her, start to cry. He did none of those things. He didn't move at all. I recall Uncle Paul saying in a soft voice that Grandfather was alive, then taking Aunt Rosalie's hand. But I'd reached her first, and I knew she was not.

"Uncle Kai-rong returned two days later. We were barricaded in the kitchen. When we heard voices in the house, Uncle Paul told Lao-li and myself to hide in a cupboard. He and Grandfather Chen seized cleavers and waited. Only when they were sure it was Uncle Kai-rong did Uncle Paul unbar the door.

"Uncle Kai-rong was devastated. Disbelieving. He wept over the garden grave Uncle Paul and I had dug for Aunt Rosalie in the dead of night. He begged her forgiveness. Then he gathered Lao-li and myself to him and said, 'You are the treasures.' He repeated it: 'You are the treasures.'

"Within days, Mao's army arrived, and order was restored in Shanghai. Number One Boy, who had been shot dead beside the gate, was sent back to his ancestral village for burial. Aunt Rosalie was given a proper funeral and reburied in the Jewish cemetery, though there were so few Jews left in Shanghai by then that some rites could not be performed.

"Uncle Paul left Shanghai a few months later, to go to America, after Mao Tse-tung made it clear Europeans were not welcome in the People's Republic. Lao-li and I grew up in the villa, watched over by Kai-rong, whom I called uncle but who treated me like a son. Until, as young men, we came to America."

A New York silence—quiet framed by a distant siren, an air conditioner's hum—suffused the room. "An old story," Mr. Zhang said

softly, "from long ago. But"—he reached for my teacup, to refill it—
"you are still wondering about the Shanghai Moon."

In truth I hadn't been. I'd been thinking about Rosalie and Kai-
rong, and how they'd never gotten to say good-bye.

"Uncle Paul," he said, "cradling Aunt Rosalie after the intruders
fled, found red marks at her throat. To Grandfather, or perhaps to
himself—certainly not to Lao-li or to me—he said, 'The Shanghai
Moon. They were after the Shanghai Moon.' Weeping, he called down
curses upon the gem and swore he wished it had never been made."

"She'd been wearing it?" I said. "I thought—"

"Though the intruders found the villa empty and bare, they continued to scream for treasure. Then suddenly, after the struggle with
Aunt Rosalie, they fled. Why? Unless by 'treasure' they meant the
Shanghai Moon, and they'd gotten what they came for. Such was Uncle Paul's reasoning. Uncle Kai-rong agreed. He cursed the gem as
Uncle Paul had, and called on it in turn to curse those who now possessed it. He ordered us never to speak of it again."

"I'm so sorry," I said, feeling how tissue-thin the words were.
"What terrible things for a child to live through."

"Many children live through terrible things. The world is a harsh
place. All we can do is try to ease one another's way."

"I suppose you're right. And I have to say, the loss of a brooch
seems so . . . trivial, in the context of this story. Of those terrible
days."

"Yes. And no. Uncle Kai-rong would have given a dozen, a hundred, Shanghai Moons, to have his Rosalie back. But it took on a different meaning to my cousin. In Uncle Kai-rong's presence we never
spoke of it, and we never spoke between us of that day, but repeatedly,
to me, in the months that followed, Lao-li vowed he would recover the
gem. He was a young child who, as you say, had seen terrible things.
The dream of recovering the Shanghai Moon gave him comfort. I—a
child also, not much older—saw no harm in his taking refuge in that
dream. I did not forsee the obsession it would become, or the trouble
it would lead to."

"Trouble?"

"As we grew to manhood, my cousin's attention was absorbed in the study of gems and precious metals. The Shanghai of the People's Republic, gray and stern, bore little resemblance to the wild city of the years before the war, or to the war years' profiteering frenzy. Luxury and opulence were banished. The European jewelers had fled, and Chinese jewelers found themselves doing little beyond repairing senior cadres' watches. Nevertheless, Lao-li found a jeweler willing to take an apprentice. After a day of Piaget screws and gears, by night he instructed Lao-li secretly on gems, their cuts, weights, colors, and flaws.

"Uncle Kai-rong was himself a senior cadre, busy with extending the generous, fierce hand of revolution to all of China. We remained in the villa—shared now, in correct Maoist fashion, with three other families—planting bok choy and beans among the sweet potato vines, giving to the poor the eggs from our chickens. For a long time, life was difficult but satisfying. Uncle Kai-rong assured us the sacrifices we were making would uplift the Chinese people through a thousand generations."

"Why didn't you dig up Rosalie's jewelry? And what about the treasures your grandfather had buried?"

"Grandfather Chen's scrolls and porcelains were retrieved and sold abroad to feed the masses. But the villa garden itself was nourishing many mouths. Uncle Kai-rong would not permit the destruction of crops to search for the jewelry, the location of which none of us knew. He felt Aunt Rosalie would have wanted it that way. As crops were plowed under or new furrows dug, of course we searched, but we were never successful.

"Then, as my cousin and I entered our twenties, the winds of the Cultural Revolution began to blow. Everyone was scrutinized, anyone could be denounced. Uncle Kai-rong was a powerful man, but his class background was incorrect. And powerful men have enemies. Being cowards, his did not take aim at him directly but whispered and hissed, inflaming others. We started to hear rumors, threats. One day, returning from his work, Lao-li was set upon by a mob in the street. Perhaps you can imagine the attitude of the Red Guards toward a young Eurasian jeweler from a landowning family?"

I could. "What happened?"

"These were the Cultural Revolution's earliest days. Some people were not yet terrified and cowed. He was rescued by neighbors and returned to us, not badly hurt. But over the months the direction of things became clear. Uncle Kai-rong, forseeing dunce caps and years of reeducation in the countryside for Lao-li, sent him to America, and me with him. He did this at great risk and no doubt would have paid a high price. But he cheated the Red Guards: He fell ill, and died not six months after I and my cousin arrived here."

"How did he die?"

Mr. Zhang smiled sadly. "We were told his heart failed him. I have no doubt that is true. Many years before, he'd lost his Rosalie. Now he lost his son, and myself. And finally, to the Red Guards, he lost his greatest love: China. I think he saw no reason to go on."

"Mr. Zhang, your family's story is extraordinary."

"No, Ms. Chin. There are many like it. Every family has its own tangles of love and consequences."

"But not all families' stories run through times like those."

"That may be, though from what I've seen that makes their stories no easier. In any case, do you now understand why it's implausible that this ministry official who stole Aunt Rosalie's buried jewelry—"

"Wong Pan."

"Why Wong Pan is unlikely to have the Shanghai Moon?"

"Because it wasn't buried with the other pieces. But yesterday you asked me about it."

"For Lao-li's sake. The search for the Shanghai Moon has given shape to my cousin's life. It's a delusion and has been from the beginning. But it's kept him from despair in the darkest times."

"So you've indulged his fantasy and, as I understand it, financed the hunt."

"The path he's followed hasn't led to the treasure he seeks. But as he wouldn't abandon this path, I have not wanted him to walk it alone."

"He's lucky to have you, Mr. Zhang."

"And I to have him. Through my young years, all I had of my own family were memories, growing faint. My mother, my father, my brother had left me behind and were gone. Yet unlike the thousands of war orphans starving alone in the streets, I grew up wrapped in the warmth of family. I was a mouth to feed, a cry to hush, but never for a moment was I allowed to think I was a burden. No, the opposite. I was part of the family's joy. This is a debt I can never repay. If I've spent money over the years helping my cousin keep hope alive, and so enabling him to live a life, with a wife and children of his own, it is no price at all. In our children and our grandchildren, the Chen, Zhang, and Gilder families still live."

I glanced at Bill, then back to Zhang Li. "I do have more questions, Mr. Zhang. But first, there's something else. You say your mother, your family, had left you behind."

"I've never blamed them. Perhaps my mother hoped to be able to come back for me, but . . . it was wartime."

"She did hope that. Still, what you think is not exactly what happened."

"What are you saying? How can you know anything about those times?"

"We've found . . . documents. Your mother's diary, for one thing. And . . ." I hesitated. I didn't want to come out and say, *And your father murdered your mother, your brother told us so.* "And some other things. I'll give them to you. They tell most of the story, and I can fill in some of the rest."

"My mother's diary! But Ms. Chin! How could you possibly have found—"

Another thing he might not need to know. Uncle Paul had it all along. "We did a lot of digging. I'll make you copies of what we have."

"Oh, my. I'd be very grateful."

"But now, Mr. Zhang: What do you know about a German named Ulrich? A soldier?"

"Ulrich? I don't think I know that name. Who is he?"

"He's mentioned in your mother's diary. He protected Chen Kairong in jail. For that Major Ulrich was promised the Shanghai Moon."

"Promised it? By Aunt Rosalie?"

"And your mother. We thought there might be a chance he'd actually gotten hold of it. But if Rosalie was wearing it years later, when the intruders came . . ."

Zhang Li just shook his head.

Another dead end, I thought, wondering if the disappointment I felt was anything like what Mr. Chen had felt over and over through the years.

"Tell me one more thing, though. Why did you ask Yaakov Corens not to speak about the Shanghai Moon?"

"Ah, Yaakov Corens." A shadow of a smile. "I was younger then. I thought in America my cousin might abandon his fixation. Begin to live in the present and leave the past behind. But only if the past really was behind us. Though he didn't know the name of the Shanghai Moon's maker, I did, having heard Aunt Rosalie and Uncle Paul as they debated selling a bracelet in our rooms in Hongkew. Many of the Jewish refugees from Shanghai came to America, and for a jeweler to come to the diamond quarter in New York would be reasonable. My cousin knew that as well as I did. I was afraid finding Yaakov Corens would only inflame his obsession, so I searched for him in secret as soon as we arrived. As it turned out, he'd gone first to Australia and only recently come here himself.

"Yaakov Corens was a true gentleman, as I've said. He understood why I was asking and he readily agreed. To this day Lao-li doesn't know who the maker was."

"But it didn't work. To help end Mr. Chen's obsession."

"No," Zhang Li said sadly. "It did not."

27

"You did that thing again," I said to Bill as soon as we were back out on Mott Street.

"Smoked too much?"

"Cut it out! Sat off to the side and watched."

"You realize, of course, that that's why I smoke? Purely as trade-craft, a tool—"

"Oh, stop it! What did you think?"

If he'd given me another smart-aleck answer, I might have socked him. Luckily, he didn't. "He's hiding something."

"Please don't say that."

"I'm wrong?"

"No." I sighed. "I think you're right. I had the same hunch, and I was hoping *I* was wrong."

"Maybe we both are."

"At the same time? That's ridiculous."

Bill shrugged.

"But what's he hiding?" I asked. "Don't tell me you think that whole sad story's not true. I wouldn't be able to stand it."

"I think what he said was true. His voice, his body language . . . But there's something anyway. Something he's not saying. Something that's also true."

"So what are we supposed to do? Part of me wants to try it Joel's way. Just go back up there and squeeze him until he gives it up."

"And the other part of you says he's an old Chinese man and you'll get nowhere."

"Right. So—" I broke off and dug out my phone, which was tinkling the *Wonder Woman* song. "Hi, Mary."

"Where are you?"

"Who wants to know?"

"Lydia—"

"Mott Street. What's up?"

"I'm at the precinct, with Wei De-xu. Can you come up?"

"That's your Chinese cop?"

"Meet us in Interview One."

"Why? I was about to—"

"Forthwith."

That's cop for "right now this minute." Mary hardly ever talks cop to me.

"Your surveillance on Mr. Chen! It turned up Wong Pan?"

"No."

"Then can't I—"

"No. I'm taking De-xu to meet the captain, but we'll be done by the time you get here."

"You guys are on a first-name basis already? What will Peter think?"

"Girlfriend, he won't care." She clicked off, so that was that.

"Nuts," I said to Bill, annoyed. "That was Mary inviting me to the precinct forthwith." Generally I'd jump at a chance to stick my nose in police business, but Mr. Zhang's hidden secret was on my front burner, and meeting a cop from Shanghai sounded like just a lot of politeness and more tea.

" 'Forthwith' isn't an invitation," Bill said.

"Hey, she did say, 'Can you?' I didn't ask if you could come, but since she's the one who called you in the first place—"

"Thanks anyway. I have some things I could more profitably be doing."

"Like what?"

"I'd like to try out these intruders on Professor Edwards, just in case there's something in his sources about people breaking into the Chen villa."

"You're just looking for an excuse to stay out of a police station."

"That, too."

"Well, go ahead. It can't hurt. Write if you get work."

The desk sergeant, a woman named Anna Bilankov I'd met once or twice, nodded and told me to go up. I took the worn concrete stairs two at a time and turned left at the top. I knew where the interview rooms were; I'd stood on the witness side of the one-way glass a few times, with clients, and sat in the customer seat once when the Fifth's former captain thought I'd been misbehaving just a little. The door to Interview One was half open, so I pushed through it.

"Oh," I said, as Mary stood up grinning from one side of the table and a Chinese woman about ten years older, four inches shorter, and infinitely tougher than either of us bolted up from the other.

Mary said, "Lydia Chin, Inspector Wei De-xu."

I shot her a glower, then bowed to Inspector Wei, who had already bowed crisply to me. "Inspector Wei De-xu," she announced in English. "Special Crimes Group of Shanghai Police Bureau." She thrust out her hand. When in Rome. Her grip stopped just short of powdering my bones.

"Lydia Chin Ling Wan-ju, private investigator. It's a pleasure to meet you."

"Investigator Chin. Detective Kee telling much about you." Wei De-xu—whose given name, meaning "virtuous order," could go either way—wore her thick hair in a heavy-banged Cleopatra framing a tanned face. She was dressed in road-movie civvies: black jeans, black T-shirt, black leather jacket. And black motorcycle boots. I bet no one messed with her in Shanghai. "One man killed, is your friend. Please accept sympathy from Shanghai Police Bureau."

"And please accept mine on the loss of your colleague."

"Inspector Sheng Yue. He is talented officer. But too eager, unfortunately."

"I'm sorry?"

"Sheng Yue is leaving Shanghai too fast. He doesn't has all informations."

Mary gestured us to sit and asked if I wanted tea.

"Luckily for me, I just had some." I turned to Inspector Wei. "Is the tea as bad in Shanghai police stations as here?"

"Of course." Wei picked up an almost empty NYPD mug and threw back a last swallow. "Even it's bad, we drinking all day."

"I'll get you some more," Mary offered and left.

"You must be exhausted," I said. "After that long flight." I knew better than to get into anything substantive before Mary came back.

"Shanghai Police Bureau doesn't sending me here to sleep. From now, going to meeting with—Midtown Squad?" She pronounced the words as though their meaning were esoteric.

"That's right," said Mary, returning with a pot of hot water, another mug, and a handful of teabags. "Inspector Wei is about to have the privilege of meeting Detective Mulgrew."

"Detective Kee telling about him also." Wei's predatory smile nearly made me feel sorry for Mulgrew.

"Before we go up there, though," Mary said, "there's something I want you to hear. From the inspector. Have you talked to Alice lately?"

"No, she's ducking me. She fired me twice. She's afraid I'll get hurt."

"Is that what she said?"

I looked from Mary to Inspector Wei. "Hey. What's up?"

Mary nodded to the Shanghai cop. Dipping a teabag as though she were fishing in her mug, Wei said, "Assistant Deputy Minister Wong Pan working in Shanghai Culture Bureau, Modern History Section. Has responsibility, artifacts, relics, all recent antiquity of Shanghai."

Now there's a government concept, I thought: *recent antiquities.* But apparently, that wasn't the problem.

"How Wong Pan is flying off to United States after stealing jewelry?" Inspector Wei asked. "Why not gets stopped leaving, or at Customs arrival? Why no record, passenger list, exit paper?"

"How could he get out so cleanly is the point, Lydia," Mary said. "The theft was noticed within hours."

"Because," Wei answered her own question, "Wong Pan has false passport, visa. New identity. Wu Ming. Stupid name. How he gets identity papers?"

I said, "I imagine it's as easy to get those things in Shanghai as anywhere."

"No. Not so easy." Wei gave me a steely look. Then she laughed. "Not so easy because some way, China still backwards. Technology some things hard to find. Easy in Europe. Easy in Switzerland."

"Switzerland? Wait—you're not saying you think Alice Fairchild had anything to do with it?"

"Shanghai Police Bureau information, very fews in Shanghai capable making papers, none of these did. In U.S., say, 'word on street?'" She looked to Mary with evident pride in her American slang. "Word on Shanghai street, Wong Pan getting papers from Europe. One other word, getting help from European woman. Small, good clothes, short hair with gray."

"Well, that . . . but it could—"

"Be anyone," Mary finished for me. "Except as far as we know, there's no one of that description connected with this case but Alice Fairchild."

"Attorney Fairchild leaving Shanghai immediately after Wong Pan," Wei pointed out.

"She was chasing him. Because he stole her clients' jewelry."

Mary said, "Or because he skipped out on whatever deal they had."

"Uh-oh," I said.

"Uh-oh, what?"

Mary and Wei both leaned forward, eyes identically glowing.

Reluctantly, I said, "The phony heirs."

"What is 'phony heirs'?" Wei leaned closer.

"Yes, Lydia, what?" Mary demanded.

I caught them up fast, so their matched cop eyes wouldn't drill holes through me.

"Why didn't you tell me about this?" Mary's voice edged toward the danger zone.

"Tell you what? My client's clients were lying to her?"

"You didn't think it was a problem I should know about?"

"What I thought was, it was a problem for my client that I didn't understand. My job isn't the same as yours."

"Catching Joel's killer?"

"Joel hired me to work for this client. Until I'm sure she's involved in something—"

"And when you're sure? What are you planning to do when you're sure?"

"*If* I'm sure," I said, "you know I'll tell you."

Mary and I locked eyes. "I know how stubbornly loyal you can be. Your clients—"

"If I were you, I'd be grateful for how stubbornly loyal I can be. Like to my best and oldest friend, for example."

Wei De-xu frowned. Whatever was going on between Mary and me wasn't helping her catch her killer. She cleared her throat. "I have theory of crime."

Mary sat back. "Go ahead."

"In Europe, peoples hear about jewelry. Go to Attorney Fairchild, make scheme together. Attorney Fairchild flying to Shanghai, suggest scheme to Wong Pan. Corrupting official, bad crime in China."

Ah, the wily *lo faan*, tempting the naive Servant of the People. Wei practically smacked her lips at the thought of bagging such a fiend.

Grudgingly, I said, "Also . . ."

"Also?" Mary repeated.

"I hate this!"

"So?"

"Yes, yes, all right. Is there still hot water in that thing?"

"Are you stalling?" Mary passed me the pot and a mug.

"Probably." I unwrapped a teabag. "It's just, the clients may not be lying. Alice may be lying. About having clients." I added milk and waited to see if it curdled. "Last time I talked to her, I told her three things. That the clients were phony, that Rosalie and Kai-rong had a son and I'd met him, and that it looked like Wong Pan had tried to call her. She said the call might be coincidence—which is true, by the way," I added, just to keep their minds open, "and she told me she'd call the clients and get back to me. And she fired me. But beyond one 'Oh, my God,' when I told her about Rosalie's son, she didn't say anything else. She didn't ask his name or what woodwork he crawled out of, how I found him, anything."

"So what are you thinking?"

"Well, he's a genuine heir with a strong claim on Rosalie's jewelry. If she's actually doing asset recovery for real clients, she'll need to contend with him. And if her clients are phony, I've inadvertently found an heir anyway. So she should have been more interested."

"But if it's not recovery, it's theft—"

"Then she wouldn't care who Mr. Chen is. The fact that he exists and knows the jewelry was found could make the pieces harder to sell. That could be a problem later on. But her problem right now hasn't changed. She needs to find Wong Pan."

Mary and the inspector traded gratified looks. I drank my foul tea and tried to calm down. If Alice Fairchild was a liar, a thief, and a swindler, it wasn't Mary's fault, or Inspector Wei's.

They just didn't have to be so damn happy about it.

28

Leaving the Fifth Precinct's wheezy air-conditioning for the muggy air of Elizabeth Street, I called Bill. I got his voice mail, which told me nothing. I already knew enough nothing. I left a message to call me and headed to my office, to try to think.

If Alice was chasing Wong Pan for a whole other reason than what she'd told Joel and me, it set a lot of things in a new light. Maybe the pay-phone call to the Waldorf meant Wong Pan had changed his mind about running out on her. Alone in the big city, he'd called to make up. Maybe I kept getting fired because they were once again thick as, well, thieves, and my searching for him was now a liability. And maybe Joel had been somehow onto Wong Pan. If so, maybe he'd also been onto Alice.

And in that case maybe Alice knew something about Joel's death she wasn't saying.

But the question still was, if Joel had found anything definitively dirty, why didn't he say that, instead of "fishy"? The impression I'd gotten was that something unexplained was bothering him. Not good, but nothing worse than that.

When the light changed and trapped me on the corner, I thumbed David Rosenberg's number into my phone. Before the light changed back, I'd asked him about Alice Fairchild. "How sure are we that she's what she says she is?"

"What do you mean?"

"A lawyer who specializes in Holocaust assets."

"As far as I know. The magazine follows recovery cases from time to time, and we wrote up one of hers a few years ago. I found her impressive. Straightforward and well prepared."

"Did she win?"

"I believe that one's still in litigation. You know these cases are hard to win."

"That's what Joel told me. Mr. Rosenberg, what if I made the same request of you that she did? Can you put me in touch with a private investigator? In Zurich?"

"What is it you need?"

"Any information at all about her."

"Is there a problem?"

"I'm not sure. I've just learned she may have supplied a Chinese national with false travel documents."

"Really? Alice Fairchild?" A moment's thoughtful silence. "Could that be what Joel knew?"

"I don't know. Can you find me an investigator?"

"Well, the system in Switzerland works differently than here. I'm not sure how to connect you. But, you know, I publish a magazine, with some very good investigative journalists on staff. Would you like me to have some research done for you?"

"I don't want to get you involved."

"This is still that same case, right? Joel's case?"

"Yes."

"Then, Ms. Chin, I'd very much like to help."

I opened the street door I shared with Golden Adventure Travel, thinking, *Okay, I have investigative journalists in Zurich digging for me, how can I lose?*

Then I walked down the hallway, unlocked my own office, and saw how.

Drawers open, books off shelves, papers everywhere. My office looked as though the Duke of Hell had had a fit in it.

Just the way Joel's had.

At first I froze, my pounding heart the only thing moving; then fury boiled me into action. Who the hell did whoever this was think he was? I drew my gun and slipped inside, back to the wall. If they were still here, they could only be under the desk or in the bathroom. *Unless it really was the Duke of Hell. He's invisible. Yeah, well, I'll plug him right between the glowing red eyes.* I kept up a silent monologue until I'd covered the entire space, which didn't take long. The breach in my security turned out to be the bathroom window, whose bars were no match for the Duke of Hell and his crowbar. I holstered my gun and called Bill. I told his voice mail about the break-in. "Watch your back and call me."

Then I called Mary. "I'm never coming up to your place anymore. It's too dangerous."

"What are you talking about?"

"While I was there, someone was here." I described the ruins I stood in the middle of.

"Are you all right?" Mary demanded.

"Of course I'm all right! They're long gone! But," I added grudgingly, "thanks for asking."

"You shouldn't have gone in alone. You should have called."

"And died from adrenaline poisoning waiting for you?"

"I'll send some uniforms right away."

"Oh, now you're hanging with the international set and you're a big shot? Come yourself, show your Shanghai buddy a genuine American burglary."

"We're in the car on our way to Midtown. I'll turn around if you want."

"Oh. No, forget it. Let Wei bite Mulgrew's head off. That might make me feel better."

"Any chance it was Wong Pan?"

"Mary, girlfriend, how would I know?" Though the thought had occurred to me, and the face I'd imagined on the Duke of Hell had been suspiciously round.

I hung up and went across the hall.

"Hi, Lydia." Ava Louie looked up from her computer with a cheerful smile. Andi Gee, on the phone, waved at me.

"You guys hear anything in my office today?"

"Like what?"

"An earthquake, explosions, a dance party? No, someone broke in."

Ava jumped up, and I had to take her to see the damage. We were joined a moment later by Andi, who gave a little shriek.

"I'm fine," I said quickly, because they were staring at me. "I wasn't here." This wasn't the first time something like this had happened. The other time had involved the travel ladies having to liberate me from a certain amount of rope. The last thing I needed was for them to decide I was a risky subtenant and evict me. "Either of you guys see or hear anything?"

They shook their heads. "We had busy afternoon," Andi said. "Lots people. This very weird. After we so nervous. We perfectly fine, but your office, this happens."

"Nervous about what?"

"Lots people, ask about flight, tour, cruise, everythings. Some maybe interested, but most, no. But sit, keep asking, talking. Actually, we worried, in case looking to see, should they rob us. But don't dare throw them out."

"Why not?"

"Because," Ava said. "White Eagles."

I left the travel ladies in their own office and tiptoed around mine, looking to see what was missing while I waited for the precinct guys.

That White Eagles had spent the afternoon researching vacation packages was beyond suspicious. Chinatown gangsters aren't *Travel & Leisure* types. A lot don't even have passports: Some are illegals, some are still serving out parole time, and others haven't used their real names in so long they don't know them. Their only purpose could have been to distract Ava and Andi from whatever was happening in my office.

Which was what? Nobody breaks into a PI's office looking for cash. Under all the paper, everything that could profitably be fenced was still here. The alley lightwell may not be Main Street, but it's not risk-free. If I were a jewelry shop, the distraction tactic and the risk might be worth it, but to break into my office?

I examined the bent bars more closely. Not a large opening. I could barely have made it through myself. Anyone slight enough to use this gap probably wouldn't have the strength to create it. So, a theory: Some muscle-bound rice-brain jimmies the bars; a ten-year-old apprentice gangster squeezes through and opens my door for some other rice-brains while yet another set distracts the ladies at Golden Adventure.

Why? What could make all that worthwhile?

Was it the same thing that had made tossing Joel's office worthwhile?

And whether or not they'd found what they came for, why didn't they steal anything else as long as they were here?

The arrival of two uniforms from the Fifth Precinct temporarily derailed my train of thought. They poked around, taking down information. "Kee told us to scare up the crime scene guys," one of them said. "But I don't know, a burglary? Even if it was White Eagles. And you don't know that. And you didn't lose nothin' . . ." He trailed off, caught between a detective's order and the sure scorn of the overworked CSI techs.

"No, it's okay," I sighed. The chances of lifting prints weren't great, and if there were any, that would just prove whoever left them had been here sometime. Since I hadn't lost nothin', what charges could I press even if I knew who to press them against?

Of course, maybe I had lost something but in this mess didn't know what. I thanked the cops and was closing the door behind them when an icy thought hit.

If whoever did this hadn't found what they were looking for, they might try looking somewhere else.

I yanked out my phone and hit speed dial. When my mother answered, I blurted, "Ma! Are you all right?"

"Ling Wan-ju? What do you mean, am I all right? Of course I am well, for an old woman. If you had not left so early this morning you would have seen how well I am."

"Don't open the door until I get there."

"Who is coming here?"

"I don't know."

At a run, I charged up Canal, headed home.

"You think those gang boys will come here?" My mother stared in dis-belief. I wasn't sure if that was for the audacity of the gang boys or for my own absurd idea that anyone, even gang boys, would climb to a fourth-floor walk-up to tangle with my mother.

"Probably not, Ma. This is just to make sure. Ted and Ling-an say they'd love to have you come back for a few days. You'll be safe out there."

"If this apartment is not safe, why will you not let me put more locks on the door?"

"Five locks are plenty, Ma. But they crowbarred my bathroom win-dow."

"Our bathrooms have no windows."

"There's the kitchen fire escape."

"The fire escape faces a busy street."

"They might come at night."

"Old Chow Lun would see them."

"He might not be there."

"Have you ever seen him when he is not there?"

How could I see him if he's not there? I tried to calm down and discuss things rationally. But this was my mother. "It won't be for long, Ma."

"How long?"

"I don't know."

"Then how do you know it will not be long?"

"Just until I find out what they wanted and whether they got it."

"How will you do that?"

"I don't know."

"And what do you think it might have been, this thing they wanted?"

"I don't know."

"I see. You do not know who they are, what they wanted, whether they found it, or how to learn these things."

"No. But—"

"But you know you want your mother to go back to Flushing, for a length of time you also do not know."

"Ma! Ma, please! I just don't want to have to worry about you."

"Oh." She peered at me. "This is not something you want me to do for myself? It is something you want me to do for you?"

"That's not what I meant! I—"

The *Bonanza* theme cut me off, which was probably just as well. "Hi," I said, watching my mother turn and walk out of the room. "Where have you been?"

"Legwork," came Bill's rational, though worried, voice. "You okay? Where are you?"

"I'm down the rabbit hole. Otherwise I'm fine."

"What does that mean?"

"I'm trying to talk my mother into going out to Queens for a few days. Those guys who broke into my office, I don't know what they were after. In case they didn't find it and think it might be here, I want her out."

"But she won't go?"

"What do you think?"

"Maybe you should tell her I agree with her. I don't think she should go."

"You don't?"

"Sure I do. I'm using reverse psychology."

"Forget it. We tried that when we were kids. There's no kind of psychology that works on my mother."

"Tell me about the break-in."

I did, leaving out the Duke of Hell.

"The White Eagles?" Bill asked. "How do you suppose they're involved?"

"I don't know. They run protection rackets on some of the jewelers, but that doesn't get me very far."

"Like your pal Mr. Chen?"

"I don't know."

"Could they have thought you had the Shanghai Moon?"

"And just dropped it in my in-box? Even White Eagles can't be that dumb. Well, they could, but I don't think so. If I could get over there and go through the mess, I might figure it out, but I don't want to leave my mother alone if—" I stopped in midsentence.

"Lydia? You still there? What's up?"

"I have to go. I'll call you back."

"What's wrong?"

"Nothing. It's fine. But I'll call you back."

I lowered the phone and gaped. My mother stood before me, traveling hat on, suitcase in hand.

29

When I finally called Bill back, from my brother's place in Flushing, I told him to meet me at my office in an hour and a half. "And bring your boy detective kit."

"Why?"

"Because my mother's a genius."

He didn't respond to that, as well he shouldn't. And admittedly it's not something I say often. On the way to Queens, though, she'd outdone herself.

Not that she'd meant to be helpful. She'd meant to keep complaining. "Send your mother all the way to Flushing again," she'd grumbled. "When she has not been back in her own home for one week yet." That was at the station, after we'd stopped at a tea shop for red bean buns. Ted's kids love them, and though you can get them at a bakery two blocks from their house, my mother swears no one in Flushing, with the exception of Ling-an when she's not too busy, can cook. We also picked up cream puffs, almond cookies, and chocolate tarts with green frosting that looked like something Bill might eat. Which I didn't mention.

Once we were on the subway, bakery boxes in pink plastic bags, my mother had another thought. "Chin Ling Wan-ju! If you are in the apartment alone when the gang boys come, who will keep *you* safe?" She stood, ready to turn and go back.

To tell the truth, I was surprised this hadn't come up sooner. I was ready. "Sit down, Ma. I'm going to get alarms for the door and the kitchen window. And I'll keep the window locked. But I really don't think anyone will come while I'm there. I was mostly worried that they'd wait until I went out and break in while *you* were there."

"Why will they not come while you are there?"

Because I have a gun. No, Lydia, don't say that. "They waited until my office was empty. They seem to not want to run into me."

She narrowed her eyes, but for a while after that she sat silent. Then, in a mutter that grew steadily louder, she picked up her earlier theme. The first words I made out were ". . . valued our elders." I guessed what was coming. "Children today, no respect," she told no one in particular. "Make their parents leave home, go far away."

"Ma, I—"

"Your cousin Danny." She gave me a dirty look, like every bad thing Danny had ever done was my fault. "Sent his mother all the way to China."

"She wanted to see her home village. Danny paid for the trip. He's very generous."

"He should have gone with her, not make her go alone."

"She's not alone. She's on a tour."

"With strangers."

"And her sister and two of her best friends!"

"And strangers. Instead of their own children. And your cousin Clifford. A very unfilial son. Made his mother go to New Jersey."

"Clifford Kwan? Armpit? He sent his mother to New Jersey?"

She frowned at me. "No wonder he is bad. People call him disgusting names."

"He's proud of that name."

"Does that make it not disgusting?"

"What do you mean, he sent his mother to New Jersey?"

"The son caused the mother so much heartache, the mother moved away."

"Oh. So he didn't send her away. She moved to the suburbs."

"He made her go away by breaking her heart."

"Ma, Clifford's been rotten from the day he was born. I'm surprised Kwan Shan didn't kick him out of the house years ago."

She rolled her eyes. Once again I'd failed to understand something basic. "It would be better if you could choose your relatives. Get ones you want, throw away bad ones. But you can't. The child you get is the child you have to keep." Her narrowed eyes told me that, by the way, I should consider myself lucky this was true. As if to emphasize her point, she added, "It was when Kwan Shan left Chinatown that her son became involved with gang boys."

I wasn't having any. "I thought you said his bad behavior made her move away."

"Now she will not come back. She is ashamed to show her face."

"She's probably just happy in her nice new apartment. With a garden. Near her grandchildren."

"What mother could be happy when her youngest son is a White Eagle?"

"Ma—what?"

"I said—"

"I know what you said. Armpit's a White Eagle? Since when?"

"Auntie Ro, at the pharmacy, told me. Her brother-in-law, who makes tattoos, drew a white eagle on Clifford three days ago. Auntie Ro says that means he is accepted as one of them."

It sure did. "Why didn't you tell me?"

"Oh, have you been home for me to tell you? I'm sorry, Ling Wan-ju, I must not have noticed."

When I got to my office, I found Bill shooting the breeze with the Golden Adventure ladies. They all but batted their eyes when he said good-bye. Well, good. Anything to keep them thinking I was a worthwhile subtenant.

"How did you talk your mother into going?" he asked as we went down the hall.

"Believe me, I didn't. I told her I didn't want to have to worry about her. She said, 'Oh, this is for you, not for me?' and I thought she was mad. Next thing I knew she was looking for her MetroCard."

"Son of a bitch."

"I hope that's for the mess and not my mother?" I could tell it was, though, by the way he'd stopped inside my door and was staring around.

"All these papers were on your desk? That's amazing."

"Oh, give me a break. They went through the files, too."

"I'd sure like to know what they were after."

"So? Get to work and I'll start digging."

Bill headed for the bathroom with his toolbox. He can be a pain, but he has his good points. One is, he has some manual skills I've never mastered: hammering nails straight, driving a stick shift. And lifting fingerprints. He can do that, too.

"Rough, dry surfaces." He examined the sill and bars. "I don't know how much I can get."

"It doesn't matter. Just be thorough. And do as much as you can from outside. And take your time."

While Bill was playing with powders and brushes, I picked up papers. The scattered folders and any papers whose provenance was obvious I refiled. Then I went through what was left. What I was doing was in the nature of carving away the marble to get to the statue. By clearing up everything I could, I was hoping to discover what wasn't there.

"Tell me about the Shanghai cop," Bill called through the window as he worked. "Is he any good, do you think?"

"Hah! A story in itself. Oh, my God, and a big one!" I stopped in the middle of my piles of paper. "I didn't tell you about Alice."

"What about Alice?"

"It's long. And bad. And involves the Chinese cop." I described Inspector Wei, which made him grin. Then I told him about the likelihood Alice Fairchild was involved in the jewel theft with Wong Pan, and the grin faded.

"That would explain a lot," he said. "And change everything."

"It sure would."

"Is Mary looking for her?"

"You bet. I called her again, too, but of course she didn't answer."

The locksmith showed up right as Bill was finishing. He raised his eyebrows at the fingerprint powder all over everything. "Run-of-the-mill B and E?" he said to me. "How come you rate?"

"Homeland Security," Bill offered without looking up.

An hour later my window had a case-hardened dead bolt and bars, my office was neater than it had been in months, and we still had no idea what had gone on. All my papers were accounted for. If the burglars were after anything besides making a mess and driving up my blood pressure, I couldn't see that they'd had much success.

Neither had Bill, it looked like. "A partial palm. A smear. And what might be a thumb up by the lock."

"I bet that's mine. Oh, well, that wasn't the point. What's 'case-hardened'?"

"Your pal Mulgrew."

"What?"

"A cop who's lost all human emotion."

"Okay, be like that." I took out my phone and dialed. I spoke briefly in Cantonese with Armpit Kwan's heartbroken mother in New Jersey. Then I called the cell phone number she gave me for her heart-breaking son.

"Yah?" Well, it was the right number. That was Armpit: nasal and aggrieved.

"Hi, Clifford. It's your cousin Lydia."

"I don't have—"

"Lydia Chin, Armpit. You do have: Our mother's fathers were sec-ond cousins twice removed." Or something. Whatever it was, he didn't know it, I'd bet on that. "Your White Eagle homies broke into my office this afternoon and I want to know why."

"Lydia Chin?" Armpit paused in pretend thought, which is the only kind he has. "Oh, *that* Lydia."

"Why, Armpit?"

"Why what?"

"My office!"

"Aw, cuz, you're tripping."

"Don't let's go through all that. They were here, they made a mess, and you're going to tell me why."

"I don't know shit about anything."

"That's *all* you know about anything, but I want to hear it anyway. You want to meet uptown where no one knows us, or you want me to come find you in Chinatown?"

"No way I'm meeting you."

"Then I'll find you, and your new friends will see us together."

"No way you're finding me, either." Armpit was stuck in a groove.

"Cousin, I'm a private eye, remember? I can do pretty much everything the cops can do"—I put a little weight on "cops"—"and I don't have to be as careful about legal niceties." I wondered if anyone had ever used "nicety" in conversation with Armpit before. "I can trace your phone. No, don't hang up, it's already too late. And I can also lift fingerprints."

A half-second delay. "So?" He was buying it, so I stepped it up.

"I have three sets of prints here. Later I'm going to send them to a private lab I use. Unless I have something better to do, like talk to my cousin. One set's small. The kid, Armpit. You sent in a kid, and once I know who it was you can bet I'm telling his parents. And their family association, and their village association, and whatever tong their village association headman belongs to. And the beauty of it, Cousin Clifford, is that all those people, who will then go out of their way to give the White Eagles as hard a time as they possibly can, will know it was *your* cousin who jammed the White Eagles up. And the White Eagles will know it, too. Now: uptown, or right there where you are?"

And bless Armpit's cowardly, probably stoned, and inarguably stupid little heart, if he didn't suggest a pizza place on Union Square. Which was a good thing, because while Bill could lift fingerprints, we had no way to ID some ten-year-old from prints even if he'd left any, which he didn't. The point of Bill dusting and lifting was to make sure the locksmith, the travel ladies, and any curious onlookers above could confirm we'd dusted and lifted. Also, though certain technologies available to the police are in fact available to PIs, I couldn't trace a cell phone call. So it was good he'd told me where to meet him, because right at that moment I had not the first idea where Armpit was.

30

Bill and I subwayed up to Union Square. We found Armpit Kwan in Vinnie's Pies, stuffing into his pasty face a slice mounded with every ingredient anyone ever thought to put on a pizza.

"Who's he?" Armpit sullenly demanded as Bill dropped into a chair.

"Bill Smith," I said. "Another detective. What's that?"

"Pizza, dumb-ass. I didn't say I'd talk to him. Just you." Or words to that effect, extruded through crust, salami, peppers, and pineapple. Sauce plopped onto Armpit's shirt, joining something brown from yesterday, or last week, or whenever his heartbroken mother had last done his laundry.

"Well, you will talk to him." I was grateful for the garlic in the air. Like most gang nicknames, Armpit didn't choose his own, and it didn't come from nowhere. "He and I work together."

"Shit, Cousin Lydia. I thought you were a big tough girl. Didn't know you were working for a *baak chit gai*." The term he used means literally "chicken roasted without soy sauce." It's what the gangs call white people these days.

"Actually," Bill said, "I work for her. I'm the muscle. So she doesn't have to get her pretty hands dirty." He crowded Armpit a little. Armpit pulled back, but all that got him was pressed against the wall.

"Listen," I said. "I want to know what the White Eagles were after in my office. And whether they got it. You tell me that, I'll even pay for your pizza."

"Oh, big whoop."

"And if you don't," Bill said in a friendly fashion, "I'll cram it and the box it came in down your throat."

"Fuck you!" Armpit, starting to rise, clonked into a badly colorized photo of Sicily.

"Armpit! Sit down! Bill, leave him alone. He's my cousin. He's co-operating." This was about the cheesiest good cop/bad cop routine Bill and I had ever done, but Armpit was a cheap date.

"Well, you lose, cuz." Armpit sank back, gave Bill another glare, and curled his lip at me. "I don't know what the deal was."

"Armpit, I know you're just a wannabe with that gang, but I need to find out—"

"Fuck you! A wannabe?" He yanked up his sleeve to expose his red, swollen shoulder, where a misshapen eagle screamed in for a landing. If this was Auntie Ro's brother-in-law's work, I hoped he had a day job. "You don't get one of these if you're a wannabe. I'm *made,* baby."

Made? Chinatown gangs were recycling Mafia slang? *Where's your cultural pride?* I wanted to ask. Instead, I said, "I don't see how that can be true, if you don't know anything about what went down today."

Trapped like a rat. Bright spots flared in Armpit's cheeks. "I didn't say I don't know *anything.* I said I don't know what the deal was, and I fucking don't."

In a flash Bill grabbed his wrist. "Clean up your language. Ms. Chin doesn't like to hear that."

Armpit tried and failed to pull away. "Ow." He stared in offended amazement.

I said, "What does that mean?"

Armpit swung back to me. "Huh?"

"You don't know what the deal was, but you don't not know any-thing? Does that mean something? I hope so. Because if it's just words, I have to tell you, Bill hates words."

Bill let Armpit go and reached for his Coke, which he downed probably so he wouldn't laugh out loud.

"Hey!" Armpit protested as his caffeine and sugar vanished. "Ly-dia!"

I gave him a benign smile. "It-tee-bit-tee fingerprints. Four fulls and two partials. Whose can they be?"

"Jesus Christ, cuz, you're a pain in the ass. *What?*" Armpit said as Bill leaned toward him. "Oh, screw it. I don't know the deal because we didn't plan the job. We don't give a shit—all right!—about your office, cuz. Some guy hired us."

"Who?"

"I don't know. I don't! *Dai lo* didn't tell us." *Dai lo*, literally "big brother," is a Chinatown gang leader's title. "He just said we'd get good money to distract the travel ladies, open the place up, and let this guy in."

"Let him in? The White Eagles didn't search the office themselves?"

"Why would we? What the— What do you have that we could ever want?"

"What did the guy want?"

"How would I know?"

"Does your *dai lo?*"

Armpit rolled his eyes.

"Find out."

"What?"

"Find out. Who it was, what he wanted."

"You're crazy."

"No, Bill's crazy," I said. Bill leered crazily. "I'm just your cousin with some little kid's fingerprints."

"I can't." Armpit's voice rose in pitch as it lowered in volume. "I can't ask *dai lo* shit like that. What if he doesn't know? If the guy didn't tell his name, ever think of that? *Dai lo* will think I'm trying to make him look bad."

"Explain you're being blackmailed. Fishface Deng, he's your *dai lo,* right? He'll understand."

"You're shitting me."

"Yes, of course. But whatever it takes, Armpit. By tomorrow morning."

"Oh, man. Don't do this to me."

"What's the problem? You're made. You're on the inside. Congratulations, by the way."

Armpit ran his greasy hand through his hair. "It's new," he mumbled.

"What?"

"The tat. Just got it."

"Yes, so I understand. You've achieved your goal, Armpit. Now achieve mine."

A look of desperation stole into his red-rimmed eyes. "*Dai lo* needs guys he can trust. For this big score coming up. That's how come." He pointed to his shoulder. "It's my chance. Don't screw me, cousin."

The third-stringer called off the bench into the big game. The understudy stepping into the spotlight. Who could fail to be moved? "Okay, you can have until tomorrow night."

"Oh, man! Oh, no, come on, give me a break."

"I'm sorry, what?"

"This bullshit"—he cringed away from Bill, but Bill only smiled encouragingly—"what happened in your office. If I rat it out, *dai lo* will kill me."

Sad to say, that might be literally true. And if I thought my mother was displeased when I'd sent her out to Queens, just wait until she learned I'd sent my cousin Clifford on to his next life.

Armpit pushed, sensing my wavering. "And the big score. I don't want to screw my chances, you know, in that. There's serious money involved. And besides money . . ." He stopped, with the wide eyes of a punk who, even stupid and stoned, realizes he's said too much.

"What, besides money? What is there for guys like White Eagles, besides money? Well, cheap sex and bad drugs. Is that what you're afraid you'll be missing?"

He glared and picked up his Coke. Discovering it empty, he slammed the can onto the table. It made a pretty feeble noise, but I nodded at Bill, who got up and came back with two Cokes and a seltzer. Armpit snapped one open, glugged some, peeled a sausage from his congealing slice, and stuffed it between slick lips. Finally he spoke. "*Dai lo* has this idea. That's why he needs guys. We're gonna be, like, a private army."

"You're what?"

"For hire."

"You're *what*?"

Exasperated, he explained. "Because the score, we got hired for that, too. Like, that was first, then your thing. But, so, we can be this private army, that's what *dai lo*'s thinking. Word'll get around. People will come to us."

I exchanged looks with Bill. "Well, isn't that wonderful? Ambition. Beautiful. Tell me about the score, Armpit."

He shook his head. "I don't know. They tell me where and when it goes down, I show up. That's all."

"Show up and do what?"

"Whatever they tell me! Nobody'll get hurt. For real, swear to God. Lydia, come on, don't fuck this up for me!"

"You don't know where, when, or what's going down, but you swear no one will get hurt?" *Oh, no,* I thought. *I sound like my mother.* "Let's go at it this way: You've been casing jewelry shop windows. How is that sleazy activity related to the big score?"

"Wasn't." If he'd been trying to send the message *I'm lying,* he couldn't have done better than the mumble and darting eyes that went with that word.

I sat back. "You're knocking over a jewelry shop."

"Uh-*uh*."

"Oh, not a jewelry shop job? So you do know what it is."

"I fucking *do not*! But it's sure as shit not something as lame as that."

I took a chance: "Mr. Chen's shop? Bright Hopes?"

"No way." His voice dripped derision, but color flared through his video-arcade pallor.

"Mr. Chen's a friend of mine." So what if Mr. Chen wasn't speaking to me? "I'd hate to see anything happen to him."

"Oh, jeez, cuz! Nothing's going to happen to Old Man Chen! He's not even—"

"He's not even what?"

"Anyone I know. He's not even anyone I know." Armpit was visibly, pitifully proud of how he'd saved that one.

Bill leaned closer. "And this big fucking deal big fucking score you don't fucking know anything about. It's related to what happened at Lydia's office exactly fucking how?"

Armpit watched Bill nervously. "Who says it is?"

"I do."

"You're full of— You're wrong." Armpit stammered, but, in an impressive display of nerve and will, he got that out.

"Armpit," I said, "did the same guy hire you for both jobs?"

"No. That's why *dai lo*'s so happy."

"Why?"

He looked at me as though I were the one whose On light wasn't lit. "Because word must be getting around already! Before we even do the first job, we get another one. The customer's happy, he tells other people, then the second customer's happy, he tells more people, and there you go: the Chinatown White Eagles, Soldiers of Fortune."

"The Chinatown White Eagles, *what*?" Mary couldn't have sounded more incredulous if I'd told her they'd all taken Buddhist vows.

"I know. But doesn't it sound like you should be keeping an eye on them?"

"You don't know anything about this big score?"

"No, except they'll never pull it off if they let Armpit anywhere near it. But I don't think it's as simple as robbing a jewelry store."

"You said Mr. Chen's name got a reaction."

"Maybe he pays his protection money to the White Eagles, so Armpit knows him. I think Armpit really doesn't know what's going on. He's a bad liar."

"And you're not going to make him find out about your break-in?"

I sighed. "It's too risky. He'd be as obvious to his *dai lo* as he was to me. I don't like the guy, but he is my cousin."

"If we break this big score, I might have to arrest him."

"Be my guest. I just can't be the one who gets him killed." She wasn't happy, I could tell, but she was Chinese, so she got it. "I did keep some leverage. He's really scared about the fingerprints, that the tongs will come down on the White Eagles and he'll be blamed. So I promised I won't use them for a while, assuming he gives me something useful at some point in the future."

"Don't hold your breath."

"I won't. But it's not a bad trade, since I don't have fingerprints."

"If the big score has anything to do with a jewelry shop, even if it's not a burglary," Mary thought out loud, "it's got to be one the White Eagles shake down. They wouldn't dare cross another gang, even if they were being paid."

"That occurred to me, too. Can you find out which real estate is theirs?"

"Patino's up on that, the maps and charts. And maybe I can get a line on one of these customers. I'll see if anyone knows who's been hanging around with the White Eagles' *dai lo*. Or I could just pick him up."

"Fishface Deng? And do what? He'd get a lawyer, you'd get nothing, and he'd know you know they have something big coming up."

"I hate to just wait and let it happen."

"I sympathize. But I'll keep the pressure on Armpit. He may come through yet. And whatever it is, and even if it isn't related to my break-in—"

"Which you're sure it is."

"I don't know. Maybe not. But even if it isn't, won't it be great for your career when you catch the White Eagles with their hands in the rice jar?"

"Where to, boss?" I pocketed my phone. Bill and I stood in the muggy evening watching the skateboarders rattle down the Union Square steps.

"You're the boss. I'm just the crazy, word-hating muscle."

"I'm tired of that. I want to be the muscle for a while. Being the boss takes too much thinking."

"Works for me. If I'm the boss, you're fired."

"Now you sound like Alice."

Wouldn't you know. As soon as I said her name, my phone tinkled the new-client song.

I threw it open and stuck it to my ear. "Lydia Chin. Alice? Is that you?"

"Lydia? Yes, it's me."

"Where are you?" One finger in my ear to block the traffic and the skateboards, I tried to make my voice normal. She didn't know how much I knew, and I didn't want to spook her.

"Lydia, I need to talk to you."

"Yes, I think we should. Are you back in New York? I'm free right now."

"How about later tonight? About eleven? In Sara Roosevelt Park."

That threw me. "That park's not the most savory place at that hour. Why not—"

"No, Sara Roosevelt Park at eleven."

"Why?"

"It needs to be someplace unexpected. I can't risk being seen."

"What are you talking about?"

Then she put an end to my attempt at normal. "Lydia, it's Wong Pan. He says he's got the Shanghai Moon."

31

"Sara Roosevelt Park at eleven?" Mary was only slightly less incredulous than ten minutes before. "Why there?"

"I don't know."

"Okay, we'll be there."

"So will we."

"No."

"Yes! Mary, she'll be casing it, you know she will. She won't show unless she sees us."

"I'll have someone there who looks like you."

"*Both* of us? Even if you did, she might not buy it. Besides, we don't know what she wants to tell me. Don't you want to know?"

"Maybe she doesn't want to tell you anything. Maybe she wants to shoot you."

"Then why call? Why not just stalk me? Come on, Mary, she may give up something you can use. Or something Inspector Wei can use. Just let us talk to her. Then you can pick her up."

"It's dangerous."

"Danger's my middle name."

"Lydia's your middle name." I could feel the friend wanting to protect me and the cop wanting to close her case. I tried to help out the cop.

"Remember, she doesn't know I'm onto her."

"How do you know?"

"She didn't have to make contact. She could have stayed disappeared."

Mary didn't answer. I was right and she knew it. "And you don't know where she is now?"

"If I did, wouldn't I have told you?" Again, no answer. "Okay, okay, but probably I would have. Anyway, she hung up as soon as the magic words—'Shanghai Moon'—were out of her mouth. And don't I get a Good Citizen Award for calling you now?"

"With a gold star. And if you hear from her again before eleven, you'd better go for another one."

"Yeah, and when you make First Grade based on my inside info, you'd better remember whose inside info it was."

"And you remember this: if you feel at any time tonight, at any *instant,* that you're in danger, you send me a signal."

"I'll scratch my head, how's that? But come on, Bill will be with me."

"Not the same Bill I called the other day, to suggest he call you? No, it couldn't be that one, you were mad about that."

Between Mary's needling and the grin that popped up on Bill's face when he heard me use him to reassure her, I felt like the ham in the sandwich.

"And," Mary said, "of course you'll be wearing your Kevlar?"

"Yes, Mom. Though if Alice wanted to do me in, I still don't see why she'd have bothered to call and arrange a meeting."

"To make sure you were in a dark park in the middle of the night?"

"Oh. Well, besides that."

Closing the phone, I asked Bill, "Are you hungry?"

He toed out his cigarette. "You're saying that after watching your cousin and that pizza, you'd ever consider food again?"

"You drank his Coke. From the same can his lips had touched."

"That was line-of-duty. Trying to impress my boss with my dedication."

"What, you want a raise?"

"No," he said. "I just want to keep the job."

I met his eyes, then turned away, not sure at all how to answer that.

• • •

We picked up vegetable dumplings, Mongolian beef, and stir-fried water spinach to take out. The place we went to is a hole-in-the-wall
with three tables. Two were empty, so we could have stayed, but I had
a strong urge to eat in my office, feet on the desk, takeout containers
everywhere.

"Reclaiming your territory," Bill said, hefting the bag off the
counter. "If you were a dog you'd be peeing in the corners."

"Thank you, Dr. Freud. It's more like I just don't want to have to
deal with other people." That's what I said, and that's what I thought.
So when we opened my office door and everything was just as I'd left
it, the relief that washed over me was a surprise. I tore off yesterday's
page from the Far Pagoda Tofu Factory calendar while Bill extracted
containers from the bag. "You know what I'm thinking?"

"I never do."

"That I'd like to pee in the corners. No, seriously. It's . . ." I tried to
frame my thoughts. "I don't care much about *stuff,* you know?"

"I know."

"And this stuff"—I waved my chopsticks around—"it's strictly Sal-
vation Army. But it's *mine.* Whoever the White Eagles let in here
didn't break anything and didn't steal anything, but I'm furious anyway. Does that make sense?"

"Absolutely."

I dipped a dumpling in sauce and made quick work of it. "You
know what else?"

"What else?"

"Rosalie. Elke. All those people having to leave their stuff behind,
or watching the Nazis take it or smash it and they couldn't do anything. And people's whole families being killed. People you loved,
cousins you didn't even know you had. It makes me think about what
Joel said about Holocaust asset recovery being a religious calling. It's
not about the stuff, is it?"

"No." Bill sat with his legs extended, just fitting alongside my desk.
It was, I realized, his usual spot; years ago I'd moved the desk over to
give him more room. "But it generally isn't about the stuff. Even when
it is. Even when the motivator is greed. It's about having. Staking out

your territory, making it bigger and bigger and giving yourself more corners to pee in as though more and bigger will protect you."

"From?"

"The fact that really, you can't control anything."

I thought about that as I speared some water spinach. "And Mr. Chen."

"What about him?"

"The Shanghai Moon. It was his mother's. He lost *her*, and he's spent his life looking for *it*. I get that, now."

We ate in silence for a while, until finally we ran out of things to eat.

"I'm still hungry," I said.

"I know."

"What do you mean, you know?"

"You always eat a lot when your adrenaline's pumping. Like when you've been in a fight. Or now."

"We should have gotten roast pork," I said.

"Uh-huh. And a *baak chit gai*."

"You know that term?"

"I'm not as white as I look."

Luckily, I didn't need to answer that. A cell phone rang, but when I grabbed mine up, it nestled in my hand in innocent silence. "Smith," Bill said into the one that was actually ringing. Glancing at me, he said, "That's great. Can't wait to hear it, but can you call back? We're at Lydia's office. We'll put you on speaker." He gave my office number, and in the ten seconds between one call and the other, he told me, "Professor Edwards."

"Oh, good. But you know, your cell phone has a speaker function." He looked at it blankly as my desk phone rang. I hit the button. "Hi, Professor. How are you?"

"Just jim-dandy," Professor Edwards's voice boomed. "My researcher found you some stuff. I might have to give her an A."

"It's that good?"

"From where I sit. No idea whether it's useful to you, though. Come to think of it, it was pretty much all in the same place—

German war records, China division—so maybe it'll just be an A minus. Ready?"

"Shoot," said Bill.

"Your boy Ulrich, Gunther. Rank: Major. Sent to Shanghai 1938. Want to know why?"

"Why?"

"He was a pain in the Führer's ass, that's why. Now, I could have told you that without wasting this young woman's time looking anything up. The only officers the Reich shipped to Shanghai to help out their very close allies and personal friends the Japanese were the ones they didn't want screwing up the home front."

"You mean incompetents?" Bill asked.

"Not necessarily. Sometimes, if a guy was a moron but well connected, yes. But they sent Robert Neumann there. The Butcher of Buchenwald, you've heard of him. He was good at his job, which was gruesome experiments and murder. But someone decided he was out of control, which by the way he was. So good-bye Dr. Neumann. With Ulrich, it was his mouth got him in trouble. He thought Hitler was misguided on some issues, imagine that. Particularly he suggested they might be focusing a tad too obsessively on Jews, gays, and Gypsies and ought to consider putting resources into defeating other countries' militaries instead of rounding up civilians—their own and everyone else's—and spending good German marks, which were less good every day, building places to put them and paying people to guard and kill them."

"A champion of human rights."

"A practical soldier. That Master Race thing drained off a lot of Nazi resources. Brought them down, in the end. But no one wanted to hear it. So they ship Ulrich to Shanghai with his wife and kid. For work, he's supposed to sniff around the Chinese puppet military, make sure no one's thinking of overthrowing the Germans' very close allies and personal friends the Japanese. So he does, and before you can say Jackie Robinson he's running around with General Zhang. The brother-in-law-to-be of your boy, Chen Kai-rong."

"Yes," I said. "We remember who he is."

"Good, you might pass after all. Ulrich and Zhang get to be bung-hole buddies, and Ulrich, that flower of Aryan manhood, flourishes in the rich Shanghai soil. Fertilized, it seems, by the dung at the bottom: gambling dens, bars, establishments of ill repute."

"Flower houses," I said.

"Show-off," he replied.

"I'm not the one who laid out the extended metaphor. Do you do that all the time?"

"If you spent your life trying to wake up stoned snoring slackers—hey, look, I can do alliteration, too. Now, shall I fast-forward to Ulrich's demise?"

My sense was that any conversation with Professor Edwards was already on fast-forward, but I said, "Yes, please do."

"February 23, 1943. Recognize the date?"

"Yes, I do, but I'm not sure why."

"You flunk. That's the day the Shanghai Municipal Police arrested your boy, Chen Kai-rong. It was the beginning of the end for Major Ulrich here."

"Why? What did he do?"

"Well, now, that's an interesting question. Seems he called his very close et cetera the Japanese, asked them to suggest to the SMP that they treat Chen Kai-rong with kid gloves. Chen was his buddy Zhang's brother-in-law, after all. Zhang must have called him."

"No. There was no love lost between the general and Kai-rong. Mei-lin asked the general to help, and he said Kai-rong was a traitor and should rot in jail. She called Ulrich herself."

"How do you know that?"

"It's in Mei-lin's diary. But we didn't know who Ulrich was."

"That's the diary that you're going to let me read any minute now."

"Yes, that one."

"As soon as we're sure people aren't being killed because of it," Bill said. "We wouldn't want to lose you."

"Obviously I'm not on your thesis committee. They all want to lose me. So. Ulrich calls the SMP. The SMP, eager to oblige, send Chen back to his cell. Actually we covered that in yesterday's lecture, working from a different source."

The professor paused, and though I couldn't see him I knew he was peering over his glasses.

"Yes," I said. "I remember."

"You, too, Smith?"

"Yessir, sir."

"Good, you might pass, too. Okay, so maybe you remember what happens next. The sister says the Commie ain't her brother, it's her husband. She hands over what she says is the general's list of agents, which U.S. naval intelligence tells us was really her brother's all along. But first she calls everyone on it and tells them to make themselves scarce. And they do. And the brother escapes. And she and Zhang escape."

"She escaped?" I said, hope springing. "I thought you said the navy said the general killed her."

"I did, they did, and he did, for sure. But the SMP doesn't know that, do they? Our historical perspective eludes them. All they know is, they've got zilch. Zero. Goose eggs. So now they're really mad. If they'd applied the usual pressure to Chen Kai-rong, the thinking goes, he might have cracked. The Japanese say, but he wasn't the spy. The SMP says, then how come he ran away? Along with, they point out, *everybody* else.

"The Japanese are embarrassed. They didn't just lose the police some crook. These were Commies! Oh, no! And the only guy they can put their mitts on is Ulrich. So they do. They haul him to Bridge House, which was a lower circle of the same hell as Number 76, run by the Japanese themselves. To make sure he comes clean, they scoop up his wife and kid and slap them in an internment camp. This was almost unheard of, interning their very dear friends the Germans, except for being Allied spies. Then the Germans straightened it out if they weren't, or the Japanese shot them if they were."

"And in this case?"

"Unfortunately for the wife and kid, this turned out to be a special case. Ulrich, in the middle of being persuaded to spill the beans, up and died."

"The Japanese killed him?"

"Seems to have been an accident. Had a seizure, bingo, the end. Whether the electrodes or the baling wire or the big tub of ice water had anything to do with it, I couldn't tell you. But it was damned inconvenient. The Japanese couldn't prove he was a Commie rat. The Germans couldn't prove he wasn't, either. So they did the only sensible thing. They forgot all about it."

"Just like that?"

"You know, get some closure, put it behind you, move on! Come on, everybody's doin' it! The Ulrich affair was forgotten and everyone lived happily ever after. Except the wife and kid. The Germans started tentative negotiations to get them out, but the Japanese were of the opinion the wife might know something. Or said they were. They were probably just saving face. But the Germans backed off. Some dame, some brat, what did they care? Keep 'em, they said. So the Japanese did."

"What happened to them?"

"They died." He sounded wistful. I suddenly wondered what it was like to be a historian, involved with people who'd lived and died long before you came across them. "Those camps weren't nice places. Not much to eat, and a lot to get sick on. The mother went first, not long after they got there, late 'forty-three, cholera. The kid died July 'forty-four."

"Dr. Edwards? How many of those internment camps did the Japanese have?"

"In Shanghai, eight. In other parts of China there were a few more, but generally they didn't ship prisoners up the river."

"Which one were Ulrich's wife and child in?"

"Chapei. Why?"

"Just wanted to know."

"Pure intellectual curiosity! Refreshing as a Tsingtao ale. Chapei wasn't any nicer than any of the others, I can tell you that."

"Are there records from the camps?"

"What kinds of records?"

"Lists of internees, I was thinking."

"It's hard to say how accurate they are. How would we know who's missing? But they exist."

"Can you find out if an American missionary family named Fairchild was also in the Chapei camp?"

"Might do. That would require my researcher to ferret out another set of documents in another language, so she might get her A after all. But you're not about to tell me why, are you?"

"Not yet, no. I'm sorry. But you've been a big help."

"I'm tickled. And now *I* have a question for *you*."

"Go ahead."

"If Ulrich's buddy General Zhang wanted his brother-in-law Chen to rot, and if Ulrich's mission was to cozy up to guys like Zhang, why did Ulrich bite when Chen's sister called? Was she Ulrich's bit on the side?"

"No. She couldn't stand him."

"Well, if it wasn't sex it must have been money."

"In a way. She promised him the moon."

Professor Edwards said he'd call us with information on the Fairchilds if he found it, and we said we'd let him know what it was all about as soon as we could. After we hung up, Bill lit a cigarette. "You said that about promising Ulrich the moon to show you're as clever as the professor."

"Don't be ridiculous. That would imply I'm the competitive type."

"Oh, right, and that's nuts, isn't it? Listen, when we get a minute we'd better copy that diary for him. I think he deserves it."

I nodded vaguely, distracted by something I couldn't quite place.

"Now, in the spirit of intellectual inquiry, I have a question, too," Bill went on. "What if it turns out Alice was in the same camp as Ulrich's wife and child? She was a kid herself. You think she learned something then that would tell her now where to find the Shanghai Moon? Why would it have taken all these years? And how does it tie into what's been going on? And what are you scowling about?"

"This isn't a scowl, it's a contemplative frown. I'm trying to re-member something."

"What?"

"How do I know? I don't remember it. Ah! Aha! Mr. Friedman!"

"Aha Mr. Friedman what?"

"I knew this sounded familiar! His book. Didn't it say something about a rumor, a German officer's widow in an internment camp having the Shanghai Moon?"

Bill, also being contemplative, drew on his cigarette. "I think you're right. But that doesn't make it true."

"But it makes it an old rumor. Look: Mei-lin gives it to Ulrich, he slips it to his wife when they come for him."

"Difficult to imagine how she could have kept it hidden in the camp, though I guess she might have. But if she had it, why didn't she use it to bribe their way out? And what happened to it when she died?"

"Maybe she didn't have it, but she knew where it was."

"Same questions."

"Okay, I admit that's all a little fuzzy. But I really, really want to know whether Alice was in that same camp."

Bill got to his feet. "Let's go ask her."

32

Twenty minutes later Bill and I were sitting in the sticky heat of Sara Roosevelt Park. If I'd had a watch, I'd have been checking it every five seconds. I did check Bill's a few times, until, with a sideways look, he pocketed it.

"She won't get here any faster if you do that."

"What if she doesn't come at all?"

"It was her idea," he said.

That didn't particularly reassure me; I have lots of ideas I don't follow through. I scanned for the moon, but the streetlights' glow saturated the haze.

"Do you see Mary? Or any cops?" I asked Bill.

"No."

"Good. Then Alice won't spot them either. Wait! There she is!" By which I didn't mean Mary, and he knew it.

A compact shape in a black straw hat and, despite the darkness, sunglasses, hurried along Chrystie and into the park. She peered around, then headed our way. Bill slid over and made a space between us. Slipping the sunglasses off, Alice Fairchild said, "Thank you both. For indulging me."

Bill didn't answer; my client, my show.

"Alice," I said, "what's going on?"

She watched her hands finger the sunglasses. "Lydia, I'm so ashamed. It's fraud."

No kidding. "Tell us."

"Yes, that's why I'm here." She shoved the sunglasses into her purse as though they suddenly annoyed her. "I can hardly believe I did it, but it's true."

"What is? What did you do?"

She took a deep breath. "I . . . It was all so wrong. It started a few weeks ago, when I heard about jewelry being unearthed in Shanghai."

"How?"

"How I heard? I maintain sources there. No one in the asset recovery community is interested in Shanghai except me. Anything that made it there was by definition not confiscated, you see? But I know how it was there. And I've always thought so much must have been lost, left behind. When I heard about this find, I thought the jewelry might have been a refugee's. I wondered who, and if they had family. Then the next day, sitting at my desk, I suddenly remembered the Shanghai Moon."

"You thought it was part of the find?"

"Oh, no. That news would have gotten out. But I remembered the name of its owner, and the story that she'd had other jewelry. So I did some research. Ambulance chasing, I guess. If I found heirs, I was going to propose that I try to recover it."

"But you didn't."

"I learned two things. One, the find certainly sounded like Rosalie's jewelry. And two, the family was gone. Horst Peretz died in Salzburg in the spring of 1938, Elke Gilder in the Stutthof concentration camp a few years later. I couldn't trace either Rosalie or her brother, Paul, as the Shanghai community broke up. So—"

"He lives in New Jersey."

"What?"

"Paul Gilder. With his granddaughter's family."

"Now? He's still alive?" Her voice dropped to a shocked whisper.

"He came in 1949. Just after Rosalie died."

" 'Forty-nine. They stayed on in Shanghai. That's why the Red Cross had no record. Oh, God. It just gets worse and worse." Shaking her head, she went on. "In any case, I didn't find anyone. Maybe I didn't look as hard as I might have. Because over the next few weeks,

I couldn't get that jewelry out of my mind. I think . . . It's probably self-serving to say I went a little mad, but I think I did. I associate Shanghai with so much unhappiness. And the business I'm in . . . You have to understand how disheartening it is. Emotions run so high. People feel *owed,* though of course what they're really owed they can never get back. Cases take years, and it's hard every step of the way. No one, collectors or museums, banks, governments, no one does anything but throw up roadblocks. And then . . ." She petered out.

"Then?"

"If we do recover anything, the heirs turn around and sell it. Almost always. You see recovered assets on the auction markets all the time. It's not because they're greedy. Once things are returned, people find they can't bear to have them around, knowing why they were lost, knowing who had them all these years. Asset recovery can give you a kind of cold satisfaction, but really, it doesn't make anyone happy."

A gust of wind mixed the shadows around on the path. "So you decided if you personally recovered *these* assets, it would make *you* happy."

"When you put it like that, it sounds awful, but I guess it's true. I got in touch with Wong Pan and went to Shanghai to 'negotiate.'" Her fingers made quote marks. "It wasn't hard to manufacture heirs. I might not have been able to fool the Swiss, or some of the Eastern European countries where a lot of assets ended up. But the Chinese aren't used to these claims.

"Wong Pan, though, turned out to be shrewder than I'd thought. He caught on, I don't know how. And he offered me a deal: He'd expose me, or I'd help him get out of China and we'd split the proceeds."

Bill said, "Sounds like he took a big risk for a hundred thousand dollars, give or take."

"I thought so, too, but I was in no position to argue. His share would have been a few years' salary at his level, so maybe that was temptation enough. Also, I got the feeling this wasn't his first step over the line. Things might have been getting a little hot for him in Shanghai.

"When he suggested the deal, I woke up. That's what it felt like, waking up. I was appalled by what I'd tried to do. I'd have given any-thing to be back in my office in Zurich, slogging through dull paper-work! But I didn't have any choice."

"I can see a few choices," I said. "But go on."

"What you must think of me," she murmured, not meeting my eyes. "In any case: I did it. I got him the papers he needed and fol-lowed him here as we'd arranged. Then everything started to go wrong."

"He gave you the slip."

"That was the first thing. That's why I hired you."

"Why didn't you just go back to Zurich, slog through paperwork, and count your blessings that you were rid of him? If you were so ap-palled at what you'd done?"

"I . . . Oh, I don't know! I think I was afraid of losing track of him. Afraid he still might expose me. I thought, if I could just find him and talk to him . . . But then more things happened, so fast. First, Joel called to tell me you'd found an heir."

"Mr. Chen? But Joel didn't know who Mr. Chen was. I didn't find out until after Joel died."

"But I did. Remember, I've been living with these people longer than you. As soon as Joel decribed his reaction to the photos, I real-ized who he might be. That made everything different, you see?"

"Not really."

"Stealing unclaimed assets is one thing, but stealing from the fam-ily? No, I couldn't. And while I was trying to decide what to do, you called and told me Joel was dead. Then I was really frightened."

"Why?"

"Because I'm sure Wong Pan killed him!"

I was sure, too: Wong Pan told me. "That call to the Waldorf. You did speak to Wong Pan, didn't you?"

"Yes, yes, I spoke to him. He wanted a truce. He needed me. Needed me? Hadn't he already gotten me in enough trouble? I was about to hang up.

"But he said there was something I didn't know: that he'd tricked me, and his bureau in Shanghai, too. I could hear him smirk. He said before I'd ever contacted him, he'd palmed something from the box, something no one else knew was there. The Shanghai Moon."

"Alice, how could he? No one saw it? He opened the box alone? He's lying."

"No, there were three people there to open it, and when they saw it was jewelry, they called the head of the bureau. They all inventoried it, and Wong Pan put it in a safe. But antiquities are his specialty, remember. The box intrigued him. He'd seen ones like it before. It was deeply carved all around, and he played with it, thinking he might find a hidden compartment. Well, he did."

"And the Shanghai Moon was in it?"

"Wrapped in red silk. Of course he'd heard the stories. He knew right away what it was. He pocketed it and was trying to figure out what to do next—he couldn't sell it in Shanghai, obviously—when I came along. Oh, I thought I was so smart! I was completely out of my league. I've never done anything like this in my life! I've been so . . . upright. And now there I was, completely tangled, like a fly in a web."

The Shanghai Moon. C. D. Zhang's words floated back to me. *Casting its web.*

"All right," I said, softening. "I think it's time to go to the police."

"No! Not yet."

"Alice, Wong Pan killed Joel. And he killed that cop who followed him from Shanghai. Shanghai's sent another cop here now. They know you made those documents for Wong Pan."

"They— You knew that? Before I told you?"

"Yes."

"Why did you—"

"We wanted to hear what you had to say."

She sighed. "I guess I deserved that."

"And I guess I understand how you got caught up in this. But it's time to let the police take over."

"No!"

"They'll understand, too. But it's not about you getting in trouble anymore. It's about catching Joel's killer."

"I'm not worried about getting in trouble. I'll take what I've earned. But I want something good to come out of all this first."

"How could that happen?"

"I have an idea."

"Your ideas don't have a stellar track record."

"I know, but this is different. The heir. Your Mr. Chen. I want to give him back the Shanghai Moon."

I didn't know what to say. Bill stepped in. "It would be his anyway. Once Wong Pan's caught—"

Alice shook her head. "It would be evidence. If it's true about the Chinese policeman, it would be evidence in *three* criminal cases—two murders and a theft. On two continents. And it's incredibly valuable. The Chinese government might not be so happy to see it returned to Mr. Chen. At the very least it will be a long battle—after the criminal trials are over. Mr. Chen's an old man. He might never get to hold it in his hand."

I thought about that. To have chased this elusive gem, this jewel that was his mother's, all his life, and then to know it had been found, and not to be able to touch it—that alone could kill Mr. Chen. "What are you proposing?"

"Possession is nine-tenths of the law. Anyone's law. Wong Pan wants to sell it to Mr. Chen."

"Wong Pan knows who he is?"

"No. He knows there are collectors who'd give anything for it. I've told him I've found one, and I want to set up a deal. I said I won't tell him who because he'll cut me out. The police can be there, waiting, you see?" *Sort of like they are right now,* I thought. "As long as they don't interfere before the exchange. Then when they arrest Wong Pan, Mr. Chen will already have the Shanghai Moon. I'm not sure he could be made to give it up. Only the other pieces were inventoried. The killings and the theft can be prosecuted using the inventoried jewelry as evidence. As far as anyone would be able to prove, the Shanghai Moon has always been just a myth."

I watched cars drift up Chrystie Street. A shaft of light and a salsa beat spilled out a half-opened door. The breeze blew my hair across my forehead. I started to reach my hand to smooth it but stopped just in time. If I looked like I was scratching my head, Mary and a platoon of cops might leap from the bushes, guns blazing.

I turned to Alice. "I think you're right."

"You do? Oh, I'm so glad."

"No," I said. "I think you're right about being a little crazy. It's a bad idea, Alice. I'm sorry. I appreciate that you want something good to come from this. But if Wong Pan's already killed two people, we can't mess around with him. We have to go to the police and tell them everything, including how you and he get in touch with each other."

Her face fell. "But . . . are you sure?" She looked to Bill, as though his opinion might be different. He gave her nothing. She said, "You're sure that's what you want?"

"Yes."

Alice nodded disconsolately. The breeze came up again, and she put her hand up to steady her hat.

"Alice," I started, "there's something else we wanted to ask you about. It's—"

A bullet's scream put an end to that. Wood splinters exploded from the bench beside me. A different scream: Alice, jumping, shrieking. What had been an empty park erupted in shouts and running footsteps. A second gunshot; I couldn't tell if it was coming or going, aimed at us or the shooter. I swung behind the bench, gun drawn. Another shot whined, slamming the earth, kicking up a dirt cloud. Bill edged around a tree. I heard Mary's commanding bark, telling her backup where to go, which ones here, which there. *Damn, girlfriend, you sound like the boss of this!* Juiced on adrenaline, I looked around for someone to shoot at or someone to run from. "Lydia! You guys *stay put*!" Mary yelled. Hey, she could read minds, too. Though, stay put behind an open-slatted bench when bullets were flying? Maybe not. But the footsteps faded, there were no more shots, and even with the sirens that wailed up Chrystie doing their best to keep nerves on edge, it soon became clear that whatever this was, it was over. Mary came running down the path, Bill emerged from behind his tree, and I stood up.

"Anyone hurt?" Mary shouted as she neared.

"Not me," I said.

"No," said Bill.

The bad news was there was no third answer. There was no one to give it: Alice was gone.

33

"I will never, never, never listen to you again."

In Interview One at the Fifth Precinct, Bill and I watched Mary pace, or more like stomp, back and forth. Bill wasn't saying anything, probably because he's smarter than I am. I tried every now and then to apologize, or explain, or offer some optimistic angle on the situation, but eventually even I could see that every word I spoke was making things worse.

"Bullets flying all over the park!" Mary fumed. "You idiots almost got killed! And now Alice Fairchild's gone, and the shooter's gone, and citizens could have been shot, and cops could have been shot! And we have nothing!"

She yanked out a chair, took a breath, and said, "All right, go over it again. This time with details."

"Only if you're really going to listen."

"Listen? So you can try one more time to twist everything and make me think it was okay to let you walk head-on into this ludicrous— All right! All right! I'm listening."

My words edged out as though any quick sound might detonate her. When she sat seething but silent, I got more articulate, expanding the outline we'd already sketched. I told her everything Alice had said, including her plan to return the Shanghai Moon to Mr. Chen.

"My God, that's insane! I'm surprised you didn't go along with it."

"That's not fair."

"Really? Now that I think about it, I'm surprised you didn't dream it up. And you didn't make her tell you where Wong Pan is, or how they get in touch?"

That was more like a disgusted statement of fact than a question, but I answered it anyway. "I don't think she knows where he is. Obviously they talk by phone. If you tapped her cell—"

"You think we haven't tried? She's a lawyer and an American citizen and not a terrorist. You tell me where to find a judge to authorize that." She turned to Bill. "What about you?"

"Me? If I were a judge I'd authorize it. I'd authorize anything you wanted."

Mary stared. "Oh, the homegirl and the stand-up comic! What a team!"

"I'm sorry," Bill said. "I'm not giving you a hard time."

"No? What was that, then?"

"I don't mean to. But I have nothing to add to what I already added to what Lydia said."

"You're both useless, you know that? The only good thing is, no one was hurt. I don't mean you two. I'm tempted to hurt you myself. But citizens or cops. Next time someone sets you up to shoot you, Lydia, have them do it someplace private, okay? Oh, now, what could possibly be funny?"

"I just remembered how careful I was not to scratch my head. But Alice adjusted her hat right before the shots. Maybe she was using the same signal." When all Mary did was stare, I said, "Okay, it's the adrenaline talking."

Maybe to keep my foot from getting any deeper into my mouth, Bill asked, "Mary? What if Lydia wasn't the target?"

"What, you think it was you? Some yellow power gang doesn't want whitey in the park?"

Being more generous than I am, he ignored her sarcasm. "If Alice set it up, why put herself in the middle? Whoever fired those shots could easily have done it while we were waiting. Maybe she was the target."

"Alice? Who, Wong Pan? You say he needs her to unload the Shanghai Moon."

"She thinks he does. But what if he's decided he doesn't? If he's figured out who Chen is, or doesn't care because he's found another buyer?"

Mary glowered but stopped yelling, so I chimed in. "Or he doesn't care because, buyer or not, Alice knows too much. Maybe he trailed her to the park."

"How did he pick her up?"

"She's probably not the world's best track-coverer. Maybe he hung around the Waldorf dressed as a bellhop. Okay, I don't mean literally, but it couldn't have been real hard."

"Well, this is just great. We're saying Wong Pan killed two people, he just tried to kill another, we don't know where he is, we don't know where Alice is, and we don't know what'll happen next."

"We may," said Bill.

"What are you talking about?"

"She seemed pretty serious about wanting to make up for what happened. Manic about it, even. She may try it anyway."

"What? Returning the Shanghai Moon to Chen?"

"It's possible."

"But if she didn't set you guys up, she must have figured out by now she was the target and Wong Pan was the shooter."

"So? Suppose she calls him, says, 'Knock off trying to kill me, we'll both make a fortune.' She says to deliver her share to a post office box or something. He'd agree, with no intention of cutting her in, but she'll have no intention of collecting. She'll wait until Chen has the Shanghai Moon. Then she'll call the cops."

"That sounds crazy."

"She may be crazy," I pointed out. "Even she said so."

Mary let a few moments pass. "So with the surveillance I have on Chen, I may get something yet." She stood. "You two? Get out. Go home. Pretend we never met."

"You want a cup of tea?" Bill asked as we left the precinct.

"No. I want to do something useful."

"At one A.M.?"

"With my life. Maybe I should join the Peace Corps."

"Maybe you should go home and go to bed."

"How would that be useful?"

"You'd wake up fresh and sharp, ready to go out and fight crime."

"Or create it. One thing Alice said is true: It just keeps getting worse and worse."

"That's your fault?"

"I'm not helping."

"You don't know that."

"May I point out I just got us into a situation where bullets were flying all over a public park? My best friend lost a collar she'd have looked good making. The jewelry I was hired to trace hasn't turned up, and some innocent old men might be about to get caught in a dangerous sting dreamed up by a client I've lost track of, who's admitted to being involved with someone who's admitted to being a killer. The killer, let me also point out, of the man I was working with."

"For."

"What?"

"You were working *for* Joel. *He* got *you* involved in this case."

I stopped and eyed him accusingly. "Are you trying to tell me I'm not the center of the universe?"

"Of course you are. But things also happen on the periphery of the universe that have nothing to do with the center."

"You," I pronounced, "are full of baloney."

"No argument from me." Bill checked his watch and fished his phone from his pocket.

"It's one A.M. Who're you calling?"

He was busy identifying himself to whoever he was calling, so he didn't answer. He listened. He said, "Are you sure?" and "Thank you." He clicked off and turned to me. "Bingo."

"Bingo what?"

"I told you I was doing legwork. That was payoff."

"For?"

"Well, I got to wondering: If Wong Pan killed Joel, how did he get past security and up to Joel's office?"

"In that building it's not hard."

"No, but it might be worth knowing. So I hit the Chinese restaurants around there and showed his photo. Nothing. But one's open all night. They told me to call back when the night manager was in. He just had a look at the photo. He says that guy got a takeout order of General Tso's chicken a few mornings ago. He remembers because the guy didn't seem to care what he ordered. And he didn't seem to care what it cost. And he ordered in Shanghai-accented English."

I called Mary. "I have a peace offering."

"What? A Trojan horse?"

I told her anyway. "He pretended to be a deliveryman," I finished. "I bet no one in the building even registered they saw him."

"How did Bill get this?" Mary wasn't done being mad yet. "He didn't throw around words like 'government' and 'INS,' did he?"

"More likely words like 'fifty bucks.' But Mary, this is something Mulgrew should have thought of. You can give it to Captain Mentzinger."

"Why? So he'll think you guys are smart?"

"No. So he'll think you are."

By the time we hung up, she was on her way to being mollified, though she wasn't about to admit it.

"So are you good like this all the time, or what?" I asked Bill as we headed down a sweltering and silent Elizabeth Street.

"Modesty forbids the truth."

"I'm annoyed at myself, though. I should have thought of this."

"It's a good thing you didn't. If you thought of everything, what would you need me for?"

I was a little surprised when I came up with a couple of answers to that. But not when I kept them to myself.

Then I did go home. Which turned out to be odd in its own way.

My mother keeps three of the five locks on our door locked at any given time, changing the formula weekly, on the theory that the bad guys will lock the unlocked ones as they pick them. Pulling my key gently out of the last one, which rattles, I stepped in, slipped off my shoes, and tiptoed into the living room. I was halfway across before I remembered there was no need: My mother wasn't here. "Oh," I said, because I couldn't think of anything smarter. I flipped the light on. Everything looked the same as when we'd left. And why shouldn't it? I got ready for bed, trying to think if I'd ever spent the night alone in this apartment. When I was a kid and Ted and Elliot were in high school, my parents would visit cousins, leaving us alone for a night or two, but there were five of us. In college I had my own apartment in Queens for two years, and I've stayed in hotels, and house-sat and pet-sat for friends lots of times, so I've spent the night alone in a lot of places. None of that ever seemed weird.

But this did.

I woke later than usual, after a night of uneasy dreams: shifting images of dark places, a sense of trying to cover a long distance in time I knew was too short. A hovering, sneering, disembodied moon face. In the kitchen I found no boiled water: Well, who'd have put the kettle on? I did that, then whipped it off to dump out the extra water I'd run to make the quart for my mother's thermos. I waved to old Chow Lun leaning on his pillow and, after investigating the fridge, sliced some scallions for congee.

Drinking tea, I ignored the echoing emptiness of the apartment and tried to decide what to make of the day. I didn't get far before the red kitchen phone rang.

"Hey, Lyd, it's Ted."

My heart pounded. "Everything okay with Ma?"

"Sure. She just wanted me to check up on you."

"On me? What could have happened to me since last night?"

"Whatever you thought was going to happen to her. But this isn't real, right? That something dangerous is going on? It's a trick to get Ma to come back out here, isn't it?"

Two of my brothers don't like my job because they worry about me; one enjoys the idea of a PI sister, and besides, he says I should do whatever I want; and one thinks I never do anything right at all and wants me to leave this profession before I embarrass the family. Ted, the eldest, is in the first group. I deflected his question with another.

"Is she driving you nuts?"

"No, she settled right back in downstairs. Went out first thing this morning to check on her melon vines."

"Oh." I felt a pang I couldn't explain. "Is that why she didn't call me herself?"

"The kids are helping her stake them. But she wanted me to tell you she talked to Clifford Kwan's mother this morning. Isn't that Armpit?"

"Yes, remember him?" Ted's eight years older than I am, so our memories of childhood are sometimes different. He, for example, remembers our mother with dark hair. By the time I came along, her older children had already turned her whole head gray. Or so she tells it.

But this time Ted and I were singing the same tune. "Sure I do. Nasty little brat. I guess he never straightened out?"

"Not even close. Why do you say that, though? Did Ma say something about him?"

"Only that I should tell you he's breaking his mother's heart worse than ever, or something like that. He was supposed to go out to Leonia for a big family picnic this afternoon, but he called and said he couldn't make it. His brothers and sisters are all going, so his mom's upset."

"Me, I think she should count her blessings."

"Yeah, but you know mothers. She really wanted him to go because his nephews will be there and she thought playing with them might awaken some family feeling in him."

"Not likely. There's no one on what passes for Armpit's mind but himself."

"That may not be entirely accurate." Ted's a professor of organic chemistry, so he can be a little pedantic. "His excuse broke his mother's heart even more. He said something important was going on in Chinatown today that he had to be there for. He wouldn't tell her what, but he said his new brothers needed him."

"His new brothers? He used those words?"

"According to Ma, that means the White Eagles. Don't you think she's exaggerating, though? Clifford? In a real gang?"

I just said, "Maybe."

"His mom asked, what did he mean his new brothers needed him, what about his old brothers? But Clifford said they'd never liked him anyway."

I was sure they hadn't and were better men for it. I thanked Ted, hung up, and speed-dialed Mary.

"No" was how she answered.

"It's today," I said before she could hang up.

"What is?"

"Whatever the White Eagles are up to. Armpit canceled out on a picnic at his mom's."

"Canceled out on a picnic? And that makes you think—"

"He said something big was happening. In Chinatown, today. That his new brothers needed him for."

"That could be a wet T-shirt party."

"You know I'm right."

"I know you'd better stay away from the White Eagles. I'll check it out, but if it turns out to be anything, I don't want you there." Then she said it again in Cantonese.

"Hey, that was good."

"You want to hear it in Spanish?"

"I think I get it. But Mary, what about Mr. Chen and Wong Pan?"

"What about them?"

"Mary! You said you'd keep an eye on Mr. Chen! Because Wong Pan might—"

"Okay, okay, I was just giving you a hard time. We're surveilling his shop. If he leaves we'll follow him. You keep away from *him*, too."

"Oh, you're acting like such a cop! And 'surveill' isn't a word, you know."

"And you're acting like an English teacher! Thinking of changing professions?"

"No, teaching's way too dangerous for me."

Mary emphasized the danger I'd be in if I were anywhere near the White Eagles today—"and I don't mean from the White Eagles"—and we said good-bye, in a manner I thought was fairly civilized for threatener and threatenee. I briefly debated whether it was too early to call Bill, decided to call anyway, and had just punched his number on the kitchen phone when my cell phone rang.

"Smith," came the rumble in my kitchen phone ear.

"I'll call you back." I hung up that one up and flipped open the other.

"Good morning, Ms. Chin. David Rosenberg here. I hope I'm not calling too early?"

"Mr. Rosenberg! Good to hear from you. No, it's not too early at all. How can I help you?"

"I've just had a call from one of my reporters in Zurich. He's been doing the background on Alice Fairchild that you asked for. Nothing he's found so far is particularly surprising, but I thought you'd like to hear it."

"Yes, I certainly would."

"Born Shanghai 1938. Father James Fairchild, mother Frances Fairchild, both Methodist missionaries. One sister, Joan Fairchild Conrad, born 1939. I met her years ago."

"Yes, I remember you mentioned that." I tucked the phone onto my shoulder and plopped congee into a bowl. "You said they were Mutt and Jeff. Different from each other." Lydia Chin, queen of the cultural reference.

"Very much. Joan's thin and frail, which I gather she always was, and more so lately, some kind of chronic lung problem from those days. Although before she retired she taught high school, so I imagine she's got a certain toughness. I remember her as humorous and outgoing. The type with a twinkle in her eye."

"Where does she live?"

"Sharon, Massachusetts. Outside Boston. Her husband died six years ago."

"Is that where Alice grew up, around Boston?"

"Yes. The Fairchilds left China in November 1945, as soon as they could after the camps were opened. They were put on one of the first ships out—both children were sick, it seems. The family settled in Sharon. Alice went on to law school—unusual for a woman of her day—and married. They divorced after eight years, apparently on amicable terms."

"Does she have children?"

"No."

David Rosenberg went on detailing Alice's career, including her move to Zurich in the eighties and her growing expertise in Holocaust asset recovery. "She's written a few articles for law journals on the fine points of that work. I've asked my staff to pull them. I'll send them to you."

"I'd appreciate that. Anything else?"

"Well, I took a look at her financials. Not my reporter, me, from here. It just seemed like the thing to do."

"Good instincts."

"I may be hidebound management now, but I did start out pounding the pavement. However, I have to admit everything I found seems in order."

"So she's not mortgaged to the hilt, anything like that?"

"Hardly. Not wealthy, but solid. She did take a hit five years ago when the capital markets fell. She'd overreached. For an estate planner it was a touch reckless, the sort of speculation that's all right when you're young and have decades to recover, but later you advise clients against it. Maybe she was feeling cocky."

"But it didn't cause her problems?"

"If things had gone her way, she'd be much closer to wealth than she is. But even though it was a large sum, she also kept a reasonable amount back. She can certainly maintain her lifestyle on what remains. Maybe that's why she did it."

"Why?"

"She was getting older, she had enough to live on. Why not take a flutter?"

"I guess I can see that. So it looks like she's more or less what she claims to be." And a number of things she didn't mention, besides. "Do you have contact information for her sister? Just to be thorough."

He did. I thanked him, hung up, and dialed Joan Conrad née Fairchild's number, not sure why. After all, if I was looking for reasons to be suspicious of Alice, I didn't need to go back any further than this week.

My mother's always saying old women don't need much sleep. That may be true, or maybe Joan Conrad was just, like me, an early riser. In any case, she certainly sounded chipper answering the phone.

"Good morning, Mrs. Conrad," I said in my best outside-Chinatown accent. I felt bad already that I was about to lie to her. But what was I supposed to do, tell her her sister was a jewel thief and a forger and I was a PI snooping into her past? "My name's Liz Russell and I'm a doctoral student at Columbia doing research for my thesis. I'm studying modern Chinese history with a focus on the Chinese civil war as it overlapped with World War II. I understand you were in Shanghai in those years, and I wonder whether you'd have time to answer a few questions."

"Well, my goodness." There followed a brief pause as Joan Conrad digested everything I'd thrown at her. "Tell me again, dear—you're writing a thesis?" Her voice was chirpy and soft, like a breathless bird.

"Yes, ma'am. I'm focusing on the relationships among the Japanese occupiers, their German allies, and the two sides in the civil war." I was on a roll. "I know you were a child in those years—"

"My, I certainly was. However did you find me?"

"I have records from some of the Japanese internment camps. They're not complete, but I've been trying to track down people who were young enough then to give me a chance of finding them now."

I heard a chuckle. "You mean we old fossils who haven't yet shuffled off this mortal coil."

"Oh, I—"

"That's all right, dear, it's not news to me that I'm gaining on Methuselah." A delicate coughing fit interrupted her. I heard another voice in the room, and waited. Joan Conrad returned. "I'm sorry, dear. Yes, thank you, Maria, please leave it here. Yes, I promise I'll drink it all!" To me again: "Such a tyrant! But a wonderful girl, my Maria."

"Your daughter?"

"Heavens, no. My caregiver. That's the word they use now. I think it's lovely, and she does give me such good care! But I'm sorry, you were asking about Shanghai, weren't you? For your thesis. About the Japanese and the Germans."

"And the camp."

"Oh, but I was such a little girl when we went to the camp. I didn't know anything about the Japanese except that they sent us there. The Germans, and the Chinese armies—why, they might as well have been on Mars. It was the Americans we were waiting for. Waiting and waiting."

"That's all part of what I want to know. How much the people in the camps knew about what was going on and how that was reflected in the camp society. First, can you verify for me which camp your family was in? It was you, your parents, and your sister, right?" I could have asked more directly, but I didn't know how good Joan Conrad's memory was, and I didn't want to plant suggestions.

Apparently, though, her memory was fine. "They called it Chapei camp. The buildings had been built as Great China University, but it hadn't been that in years."

Bingo! Keeping my voice level, I said, "Chapei, yes. That camp particularly interests me for my research because it's one of the few where they held Germans."

"Germans?"

"For example, a woman and child. A Frau Ulrich, wife of a German officer."

"Oh, you mean poor Mrs. Ulrich! Goodness, I haven't thought of her in years." Another round of coughing broke into Joan Conrad's reminiscences. "Excuse me, dear."

"Are you all right?"

"Oh, yes, of course. Mrs. Ulrich!" she marveled. "My, she was beautiful. But I think she was the only German I knew."

"And her child, isn't that right?"

"Did she have a child?" A note of doubt wavered in Joan Conrad's voice. Maybe her memory wasn't so perfect after all.

"The child died about a year after they'd come to the camp. A few months after Mrs. Ulrich herself."

"Died. Yes, I suppose so. I think that's right." After a moment, in a steadier voice, Joan Conrad said, "Mrs. Ulrich was a friend of my mother's, you know." She continued in her cheerful vein; I guessed she was back on solid ground. "She lived in the next room. Oh, but they weren't really rooms! The building we were in had been a dormitory, you see. Most families had individual rooms, but when we came those were occupied. We were put into the big lounge with some other families. The men were given asphalt boards and old wood, and everyone hammered and sawed. They divided it like a rabbit warren, a room for each family and sometimes dividers inside those, too. Mrs. Ulrich was there without her husband, so my father and some of the others built her room. You could hear everything—people talking, babies crying. Even the men snoring! At the mission in Shanghai my sister and I . . ." Again, a hesitation. "We'd each had our own rooms there. But the camp, with everyone on top of each other! And the food was monotonous and didn't taste good. At first it was an adventure, but then I wanted to go home."

Joan Conrad's description of Chapei Camp sounded just like Rosalie's account of the Jewish refugees' shelter. Displaced people, on top of each other, disoriented, frightened, and missing home: everyone's story the same.

But not exactly the same. Sometimes there were surprises. Like the fact that Frau Ulrich, wife of the intended recipient of the Shanghai Moon, had lived in the same *room* as Alice Fairchild.

"Mrs. Conrad, can you remember anything about Mrs. Ulrich? I'm interested in her case."

"Oh, I was so young . . . but I remember she was glamorous! The women I was used to were missionaries, very plain, you see. Mrs.

Ulrich worked at keeping up appearances. She'd brought cosmetics to the camp, rouge and powder and all sorts of things missionary children didn't see. She hadn't packed very practically. As though she weren't intending to be there long. Nobody was, of course not, but we weren't allowed to bring much, so most people packed clothes and personal items, practical things. But now that I think of it, Mrs. Ulrich had a number of suitcases. I don't know how many, but more than one. We were only allowed one each, the Japanese made that rule. I remember because my sister and I had to both sit on my suitcase to close it again after I opened it to sneak my teddy bear in. But Mrs. Ulrich had more."

"Maybe because she was German? Maybe the Japanese treated her better than they treated Americans, could that be?"

"You know, dear, I think you're right. I do remember the guards bowed to her. Not that that kept them from ordering her around. And she certainly didn't feel well treated. I was a bit frightened of her, actually, as I think about it. Oh, such times are coming back to me!"

"Why were you frightened?"

"She was angry. All the time, so angry. My mother was usually able to calm her with a word or a cup of tea, but she never stopped being angry even when she didn't act it. Children sense that sort of thing."

"Angry at who? The Japanese?"

"Whom, dear," Joan Conrad said mildly. "At the graduate level there's really no excuse for sloppy grammar and syntax."

"Yes, my adviser is always telling me that. Whom was Mrs. Ulrich angry at?"

"With whom was she angry, you mean. Partly the Japanese, of course, the way all the adults were. She was also furious with her husband. I remember that! He wasn't in the camp. I think she might have lost him, though I'm not sure. But, no, that must be wrong, because I can't imagine she'd speak so badly of him if he'd passed away! And she did harp on it. What a stupid, greedy man he was. She'd say that to anyone who'd listen. That it was his fault they were there at all—" She stopped. "They! She said 'they'! 'We,' I mean. Oh, I can hear her, that soft German accent she had. Not one of the grating ones, but the other kind. 'Vee vouldn't be here iff he vassn't so greedy.' It would have been nice to listen to her if I hadn't felt frightened. But she said 'we'! If her husband wasn't there, you must be right. She must have had a child, mustn't she? Oh, my. And toys. In those suitcases, toys, yes, yes. The little wooden horse, I still have it, over there on the shelf with my teddy bear. From one of her suitcases." Again, Joan Conrad's voice faltered. "The wooden horse . . . And Alice, Alice has a top . . . In any case, if she had toys she must have had a child. But I don't remember. I'm sorry, my dear. I was young . . . some of those memories . . ."

"I understand. The camps were difficult places, I know."

"Harder for the adults than the children, though. Children are so resilient! We played marbles and tops in the dust. We made up games and had dolls that we brought with us or that our mothers made from sticks and rags. Even when we were ill, and we were ill most of the time. Dysentery, croup . . . That's where my cough came from—and here it comes again." I waited while she coughed; then she laughed. "That was well timed, wasn't it?"

"You seem very comfortable with your memories of those days, Mrs. Conrad."

"Oh, children adjust. It just became our life. It was hardest toward the end, when there wasn't much to eat . . . to this day I can't bear sweet potatoes. I can't get over the idea they have worms in them! The scariest part, I think, was that the adults were frightened. During roll call, when if you'd done something against the rules you'd get summoned for punishment. You never knew if you'd done anything until then, you see. Or the Japanese would order us to assemble when something had happened that made them angry, in the war, I mean, not the camp. Then someone would get punished, an American or English person would be beaten, because of where their country's planes had dropped a bomb. Sometimes rations would get cut, or there'd be no water for a day or two. Of course, I didn't know about those things then, I mean the reasons why these scary things happened. For us, for the children, it was just our life. And Alice always took care of me, so I was shielded more than most." She paused. "Oh, dear. Is any of this what you wanted to know? Am I helping you at all?"

"Oh, very much. This is fascinating. May I ask you about something specific that's come up in my research? Something curious?"

"Yes, of course."

I took a breath and, trying for no change in my voice, asked, "Mrs. Conrad, have you ever heard of a gem called the Shanghai Moon?"

"The Shanghai Moon . . . That rings a faint bell, but no more. Is it something I should remember? Oh, dear."

"Maybe not. It's just something I've come across. It was a brooch, very valuable, and there was a rumor it was in Chapei Camp."

"The Japanese had it, you mean?"

"No, actually, the story I read said a prisoner might have had it."

"Oh, I don't think that's possible. None of us had anything valuable. The Japanese took all that, you see. For safekeeping, they said, though of course it never came back."

"What if someone had hidden it? Didn't anyone conceal anything?"

"In the beginning, I think so. A widowed friend of my mother's hid her wedding ring. But when her children got sick, she sold it to the camp commander for medicine. And another woman, alone and very beautiful . . . Miss Montgomery, she'd been a Sunday school teacher, yes, that was her name! One day she was gone, and I heard some adults say the Japanese had suddenly discovered she wasn't American, but Swiss, and put her on a repatriation ship. The way they were talking, I knew something was odd, but I didn't know what. Later I learned everyone thought she'd bought her way out of the camp. She had nothing valuable, though, and I couldn't imagine what she'd sold." Mrs. Conrad said that sadly, letting me know that now, she could.

"So the Shanghai Moon . . . ?" I said gently.

"No, dear, I don't know about it. But I don't think anyone in the camp had it. No matter how much they might have wanted to hold on to it when they arrived, after the first year, or the second, they would have given it and much more to get out."

We talked some more, Joan Conrad offering whatever memories she had, me gently steering the conversation, until I was finally convinced she had no further light to shed.

"Mrs. Conrad, I want to thank you very much. You've been an invaluable aid to my research. If I can ask you one more thing?"

"You *may,* dear. You certainly may."

"Yes, thank you. Your sister, Alice. I'd like to speak to her, too. Can you tell me how to find her?"

"Oh, Alice lives in Zurich now. She's a lawyer. But you may be lucky. She's in the U.S. at the moment, in New York. Isn't that where you said you were?"

"Yes, at Columbia."

"Good for you! You must be quite bright, studying at such a prestigious university. All the more reason to take care with your language usage. Yes, Alice is staying at the Waldorf-Astoria. Do you know where that is?"

"Yes, I do."

"I'm not sure how much longer she'll be there. She was up here yesterday, just for the day."

Oh? When she said she was in Washington?

"She comes over every few months. She's such a dear, but my goodness! I've told her she doesn't have to make that costly long trip just to tell me to take my medicine! Maria will certainly do that!" She laughed. "But Alice has always taken such good care of me, since we were little. And now that I'm alone . . . Well, I do enjoy seeing her, so I suppose I don't put my foot down the way I ought. In any case, try her at the Waldorf."

"Thank you, I will. Could I—may I also have her address in Zurich? In case I miss her?"

"Of course you may." She all but audibly beamed at my self-correction. "I'll get it for you." I heard the phone clunk down, and before long she was back. She read off an address and phone number in Zurich, both the same as on Alice's card.

"Thank you. And I have just one more question."

"Ask as many as you like. This has been so interesting. You know, when we came back, what with the horrible news from the concentration camps in Europe, and the prisoner of war camps in the Philippines and so on, no one wanted to listen to us talk about our war. Most people didn't even know where Shanghai was. My parents never spoke about the camp, either. I suppose they didn't want to bring up bad memories. And our family had other things to adjust to, after all. Alice and I had never been to America. We saw snow! And we were both sick when we got here. Then we got well and we started going to school and that was that. So I haven't talked about it very much at all. So many memories! Even if most of them are muddled." She stopped, coughed, then said, "Yes, I'm sorry, dear. You had another question?"

The needle on my guilt-o-meter had flown into the red zone, but I asked my question anyway. "After people died, what became of the things they'd brought with them? Mrs. Ulrich, for example. What would have happened to her suitcases?"

"Her suitcases?" A pause. "This won't sound very nice, I'm afraid. I don't remember about Mrs. Ulrich's things specifically. But when people passed on, their things were . . . divided up. None of us had enough, you see. Clothes, or shoes, blankets, toiletries, medicines. Hairbrushes or sewing kits. Even the suitcases themselves—people made furniture from them, and cribs for the babies. So that would have been what happened. When poor Mrs. Ulrich took ill she died very quickly, a matter of days, I think. My mother was probably in charge of deciding what to do with her things, and they were put to good use, I've no doubt about that."

I thanked her, promising to call again if my research needed anything else, and hung up. It crossed my mind she might call Alice and gush about the nice young graduate student from New York who was so interested in Shanghai. Well, it couldn't be helped. What possible rationale could I give for asking her to keep mum?

I poured a cup of tea and thought about Mrs. Ulrich's things being put to good use. It was likely they had been, but unlikely that, if she'd had the Shanghai Moon, anyone had knowingly ended up with it and kept it secret all these years. Why would they? But unknowingly? Could someone have it now—sewn into Mrs. Ulrich's sewing kit, concealed in one of her many suitcases the way Rosalie and Paul had hidden Elke's jewelry? Could it be languishing in some airless attic, tossed onto a moldy pile of World War II keepsakes? That was possible, and if so it was as good as gone forever. But that left Bill's question unanswered: If Frau Ulrich had had the Shanghai Moon, or even knew where to find it, why hadn't she used it to buy her way out of the camp?

So probably she hadn't had it and couldn't have laid her hands on it. But it was clearly way beyond coincidence that Alice had been locked in the same camp, in the same room, with the Ulrichs. Especially since that fact, like so many other things—say, the existence of the Shanghai Moon itself—was one Alice had failed to mention. But if something from those days gave her a clue to where the Shanghai Moon was now, why had it taken this long, and the discovery of Rosalie's other jewelry, to get her moving on it? And if, as Wong Pan claimed, it had been in a secret compartment with the other jewelry all along, and he had it now, what was I supposed to make of Alice's relationship with the Ulrichs? Or of Zhang Li's contention, echoed by his brother C. D. Zhang, that it was stolen in a robbery in 1949?

I called Bill.

"Who're you?" he drawled.

"I'm sorry."

"And I'm pissed off. Pleased to meet you."

"Are you really?"

"Pleased to meet you? I already know you. So I wasn't surprised that you called and woke me to tell me you'd call me back. So no, I'm not really pissed off."

That being the case, I told him about my morning.

"Whoa. You've been busy. Maybe there's something to this early morning thing after all."

"You think?"

"No. But this business about Alice Fairchild and the Ulrichs— God, I wish I knew what it means."

"So do I. The other thing I wish I knew is what the White Eagles are going to be up to this afternoon."

"You think this is it? The big score?"

"Don't you? Mary said we have to stay away. But—"

"No buts. If the NYPD is all over it, we're not. For one thing, it may have nothing to do with us, with this case. And come on, Mary will tell you all about it."

"If she ever starts speaking to me again."

"Doesn't she owe you one, for calling me in the first place?"

"She doesn't see it like that. Bill?"

"Uh-huh?" I could hear the snap of a match as he lit a cigarette.

"Do you think my mother could have done that on purpose? Called Armpit's mother to see if she could find out anything to help me?"

Silence while he drew in that first nicotine hit. "I'd say yes."

"But this is my mother!"

"Did she have any other reason to speak to Armpit's mother?"

"Not that I know of. But . . ." I couldn't think of anything more to explain my inability to believe this than "This is my mother."

34

Bill and I made plans to meet; then I spent a useless half hour on the phone and online while Bill showered and pulled himself together. I called Mr. Chen, so Irene Ng could tell me he wasn't in, and Mr. Zhang, so Fay could tell me he was out. I called Alice, so her voice mail could tell me she wasn't available. I Googled the Ulrichs, the Fairchilds, and Chapei Camp in all the combinations I could think of, so the Web could tell me the Shanghai Moon wasn't anywhere. I stared at my cell phone, trying to hypnotize it into ringing the *Wonder Woman* song so Mary could tell me anything at all. It just sat there.

I did my dishes, swept up, and straightened this and that. When the phone finally played something, it was the *Bonanza* theme. I grabbed it up. "Took you long enough!"

"Why, something happening?"

"No, and I'm sick of it!"

"A little antsy?" Bill asked sympathetically.

"So antsy I can't stand it. Come on, I'll buy you coffee. Meet me at Tai-Pan."

"Uh-oh. Do I detect disobedience of a direct NYPD order?"

"No way! Do you see me anywhere near the White Eagles? And why can't I buy my partner breakfast at my favorite bakery?"

"Since when is Tai-Pan your favorite bakery?"

I didn't bother to answer, because he knew: since we found out how handy it was to Mr. Chen's shop. I also didn't comment on how he didn't comment on my slip of the tongue that brought out "partner."

My congee being a fairly recent event, I contented myself with tea and a red bean bun at Tai-Pan. I put this measly array on an unnecessary plastic tray and added napkins and knives and forks, the better to colonize space at the counter. Bill showed up soon after and ordered a large coffee and an ugly cream-filled pastry, something Chinese people wouldn't have dreamed of eating until the Hong Kong British introduced what passed for food back home. When Bill took out his wallet, though, the stone-faced woman at the register waved him off with a nod to me.

"I told you I was buying." I slid the placeholder tray off his part of the counter.

"You're a class act. How'd she know it was me?"

"You're kidding, right?"

He turned and looked at tables crowded with Chinese grandmas chattering in Chinese, Chinese waiters on their way to work in Chinese restaurants, Chinese mothers with Chinese babies. The only *lo faan* besides Bill were a tourist couple trying in whispers to guess the ingredients in the pastries.

"Okay, I get it." He sipped his mammoth coffee. "So what's the plan?"

"We have no plan. Mary has people keeping an eye on Mr. Chen and other people keeping an eye on the White Eagles. I'm obediently staying out of it, even though both leads came from me. If the police department gives a civilian medal of honor, I think I should get one."

"For leads, or obedience?"

"Both."

"So we're just here for breakfast?"

"You don't like the coffee?"

"It's great. And this cream horn is even better."

"Don't even tell me about that thing."

"And if Wong Pan shows up?"

"If he does, I want to . . ."

He gave me a moment, then prompted, "You want to what?"

"See him. I just want to see him."

"I don't believe you."

"I'm lying."

Across the street, sunlight flashed off the door at Bright Hopes as Irene Ng stepped outside to inspect the window display.

"I wonder if Chen's in there?" Bill said.

"I would really, *really* like to go over and find out."

"Tell me again how long you and Mary have been best friends?"

"Okay, all right," I grumbled. I sipped tea and watched the comings and goings. I was trying to convince myself the chewy dough and spicy sweet filling of my red bean bun were enough compensation for being forced to sit on the sidelines when Bill nudged me.

"There's your cousin."

And damned if Armpit Kwan wasn't slouching up the other side of the street. His greasy hair flopped over his forehead, and if he'd changed his shirt since yesterday, it only proved his entire wardrobe was equally spattered and disgusting.

"Those two guys," I said. "The one next to him and the one who just stopped at the noodle cart? They're White Eagles, too."

"Big deal ones?"

"I don't think so. Junior nobodies, like Armpit. I wonder where Fishface is. Or his lieutenants."

We watched Armpit and his boys meander. They stuck to that block but didn't pay much attention to Bright Hopes. They smoked, they ate, they ogled girls.

"Must be waiting for the boss to show up," Bill said.

I agreed; if this was the White Eagles's big score, nothing would happen without their *dai lo*.

"That guy with the map, by the mailbox." Bill pointed. "Fifty cents says he's a cop."

"And the man selling folded-paper animals. And the Xpress Messenger van, which doesn't seem interested in expressing anything and isn't getting a ticket after twenty minutes in a no-standing zone."

"Well, everyone's ready."

I grabbed his arm. "Maybe not for everything."

Making his way along the sidewalk was C. D. Zhang, carrying a leather briefcase. He entered Bright Hopes, where Irene Ng led him toward the back. She returned to the counter alone. C. D. Zhang must be in the office with his cousin, Mr. Chen, and I'd have bet a nickel his brother, Zhang Li, was there, too.

"Family conference?" Bill asked.

"Did you see Armpit checking out C. D. Zhang when he went in?"

"Yes."

"I just got a bad feeling."

"About what?"

"Our two upcoming crimes. They may be the same. Do you think the White Eagles could have heard about the Shanghai Moon? And they're waiting for Wong Pan to bring it to sell to Mr. Chen so they can steal it?"

"Well, if that's the case, they're walking into the biggest mousetrap in Chinatown."

We waited for more mice, but none showed. Just as I finished my tea, C. D. Zhang came out again. He headed briskly off in the direction he'd come from.

"What was that about?" I asked, but rhetorically. I pulled my phone out.

"You'd better be calling from Florida," Mary said.

"C. D. Zhang just went in and out of Bright Hopes."

"How do you know that?"

"I have a periscope. Look, I know you have people watching the place, but I wasn't sure they know who he is."

"I'm watching it myself," she grudgingly admitted. "That was him just now?"

"You're in the van?"

"Never mind. That was him?"

That was the cop speaking, not the friend, so I just said, "Yes."

"He's family and in the business. Why shouldn't he drop in?"

"I don't know. But on a day like this—"

"We don't know it's a day like this."

"Oh, come on! There are three White Eagles loitering on that block, including Armpit. Wait—four. Warren Li just turned up."

"Another bottom-feeder. No big score is going down just because those four punks are hanging out. Besides which, I know Li's here, be-cause I have two surveillances going, one on Chen and one on your no-good cousin. On your say-so, Lydia. If at least one of them doesn't pan out my captain's going to bust me back to the street and the over-time for all this will come out of my paycheck. And you're about to ask me to put a tail on another old man who dropped by his cousin's store? Don't tell me you weren't, I know you were. By the way, where are you?"

"In Tai-Pan. Mary—"

"*Lydia! I told you—*"

"I know: Get lost."

"And when were you planning to do that?"

"Now. Right now. 'Bye." I clicked off, jumped down from the stool, and told Bill, "Come on."

"Where are we going?"

"Mary said to get lost."

We burned rubber out of Tai-Pan—Mary probably watching us scurry—and managed to pick up C. D. Zhang two blocks west. He threaded through the gray-market car stereos, fake Rolexes and coun-terfeit handbags with the practiced sidestep of a Chinatown local.

And returned to his own office.

Standing on the south side of Canal keeping an eye on a business on the north side might not have qualified as "lost" in Mary's book, but really, there's nowhere in Chinatown I could get lost anyway. I did *feel* a little lost when, after about twenty minutes, Bill asked, "Why are we doing this?" The answer was obvious, though: I had to be doing *something*.

"Anyway, it's weird," I said. "Mr. Chen and Mr. Zhang don't hang out with C. D. Zhang. He said so, Mr. Zhang said so, and Irene Ng said so. If C. D. had something to tell them or ask them, why didn't he just call? Why go over and then not stay long? They hardly had time for a cup of tea. No, something's up. Definitely. Positively. Why are you being so quiet?"

He grinned around his cigarette. "Adrenaline affects different people differently."

We hung out across from C. D. Zhang's office for close to an hour as the day got hotter and stickier. Two more White Eagles passed us, one I knew and one I didn't but both with tattoos conveniently exposed.

"They don't seem to feel any need for discretion," Bill said.

"What good's a gang tattoo if you can't intimidate people with it?"

I restrained myself from leaving Bill on C. D. Zhang watch and charging up Canal to see what the gathering gang cloud was up to. I didn't want to find out that Mary had ordered me arrested if I got too close to that end of the street; it wouldn't be good for our friendship.

As the sun mounted, I began to wish I had a hat. Or a bottle of water. Or a purpose. Traffic snarled and flowed, snarled and flowed in a mesmerizing rhythm. We stood there breathing fumes, fried turnip cakes, and other people's sweat. Wiping my forehead, I said to Bill, "I'm starting to feel like one of Armpit's T-shirts."

"That's pretty serious. You want to take turns grabbing a drink in someplace air-conditioned?"

"No, but tell me something. Am I crazy, standing here like this? And are you just humoring me, or proving your loyalty or something?"

He shook his head. "I'm here because I think you're right."

I was about to demand proof of this ridiculous assertion, but I didn't get the chance. Because proof came hurrying up the block: Wong Pan.

35

"Wong Pan?" Bill asked. "You're sure?"

"If it's not, then whoever it is needs to be arrested for looking too much like Wong Pan. That's got to be a crime." I was speed-dialing Mary as I spoke. Her phone rang as Wong Pan or his evil twin passed C. D. Zhang's building. As he ducked into a greasy chopstick a few doors up, her voice mail came on. "Oh, *no*!" I said. "Girlfriend! Pick up! Wong Pan's on the west end of Canal, at New Day Noodle, north side near Church. I'll—" I stopped as Bill touched my arm and nodded across the street. C. D. Zhang was coming out of his door, briefcase in hand. We watched him walk up the block, and sure enough, he was interested in noodles, too.

"Mary's voice mail," I told Bill. I dialed 911 and reported the location of a dangerous fugitive. Then I snapped the phone shut. I had my arguments all in a row about why we absolutely had to go over there, but I didn't need them: Bill was off the curb, searching for a break in the traffic.

"If Wong Pan's killed two people—" he said over his shoulder.

"My thought exactly." Our chance came, and we dashed across in a storm of honks and curses. "Do you think C. D. Zhang knows who he's meeting?"

"Damn right he does. I think we've been conned. Chen and Zhang know the cops are onto them. They're decoys. C. D.'s making the exchange."

"He was at Bright Hopes picking up the money?"

"I'd bet on it."

In the garlicky shop, a dozen customers were ordering noodles, slurping up noodles, or picking noodle remains from their teeth. None of them was Wong Pan or C. D. Zhang. Bill and I made it through the dining room to the kitchen and through that to a door in the back wall before anyone stirred.

"Hey, you can't go there!" the manager shouted in Cantonese.

"So call the cops!" I yelled, hoping he would.

When we burst into the back room, two men looked up from a banquet table. The question of who'd have a banquet in a noodle-shop back room cramped by twined-up linens and sagging cardboard boxes, near a rear door bubbly with rust, was an interesting one, but I had no time to ponder it.

"Ms. Chin." C. D. Zhang's leathery face registered both surprise and displeasure. "And Mr. Smith. What—"

"Do you know who this is?" I pointed at the round countenance of Wong Pan, which, after momentary alarm, had settled into an odd superior smile.

"This gentleman is a valued customer. And forgive me, but this is private business."

"This business is you buying the Shanghai Moon from Wong Pan. And his business was killing two people to get it this far."

"And you, no business here," said Wong Pan. "You go away."

"The police are coming." Assuming Mary picked up her voice mail. Or 911 didn't think I was just another nut and actually followed up my tip. Or the noodle shop manager was incensed enough at the intrusion that it trumped his distaste for cops; though since nobody had even cracked the door to see what was going on in here, that one seemed unlikely. "You're the one who's going away."

Fear flashed in Wong Pan's eyes, but after consideration he shook his head. "Police coming, would be already here." He began to reach into his jacket.

"Easy!" Bill said. All movement stopped as Wong Pan and C. D. Zhang registered Bill's snub-nosed Colt, unholstered as we passed through the kitchen but until now discreetly palmed.

Wong Pan snickered, theatrically lifted one hand in the air, and with the other drew out a small cardboard box. "We have business. You go away."

"Both hands on the table," Bill told Wong Pan.

Wong Pan, looking amused, did as Bill said. I glanced to C. D. Zhang. He stared at the box under Wong Pan's hand with the eyes of a parched man seeing an oasis. He reached; Wong Pan, eyebrows raised, pulled the box back. Bill sent me a look. I nodded: Let them finish. Let C. D. Zhang hold it in his hand before it becomes evidence, before it becomes Chinese cultural patrimony, before it's lost to him and his family forever. C. D. Zhang picked up his briefcase and placed it on the table.

At which exact moment the kitchen door opened.

The manager had actually called the police?

Absolutely not. White Eagles filled the doorway. And they had more guns than we had.

They stared. We stared. The gang sea parted, and Fishface Deng strolled in. His own gun, still in his belt, telegraphed through his untucked shirt. Behind him the White Eagles fanned out. Six guns: one on each of us, with two for extras. Seven White Eagles, including Deng and his two top lieutenants. And notably not including Armpit. Or Warren Li, or any of the losers up on the east end of Canal.

Lydia! You are a MORON! I silently screamed at myself. Mr. Chen and Mr. Zhang weren't the only decoys. Two stakeouts; two sets of decoys. I stared at Fishface Deng's bulging eyes and sharp little overbite mouth. "You knew."

"What, that the cops were watching us?" He gave a shrug of modest pride. "Your cousin's a good kid. Dumb as a box of rocks, but loyal. He said you were onto us. He said there was no way to scare you off or buy you off, but he asked me not to kill you." He shook his head. "I tried to help the guy out, dammit. Didn't I?" He looked to one of his lieutenants, who nodded seriously, backing up the boss's story. "But you had to show up here. Now I gotta do what I gotta do. Well, he's a good kid. He'll understand." Fishface turned to Bill. With no change of tone, he said, "If you don't put down that fucking piece, these guys will blow you away, and her, too."

Wordlessly, Bill laid his Colt on the table. In view of Fishface having said he was gonna do what he hadda do, there might not have been much point in Bill's relinquishing the gun. Except that as far as getting blown away, later was better than sooner. Every moment you were intact was a moment you could be thinking your way out of your situation, which Bill was obviously already doing and I was going to start doing as soon as I got my adrenaline tsunami under control.

"Lydia?" Fishface said almost solicitously. "Are you carrying, too?"

I lifted my shirt to show him the .25 clipped to my waistband. He relieved me of the gun and its holster, too. I couldn't blame him; the gun would probably sell for more on the street with a nice leather rig.

The *dai lo* turned his attention to the men at the table. They were taking this hijacking in different ways. C. D. Zhang wore a stricken look. Fishface offered him a smile of recognition, and I guessed I knew now who got C. D. Zhang's red envelopes at New Year's. Wong Pan still smirked. I wondered if that was shock, or if he thought he could tell all these guns to go away, too.

Just sit there, I thought at them both. *Don't make a move until us professionals come up with something.*

I glanced at Bill. His nerves might have been riding as high as mine, but he stood completely still, except for his eyes. They methodically searched the room and the people in it, looking for our opening, our chance.

And suddenly, as a solemn White Eagle was reaching for Bill's gun, as Fishface was pocketing the cardboard box and leaning toward the briefcase, leaving stone-faced Wong Pan and pale C. D. Zhang with nothing, nothing, nothing at all, a bullhorn blared.

"Wong Pan! C. D. Zhang! White Eagles!" It was Mary, a commanding cop thunder. "This is the police! Come out slowly! One by one, hands up and empty. You're surrounded."

Fishface's bulging eyes flew to the rusty back door. He nodded. One of his boys edged it open enough to peek into the alley and then slammed it shut. "Fuck!"

Now Fishface pulled out his gun, too, a big Glock. "You bitch! You called the cops!" He said this as though he couldn't believe it, as though he'd caught me cheating at a friendly game of cards.

"Not on you," I pointed out. "On those two."

The distinction didn't impress him. He looked from the back door to the kitchen one. "Well, so, a change of plans. Take them." He waved the Glock at Wong Pan, C. D. Zhang, and Bill. He grabbed my elbow, to escort me personally.

"What are you talk about, Deng *dai lo?*" Wong Pan sputtered. "I don't going!"

"Oh, you do so going, old man." Fishface changed his grip on me to a choke hold and pressed the gun to my temple. I heard chairs scrape and had to assume similar things were going on behind me. As he steered me to the kitchen door, my brain juggled three thoughts.

I hope the NYPD has better control of its adrenaline than I do.

Old man? Fishface, you punk, Wong Pan's not even sixty.

And *How does Wong Pan, fugitive from Shanghai, know a Chinatown gangbanger's title and name?*

I had to stop thinking for a minute as Fishface barked in my ear, "Open the door."

In the vacated kitchen a cauldron steamed and greens sat in a wok getting soggy. Congealing *chow fun,* scattered chopsticks, and pots of tea dotted the empty dining room tables. New Day Noodle looked like a restaurant that had just sailed into the Bermuda Triangle.

Outside, things were different. Red and white lights flashed. Traffic on Canal was blocked by cop cars parked at all kinds of angles. Behind the cars, cops in blue and cops in streetclothes wore Kevlar, held guns, shouldered rifles. I thought about the overtime and almost laughed. Through the window I spotted Inspector Wei, wearing an NYPD vest and the rapt glow of a runner at the starting line. Next to her crouched the Fifth's big, mustached captain, Dick Mentzinger. Beside him I saw Mary, and caught the dismay in her eyes when the first person to lurch out of the restaurant, with Fishface Deng's arm wrapped around my neck, was me.

"We're leaving," Fishface shouted. "We have four people. Let us through or we'll shoot them right here."

Mentzinger took the bullhorn. "I can't do that."

"Do it!"

"If this ends here it's not so bad. No one's hurt. You and your boys can—"

"Shut the fuck up! I don't want to hear any bullshit cop promises." *Or more likely,* I thought, *you don't want your boys to hear them.* He squashed the muzzle harder against my head. "Put down your fucking guns!"

Mentzinger, after a moment, gestured to his cops. Rifles lowered slowly.

"Now back off. Back off! First shot we hear, or if anyone follows us, we're gonna make a bloody mess of all these people. This cute one first."

Mary took the horn. "You have no place to go, Deng *dai lo*," she said in Cantonese.

Fishface laughed. In English he answered, "Lady, in case you haven't heard, there's Chinese people in every country on the fucking earth! An hour from now you'll never find me." He tightened his arm against my windpipe. *It's getting near time to do something,* my pounding heart suggested to my brain. It would be good to make a move before these gangsters started hustling us through Chinatown and realized what trouble we were to hold on to, and how we'd messed up their lives.

So a few steps down the sidewalk, between the empty storefronts and abandoned vendor's trays, I stumbled. Fishface yanked me up with the arm around my neck. Expecting that, I went with it, throwing my weight back into him. After an eternal thrashing moment he thudded heavily down, extra heavily because I landed on top of him. I dove for the gun. We writhed, scraping flesh on concrete. He punched me in the head. I saw blinding colors but by then I had hold of the pinkie on his gun hand. His adrenaline might be high enough to mask the pain but he couldn't pull the trigger with his finger bent to his wrist. He yanked at my shirt, my hair. When I felt his finger snap, I almost lost my grip. He yowled. I yanked at the gun; it skidded along the sidewalk. I rolled, grabbed it, and heard the roar of a gunshot. More roars, and the whine of bullets. I flattened and looked around. And was once again reminded I wasn't the center of the universe.

The sidewalk churned with cops, White Eagles, guns, and silver handcuffs. Two uniforms had slammed onto Fishface as soon as I'd rolled away. Shouts and grunts punctuated the honking of traffic probably backed up to New Jersey. A White Eagle made a break, dashing halfway across Canal before he was downed by a flying tackle so long and accurate it would be cop legend before the cop who made it got back to the precinct. Two more White Eagles lay on the sidewalk, hands on their heads, faces pressed into a glittering scatter of Rolex knockoffs. Straddling a third, yanking his hands behind to snap on cuffs, was a flushed and glowing Inspector Wei. Just beyond her, Mary had Wong Pan bent over the hood of a car. I hoped it had been parked in the sun all day and was damn hot.

I scanned the ruckus, looking for Bill. My heart lurched when I saw him doubled over in a doorway, but then he started to stand. Before I reached him he was on his feet, breathing heavily above Fishface's lieutenant. "You okay?" I asked. He grinned and flexed his hand like a man who'd just punched a White Eagle's lights out.

I heard more sirens, wondered why, since the action was pretty much over, and then, looking around, realized it wasn't more cops, it was ambulances.

C. D. Zhang lay on the sidewalk, a red hole in his chest.

36

Interview One, my home away from home.

I'd been here for an hour. Bill, last I'd heard, was in Two. In widely separated nooks and crannies, handcuffed White Eagles waited their turns to rotate through Three and Four. I didn't know where Wong Pan was, and it clearly wasn't on anyone's to-do list to tell me.

Leaving a suspect alone to sweat is standard NYPD procedure, and though I didn't get the idea anybody actually considered me a suspect in the day's proceedings, Mary was probably mad enough to let me sit here until I grew moss.

I could, of course, make a stink, demand to be charged or released. But that would make my best and oldest friend even more furious. And completely blow my chances of finding out, from anyone's point of view but my own, what had gone on since we'd all been piled into cop cars outside New Day Noodle.

Besides, I had hope: the backup of White Eagles. The NYPD couldn't keep me here forever; they needed the room.

After another ten minutes my hope panned out. The door opened and Mary came in, her face one big, dark scowl. Following her was Wei De-xu. Behind Mary's back the Shanghai inspector gave me a quick grin, then went pokerfaced again as they rattled out chairs.

"How's C. D. Zhang?" I asked before Mary had a chance to yell at me.

"Luckily for you," she said icily, "not too bad. A clean through-and-through. Chen and Zhang are at St. Vincent's with him. He's sewn up and conscious and not talking."

"Why would he? He was buying stolen jewelry."

Mary exchanged a look with Inspector Wei.

"What?" I said. "Are you charging him?"

"Not right now." She added, unnecessarily, I thought, "He's an old man."

"I'm sorry."

"I doubt it."

"No, I—"

"Lydia!" She cut me off. "Can you just *tell* me what you idiots thought you were doing?"

"I called you!" I protested. "And I called nine-one-one. But Wong Pan was dangerous, and we didn't know if C. D. Zhang knew who he was. We couldn't just leave him in there with him. And we didn't know the White Eagles were coming!"

"Bill says you were pretty sure C. D. Zhang knew exactly who Wong Pan was."

"You talked to Bill already?"

"And every White Eagle we took up. And some of the witnesses. And I tried Chen and Zhang at the hospital, even though I got nowhere. Captain Mentzinger finally said if I didn't come in here and interview you I'd have to cut you loose. Which I don't want to do. What I want is to throw you and your idiot partner into a cell way out at the end of Brooklyn for a few months. For being hopelessly stupid."

Inspector Wei looked up with interest. "Can do here?"

"No," Mary answered, still glaring at me.

Wei shook her head ruefully. "In China, can't do also."

"But as it happens, Lydia," Mary went on, "Captain Mentzinger is more laid back about your part in this than I am, maybe because if you get killed he's not the one who'll have to explain it to your mother. And you have to thank Inspector Wei, too. She pointed out to the captain that, though we had a firefight on Canal Street that resulted

in costly property damage and a citizen injured, said citizen was attempting to procure stolen goods at the time of the incident, which,
not your presence, was the precipitating factor. Also that we've appre-
hended an internationally sought homicide suspect."

"Plus suspect in theft from Chinese people," Inspector Wei added.
"So NYPD has gratitude of Shanghai Police Bureau, also government
of People's Republic."

"And," Mary finished, "we also took up seven armed gangbangers
as a result of your information."

I was impressed that Mary could produce such an abundance of
cop jargon, but this wasn't the time to mention it.

"Also, Captain Mentzinger wants something from you. So he'd
rather I didn't keep you on ice for the rest of your life."

"What does he want?"

"We'll get to that. First, I'm going to ask questions, and you're going
to answer as though you were a good, cooperative PI." I sat in cooperative PI silence. "One: You did think C. D. Zhang knew who Wong Pan
was when you went charging in there, right? The way Bill says?"

"Bill did. I thought maybe." I didn't like this shift that made Bill
the good guy and me the bad guy in Mary's eyes.

"And it had occurred to you the White Eagles might be after the
Shanghai Moon."

"Maybe. Possibly. But I thought that's why they were all gathering near Bright Hopes. I had no idea Fishface Deng knew about the
noodle shop! I mean, how did he?" I asked that even though a theory
on it was one of the things I'd come up with sitting here in silent
meditation.

But if I thought I was going to slip in a question and get Mary to answer it, I was mistaken. A glare, and she said, "It didn't occur to you just
to keep an eye on the place and wait for us? Never mind, that would be
only if you'd wanted to help us take up Wong Pan. But that wasn't it.
You wanted to see what was going on. Right?"

"Oh, Mary, of course I did! All right, that was bad judgment. But
after all this, to actually see the Shanghai Moon—"

I stopped as Mary reached into her pocket and pulled out a Ziploc holding a cardboard box. "Go ahead. This is what it was all about? Open it." She tossed it over.

The box was the worse for wear, probably from things like when I landed on Fishface, and it was dusty with fingerprint powder. Despite my new theory, my heart pounded as I lifted the top and pulled off cotton batting. On more batting, stuffed in tight so it wouldn't roll around, lay a big green cat's-eye marble.

I sat back heavily against my chair. "Damn."

"Damn? That's all you have to say?"

"It's a marble."

"That's right. Not some romantic mysterious lost gem. A piece of glass."

"Wong Pan never had the Shanghai Moon."

Mary looked to Inspector Wei, who shook her head. "After you tell story from Attorney Fairchild, Shanghai Police Bureau investigates carved box. Have two expert try. Take to hospital so can make X-ray. Box doesn't has secret compartment."

A tide of futility and failure washed over me. *Oh, Rosalie, Kai-rong! I'm so sorry!*

"Lydia?" Mary's tone gave me a chill. "You know, you don't seem surprised. What are you holding back? Girlfriend, I swear—"

"I only just figured it out," I said wearily. "While you kept me sitting here for an hour. Girlfriend." I looked from one cop to the other. "Did you find out how the White Eagles knew about the meeting in the noodle shop? Or how Wong Pan knew who Fishface was? No, stop, don't tell me you're the one who asks the questions. This"—I pointed at the marble—"confirms what I was thinking. The whole thing was a sting."

"Go back," Mary ordered. "Wong Pan knew Fishface?"

"He called him 'Deng *dai lo*.' Not just his name, his title. How would anyone from outside Chinatown know that, let alone some guy from Shanghai? Unless they'd met. And a marble? Wong Pan can't have expected C. D. Zhang not to look in the box. He didn't care. The box was showmanship. It wasn't supposed to be opened. Wong Pan hired the White Eagles to knock the meeting over."

Neither cop said anything. That made me suddenly crabby. My best friend keeps me on ice for an hour and then doesn't buy my theory? "This was the big score. Not some jewelry store stickup. This was the gig that was going to launch their soldier-of-fortune careers. The big score had a *client*. Wong Pan was the client. Ask him. Or ask Fishface."

Mary said, "I talked to Fishface. He says any story about clients is bogus. Everything the White Eagles have ever done was his own idea. Not that they've ever done anything, a friendly little social club like them. But if they ever *had* done anything, it would have been his idea."

"What does he say his social club was doing in New Day Noodle waving guns around?"

"Funny, I asked him that. He said they smelled smoke and went in to help, and what guns?"

"What do you mean, what guns? They were all carrying, every one of them."

"That's what you say. As soon as they saw how trapped they were, it was raining guns on Canal Street. Not one White Eagle was found with a weapon."

"But—! Oh, never mind. This was a sting. And Wong Pan was the client."

"You really think so?"

"Fishface didn't think this up. It's way above his pay grade. There has to be a client."

"Agreed. I mean, you think it was Wong Pan?"

"As opposed to who? Whom? What?"

"Wait here." As though I had a choice. Mary got up and left. Inspector Wei went with her, and I thought I might be in for another meditation session, but she came back a minute later with two mugs. "Terrible." She handed me one. "Worse than Shanghai police station. How is possible make such bad tea?"

"They say the coffee's worse."

Wei nodded, considering that. "In China, not many private investigators. Only study mens for wives, for divorcing. Not useful to police, like you, like Investigator Smith."

"Useful? Are you kidding? Do you see how furious Mary is?"

"Detective Kee your friend, wants you not get hurt, Investigator Smith also. But your informations, valuable to her, for case, for career."

"You think?"

"Behind furiousness, eyes full of pride, having smart, brave friend like you. You can't see?"

I sure couldn't. While I was wondering whether there was any truth in that or if it was just a case of cultural misinterpretation, Mary came back. She held a briefcase I recognized, having watched it swing from C. D. Zhang's hand down the length of Canal. Dropping it on the table, she repeated herself. "Go ahead. Open it."

I did. It was stuffed tight with a month's worth of *Tsingtao Daily.* "Wow. What?" I looked up. "I don't get it."

I could see the cop and the friend warring in Mary. Actually, not: Both obviously wanted to tell me "Hah!" and send me away not getting it. But the cop, who had a case to crack, grabbed the lead. "Right now we're thinking C. D. Zhang stole the cash. Not that anyone's admitting there was any cash, so we don't know how much, but Bill says the Shanghai Moon would be worth at least a million."

"That's what we were told. But C. D. Zhang, stealing it? That's nuts."

"That doesn't make it wrong. People have ripped off relatives for a lot less."

I thought of C. D. Zhang's eyes glittering as he warned me, *The Shanghai Moon's a quicksand, tread carefully.* And something else: Fishface Deng smiling at C. D. over the back-room table. I'd thought that was a red-envelope familiarity, but it could, I supposed, have meant something else. "You're saying C. D. Zhang steals the money, then fakes getting robbed by the White Eagles? But what about the newspaper? Why substitute if he wasn't really being robbed?"

"Showmanship, like the marble. Make the weight of the briefcase look right."

"But the marble . . . If C.D. hired the White Eagles—"

"I think they both did. Wong Pan and C. D. Zhang. That's why the meeting was in a public place. So the world would know they'd been robbed. The whole thing was a sting on Chen and Zhang."

I didn't like that, not at all. But there was the briefcase in front of me, full of no cash. "Wong Pan and C. D. Zhang were both the client? What do they say?"

"I told you! C. D. Zhang isn't talking, and I can't lean on him unless we charge him. My captain doesn't want to do that right now, to avoid, you know, another stupid mistake."

Brought about by your best friend, okay, I get it. "And Wong Pan?"

"Wong Pan. Now, Wong Pan is exactly the problem."

Both cops regarded me evenly, as though Mary had said something I was supposed to do something about.

"What?" I demanded. "He killed Joel. And Sheng Yue, too, whatever he says."

"Oh, he killed them both. He's all but admitted it."

"So what's the problem?"

"Well, for one thing, we didn't exactly take him up neat and clean. We had guns, bullets, SWAT guys. Streets closed, tourists diving for cover. A wildly expensive operation and a public relations nightmare. Captain Mentzinger's fielding hysterical calls from every civic group in Chinatown. And he's expected at One PP in an hour to explain himself." One Police Plaza, NYPD headquarters, where precinct commanders go to be chewed out by brass. Mary leaned forward. "For another thing, Wong Pan, on the verge of signing off on both homicides, has suddenly clammed up."

"Why?"

She gave me a drama-department pregnant pause. Then she turned to Inspector Wei and cued her with a nod.

"Shanghai Police Bureau sends me here, bring back killer of Inspector Sheng Yue." Wei spoke evenly, but her resolve was unmistakable. "Wong Pan doesn't want coming back."

I ventured, "I don't blame him."

"The State Department is pressuring the DA to send him back, though," Mary said. "Closing two homicides means less to them than our relationship with a friendly foreign power. But the DA doesn't want to, and Captain Mentzinger sure doesn't, either. China gets the prize and we're left empty-handed with a mess to clean up?" She gave me a look to remind me who made the mess. "And this is where you come in."

"In the middle of a tug-of-war between the DA and the State Department?"

"I know, amazing, right? For someone who should be locked up in Brooklyn."

"Are you threatening me?"

"I would if I thought it would work. Anyway, keeping *you* locked up isn't my problem. It's the seven White Eagles we might have to cut loose."

"Why would you?"

"What can we charge them on?"

"Attempted robbery?"

"What robbery? Grand theft marble? Receiving stolen newspaper?"

"Breaking and entering?"

"A public noodle shop?"

"Oh, come *on*! Kidnapping?"

"Their lawyers already told the press these misunderstood Samaritans got scared when they saw all the firepower outside, since they've been harassed by cops all their lives, and you and Bill had guns, and they didn't have any guns, so they panicked and used you as shields to escape the police brutality they'd come to expect, which was bad judgment and they're very sorry, and of course they were planning to let you go."

"Are you— What was that thing Fishface had against my head if they had no guns? What about all the guns all over the street?"

"Every one we found had been filed rough. Not a usable print anywhere."

"But—"

"Lydia! It's not what it *was*, it's how a lawyer can make it *look*. At the very least they'll make bail. Then they'll disappear."

I let out a disgusted breath. "All right, I get it. I can't believe it, but I get it."

"Good. Now get this, too: Captain Mentzinger is very, very reluctant, under the circumstances, to let these guys walk."

"I'm with him. But he thinks there's something I can do? Armpit? I can try, but—"

"No, he's useless. We picked those guys up, but we have nothing on them, so why would they roll?" She paused for effect again. It was effective. "But if there *were* a client? Someone to testify the White Eagles *had* been hired to knock over the meeting? That's criminal conspiracy. And C. D. Zhang got shot in the course of it, which, according to the DA, makes the White Eagles responsible even if it turns out a cop shot him. Then we could put them all away. That would make the DA and Captain Mentzinger very happy."

"But Wong Pan *was* a client. Can't he testify?"

"He could. And he will—if, and only if, he gets a promise we won't extradite."

I looked at Inspector Wei. "And he's not about to get that, is he?"

Wei smiled. "No."

Mary said, "So we have to get the White Eagles another way. Then everyone has face and everyone's happy."

"You know how much I like for everyone to be happy. But how can I—"

"Alice Fairchild."

"*What?*"

"She must be in on it."

This is what your best friend can do: voice thoughts you were trying to pretend to yourself you weren't having.

I said, "I can't give her to you. I'm sorry. I really am. But until I'm sure she's involved, I have to protect her."

"I know what I'm asking," Mary said in a softer voice. "I know she's your client."

"More than that. She was Joel's client."

Mary sat back and considered me. "For what it's worth, Bill said the same thing."

"I'm not surprised. Except that you're telling me. Aren't you supposed to be playing divide and conquer?"

"With anyone else, I would be."

I nodded slowly.

"Okay, see if this persuades you," she said. "This non-extradition deal wasn't Wong Pan's idea."

"I'm assuming it was his lawyer's."

"No. By the time he got a lawyer, someone had already filled his head with ugly pictures of what would happen if he went home, and others of the relative delights of American prisons."

"Who did that?"

"Mulgrew."

"Mulgrew? Who asked him?"

"That's where Wong Pan is. Up there."

"At Midtown? Why?"

"They're not happy with us. They've been two steps behind all along and it's made them look bad."

"So for being smarter than they are, you have to give them the prize?"

"Their captain made a grab. The second it was over. The homicides are theirs, remember, and we had nothing else to charge him with."

"Nothing to—"

"Down here? He was minding his own business, having a meeting in a noodle shop, when gangsters broke in and kidnapped him. He wasn't a criminal. He was a victim."

"I—"

"Besides, Captain Mentzinger has his own troubles. Something about SWAT teams and bullets flying."

"Okay, okay. So what's Mulgrew up to?"

"Closing his homicides. Wong Pan confesses, pleads it out, saves the cost of a trial, Mulgrew's a hero. And if Wong Pan gives him the White Eagles on a deal that makes me and Captain Mentzinger look stupid, that would ice his cake."

"I'd like to ice his cake myself. What if Wong Pan doesn't get his deal, gets sent back, and never gives up the White Eagles?"

"What does Mulgrew care? They're our problem down here."

"What a dirtbag."

She leaned across the table. "So shut him down. Give me Alice."

I bit my lip. "I don't know, Mary."

We looked at each other for a while, neither of us happy. Mary breathed a sigh. "Okay, you can go." She stood and headed for the door.

"Mary, really! I don't know where she is anyway. But I'll see what I can do. Can I ask a question?"

"I can't wait."

"Do you have Armpit stashed around here somewhere?"

"No. We leaned on those losers, but all they'd tell us is Fishface said to go hang around that corner and stay there until he said otherwise. You know what's scary?"

"What?"

"As long as we have Fishface and the All-Stars locked up, your idiot cousin and his homies *are* the White Eagles. I may take them up again so they don't shoot their own feet off."

"I have a better idea."

"You always do."

"Can you let word leak out that you wanted to charge them, that whole loser crowd, but I asked you not to, and as a favor to your best and oldest friend, you didn't?"

"That would give him big face. Using his family influence to protect his friends."

"Yes, but he'd owe me."

"He already owes you for not using fingerprints you don't have."

"So maybe we'd reach a tipping point and actually get something useful out of him. I'll call and give him a squeeze."

"Yeah, right."

Inspector Wei said, "I think is good idea."

Mary turned to her. "You do?"

"If can't get anything by arrest Cousin Armpit, good idea, create *guanxi* debt. For this case, or for future."

"Oh, fine. Though if Cousin Armpit comes through, Lydia, now or ever—"

"You'll be the first to know. One more thing?"

"Please, be my guest."

"If C. D. Zhang ripped off Mr. Chen and Mr. Zhang for a million dollars, why are they sitting at his hospital bedside?"

"Maybe," Inspector Wei said, "they want to know where is."

"Or maybe because whatever he did," said Mary, "he's still family."

37

The Fifth Precinct air conditioners may have been wheezy, but they'd been getting the job done. The minute I walked out onto Elizabeth Street, my shirt melted around me. Car exhaust and the aroma of roasting chickens thickened the sluggish air. I took out my phone and called my cousin.

"Yah?"

"It's Lydia, and I just saved your skinny ass."

"Huh?"

I explained how close he and his homies had come to protective custody. "But the detective's a friend of mine. So I told her to leave you alone."

"Why?"

"You're welcome. Because you're my cousin and I have a certain amount of family feeling. And because I really, really want to know who the White Eagles' clients were, for the noodle shop job and for my office."

"No way—"

"Armpit, the private army thing is over. The way this went down today, no one will hire the White Eagles to take out the garbage. If you don't find out who the clients were, I may have to tell Mary I've just run out of family feeling." I hung up on him. Then I called Bill. "Where are you?"

"In my kitchen drinking coffee. You?"

"On my way home, to take a shower. Who ever said I didn't know when to quit?"

"Everyone. You want to get together when you're done?"

"Of course."

In the empty apartment I showered, dressed, and got ready to hit the street again. I wore a big linen shirt. I'd have been happier in a sleeveless top and shorts, but with the way bullets had been flying around lately I'd have felt uncomfortable without a gun. The NYPD still had the .25 Fishface had taken off me, but a .22 can do in a pinch. Just before I left, I called my mother. Someone was sure to tell her about the scene outside New Day Noodle, and I wanted her to think whatever they said was greatly exaggerated.

Barry answered the phone. "Auntie Lydia! Po-po's teaching us to play fan-tan! I won three dollars and eight cents!" He ran to get my mother.

"Ling Wan-ju? Are you all right?" my mother demanded. "Those gang boys, did they come?"

"No, Ma." *We went to them.*

"I see." I could hear her relax. "Then you had no reason to send me out to Flushing."

"I sent you so I wouldn't have to worry, remember? How are you?"

"If you are not worrying, why did you call?"

Sigh. "Just to check up. Listen, Ma, there was some excitement, and a bunch of White Eagles are in jail."

"Your cousin Clifford? Oh, his poor mother!"

"No, Clifford's okay. But if you speak to Kwan Shan, tell her to tell Clifford to behave himself. His *dai lo*'s been arrested, and the cops are watching him and his friends."

"Kwan Shan can say what she wants. Clifford will not listen. Some children never listen to their mothers. Your brother is painting the downstairs kitchen white, to make it brighter."

If a more pointed remark was ever made, I couldn't think of it. "That's great, Ma. I have to go. Talk to you later." I locked up and headed to Excellent Dumpling House.

Bill was there waiting. "You look fresh and sharp."

"You're such a liar."

"Mixing it up with the White Eagles took it out of you?"

"No, but I just got off the phone with my mother. You okay?"

"Fine. Mary yelled at me, but she didn't arrest me, so I came out ahead. She wanted to know whether crashing the noodle shop meeting was my stupid idea or your stupid idea."

"What did you tell her?"

"I said we're such a perfect team, so much in sync, it's impossible to tell which of us originated any particular stupid idea."

"I'll bet she loved that."

"Not even a little. You want pork, chicken, or shrimp?"

"All three. And dry-fried green beans."

He raised his eyebrows, but I ignored him. He was the one who'd pointed out I get hungry when my adrenaline's high. I didn't mention the orange and the banana I'd eaten when I got home, or the Fig Newtons I'd grabbed on my way out the door.

"We have a problem," I said while we waited for the dumplings.

"Mary wants Alice, I know."

"What are we going to do?"

"We?"

"Don't give me that look. We, white man."

"Can I say something serious?"

"I don't know, can you?"

"If Wong Pan killed Joel, then whatever else, you did what you promised Joel. You caught his killer."

I sipped tea, and when it was gone, I said, "We," again.

Bill gave me a grin, I gave him a slow smile, and we probably looked like idiots by the time the waiter settled bamboo steamers on our table.

For a while we focused on dumplings and beans. The clatter, the rush, the familiar smells and tastes finally relaxed me. "Maybe it doesn't matter." I poured the remains of the tea. "About Alice. I have no idea how to find her."

"You have her sister."

"I was hoping you wouldn't mention that. Do I have to give her to Mary? She's so . . . cheerful."

He said nothing, which said everything.

"Oh, you're impossible! Can I finish lunch first?" Without waiting for his answer, in case he said no, I pulled out my phone. Not to call Mary, though. I wanted to try Alice once more.

"It's Lydia," I told her voice mail. "The entire NYPD is looking for you. You're in serious trouble. I'd like to talk to you before they do. Call me."

I put the phone away. "You know what really bothers me?"

"The Shanghai Moon. That it wasn't here."

"You're impossible, but you do have your moments. Yes, the Shanghai Moon. That it's no more real now than when you were hearing about it in sailors' bars. It hasn't come back. It hasn't been seen at least since Rosalie died, probably longer than that. Everyone told us that, but I didn't listen. I've never even seen the thing, and I got all tangled up, just like all those other people over the years. I wanted to believe. Because of Rosalie and Kai-rong. I wanted—"

"Lydia?"

"Stop. If you're about to tell me not to be hard on myself, I don't—"

"I'm not. Listen. Zhang said he'd never told that story before, about when Rosalie died. To anyone."

"So he wouldn't call down more bad luck. My mother would understand that."

"Right. So how did C. D. know? He told us Chen and Zhang always thought robbers took the Shanghai Moon. How did he know about the robbers?"

"Mr. Zhang must have told *him*. He's his brother."

"He said no one, ever. He tried not to even think about it because of the bad luck. And he didn't see C. D. again until twenty years later. Why would he tell him then?"

I thought about it. "Maybe Mr. Chen told him?"

"Zhang said neither of them talked about it."

"Paul Gilder?"

"C. D. said he hardly knew him."

"Still . . ."

"It's possible. But don't you want to know?"

"What are you thinking?" I asked, as it began to dawn on me what he was thinking.

He stood and dropped two twenties on the table.

I stood, too. "We're going to get in his face in the hospital?"

He didn't answer, and I didn't ask again. Of course we were.

"There might be cops here," I said as we rode the elevator to C. D. Zhang's floor. "In case he changes his mind about talking."

"Not if they're not charging him. It's not in the budget. But aren't Chen and Zhang supposed to be here? That might put a crimp in his willingness to talk to us."

"What willingness? Especially given what we've come to talk about."

But in C. D. Zhang's room no visitors were in evidence. A jovial man, watching TV from the near bed, tipped his head helpfully toward the curtain around the bed by the window. "He's sleeping."

"That's okay," I smiled. "We'll be quiet." I tried to look like a concerned relative, though I wasn't sure what Bill looked like. We pushed through the curtain, and there was C. D. Zhang, looking old and frail. His eyes were shut, but he wasn't sleeping, or if he was, we woke him. He turned his head, looking at us but saying nothing.

"Hello, Mr. Zhang," I said. "I'm sorry you got hurt."

After a moment he gave what, if he'd been stronger, might have been a snort. "I'm not sure, Ms. Chin, whether you endangered my life or saved it," he said in a voice weak but clear.

"I'm sorry," I said again. "Mr. Zhang, we've come to ask you some questions."

He turned his head away. But he didn't tell me to stop.

"Wong Pan. You knew who he was?"

"Of course I did."

"And you knew what he was selling?"

"Why else would I have been there?"

"Why were the White Eagles there?"

"To steal both the jewel and the money, I can only assume."

"But there was no money."

He gave me a long look. "It's true, then? That was what I understood the police to tell me, though I've been given so much medication I thought perhaps I'd imagined it."

"No, it's true."

"Nor any jewel, I understand."

"Mr. Zhang, why was there no money?"

He smiled sardonically. "Thank you for the courtesy of the indirect question. What you really mean is, at what point did I steal my brother's million dollars and where is it now?"

"I didn't—"

"I think you did. No matter! The police certainly did. They think I hired the White Eagles, in a clever scheme."

"You obviously knew them."

"They bring me orange trees at the New Year! For which I pay a considerable amount, I promise you."

That's how protection works: The gang brings a good-luck orange tree, the merchant gives them a good-luck red envelope. Luck smiles on everyone all year.

"I didn't, though. Hire them. Nor did I take the money. I thought that briefcase full of cash."

Bill asked, "Was it ever out of your sight, the briefcase?"

"I had it with me every minute."

"And you're sure it had the cash in it when you got it?"

"No." C. D. looked away again. "It was locked when my brother gave it to me."

"It was?" I asked. "Why?"

"Perhaps they didn't trust me not to help myself."

"They trusted you to make the buy, but not to leave the cash alone? Weren't you offended?"

He sighed. "With the exception of sponsoring them to come to this country, my cousin and my brother have never asked anything of me. An introduction, a loan, advice on a business venture . . . the small good turns of families. Nothing. This was the first time. And on a subject so vital! If I was offended, that was secondary. I was honored and delighted and I'd have accepted the charge on any terms they'd proposed." He paused. "Ms. Chin? Mr. Smith? When the police left and Li and Lao-li were allowed back in this room, I told them what I'd learned about the money in the briefcase. My cousin seemed quite startled."

"And your brother?"

"He only said, 'The important thing is for you to get well, brother. The rest means nothing.'" C. D. Zhang smiled in a way not at all sardonic but sweet and sad. "I've been waiting all my life to hear words like that from him. If I'd known the way to do it was to get shot, I'd have made the effort sooner." The smile faded. "But I don't know if he believes I didn't take the money. I think, to the contrary, he believes I did, but, since the Shanghai Moon was not lost as a result of my pilferage, he's willing to forgive me. He probably expects I'll return it to him when I'm well, and all will be as before. But I didn't take it. I can't return it. His anger, kept in check now by a family feeling I've been hoping for all my life, will erupt." A pause, and then, tentatively, "Can you . . . talk to him? Ms. Chin? Can you persuade him this is the truth?"

"I don't know. Is it?"

"Yes. Yes, of course it is."

"Well, maybe it is. And maybe I can convince Mr. Zhang. But you haven't been entirely devoted to the truth in the stories you've told so far."

"What do you mean?"

"Or maybe you told a little too much of it."

"I still don't—"

A brief moment, while I reminded myself this was not just an old man but an injured one. Then I shoved that qualm aside. "Why weren't you and your father together on the day you left Shanghai?"

"But we were. On the *Taipei Pearl.* I told you."

"Not on the ship. Before that."

"In the wailing and screaming, in the crush in the streets, people flying every which way with their pitiful possessions—the miracle would have been if any two people had been able to stay together as they made their way through Shanghai."

"Especially if they had different destinations."

"What do you mean?"

"You were going to the wharf. Your father went somewhere else, didn't he?"

"Once we'd lost each other, I don't know what he did."

"He went to the Chen villa with two other men and tried to rob it. He killed Rosalie Gilder when she fought back. That was what your father did before you met him on the *Taipei Pearl.*"

Pale already, C. D.'s face drained of all color. "Ms. Chin! How can you—"

"You told us your cousin and brother are sure robbers took the Shanghai Moon. But neither Mr. Chen or Mr. Zhang ever told the story of that day. To anyone. How do you know about the robbers?"

We could have been wrong. If he'd said of course his brother had told him the story, what could we have done? But this was the answer Bill had proposed to the question he'd asked. I'd agreed, and my instincts told me we were right.

And we were. But wrong, also.

"Did your father take the Shanghai Moon from Rosalie?" I asked, more gently, when he didn't respond. "Have you had it all these years?"

"No." C. D.'s voice was dry and rustling. "No. My father didn't kill Rosalie."

"I'm sorry, but there's too much wrong. Your knowing what went on. Rosalie not having the gem. You and your father not staying together. Maybe the reason you didn't take your brother's million dollars is that you already have his jewel."

"Is that what you believe? Is that what you'll tell my brother and my cousin?"

"I don't know what I'll tell them. I don't know what to believe. Except that this all needs to be explained. If your father didn't give the Shanghai Moon to you—"

"He didn't give it to me. Or to anyone. He never had the Shanghai Moon. My father didn't kill Rosalie Gilder, Ms. Chin. I did."

38

I stood in stunned silence at C. D. Zhang's bedside. I didn't know what to say, and neither, obviously, did Bill. C. D. suddenly grinned a shadow of his old, ironic grin. "I see you didn't know that."

I said in astonishment, "No, of course not."

"In that case, Ms. Chin, I must apologize for the mayhem in your office."

"My office?"

"I asked Deng *dai lo* to provide entry, and I must say he made a creative and efficient job of it."

"You were the client?"

"Your documents, the newly discovered sources from that time. I was afraid somewhere there was a trail that would lead to me."

"That's why you offered to read them for me."

"Yes."

"But you didn't find them. I had them at home. Why didn't you try that next?"

"Ms. Chin! Where your aged mother lives?" His look said I should be ashamed of myself. "No, I decided I would be forced to take my chances. And I can see now it was not the documents that betrayed me."

"No. But I don't understand. The way you've spoken about Rosalie . . . and your brother was there . . . how could you do that?"

"I'm not sure I can make you understand. But if you want to hear the story, and then judge me as I've judged myself through all these years, I'll tell you."

"Yes," I said. "We certainly do."

C. D. Zhang gazed at the ceiling as though a grainy old film were flickering there. After a long pause, he began to speak.

"I was twelve when we left Shanghai. I was eighteen when we returned, and a soldier. My body had grown, my face hardened, my voice deepened. I was not with my father, had not been together with him for weeks. He'd gone ahead, to make sure of our arrangements on the *Taipei Pearl*. I entered Shanghai with two men from my unit, no older than I. Through terrible days and nights these companions had followed me without question. But now I was leaving Shanghai, and they were not. They had no fathers to buy them passage with stolen wealth, as I had."

"Stolen?" As soon as I said it, Bill shot me a glance, and I could have kicked myself for interrupting. But the word had grabbed my attention. C. D. Zhang didn't seem to notice.

"By 1949 anyone with eyes unclouded by doctrine could see Chiang Kai-shek's army wouldn't win the civil war. Abandoning any pretense of fighting for a cause—which had only been pretense in any case—my father had his troops lay siege to villages and towns, for no reason but thievery. They killed those who resisted, chased off the rest, and divided the spoils. Oh, don't think he was the only officer who did this, or even the worst! There was no order toward the war's end, no rule of law, or sense, or kindness. War is a madhouse of fear, hunger, and death. We were all mad.

"Myself included. My unit—a tattered and pitiful bunch, wrapped in rags, living on crickets and field mice, filthy, diseased—tried, in those last days, to work our way toward Shanghai. Not to fight, not to hold the city for our glorious Generalissimo, oh, no. To escape! Our captain had died of a fever, and we had no leader, except myself. Not from rank but because, as I told you, I seemed to have a skill for finding food and shelter, what little there was to be had. My fellows followed me, and I carried their hope like a heavy weight.

"But I wasn't up to the task. Under my inadequate command we stumbled into an ambush. Remembering a flooded marsh outside Shanghai where frogs were plentiful when I was a boy, I led the way.

But Mao's soldiers had reached the area before us, situating themselves on high ground. I might have seen evidence of their positions, had I known what to look for, but I didn't. They pinned us down, and over three days they picked us off.

"At first we took aim, but shooting only drew their fire. So, in the steaming heat, soaked and starving, we waited to die. Crickets whirred and the wounded moaned. Otherwise all was still. Only when one of us, unable to bear it, tried to bolt, did we hear the whine of bullets. The wounded died and the dead began to rot. Crows circled and landed to feast. Mao's troops amused themselves firing at the birds.

"Days and nights of this, until all around, floating in brown water, were the staring bodies of my friends. I thought, finally, I was the only man living. I decided to show myself and let the enemy end my miserable life.

"So I jumped up, arms wide, and shouted for the soldiers to shoot. There was no response. They were gone.

"I started to laugh. Unable to control myself, I collapsed in the mud. I'd have drowned there, laughing, if not for another soldier who'd seen my suicide attempt. He pulled me to drier ground, shouted and slapped me until the hysteria passed. As we struggled together from the swamp, we found one more man alive. Just one.

"Together we three resumed our stumble toward Shanghai. We stole clothing from the bodies of civilians—thousands to choose from, thousands!—so we could discard the tatters of our uniforms. We had rifles, but still we exhausted ourselves crossing fields and paddies to avoid the Red Army, which filled the roads. The details of that flight do not bear repeating. Until finally, four days later, we entered the city, to fight our way to the wharves.

"I couldn't leave these men, do you understand that? They'd followed me into that swamp, and after what had happened, still they followed me out. But I knew I had passage on the *Taipei Pearl,* if I could reach the wharf. And they did not."

He broke off, coughing. He gestured to a cup on his bedside table. Bill held it for him. When C. D. Zhang spoke again his voice was weaker, and I leaned to hear him.

"I was starving. I was beyond the end of my strength. That's how I've explained my decision to myself, over the years. I was mad.

"Chen Kai-rong was responsible for my desperate situation. That was my logic. His escape was the reason my father and I had been forced to flee Shanghai and suffer the privations of war, while his family remained, comfortable in their villa, surrounded by their wealth. Of course that was absurd—if I'd looked I could have seen what the war had done to Shanghai. No one had comfort, no one had wealth. But I was mad.

"I led my companions to the Chen villa. We would steal what we could and barter what we stole to buy them passage on the ship. As we neared, my mind burned with the thought of the carpets, the paintings, the delicate porcelains. And one treasure more than all the others: the Shanghai Moon. I hadn't seen it since I was a boy. Any of the hoard I imagined the Chen family to possess would have done to save my friends. But it was the Shanghai Moon that consumed me. Because it was not only a treasure of the Chen family but of the wife of Chen Kai-rong. He was responsible for my nightmare. As recompense for my suffering, I deserved the gem!

"By the time we reached the villa, I was aflame with fury and righteousness. We broke in easily—I knew the gates, the walls, their weaknesses, from days of childhood play. Screaming, waving our rifles, we forced everyone to the study. I must tell you, my resolve nearly broke when I saw my brother, thin and trembling. In my feverish visions of triumph and revenge, he had not appeared.

"But my companions were dismayed and panicked by the bare walls, the empty shelves. Where were the treasures? A smaller boy, a child I didn't know, began to cry, and both Rosalie and my brother stepped forward to comfort and protect him. My brother, safeguarding a strange child! My duty to my friends became all I could see, all I lived for. I seized old Chen Da, Kai-rong's father. Something must remain, some hidden treasure—the Shanghai Moon must be in the villa, I was sure of it. I beat him, an old man; I beat him and he would tell me nothing.

"Then . . . I don't know. I don't know precisely what happened. I heard a shot, and when I turned to look, it was not one of my men but the old houseboy—I remembered him, always slipping sweets to the children—and he aimed a rifle at me! I fired first. And my shot struck Rosalie.

"When Rosalie fell, the fog of madness cleared instantly. What had I done? Both children reached for her, wailing. I called out, ordered my companions to leave with me. As they had for weeks, they obeyed. The old houseboy chased after us. One of my friends stopped him with one shot."

C. D. Zhang's labored breathing and his pallor made me think he wouldn't go on, but after a few moments he turned his gaze to me. "We took nothing with us. Do you understand? Nothing. If Rosalie wore the Shanghai Moon, my companion didn't find it."

It took me time to regain my voice. The Shanghai Moon seemed almost beside the point. Still, I asked, "How do you know? What's to say he didn't keep it from you?"

"Because he died! They died, both of them, fighting to force their way onto a ship on which they could not buy passage! The Shanghai Moon would have saved them. But they—we—didn't have it.

"So I and my father sailed for Taipei, and my fellows died. We came to America, and I started a new life. But there's no putting the past behind you, no matter what you're told. The sight of my companions' hands reaching out to me from the gangway has haunted me always. And another sight, so similar: those two young boys, reaching for Rosalie."

Another cough; then, with clearly slipping strength, he resumed. "Twenty years later, when I received that letter from Shanghai, I felt I'd been given a new chance. I could help my brother and my cousin, I could save them, and we could be a family. But of course that hasn't happened. It would have been much more than I deserved. My brother especially has always felt a discomfort in my presence. He's a sweet-natured man and regrets this sentiment he doesn't understand. As though his unease were the result of some flaw in himself."

C. D. Zhang's eyes slowly closed. "I didn't take their money," he murmured. "I'd taken far too much from them already."

39

Bill and I had left the hospital and were back in Chinatown, but even these familiar streets didn't give me any sense of being on solid ground.

"You think it's true?" I asked. "What he said?"

"Could you tell a story like that if it weren't true?"

"He killed Rosalie? But . . ."

"But you like him."

"And he was family!"

"Families are complicated things." He lit a cigarette and didn't look at me.

I trudged on glumly. I didn't like this new knowledge; it was weighty and disheartening and didn't seem to offer any compensation, like for example help in figuring out where the million dollars was. Or the Shanghai Moon.

"We have a plan?" Bill asked.

"Are you kidding?" I turned down Mulberry for no good reason. At Bayard we stopped for a funeral to go by. In my mood, I wasn't surprised; I might have conjured it. Red and yellow flowers frothed on the grille of the hearse, surrounding a photo of the deceased. A youngish man; I could see his wife and children in the next car, stunned and still. I wondered who was at home preparing the funeral meal, and whether it would be as chaotic as Joel's shiva.

And suddenly I was struck by a bolt of lightning.

I grabbed Bill's arm.

"What?"

"Wait." I ran it through in my mind once more, to make sure I was right. I was. "Joel's fishy thing. It *was* in the call with David Rosenberg. Oh, damn! Why didn't I see it sooner?"

"I don't see it now. Care to explain?"

"Alice asked him for a PI!"

"And?"

"In Zurich! At a cocktail party. Before she left for Shanghai. Before she met Wong Pan, before he skipped out. Before this all started!"

Bill didn't answer. I could see in his eyes he was doing what I'd done, playing the conversation with Rosenberg over in his mind.

Three more funeral cars rolled by, holding more solemn children. Nieces, nephews? Cousins? The kind I had, so many and so distant that even my mother couldn't run down the lines of connection? But it didn't matter; family was family. *Better if you could choose relatives,* my mother had said. *But you can't.*

"But you can!" I burst out as the second bolt hit. I saw not the black cars in front of me but other funerals, plain pine boxes, garden graves, winding sheets. Swampy water and bricks weighting bodies down.

"You can what?"

"You just said it. Families are complicated things." I whipped out my phone and dialed Rosenberg's number.

"Hello, Ms. Chin. How are you?"

"Fine, thanks." If you didn't count the guns, the sidewalk scuffle, the police station, C. D. Zhang's depressing revelations, and the jolts from the lightning. "But I have to ask you something. When you talked to Joel, you told him Alice had asked about a PI in New York. Did you tell him when she asked?"

"Not precisely. I think I said a few weeks back."

"Thank you! Talk to you later."

"Wait. Are you in a rush, or shall I tell you what I've learned about the forged documents? My reporter's spoken to his street source. I was waiting until my information was complete, but I can give you what I have now if you'd like."

"Oh. Oh, yes, please."

"Alice Fairchild probably did have them made, in Zurich. There were a Chinese passport and a U.S. visa in the name of Wu Ming."

"Thank you. And"—a wild guess, but it was so clear to me now—"a Swiss passport, too?"

"Yes. How did you know that? For herself, though why—"

I interrupted. "In what name?"

"Helga Ulrich."

"Thanks! Good-bye." I speed-dialed Mary. "Unbelievable!" I said to Bill while I waited.

"What is?"

"How stupid I am."

Mary answered her phone with "If you're in trouble, I don't want to hear about it."

"Trust me, I wouldn't tell you. Listen, this is important. Alice Fairchild has a Swiss passport in another name. She's probably registered at a hotel using it."

"What name?"

"Helga Ulrich."

"What kind of a name is that?"

"Swiss. No, seriously, it's a long story."

"Do I want to hear it now?"

"No, you want to go looking for Alice."

"You're right, but first tell me how you know this."

I was tempted to remind her PIs have an ecological niche in the crime-fighting world, too, but I just gave her the facts.

"Oh," she said grudgingly. "Not bad."

"You're welcome. 'Bye." I clicked off before she could ask what I was up to next, even though I didn't know what I was up to next. But fresh adrenaline was sizzling in my veins. Turning to Bill, I said, "Alice has—"

"I was eavesdropping. Helga Ulrich?"

"How about that?"

We stood on the sidewalk and discussed how about that. We were on our way to a hell of a theory, I thought, when we were interrupted by my phone ringing again. It wasn't the *Wonder Woman* song but, hoping it was Mary calling from some landline to tell me my tip had panned out and they'd found Alice, I answered anyway.

"Yeah, yeah, yeah. It's your cousin, cuz. I got some shit for you. You want it?"

Crabby because it wasn't Mary, I said, "If that's all you have."

"What?"

"Nothing. Go ahead, I'm listening."

Warily, he said, "That shit you asked about before, I don't know nothing, like I said."

"Armpit—"

"Just listen! That fat dude, got picked up today when *dai lo* got grabbed—anything you can do about that, by the way? Cuz?"

"No."

"I just thought, since you're tight with the cops—"

"You thought wrong. Keeping them off you is about all I can do, and it's getting harder every minute. Armpit, I'm busy here. You have something for me or not?"

"Jesus, take a chill pill. That fat guy, like I say. Warren says he saw him. With *dai lo*, twice. You know, at meetings I couldn't make."

Or wouldn't have been invited to if you were the last White Eagle standing. "You're telling me Wong Pan and Fishface Deng knew each other. It's nice to have that corroborated, Armpit, but we'd kind of figured it out by now."

"Shit, cuz! Cut me some slack, will you? I'm trying to help you out here. The second time, Warren says the fat dude was with a lady. *Baak chit gai.*"

Oh. "Who?"

"No idea. But you want to see her, she just went into old man Chen's store."

Bill and I charged to Bright Hopes on a dead run, as far as that's possible in weekday Chinatown. I called Mary, got voice mail, left a message, and stuck my phone in my pocket so I could dodge grandmas,

school kids, and melon vendors. Drenched in sweat, we pushed into
and through Bright Hopes past a first smiling, then confused Irene Ng,
who gave us a token "Wait."

"It's okay. We were invited." I threw open Mr. Chen's office door.

Three heads turned.

"Lydia!" Alice Fairchild's voice was filled with dismay. She sat opposite Mr. Chen and Mr. Zhang, the same as when I'd met them in
here. The differences between that meeting and this were, one, no
one had served tea; and two, Alice was rather impolitely pointing a
pistol at the two old men.

40

"Alice, put it down," I said quietly.

"Lydia, go away!" Hysteria edged Alice's words. "I don't want to hurt anyone. I'm just asking these gentlemen for money. I need money."

"For your sister, right?" I spoke gently. "She told me you were taking good care of her."

"You talked to her? To Joan? Lydia, for God's sake, leave her out of this!"

"But she's what it's about, isn't she? Only she's not your sister."

Alice's eyes widened. She didn't answer, but she also didn't let the gun waver. Her finger was on the trigger, not beside it where a practiced shooter's would be. I'd have bet it was the first gun she'd ever held. So I went on in a calm, reassuring voice, because nothing's as scary as a scared amateur. "You're Major Ulrich's daughter. Your mother died in Chapei Camp. Alice Fairchild died, too, didn't she? You're not really Alice Fairchild."

For a long moment no one moved.

"Chapei Camp made a lot of orphans, and orphans didn't do well," Alice said quietly. "The Fairchilds took me in. They had nothing, the same as everyone else, but when my mother died they took me in and loved me and saved my life.

"Then a few months later Alice died. Joan was very sick. In her fever she called me Alice and cried when I said I wasn't. So we all started to pretend I was her sister. For her sake. Lydia, I know you have a gun, and Bill, you, too. Please put them on the table here. One at a time, please, Lydia first."

"But after the war?" I said, to keep her talking. "The Japanese must have known who you really were."

"Do you think they cared? Father—Reverend Fairchild—told the Americans the Japanese records were wrong. That's all, just wrong. That's all there was to it. Thank you," she said when I put down my rig, as though I'd poured her tea. "Now Bill, please."

Bill put his .38 beside my .22. As he straightened he stepped back, to spread Alice's field of vision.

Alice turned to the old men, who'd been sitting in silence, Mr. Chen with wide, frightened eyes, Mr. Zhang less visibly scared but not looking as unperturbed as usual.

"Now, gentlemen, I'm very sorry, but really, I need a lot of money. Joan's very ill and she needs to stay in her own home. I'm not going to put her in an institution. They're like the camp, those places, crowded with people you don't know, nothing beautiful, everyone sick . . ."

The hysteria had crept back into her voice. Conversationally, I said, "You made some risky investments a few years ago. Was this why? Because Joan needed money?"

"Tom died. His pension stopped. I'd tried to tell him, to help him plan, but he said Joan would be all right. He didn't know, he had no idea how much it costs when you're sick . . . So I tried to make it up. But I couldn't. Now. Now." She turned to Mr. Chen. "I know you were going to pay a million dollars for the Shanghai Moon, and I'm sorry that money's been confiscated, but you'll get it back. I was supposed to get half of that, and I really need it. Please."

That "please" wasn't a request; it was an order for the old man to go fetch her money. No one moved, though. Alice frowned. To distract her, I said, "And the Shanghai Moon was at the root of everything. Your father had been offered it, to save Kai-rong."

Mr. Chen blanched. "*What?* What are you saying?"

I raised my hand gently, telling him to stay calm. "But he never got it, did he?" I asked Alice.

"He told my mother about it." She smiled a bitter smile. "It was going to make us rich. Rich! He was arrested on his way to meet Rosalie."

"How do you know that? You were a child."

"Oh, my mother repeated it, over and over, every day in Chapei Camp. How my father's greed sent us there. And how the Germans could have gotten us out but they didn't. Germans! I hated them. They left us to rot in that horrible place, left my mother to die."

"Holocaust asset recovery," Bill said. "That's why you do it. To get back at the Germans."

Expressionless, she looked at him. "My mother had a silver dressing-table set, with grapevines on it. A mirror, combs, and brushes. A magnifying glass, and a delicate thing for stretching the fingers of kid gloves before you put them on. When she got sick, I had to ask the camp commander to take them in exchange for medicine. *Ask him!* Then she died. Over the next few years we traded everything away. When the camp was liberated, I had nothing of hers."

"But the camp was run by the Japanese," I said.

"We didn't have to be there! The Germans could have saved us!" Alice's shrillness made Mr. Chen jump. Mr. Zhang put a hand on his arm. Alice went on more calmly, "It was their fault. And Rosalie's and Mei-lin's, for tempting my weak, greedy father."

"But what was the point of getting Joel and me involved?" *Where the hell was Mary?* "Why not just sell the jewelry after you and Wong Pan stole it?"

At the mention of Joel she lost a little starch. "It wasn't worth enough. Joan needs much more money than that. Mr. Chen and Mr. Zhang had to believe Wong Pan had the Shanghai Moon and was desperate to sell it before I caught up with him. So they wouldn't ask why it wasn't offered on the open market."

"You knew who they were?" *Mary? Girlfriend? Any time now.*

"Of course. But they had to believe I didn't. That Wong Pan was ahead of me. I thought it was a clever plan, but I'm a plodding lawyer, not a strategist. Joel called that morning to ask why I'd inquired about a detective before I'd even left Zurich. I put him off with a promise to come in and talk about it. Then I called Wong Pan. Just to say we had to hurry. I didn't know he'd already made a deal with the White Eagles, already gotten a gun from them, already killed that Shanghai policeman. Lydia, I'm so sorry."

"I knew it. I knew you didn't mean to have anything to do with killing Joel." I tried to sound as if I'd had faith in her all along. "Alice, put the gun down. This can all be worked out."

"No. I'm going to jail, I don't doubt it. And I should. So many bad things were my fault. But I've got to take care of my sister first."

"I'm very sorry." Mr. Zhang spoke up, and he really did sound sorry. "But my cousin and I don't have the money you're asking for."

"You were going to pay a million dollars for the Shanghai Moon. I've looked into your history of chasing it. That was part of my research for my plan. Like asking about a detective." She shook her head sadly.

"Yes. And earlier today we had it, and could have given it to you. Now it's gone. Even the police don't know where."

"Someone stole it, Alice," I said. "Before the noodle shop."

"What are you talking about? Who?"

"We don't know. So you see—"

She shook her head. "No. No."

"Yes. I—"

"No!" In rising panic, she said, "There must be more! Anyone willing to spend that much, there must be more."

"No." Mr. Zhang's voice was gentle with regret. "No more."

Maybe I should go for the gun, I thought, *even in this crowded room, before Alice totally loses control.*

Suddenly her face brightened. "Jewelry! Oh, yes! I'll take what you have here and sell it, and Mr. Chen, I'm sure you're insured! Everyone will be fine! Oh, I wish I'd thought of this sooner!" Smiling happily, she stood and gestured for Mr. Chen and Mr. Zhang to get up. Mr. Zhang rose and helped his cousin, whose pale face was sweating.

Okay, I thought. *We'll go to the front, and someone will see this crazy lady with a gun and call the cops. Or I'll distract her and Bill can jump her. Or Mary will finally turn up.*

I followed Bill, who followed the cousins, with Alice behind us.

Irene Ng's confusion when Bill and I charged in was nothing to her shock as our little parade came out.

"It's all right, Irene," Mr. Zhang said soothingly. Mr. Chen didn't speak.

"Lock the door," Alice told Irene. The young assistant seemed rooted to the spot, but Alice moved the gun an inch or so, and Irene hurried to the front.

Mr. Zhang spoke again, calmly. "Irene, please open that case"—he pointed to a display of diamonds, sapphires, and emeralds in gold settings—"and put everything into a bag." Irene's wide eyes found Mr. Chen, who managed a nod. With shaking hands she unlocked the case, took a velvet sack from a drawer, and slipped necklace after bracelet after ring into it. I glanced at Alice, hoping her hands weren't shaking, too. *All right*, I thought, *bystanders, it's time to show some Chinatown spirit. Get involved! Call a cop*! I mean, here was a daylight robbery on Canal Street. Someone had to care.

Someone did, too. Just not someone I was expecting.

Irene had the case emptied when shattering glass tinkled and the burglar alarm started to shriek. Shards rained, a brick hit the floor, and seconds later so did my cousin, Armpit.

Bill, less dumbfounded than I—or just more able to function in surreal situations—yanked Alice's hand ceilingward. A bullet screamed and brought down a spray of plaster.

And that was it. Bill had the gun. Alice's face crumpled into disbelief, then defeat. She leaned heavily on the emptied case.

As the alarm howled, everyone but Alice stared at my cousin. Blood oozed onto his skeevy tee from a cut down the center of his new tattoo. His face was scratched, too, from his dive through the broken window. Bill asked Irene to turn off the alarm, and by the time the screeching stopped I'd located my voice.

"Armpit? What are you doing?"

He looked up at me as though I'd just won the Year's Dumbest Question prize. "She was holding up the store."

"You didn't have to come crashing through a window. You could have called the police."

"The police? Are you tripping, cuz? Old Man Chen pays good money for his orange trees."

I just stared, and stared some more. Could I really be related to the only gangster in Chinatown dumb enough to think a protection racket was about protection?

Apparently I was.

"*Dai lo* and all are in jail," Armpit explained. "Someone has to take care of the customers."

Armpit's astounding brainlessness and attendant bravery merited hours of discussion, which they would certainly get. For one thing, I couldn't wait to tell my mother.

But I'd have to wait. Mr. Chen, pale and sweating, collapsed in a heap on the glass-strewn floor.

41

"You wouldn't consider"—Mary stirred honey into her tea—"moving to, say, New Smyrna Beach, Florida?"

"Why would I?"

"Because I understand they have no crime there."

Bill and I were sitting with Mary and Inspector Wei over debriefing caffeine in a diner near St. Vincent's. Mr. Chen's heart attack, serious but survivable, had put him on the same floor in the same hospital as his cousin C. D. Zhang.

"If I did, you'd have to explain to my mother why you made me go all the way there."

Mary had a solution to that: "Take her with you."

That was a laughable idea, but I wasn't ready to laugh in Mary's company yet. I was cautiously optimistic, however, that her attitude toward me might have improved, based on her afternoon. The Helga Ulrich tip had given her Alice's hotel room at the Peninsula and Rosalie's jewelry in the hotel safe. And though Fishface Deng and his attorney were still swearing the White Eagles had been up to absolutely nothing, Alice, completely deflated, had already told her story on NYPD videotape. Plus one more thing: that she'd hired Fishface to shoot at us—and miss—in Sara Roosevelt Park. As a diversion, in case I'd brought cops along to hamper her escape. Since in fact I had, I could only admire her foresight.

"You know, Lydia," Mary said, "for someone who was supposed to be your client, you've messed up her plans right and left."

"I thought her being my client didn't matter to you."

Mary gave me a searching look, and then a sigh. "I know how hard this was for you guys, turning a client over. I appreciate it."

From Mary, at that moment, that was huge. "You do know we wouldn't do this for just any cop?"

Inspector Wei grinned slyly. "You mean, if officer needs informations is Detective Mulgrew, you don't give?"

"If officer needs a Kleenex is Detective Mulgrew, I don't give."

"Well, as long as we're talking about things no one likes," Mary said, "I might as well tell you this: The DA wants to charge C. D. Zhang as a co-conspirator."

"What?" My tea took on a bitter taste. "You can't."

"Not us, the DA. He stole the money."

"Um. I don't think he stole the money."

"He had to. Who else?"

Keeping things from Mary made my tea taste even worse, but I just said, "Well, what if he did? If Mr. Zhang won't press charges—"

"If it's part of the conspiracy, it doesn't matter. They won't charge him with theft, just racketeering. The DA doesn't really want him. They want to squeeze him into rolling on the White Eagles."

"What if he doesn't?"

"Then I guess he'll go to prison."

"Mary! He's an old man!" Which she'd pointed out to me just a few hours ago.

"That's why he'll cooperate. I'm sure he'd rather have his relatives know he stole their money than end up in Green Haven."

"What if he didn't?"

"Cooperate?"

"Steal it."

She shrugged. "Then maybe he can help figure out who did."

That was it for the diner meeting, besides Mary's suggestion that I leave town, which was looking better and better. Bill and I declined her offer of a ride and stood on the corner watching her and the inspector drive away.

"I would seriously hate it if C. D. Zhang went to prison for not stealing his brother's money," I said.

Bill didn't answer, just lit a cigarette. I waited, in case it helped him think. "If he didn't steal that money—"

"Then who did? I know," I said crossly. "But—"

"No, wait. If he didn't, it might be because it wasn't there."

I eyed him. "The briefcase was full of newspaper from the beginning? Why?"

"There are only two possibilities I can think of."

We discussed them. Neither was pleasant, and it didn't take long. We didn't discuss what to do next. But as if we had, we stepped off the curb and headed for the hospital in perfect sync.

We found Mr. Zhang sitting in Mr. Chen's room, drinking vending-machine tea. He smiled when he saw us. "It's kind of you to come," he whispered. "I'm afraid my cousin is asleep. Can I offer you tea?"

"Thank you, we just had some," I said. "Mr. Zhang, we need to talk to you."

Mr. Zhang glanced at his cousin, hooked to a bank of blinking, peeping, and line-drawing machines. He stood and led us down the hall to a sitting area. We settled on bright vinyl chairs, which didn't match my mood at all.

"How's Mr. Chen?" I asked, before we started on the real business.

"Doing well, thank you, for which I'm grateful. His son is on his way here."

"And your brother?"

"Also recovering nicely. He'll be going home soon, I believe."

Then came an awkward silence while Mr. Zhang waited politely to hear the reason for our visit and I mentally tried out and trashed a number of openings. Bill gave me a look that asked, *Want me to do it?* I shook my head. These old Chinese men were my problem.

"It may be," I told Mr. Zhang, "that your brother won't be going home. The district attorney is planning to arrest him."

"Arrest him? For what?"

"They think he was part of the conspiracy with Alice Fairchild and Wong Pan. That together they hired the White Eagles. Then he double-crossed the others, stole your million dollars, and was planning to blame the gang."

Mr. Zhang's round face turned pale. "Oh, but that's nonsense. My brother, the White Eagles? It's ridiculous."

"Maybe, but they're going to charge him."

"He's my brother. I won't have him arrested. I don't care what he did."

"They don't either. It's a pressure tactic. They want him to give them the White Eagles."

"I'll say there was no theft. I'll say I told him he could have the money."

"It's not the money that matters. It's the conspiracy."

"They cannot do this!"

Bill, with all the authority of a large white man, said, "Yes, they can."

I gave Mr. Zhang a moment to worry. "But here's the thing. He told us he didn't take the money. And we believe him."

"It makes no difference whether he did or didn't," Mr. Zhang tried stoutly once more.

I hated this. I gave Bill back that look: *Yes, you do it*.

"I'm sorry," Bill said, quiet, respectful, "but you're wrong. What matters is that he didn't. Because when all he does is tell the truth, even under threat of prison, when all he says is he got a locked brief-case from you and when it was opened it was full of newspaper, they'll begin to doubt their theory. Then they'll start looking around for the real conspirator."

Out the window, summer twilight was falling. In here, hospital fluorescents notwithstanding, it seemed already dark.

"There never was a million dollars in that briefcase, was there?" Bill asked, though we all knew the question was rhetorical. "Or maybe there was, but not by the time your brother got it. Maybe when you got it from Chen. Your brother told us most of the money behind this hunt was yours, but most isn't all. This money was your cousin's. And you're the one who stole it."

Mr. Zhang's eyes widened in what looked like true surprise. "No! Certainly not. Steal from Lao-li? I would never do that."

"It's the only way it makes sense," Bill said, "if your brother didn't take it. Are you saying he did?"

Slowly, Mr. Zhang shook his head. "No. No, he did not."

"Well, there's only one thing left," I elbowed back in. It wasn't fair to make Bill do it all. "If your brother didn't take it and you didn't take it, Mr. Chen must have stolen the money from *you*."

There it was, the heart of the matter, the theory Bill and I had worked out on the street corner, the theory I hated so much. One of these close, loving cousins was swindling the other.

And as had happened so often in this case, it turned out we were right.

And wrong.

"No," said Mr. Zhang. "Lao-li would no more steal from me than I from him."

"Sir," Bill said, "even if we believe you, the police won't. That newspaper's going to eat at them. They won't stop until they find out where it came from and where the million dollars went. One of the three of you knows."

An orderly rolled a tinkling cart down the corridor, passing us just as Bill said "million dollars." He raised his eyebrows and grinned. Mr. Zhang abruptly stood. "Come with me."

We got on the elevator, but we weren't alone there, so it wasn't until we were outside in the damp twilight that Mr. Zhang said angrily, "The million dollars went nowhere. There was no million dollars."

"I don't believe you," I said flatly. "How were you going to buy the Shanghai Moon?"

"We were not going to buy the Shanghai Moon. Wong Pan didn't have it."

"That's clear now, but you couldn't have been so sure before."

Mr. Zhang gave no answer.

"You were taking a big risk," Bill said. "Losing what you've been after for so long."

"There was no risk. My brother would have known whatever Wong
Pan presented him with for what it was—a fraud."

"Your brother hadn't seen the gem since he was a boy."

"He's a man of fine eye. He wouldn't need to be able to recognize the
Shanghai Moon to know that Wong Pan was attempting to pass off, at
best, some other gem, and more likely a worthless piece of glass."

I said, "But what if he wasn't?"

"He was."

"Then why go through the charade?" Bill asked. "Why send your
brother to the meeting at all, if you were so sure?"

"I was sure. My cousin wasn't."

"Why not just tell him your reasons?"

"Oh," he said, almost too softly to hear. "I have."

"No," I snapped. "No, I don't buy it. You've been hunting this gem
for forty years, racing around the world. An offer as promising as this
comes along and you're absolutely sure it's not worth following up?
Then you go through a whole dangerous farce just to humor your
cousin? I don't believe it."

"However, it's the truth."

Wham. I'd had it. Why was I arguing with this old man? So much
love, so much loss wrapped around this jewel across sixty years, and
these guys were screwing with each other over *money*? "Okay. You
know what? It's not my problem. Joel's killer's been found, Rosalie's
jewelry's been found. We're done. Good-bye, Mr. Zhang. Maybe you'll
be lucky and the police will forget about the missing million dollars.
But don't count on it."

I'd stepped from the curb and raised my arm for a cab when I
heard, "No, Ms. Chin, please."

The taxi sped away again as I turned. "What?"

Mr. Zhang drew a breath. "I have no right to ask for your help, but
I must. This investigation cannot continue. This is a private matter,
involving only my brother, my cousin, and myself. We must be allowed
to settle it."

"A private matter? Two people dead, fake passports, stolen jewelry, missing money, gangsters shooting up the streets? Oh, no, this investigation is going to continue. The next thing they'll do is subpoena your bank records, yours and Mr. Chen's. They'll find out whose money it was and who was cheating whom." *Would you look at that? The world's falling apart and Lydia Chin finally gets her grammar right.*

"You can't let them do that."

"I can't stop them."

"My cousin is a sick man! Knowing that money wasn't there could prove dangerous! Thinking I was cheating him—!"

"But you were."

"Not in the way you think." Mr. Zhang's accustomed calm had vaporized. His voice was hot and his eyes pleaded.

"But you were." I heard the sorrow in my own words. Right up until this moment I'd been waiting for another explanation, one that would make all this make sense and these old men still turn out to be the close and caring family they appeared.

Bill spoke, probably because he knew I couldn't. "Mr. Zhang? Even if we knew the truth, I'm not sure there's anything we could do. But without it . . ."

Mr. Zhang shook his head desperately. He stepped from the curb and flagged down a cab. I expected him to get in and speed away, but he held the door, all anger and impatience. We got in with him and in silence drove back to Chinatown.

42

The silence continued as we climbed the stairs to Fast River Imports, as Mr. Zhang unlocked the door and shut down the alarm, and as he switched on lights and took us through to his office. The terra-cotta soldiers on the windowsill seemed suspicious and alert.

A weary hand wave told us to sit. We did, on the glazed ceramic stools, and watched Mr. Zhang unhook a scroll from a nail on the wall. Behind it was a safe door. He twirled the combination, removed papers and cash, and then, with a screwdriver, pried a false bottom from the safe. This was something I'd never seen before. Even Bill raised an eyebrow. Still, neither of us said anything. Nor was a word spoken when Mr. Zhang lifted a velvet box from the hidden compartment and held it out to me.

Until I heard my own disbelieving voice. "You have it?"

And the reply, a command with edges of fear: "Ms. Chin, Mr. Smith. You must never let this knowledge leave this room."

"You *have* it? And your cousin doesn't know?" My voice seemed to be going on without the rest of me, which was unable even to reach out and take the box.

Bill did that. He opened it, peered in, looked up at Mr. Zhang, and turned the box toward me.

On a pillow of blue velvet sat a minute brooch. Eight tiny diamonds circled a diminutive jade disc. No other stones, no grand setting, no filigree or fretwork or chasing. The whole thing wasn't an inch wide.

"Behold," Mr. Zhang said. "The Shanghai Moon."

"*This?* No. It can't be. This isn't—"

"Worth a million dollars. It's not worth ten thousand. The jade, because of its antiquity, has some value, but as you can see it's cracked. The diamonds are small, and two are flawed. The only worth of this piece is based on its story, but most collectors, seeing it, would react as you have."

I took the miniature thing from the box and rested it in my hand. The jade, split along its length, felt cool to the touch, as jade always does; and tiny and flawed though they were, the diamonds sparkled.

Mr. Zhang looked as though he wanted to reach out and grab it back from me, but he didn't. "The jade Kai-rong gave Rosalie was not the most valuable stone his family possessed. It was the oldest. Though cracked and small, it was created for a Chen ancestor's wedding and had been in the Chen family for fifty generations. To Kai-rong it represented enduring family love. The necklace Rosalie chose to dismantle for its diamonds was not the most valuable piece she brought to Shanghai, either. It was the one that meant the most to her."

I looked up. "How do you know that?"

"Yaakov Corens told me."

I held the brooch to the light as he went on, "By the time my cousin and I came to America, Lao-li's obsession with the Shanghai Moon was total. Its legend had grown in the decades since it vanished, both in his mind and in the world of collectors. When I found we were in the same city with its maker, I could not risk Lao-li discovering its truth."

"Why not? Did you have it by then?"

As though the words were cumbersome, Mr. Zhang spoke slowly. "I have always had it."

"Then what are you talking about, 'the decades since it vanished'? It never vanished. *You had it!*" I thrust out my hand, the brooch sparkling in it. "How could you do that to Mr. Chen? How could you let his obsession ever get started? Why didn't you *tell* him? What was the *point?*"

The silence returned, and lasted so long I was starting to think Mr.

Zhang had no answer. And really, what answer could there be? Greed? A family bitterness, a rivalry? Something to lord over his cousin, a way to control him?

Softly, Mr. Zhang spoke. "The seed of the legend of the Shanghai Moon was planted in desperate, dark times. It was watered with tragedy and tended in heartbreak. Public and private. Private and public.

"The truth you hold you in your hand, that small, flawed thing, was meaningless in the face of people's need—Chinese people and exiled Jews and others besides—to believe something glorious could exist outside the despair and horrors of wartime Shanghai. No, more: could exist *amid* that despair and horror. From the moment it was made its legend began. That Rosalie would not show it only helped the legend flourish. In whispers, in rumors.

"Those rumors were why, years later, the robbers came for it." He reached out and took the brooch from me. "But they did not leave with it."

Mr. Zhang turned the gem in his hand, watching it gleam. "The moment he shot Aunt Rosalie, the robbers' leader panicked. He commanded the others to retreat. They did. When I reached Aunt Rosalie—as I told you, I was the first—I found the Shanghai Moon's gold chain broken but the gem still on it, on the floor beside her. I put it in my pocket. I wanted to be the one to give it back to her, when she was well. I wanted to be the one to bring her that happiness.

"But of course there was to be no happiness. Rosalie was dead. When Uncle Paul found her so, and saw the Shanghai Moon gone from about her throat, he wailed and, shocking me, began to curse the gem and those who now possessed it, calling down all manner of misery upon them. They had stolen it, they had killed for it, and now let them suffer all the torments of hell for it. His inconsolable grief and anger frightened me as much as the robbers had. He saw that, and calmed; he embraced me; he asked me to attend to my young cousin while he cared for Grandfather, who was badly hurt. I did so. For many hours I tried to comfort Lao-li with sweets and stories, sang to him, made tea. I brought water for Uncle Paul and tore cloth into bandages. I helped without question in whatever way I was asked. Trying to be good. Trying to hide my guilt and my terror. Because as day turned to night I'd come to understand that the loss of the Shanghai Moon had killed Aunt Rosalie. Also that punishment was assured to—and deserved by—whoever possessed it now."

Mr. Zhang paused, sad eyes still on the gem. He seemed to have shrunk.

"Oh," I said, "but that's—"

"Yes." He nodded without looking up. "But I was eight years old.

"Over the next few days, barricaded in the kitchen, Uncle Paul nursed Grandfather while I tried to comfort and distract my cousin. In the dead of night we stole to the garden to bury Rosalie. Uncle Paul chanted prayers and shed tears. And I kept my terrifying secret.

"When Uncle Kai-rong surprised us with his return, he echoed Uncle Paul's shock, his grief and his curses. Echoed and multiplied them. He forbade us ever to speak of the gem again. And with tears in his eyes he said Lao-li and I were his treasures. A treasure—that was what I wanted to be! Not a thief! Not a cursed killer!

"I thought many times to bury the Shanghai Moon in the garden. To throw it in the river. As though that would remove the curse! Always I was stopped by the thought of Aunt Rosalie. How she had loved it. I hid it among my things.

"In the weeks that followed, I found my young cousin shared my understanding that the loss of the gem had caused Rosalie's death. Hadn't Uncle Paul and Uncle Kai-rong said exactly that? At first we returned to that day over and over, trying to comprehend, but finally, terrified of its power, we made a pact never to speak about it. We kept to our word until my cousin stunned me, weeks later, with an idea spoken casually, as simple truth: Finding the gem would bring his mother back.

"I was a child, at the limit of my understanding, but I knew this was wrong. He went on to confess his greatest fear: that he was not up to the task, and that she could not come back until he accomplished it.

"What I would have given for adult counsel! But I could ask for none. But I also could not bear for my cousin to shoulder this impossible task and the guilt that would accompany his inevitable failure. I was racked with enough guilt for two already! I determined to take the only course I saw. I would show him the Shanghai Moon. I had no doubt this would bring down on my head the punishments the gem's thief and possessor deserved, but it had to be done for my cousin's sake.

"Some nights later, by the glow of a forbidden candle, and with my heart pounding, I retrieved the Shanghai Moon and held it out to him. He took it from me with a child's interest in a sparkling, pretty thing, admired it, and gave it back. He didn't seem to understand. 'This is the Shanghai Moon,' I said. 'It was Aunt Rosalie's. Cousin, in this life she cannot come back.'

"He smiled as though I was kind but simple-minded. 'No,' he said. 'When I find the Shanghai Moon, she will come back.'

"Possibly you can imagine how it was for me then. A child alone with this secret, this quandary! Three more times in the next months I tried to show the gem to him, and three times he denied the jewel I had was the missing Shanghai Moon. Until finally he became angry with me. His shouting and his tears brought Uncle Paul running to see what the trouble was. Neither of us would say. In my terror of being discovered I professed ignorance, and my cousin said only that I had been teasing him. Uncle Paul asked us please to find ways to be kind to each other. Then he sat us down and said he had something to tell us that would make us sad, so he was going to tell us now, when we were sad already. He was going away, he said, leaving Shanghai. He was on his way to America, a beautiful place, and we were to stay with Kai-rong and Grandfather, but someday we could come see him in America, too. A few weeks later, he sailed from the harbor.

"I never again showed the Shanghai Moon to anyone, from that day to this. Aunt Rosalie's death, my cousin's anger, Uncle Paul's leaving us—all these things were bound in my mind to the gem. As I grew to manhood, of course, I came to understand that the truth was both simpler and more complex than my childhood fears had made it. Still, it was years before the magic powers of the Shanghai Moon ceased to hold me, and to frighten me."

Mr. Zhang turned the brooch in his fingers. "Those powers have never ceased to hold my cousin. He grew up obsessed with the gem. In time he began to laugh at his former connection between its return and Rosalie's. The fantasy of a grieving child, innocent and foolish. Or so he said, and no doubt believed he believed. But his obsession did not diminish. Nothing interested him but gems. He read and studied, became an authority, and when we arrived here he took up his profession without hesitation. And, freed of the embargo against the world outside China under which we had grown up, he immersed himself happily in the search for the Shanghai Moon."

Mr. Zhang's deep brown eyes moved from Bill to me. "Mr. Smith? Ms. Chin? My cousin was mad. He *is* mad. The report of Kai-rong's death soon after we arrived here sealed his folly, but really it had been complete for many years. His madness, though, has only one dimension. As long as he can continue the hunt for the Shanghai Moon, he's as able to function in the world as you or I. He courted and wed and fathered two fine children. He has run a business honorably and participated in the life of his family and community. He's been kind to me, and to my brother—kinder, I think, than I have been—and to Uncle Paul. All he ever asked was that I join him in the search. How could I refuse?"

The question floated in the air. The vigilant terra-cotta soldiers, the cricket cages and the scrolls, the traffic sounds and the shadows in the open safe all seemed part of it, this same question.

"The search . . ." I began.

"I'm not a wealthy man, but my business does well enough. When we were younger, one or the other would travel where the rumors led. Later, sometimes, we sent agents. The cost of travel was easily manageable. The larger cost, the cost my cousin counted on me for—the purchase of the gem itself, when we found it—I knew I would never have to pay."

"Your brother—does he know this?"

"No. He's looked skeptically upon our enterprise from the beginning, but for my part I've scoffed at his scoffing. As though I didn't know he was right. My brother has no patience for memory, for nostalgia." An ironic smile lifted the corners of Mr. Zhang's mouth. "My cousin and I were taught the past must be smashed. My brother fought against that philosophy. Now I sell reminders of the past. My cousin seeks it. And my brother scorns it. No, he doesn't know the truth. About the Shanghai Moon, or me." *Nor you about him,* I thought. "My brother's interest in gems is solely a function of their value. To him they have no deeper meaning."

If you didn't count purity or immortality. I wondered if the brothers had ever once, over the years, actually talked about the deeper meaning of anything.

"It seems to me," Bill said, "that a lot of people have gotten caught up in your game over the last sixty years."

"Please believe me, it was never a game. Yet what you say is true, and a source of regret. Many collectors, not just ourselves, have expended time and money in this search. I've comforted myself that to collectors the joy is in the chase, not the capture. Some other gem would have kept them running, if not the Shanghai Moon."

"It wasn't the thrill of the chase that drove Alice Fairchild," I said.

Heavily, Mr. Zhang stood. He walked to the window and looked out over Chinatown. "No. And now two men are dead. My brother is hurt and my cousin very ill. Lives have been disrupted, and more heartbreak lies ahead. Because of me. Because instead of reality, I fostered illusion. Instead of truth, I encouraged dreams." He turned to us. "Do you see? This is what was spoken by Uncle Kai-rong and Uncle Paul. This is the curse of the Shanghai Moon."

43

A weary Mr. Zhang busied himself with kettle, tea canister, and little cups. Bill lit a cigarette and went to the window. I watched the Shanghai Moon sparkle against my fingertips.

It didn't look cursed. On the contrary: The tiny diamonds' sparkle and the green marbling of the jade made me hopeful, comforted me. As though, through everything, Rosalie and Kai-rong's love still glowed.

But Mr. Zhang must be right. Look at all that had happened because of it. It must, in fact, be cursed.

Ah, what do you know, Chinsky? What was the last cursed thing you saw? I jumped at the voice in my head.

What, Pilarsky, you think this is funny? I silently demanded.

Hey, I'm one of the guys the thing took out, why would I laugh? I must've been losing it anyway, falling for Alice like that. But listen: That's not the problem anymore.

What's not?

In the first place, you can't be serious, blaming that chatchke for all this tsuris. People made the mess, like always. Second, the bad guys are in jail. We're square, you and me. Thanks, by the way.

Thanks? But I—

I said thanks, that's it, no more, the end. Stick to business: You've got a bunch of old Chinese men here who still have troubles.

And? What am I supposed to do about it?

I should know? But you always said the old Chinese men, they were your problem.

"Ms. Chin? Are you all right?"

I looked up to see Mr. Zhang holding out a cup of tea. How long he'd been standing there, I couldn't tell, but he seemed concerned. "Yes. Thank you. I'm fine."

Bill had a teacup by his side at the windowsill. He was looking at me, too, quizzically but without worry. As though, whatever was going on, he knew I could handle it.

And of course, I could.

After all, I was Lydia Chinsky.

Mr. Zhang sat down and leaned toward me. "Do you understand, now, why this investigation must stop? If my cousin were to learn I never intended to buy the Shanghai Moon, and why . . . He's just had a heart attack. Another might end his life."

I sipped my tea. An idea began to glow in my mind, just a tiny pinprick at first, then brighter. *Go, Chinsky!* I had some more tea, to stall. Was I really about to do this? "Your brother," I heard myself say to Mr. Zhang. "You know he would do anything you ask?"

"Yes," Mr. Zhang said sadly. "And the one thing he's asked, a brother's love, I've been unable to give."

"Maybe now," I told him, "you can."

Of course, I wasn't there to see it. Bill and I had to content ourselves with Mary's report. She was there because C. D. Zhang had requested "that Chinese detective," just as his brother had instructed. For all Mary knew, we had no idea what was even going on.

Right.

"You made this happen." She hadn't sat down at our Taiwanese tea place before the words were out of her mouth.

"I got ginger black with condensed milk." I lifted the teapot.

"Never mind that." She held out a cup anyway because ginger's her favorite. I poured for her and for Inspector Wei, who gave the tea a skeptical sniff. "C. D. Zhang's confession," Mary said. "You guys' pawprints are all over it."

Bill held up innocent hands.

I shrugged. "I owed you, girlfriend."

"So, what, you manufactured a confession and found someone to deliver it?"

"I just suggested to C. D. Zhang that he admit he did his brother dirt." And if the crime he confessed to wasn't the one he committed, was that so terrible?

"Of those three, C. D. was my least likely suspect."

"Sometimes that's who did it."

"And sometimes"—Mary put her cup down—"a guy admits to stealing his brother's million dollars, his brother declines to press charges, and we have no one to prosecute."

"For *that*. But Alice rolled on the White Eagles. You have your conspiracy."

"True. So it just so happens we no longer need Wong Pan. So when he slips Midtown's clutches and gets shipped back to Shanghai with the DA's blessing, everyone will be happy."

At that, Inspector Wei lifted her cup. We all clinked. "This tea," she said. "Well made. But condensed milk, so sweet, terrible."

"Sorry."

"Oh!" Mary said, as though something had just hit her. "Except there's one guy who'll be left with nothing, so he won't be happy. And just by coincidence, it's Mulgrew."

"Well," I said, "some days the bear gets you."

"You know Mr. Chen will never forgive C. D. for endangering his chance at the Shanghai Moon, even though it wasn't a real chance."

"I'm afraid that's true. But Mr. Zhang will. He already has. That's why he's not pressing charges."

"In fact, he turns out to be quite a humanitarian. I hear he's offered to help pay for home health care for Alice's sister. Oh, didn't you know she has a sister? In Boston."

"Yes, Alice mentioned her when she was, you know, holding up the jewelry store. That's very kind of Mr. Zhang."

Mary narrowed her eyes. "Lydia. Something else is going on here, isn't it?"

"Probably. Families are complicated things."

That was the truest thing I'd said since Mary sat down.

What C. D. Zhang was getting in return for his "confession" wasn't his brother's forgiveness, since what he'd done sixty years ago he wasn't admitting, and what he was admitting he hadn't done. What he was getting was much more. Gratitude. Appreciation. A secret shared with his brother. A bond between them.

What Zhang Li was getting was a solution to the million-dollar mystery that Mr. Chen would buy.

What Joan Conrad was getting was the ability to go on living in her own house.

What I was getting was a dubious look from my best and oldest friend.

But rumor had it what she was getting was a commendation. So I didn't think she'd be upset for long.

I poured more tea, and as I turned the lid upside down so they'd know to bring us another pot, my phone rang. It was my brother Ted's number in Flushing, but when I answered it, it was my mother. I excused myself and skipped outside. "Hi, Ma."

"Ling Wan-ju! Are you all right?"

"Of course. Why wouldn't I be?"

"Now you surely will be. Kwan Shan tells me the gang boys are all in jail."

"Did she tell you what a hero Clifford was?"

"Oh, so much big talk from her! She said Clifford saved your life. I told her that was ridiculous."

"It's pretty close to true. Anyhow, the White Eagles are off the streets, so I'll come out and bring you home whenever you want."

"That's why I'm calling. I've decided to stay here some days longer."

"You have?"

"Now that the apartment is painted white, it's not so dark. And your brother's children want me to teach their mother to make *har gow*."

"Oh," I said. "Oh. Okay, Ma. Just let me know when you want to come home."

I lowered the phone and stood in the churning river of China-town's streets. A vendor's flying fingers folded a paper dragon. Shoppers flowed around him without a break in stride. A girl guided her grandmother, bent and leaning on a stick. The grandmother scolded; the girl ignored her words but took great care to steady her.

I went back inside. "Oh, here is," Inspector Wei said, raising her cup. "This time, drinking jasmine tea. Much better." She waited for Mary to pour me some. "Investigator Chin. Investigator Smith. Shanghai Police Bureau asks me, give you official gratitude. Anytime you coming to China, please accept hospitality of Shanghai Police Bureau."

"Thanks," Bill said. "Can't wait."

"Me, too." I raised my cup in return. "To Inspector Wei De-xu and the Shanghai Police."

Wei, with her sharp smile, said, "To Investigator Chin."

I turned to my left. "To Detective Mary Kee and the NYPD."

Mary tried to keep the suspicious look going but gave up and grinned. "To Lydia."

I turned to my right. I hesitated; then in my head I heard, *Chinsky! Come on, just say it!* So, because Joel always gave good advice, even though, as usual, I hadn't asked, I said, "And to my partner."

Bill's smile was small and his words were quiet, but I loved them. "And to mine."

I ambled to my office through the bright sticky heat. At Golden Adventure's door, Andi waved me in. "Hi, Lydia! Package for you. FedEx man wants to know, you *that* Lydia Chin?" Notoriety has its uses. The travel ladies had been dining out for days on my part in the Canal Street shootout and their own close call when the White Eagles came to their office. I figured that meant my lease was safe for a while.

The return address on the box was Teaneck: Anita Horowitz, Paul Gilder's granddaughter. I thanked Andi and took the box to my office.

Small, dim, messy; but mine. I opened the box and slid out a padded envelope with a note attached.

Zayde's been asking if Mei-lin is coming back, and he insists Mei-lin should have this. Rosalie had it taken to send to Elke before they knew she'd been arrested. Zayde keeps it by his bed. I know it's a big favor to ask, but he seems so happy when he talks about seeing Mei-lin again. Would you mind coming out here, if you have the time? You wouldn't have to stay long.

Would I mind? To hear the stories Paul Gilder could tell, about Rosalie, about Kai-rong, about Shanghai in their time?

I had a copy made, and I'm sending it to you so if you do come back and he asks about it you'll know what he means. Hoping to see you again, Anita.

Inside the envelope was a black-and-white photo. In a garden under a blossoming acacia tree, five people smiled from thin-armed rosewood chairs. Two I recognized; three I'd never seen, but I knew them.

On the left, Rosalie, her hair stirring in the breeze. Beside her, a handsome Chinese man in a European suit and tie. The older man in the center wore a traditional silk scholar's robe, and the young woman next to him a *qi pao*—and, I was delighted to see, high heels. On the right, Paul, leaning forward, ready to jump up as soon as the shutter clicked.

Peering closer, I could see the tangle in the grass beside the tea table was really lines of handwriting, faint, but neat and familiar. I called Bill.

"Could you translate some German?" I read the words to him. "I can tell 'Kai-rong' and 'Mama,' but besides that I'm lost."

"Give it to me again, slowly."

I read it again.

"Okay, loosely, 'Here are Kai-rong and his father and sister. Our new friends! People to care about, and who care about us—what treasure, not to be taken lightly in these times. I'm so anxious for the day when you meet them yourself. Until then, all my love, Mama. Your Rosalie.'"

Lost in the photo, I almost didn't hear Bill ask, "What was that from?"

People to care about, and who care about us. What treasure, not to be taken lightly.

"Come to my office," I said. "Bring a cup of coffee. I'd like to show you."